PI

GEORGE C

PENGUIN
GENERAL

GEORGE CRABBE was born in 1754 in Aldborough (now Aldeburgh) in Suffolk, where his father was a collector of salt-duties. After a period of apprenticeship and unsuccessful practice as an apothecary and surgeon, during which he met his future wife Sarah Elmy, Crabbe went to London in 1780 to make his way as a writer. He became almost destitute before being befriended by Edmund Burke who helped persuade James Dodsley to publish *The Library* (1781) and *The Village* (1783). Burke's influence also enabled Crabbe to embark on a career in the church, first as curate at Aldborough (1781–2) and domestic chaplain to the Duke of Rutland at Belvoir Castle (1782–4), then as curate or vicar of various rural parishes in Leicestershire and Suffolk (1784–1814) and finally as Rector of Trowbridge in Wiltshire until his death in 1832.

Crabbe had two literary careers. His brief eighteenth-century career reached its climax with the bitter attack on literary idealizations of rural life in Book One of *The Village*. Between *The Newspaper* (1785) and *Poems* (1807) Crabbe published some botanical studies, but no poetry. His nineteenth-century literary career was longer and more prolific and successful, producing two overlapping bodies of remarkable and original work: his studies of provincial communities in 'The Parish Register' (1807) and *The Borough* (1810) and his fictional tales in verse, most notably the *Tales* of 1812.

GAVIN EDWARDS lectures in the Department of English at Saint David's University College, Lampeter. He is the author of *George Crabbe's Poetry on Border Land* (1990).

PENGUIN CLASSICS

GEORGE CRABBE: SELECTED POEMS

PENGUIN SELECTED ENGLISH POETS
EDITOR: CHRISTOPHER RICKS

GEORGE CRABBE
Selected Poems

EDITED WITH AN INTRODUCTION AND NOTES BY
GAVIN EDWARDS

PENGUIN BOOKS

FOR DEBORAH

PENGUIN BOOKS

Published by the Penguin Group
Penguin Books Ltd, 27 Wrights Lane, London w8 5tz, England
Viking Penguin, a division of Penguin Books USA Inc.
375 Hudson Street, New York, New York 10014, USA
Penguin Books Australia Ltd, Ringwood, Victoria, Australia
Penguin Books Canada Ltd, 2801 John Street, Markham, Ontario, Canada l3r 1b4
Penguin Books (NZ) Ltd, 182–190 Wairau Road, Auckland 10, New Zealand

Penguin Books Ltd, Registered Offices: Harmondsworth, Middlesex, England

First published 1991
1 3 5 7 9 10 8 6 4 2

Introduction and Notes copyright © Gavin Edwards, 1991
All rights reserved

Filmset in Ehrhardt (Monotype Lasercomp)

Printed in England by Clays Ltd, St Ives plc

CONTENTS

CONTENTS

from TALES OF THE HALL

from POSTHUMOUS TALES

INTRODUCTION

George Crabbe published a small number of poems in the 1780s, but most of his poetry – well over four-fifths of it – was both written and published in the nineteenth century. *The Cambridge Bibliography of English Literature* nevertheless includes him only in its '1660–1800' volume, and many libraries still puzzle readers in search of Crabbe by shelving him with Johnson and Cowper rather than with Wordsworth and Shelley. Volume One of the widely used *Norton Anthology of English Literature* prints Book One of *The Village* (1783), while correctly noting that 'Crabbe belongs to the early nineteenth rather than the eighteenth century'; but the section of their Volume Two covering the early nineteenth century contains no Crabbe: *The Borough* and *Tales* are removed from literary history by the familiar device of calling the years in which they were written and published 'The Romantic Period'.

Crabbe's early-nineteenth-century contemporaries, who did not know they were living in The Romantic Period, knew better. Reviewing Crabbe's *Poems* (1807) in the *Edinburgh Review* for April 1808, Francis Jeffrey described Crabbe as 'one of the most original . . . poets of the present century'. What was remarkable about Crabbe was – and is – his originality, not his belatedness.

A selection of Crabbe's work should represent him as principally a nineteenth-century writer. The decision to represent him as a writer of verse tales rather than as the author of 'The Parish Register' and *The Borough* has been more difficult. The sensible policy of this Selected English Poets series is to print only whole poems, not excerpts from poems. In Crabbe's case of course this rule has to be interpreted liberally since most of his poems originally appeared as parts of larger wholes. The 1812 volume *Tales* is given in full because almost all its constituent poems are among Crabbe's most interesting and because it is a more integrated volume than might at first appear. But 'Peter Grimes', for instance, is separated from its original context in *The Borough*, and 'Delay Has Danger' from its original context as one of the *Tales of the Hall*. They function here as examples of Crabbe's verse tales rather than as samples of the larger wholes from which they have been removed. The only way to represent 'The Parish Register' or *The Borough* effectively would be to present them in full, which would have pushed aside the verse tales. If *The Borough* is a single work in a way that *Tales* is not, then I can agree with Jerome McGann that *The Borough* is 'one of the three most important works of poetry published in the Romantic period' (*London Review of Books*, 16 March 1989); but I share the general view that Crabbe is equally original, and more consistently powerful, in his verse tales.

Crabbe's development as a poet can best be displayed by presenting his poems in the chronological order of their composition and of their publication: so far as we know, and for the poems selected here, there is no significant discrepancy between these potentially distinct chronologies. Almost nothing is known about the composition of *Tales* but it seems likely that most of the writing was done after the writing of *The Borough* was completed. Nor is anything known about the order in which Crabbe wrote the four poems selected here from *The Borough* or the twenty-one poems in *Tales*. Nothing is therefore sacrificed by presenting them – as they should in any case be presented – in the order of their first appearance. 'Sir Eustace Grey' (written 1804–5) was printed before 'The Hall of Justice' (written 1798) in *Poems*; but although there is some significance in the ordering of the poems in *Poems* it is less integrated than any of Crabbe's subsequent volumes; more is gained than lost by presenting the two poems selected from it in the order of their composition. 'Fragment, Written at Midnight', taken here from the *Poetical Works* of 1834, comes first in the present selection according to the probable date of its composition.

The present selected edition is very much indebted to the recent, and excellent, *George Crabbe: The Complete Poetical Works* (1988), edited by Norma Dalrymple-Champneys and Arthur Pollard (General Editor: Norma Dalrymple-Champneys). For full bibliographical information and for variant readings, *CPW* should be consulted. The present edition is however based on independent study of early printed editions and of copies of most of the relevant known manuscripts, and the texts presented differ in certain respects from those offered by *CPW*.

The text is in most cases based on the earliest printed version that Crabbe had had an opportunity to correct. In the case of *The Village*, and a number of poems not included in the present selection, Crabbe made some alterations to the second editions which he would not have made to the proofs of the first: notably alterations made in response to his own changing views or to pressure from reviewers. These rewritings affected Crabbe's footnoting of the poems in this selection rather than the poems themselves (for *The Village*, see below); consequently Crabbe's own notes to first editions have been retained here, as footnotes, but not those added by him in subsequent editions. A similar policy has been followed with the summarizing Arguments which precede some poems in the early editions. The Pforzheimer Library's fair copy of *Tales of the Hall* includes these summaries in Crabbe's hand and Crabbe seems to have at least gone along with the practice in *Poems*, *The Borough* and *Tales of the Hall*; the Arguments have therefore been retained for these volumes, but not for *The Village* where no Argument appeared in the first edition.

The text of *Tales*, for which no manuscripts survive, is based on the second (two-volume) edition, printed by John Brettell for John Hatchard, which appears to incorporate Crabbe's corrections to the proofs of the first edition (the first edition itself does not do so). Although we do not know whether Crabbe corrected proofs of *The Village* (1783) the present text is based on that edition rather than on the poem as Crabbe revised it more than twenty years later for inclusion in *Poems*. There is no evidence that Crabbe was directly involved in the 1823 *Works*, printed by Thomas Davison for John Murray, on which some twentieth-century editions of the poems up to 1823 have been based. Poems not published in Crabbe's lifetime are (with the exception of 'The Family of Love') based on the original manuscript or, if none exists, on *1834*. 'The Family of Love' is based on *1834* because it is likely that the editors had access to manuscript material additional to the surviving manuscripts in the Murray Archive and in the Victoria and Albert Museum.

Following the policy of the series, Crabbe's spelling has been modernized, except where a very clear prosodic change would result or where archaism, dialect or ideolect seem to be intended. Where past participles are used as adjectives ('griev'd') they have been expanded to end in 'ed', except in a few cases where no unaccented modern form exists. In *Tales* xxi 'a learned point' becomes 'a learnèd point' (though the title remains 'The Learned Boy'). The spelling of regular verbs in the Past Simple has been standardized so that they all end in 'ed' as opposed to some ending in 't' or 'd'. In modern English, different written forms are not required to produce these different sounds: for example 'tript' and 'tripped' sound the same because the unvoiced /p/ has to be followed by an unvoiced /t/ sound. Similarly, in a verb like 'begg'd' the voiced /g/ is followed by a voiced /d/ sound. The use of an apostrophe to mark unsounded vowels in parts of speech other than the verb (in nouns like 'Heav'n' for instance) has also been modernized. The abbreviated forms tho' and thro', and all ampersands, have been expanded. Th' has been expanded except where a very definite and awkward prosodic change would result. The alternative forms 'sat' and 'sate', which do sometimes indicate a difference of sound, have been retained.

Crabbe's hyphens present a problem. He frequently uses a hyphen to separate words we would not separate (*Sea-port*) and join words we would not join (*Sabbath-day*). But the rules of modern hyphenation are not hard and fast, and Crabbe's hyphenation frequently seems purposeful (it is appropriate that 'Peter Grimes', a poem about a man and a terrain which are a part of the world but apart from it, should be especially full of hyphenated words). Consequently Crabbe's hyphens have been retained.

Crabbe's punctuation has been altered only in the few occasions where the original seems both purposeless and very awkward. The text of 'Infancy', reconstructed from a manuscript which is almost unpunctuated and sometimes illegible, has been lightly punctuated; the punctuation in the fair copy (not in Crabbe's hand) of ' "Peasants Drinking" by Miss Ford' has been preserved. The fair copy of 'The Flowers' in the Murray Archive is lightly but deliberately punctuated: only two punctuation marks have been added here, both from an earlier manuscript version of the poem.

Running quotation marks have been removed; the use of single and double quotation marks has been altered so as to conform with modern practice. But Crabbe's use of quotation marks for what we now call free indirect speech is retained.

A notable feature of *CPW* is its decision to retain the varying pattern of capitalization in its copy texts. The present edition follows the same policy with respect to capitalization and to the italicization of proper names. There is some evidence that the choice between upper- and lower-case initial letters for words other than proper nouns is purposeful, though it is not systematically purposeful and it is the printers as well as the poet whose purposes are involved. Crabbe's literary career spanned a period in which the practice of writers and printers was in confused transit between an older practice – in which the initial letters of most nouns were capitalized – and the modern practice of reserving the capital letter for proper nouns. Crabbe's capitalization in his handwriting remained erratic throughout his life, though it tended to be heavy. The capitalization of the early printed editions depends very much on the practice of his printers. Of course the distinction between an upper-case and a lower-case letter need not be so clear in handwriting as it is in print, and there is reason to believe that it was when he was presented with printed versions of his poems that Crabbe came to see semantic significance in the choice between the two forms. In *Poems* (1807) and *The Borough* (1810) the capitalization is erratic, though in his corrections to the first editions Crabbe seems to be aiming for various kinds of special emphasis. It is with *Tales* (1812) that one particular kind of emphasis comes into focus, and is drawn to our attention by the approximately eighty changes between upper and lower case incorporated into the second edition (the largest number of changes, fourteen, are in 'The Frank Courtship'). Apart from proper names and the occasional personification, capital letters are used in *Tales*, almost exclusively, and in some poems quite systematically, for the names of positions in the social and kinship order (I have discussed the possible semantic significance of Crabbe's practice in 'Crabbe's So-Called Realism', *Essays in Criticism*, XXXVII, 1987, pp. 303–20, and in 'The Essential Crabbe', *Essays in Criticism*, XXXIX, 1989, pp. 84–91). After changing publishers in 1819 (from

Hatchard to Murray) Crabbe seems to have gone along with the much lighter capitalization used by Thomas Davison for *Tales of the Hall* and for subsequent editions of the earlier and collected poems. But the two manuscript versions of 'The Flowers' in the Murray Archive encourage the view that Crabbe's capitals can be purposeful. Probably intended for Mary Hoare's album, the fair copy is far more selectively capitalized than the earlier draft: for a poem not intended for publication, and where the handwritten form was to be the final form, Crabbe gave the capitalization a kind of attention he might normally have reserved for printed proofs.

Crabbe's epigraphs from Latin authors are translated in the Notes, normally from Loeb. The epigraphs from Shakespeare contain many mistakes and undoubtedly some deliberate emendations of the original, though it is not always possible to be sure which edition of the play he was using (see *CPW*, i. 600–601). The passages have been reproduced here as they stand, together with Crabbe's attribution of them to Act and Scene. The Notes supply Act, Scene and line numbers from the New Penguin Shakespeare (for *Cymbeline*, from the Arden Shakespeare), and indicate especially significant textual discrepancies. The names of the Shakespearian characters involved are given, to indicate the original dramatic context of the epigraph.

ACKNOWLEDGEMENTS

My chief debt is to the previous editors of Crabbe's poems, especially to Norma Dalrymple-Champneys and Arthur Pollard. I should also like to thank Barbara Dennis, Kelvin Everest, Thomas Faulkner, Anne Ferris, Brian Ferris, Deborah Ferris, Doreen Kay, John Lucas, Peter Miles, Virginia Murray, Lawrence Normand, Christopher Ricks, Gareth Roberts, Mrs D. A. Staveley and Gordon Williams who have helped me with information, advice and assistance of various kinds.

I should like to acknowledge the expert assistance provided by the library staff of Saint David's University College, Lampeter, and by the staff of Exeter University Library and the National Library of Wales. I am also grateful to the following libraries and museums who have provided me with copies of manuscript or early printed editions of Crabbe poems: The Bodleian Library; Colorado College, the Tutt Library; The Henry E. Huntington Library; the National Library of Wales; the Carl H. Pforzheimer Library; the Victoria and Albert Museum; Wellesley College, the Margaret Clapp Library; Yale University, the Beinecke Library.

I am especially glad to have this opportunity to thank the Duke of Rutland and John Murray Ltd for generously allowing me to use manuscript material in their possession.

TABLE OF DATES

1754   *24 December* Born at Aldborough (now Aldeburgh), Suffolk, son of George Crabbe (customs official) and Mary Crabbe (née Lodwick).

1762–6 Pupil at Richard Harvey's School, Bungay, Suffolk.

1766–8 Pupil at Richard Haddon's School, Stowmarket, Suffolk.

1768–71 Apprentice to an apothecary and farmer at Wickhambrook, Suffolk.

1771–4 Apprentice to a surgeon-apothecary at Woodbridge, Suffolk.

1772   Meets his future wife, Sarah Elmy (b. 1751) at the Parham home – near Woodbridge – of her aunt and uncle Tovell, wealthy yeoman farmers, with whom she frequently stayed. *September* Publishes 'Poetical Essay on Hope' and 'To Mira' (Sarah Elmy) in Wheble's *Lady's Magazine* and 'Solitude' in Robinson's *Lady's Magazine*.

1775   Works as a labourer on the quay at Slaughden (next to Aldborough), then as an apothecary; appointed surgeon to the poor by Aldborough Vestry. *Inebriety*, imitating Pope's *Dunciad* and *Essay on Man*, published anonymously at Ipswich, Suffolk.

1776   Lives in London (Whitechapel), attending medical lectures, visiting hospital wards.

1777–9 Attempts to survive as apothecary in Aldborough. Starts to learn Latin seriously in order to read botanical books.

1780   Returns to London, to make a career as a writer. Associates
        with mathematicians and scientists (John Bonnycastle, Isaac
        Dalby, Reuben Burrow). Rejected by publishers and aristo-
        cratic patrons. Records his increasingly desperate life for
        Sarah Elmy in his 'Poet's Journal'. Witnesses Gordon
        Riots.
        July Publishes, anonymously, *The Candidate; a Poetical
        Epistle to the Authors of the Monthly Review.*
        Death of his mother.

1781   Successfully appeals to Edmund Burke for patronage. Intro-
        duced to Duke of Rutland, Charles James Fox, Joshua
        Reynolds.
        July Publishes, anonymously, *The Library*, with James
        Dodsley.
        December Ordained deacon; returns to Aldborough as
        curate.

1782   Ordained priest; moves to Belvoir Castle as domestic
        chaplain to the Duke of Rutland.

1783   Samuel Johnson emends manuscript of *The Village*.
        May The Village published by James Dodsley.
        December Marries Sarah Elmy.

1784   Moves to Stathern, Leicestershire, as curate.

1785   *March The Newspaper* (his last published poem till 1807)
        published by James Dodsley.
        Birth of son George, later the poet's biographer.

1786   Death of Crabbe's father.

1787   Visits the Doncaster factory of his friend Edmund Cart-
        wright, inventor of the power-loom.

1789   Successfully examined for LL.B. Moves to the Crown
        living of Muston, Leicestershire. Death of daughter Sarah
        Susannah, born earlier same year (first of four offspring to
        die in infancy or childhood by 1797).

1790   He is first prescribed opium (for vertigo) about this time and 'to a constant but slightly increasing dose of it may be attributed his long and generally healthy life' (*Life*). Publishes 'The Natural History of the Vale of Belvoir' in Nichols's *Bibliotheca Topographica Britannica*.

1791   On the death of Sarah's uncle Tovell, the Crabbes move to Ducking Hall, Parham, where they stay till 1796.

1794   Becomes curate of nearby parishes of Sweffling and Great Glemham. Sarah starts to suffer mental (manic–depressive?) illness.

1796   John Davies, Vice-Master of Trinity College, Cambridge, dissuades him from publishing a treatise on botanical classification because it is written in English. The Crabbes leave Parham for Great Glemham Hall.

1798   Publishes 'A Catalogue of Plants growing in and near the Parish of Framlingham' in Hawes and Loder's *History of Framlingham*. Probably writes 'Aaron, or The Gipsy' (subsequently 'The Hall of Justice').

1801–2 Leaves Glemham for nearby Rendham. Writes, and destroys, three novels, including 'The Widow Grey' and 'Reginald Glanshaw, or the Man who commanded Success'.

1802   Probably starts 'The Parish Register'.

1804   Probably writes 'Hester' and starts *The Borough*. 'Sir Eustace Grey' probably written in the winter of 1804–5.

1806   Laws against absentee clergy require his return to Muston.

1807   *Poems* published by Hatchard, including 'The Village' (slightly revised), 'The Library' (revised), 'The Parish Register', 'Sir Eustace Grey', 'The Hall of Justice'. Francis Jeffrey in the *Edinburgh Review* praises him as 'one of the most original, nervous, and pathetic poets of the present century', contrasting him with 'Mr Wordsworth and his associates [who] show us something that mere observation never yet suggested to anyone'.

FURTHER READING

EDITIONS

Norma Dalrymple-Champneys and Arthur Pollard (eds.), *George Crabbe: The Complete Poetical Works*, Clarendon Press, Oxford, 1988.

Thomas C. Faulkner (ed.), *Selected Letters and Journals of George Crabbe*, Clarendon Press, Oxford, 1985.

BIOGRAPHY

George Crabbe, jun., *Life of the Rev. George Crabbe, LL.B.*, Vol. I of *The Poetical Works of the Rev. George Crabbe: With his Letters and Journals, and his Life, by his Son*, 8 vols., London, 1834. There have been twentieth-century editions of the *Life* in the World's Classics Series (Oxford University Press, 1932, Introduction by E. M. Forster) and from the Cresset Press (1947, Introduction by Edmund Blunden).

CRITICISM

Contemporary and nineteenth-century opinions (including those of Jeffrey and Hazlitt) are collected in Arthur Pollard's *George Crabbe: The Critical Heritage*. Much of the best modern criticism can be found in books devoted principally to other or broader topics: the Notes to the present edition should be consulted.

Terence Bareham, *George Crabbe*, Vision Press, 1977.

R. C. Chamberlain, *George Crabbe*, Twayne Publishers Inc., 1965.

Gavin Edwards, *George Crabbe's Poetry on Border Land*, Edwin Mellen Press, 1990.

Lilian Haddakin, *The Poetry of Crabbe*, Chatto & Windus, 1955.

Ronald B. Hatch, *Crabbe's Arabesque: Social Drama in the Poetry of George Crabbe*, McGill–Queen's University Press, 1976.

Peter New, *George Crabbe's Poetry*, Macmillan, 1976.

FRAGMENT, WRITTEN AT MIDNIGHT

Oh, great Apollo! by whose equal aid
The verse is written, and the medicine made;
Shall thus a boaster, with his fourfold powers,
In triumph scorn this sacred art of ours?
Insulting quack! on thy sad business go,
And land the stranger on this world of woe.
    Still I pass on, and now before me find
The restless ocean, emblem of my mind;
There wave on wave, here thought on thought succeeds,
Their produce idle works, and idle weeds: 10
Dark is the prospect o'er the rolling sea,
But not more dark than my sad views to me;
Yet from the rising moon the light beams dance
In troubled splendour o'er the wide expanse;
So on my soul, whom cares and troubles fright,
The Muse pours comfort in a flood of light. –
Shine out, fair flood! until the day-star flings
His brighter rays on all sublunar things.
    'Why in such haste? by all the powers of wit,
I have against thee neither bond nor writ;   20
If thou art a poet, now indulge the flight
Of thy fine fancy in this dubious light;
Cold, gloom, and silence shall assist thy rhyme,
And all things meet to form the true sublime.' –
    'Shall I, preserver deemed around the place,
With abject rhymes a doctor's name disgrace?
Nor doctor solely, in the healing art
I'm all in all, and all in every part;
Wise Scotland's boast let that diploma be

30   Which gave me right to claim the golden fee:
      Praise, then, I claim, to skilful surgeon due,
      For mine the advice and operation too;
      And, fearing all the vile compounding tribe,
      I make myself the medicines I prescribe;
      Mine, too, the chemic art; and not a drop
      Goes to my patients from a vulgar shop.
      But chief my fame and fortune I command
      From the rare skill of this obstetric hand:
      This our chaste dames and prudent wives allow,
40   With her who calls me from thy wonder now.'

THE VILLAGE

BOOK I

The village life, and every care that reigns
O'er youthful peasants and declining swains;
What labour yields, and what, that labour past,
Age, in its hour of languor, finds at last;
What forms the real picture of the poor,
Demands a song – The Muse can give no more.

Fled are those times, if e'er such times were seen,
When rustic poets praised their native green;
No shepherds now in smooth alternate verse,
Their country's beauty or their nymphs' rehearse;   10
Yet still for these we frame the tender strain,
Still in our lays fond Corydons complain,
And shepherds' boys their amorous pains reveal,
The only pains, alas! they never feel.

On Mincio's banks, in Caesar's bounteous reign,
If TITYRUS found the golden age again,
Must sleepy bards the flattering dream prolong,
Mechanic echoes of the Mantuan song?
From truth and nature shall we widely stray,
Where VIRGIL, not where fancy leads the way?   20

Yes, thus the Muses sing of happy swains,
Because the Muses never knew their pains:
They boast their peasants' pipes, but peasants now
Resign their pipes and plod behind the plough;
And few amid the rural tribe have time
To number syllables and play with rhyme;

Save honest Duck, what son of verse could share
The poet's rapture and the peasant's care?
Or the great labours of the field degrade
30   With the new peril of a poorer trade?

From one chief cause these idle praises spring,
That, themes so easy, few forbear to sing;
They ask no thought, require no deep design,
But swell the song and liquefy the line;
The gentle lover takes the rural strain,
A nymph his mistress and himself a swain;
With no sad scenes he clouds his tuneful prayer,
But all, to look like her, is painted fair.

I grant indeed that fields and flocks have charms,
40   For him that gazes or for him that farms;
But when amid such pleasing scenes I trace
The poor laborious natives of the place,
And see the mid-day sun, with fervid ray,
On their bare heads and dewy temples play;
While some, with feebler hands and fainter hearts,
Deplore their fortune, yet sustain their parts,
Then shall I dare these real ills to hide,
In tinsel trappings of poetic pride?

No, cast by Fortune on a frowning coast,
50   Which can no groves nor happy valleys boast;
Where other cares than those the Muse relates,
And other shepherds dwell with other mates;
By such examples taught, I paint the cot,
As truth will paint it, and as bards will not:
Nor you, ye poor, of lettered scorn complain,
To you the smoothest song is smooth in vain;
O'ercome by labour and bowed down by time,
Feel you the barren flattery of a rhyme?
Can poets soothe you, when you pine for bread,
60   By winding myrtles round your ruined shed?
Can their light tales your weighty griefs o'erpower,
Or glad with airy mirth the toilsome hour?

Lo! where the heath, with withering brake grown o'er,
Lends the light turf that warms the neighbouring poor;
From thence a length of burning sand appears,
Where the thin harvest waves its withered ears;
Rank weeds, that every art and care defy,
Reign o'er the land and rob the blighted rye:
There thistles stretch their prickly arms afar,
And to the ragged infant threaten war;   70
There poppies nodding, mock the hope of toil,
There the blue bugloss paints the sterile soil;
Hardy and high, above the slender sheaf,
The slimy mallow waves her silky leaf;
O'er the young shoot the charlock throws a shade,
And the wild tare clings round the sickly blade;
With mingled tints the rocky coasts abound,
And a sad splendour vainly shines around.

So looks the nymph whom wretched arts adorn,
Betrayed by man, then left for man to scorn;   80
Whose cheek in vain assumes the mimic rose,
While her sad eyes the troubled breast disclose;
Whose outward splendour is but Folly's dress,
Exposing most, when most it gilds distress.

Here joyless roam a wild amphibious race,
With sullen woe displayed in every face;
Who, far from civil arts and social fly,
And scowl at strangers with suspicious eye.

Here too the lawless vagrant of the main
Draws from his plough the intoxicated swain;   90
Want only claimed the labour of the day,
But vice now steals his nightly rest away.

Where are the swains, who, daily labour done,
With rural games played down the setting sun;
Who struck with matchless force the bounding ball,
Or made the ponderous quoit obliquely fall;
While some huge Ajax, terrible and strong,

Engaged some artful stripling of the throng,
And foiled beneath the young Ulysses fell;
100 When peals of praise the merry mischief tell?
Where now are these? Beneath yon cliff they stand,
To show the freighted pinnace where to land;
To load the ready steed with guilty haste,
To fly in terror o'er the pathless waste,
Or when detected in their straggling course,
To foil their foes by cunning or by force;
Or yielding part (when equal knaves contest)
To gain a lawless passport for the rest.

Here wandering long amid these frowning fields,
110 I sought the simple life that Nature yields;
Rapine and Wrong and Fear usurped her place,
And a bold, artful, surly, savage race;
Who, only skilled to take the finny tribe,
The yearly dinner, or septennial bribe,
Wait on the shore, and as the waves run high,
On the tossed vessel bend their eager eye;
Which to their coast directs its venturous way,
Theirs, or the ocean's miserable prey.

As on their neighbouring beach yon swallows stand,
120 And wait for favouring winds to leave the land;
While still for flight the ready wing is spread:
So waited I the favouring hour, and fled;
Fled from these shores where guilt and famine reign,
And cried, Ah! hapless they who still remain;
Who still remain to hear the ocean roar,
Whose greedy waves devour the lessening shore;
Till some fierce tide, with more imperious sway,
Sweeps the low hut and all it holds away;
When the sad tenant weeps from door to door,
130 And begs a poor protection from the poor.

But these are scenes where Nature's niggard hand
Gave a spare portion to the famished land;
Hers is the fault if here mankind complain

Of fruitless toil and labour spent in vain;
But yet in other scenes more fair in view,
Where Plenty smiles – alas! she smiles for few,
And those who taste not, yet behold her store,
Are as the slaves that dig the golden ore,
The wealth around them makes them doubly poor:
Or will you deem them amply paid in health,   140
Labour's fair child, that languishes with Wealth?
Go then! and see them rising with the sun,
Through a long course of daily toil to run;
Like him to make the plenteous harvest grow,
And yet not share the plenty they bestow;
See them beneath the dog-star's raging heat,
When the knees tremble and the temples beat;
Behold them leaning on their scythes, look o'er
The labour past, and toils to come explore;
See them alternate suns and showers engage,   150
And hoard up aches and anguish for their age;
Through fens and marshy moors their steps pursue,
When their warm pores imbibe the evening dew;
Then own that labour may as fatal be
To these thy slaves, as luxury to thee.

Amid this tribe too oft a manly pride
Strives in strong toil the fainting heart to hide;
There may you see the youth of slender frame
Contend with weakness, weariness, and shame;
Yet urged along, and proudly loth to yield,   160
He strives to join his fellows of the field;
Till long contending nature droops at last,
Declining health rejects his poor repast,
His cheerless spouse the coming danger sees,
And mutual murmurs urge the slow disease.

Yet grant them health, 'tis not for us to tell,
Though the head droops not, that the heart is well;
Or will you urge their homely, plenteous fare,
Healthy and plain and still the poor man's share?

170   Oh! trifle not with wants you cannot feel,
Nor mock the misery of a stinted meal;
Homely not wholesome, plain not plenteous, such
As you who envy would disdain to touch.

Ye gentle souls who dream of rural ease,
Whom the smooth stream and smoother sonnet please;
Go! if the peaceful cot your praises share,
Go look within, and ask if peace be there:
If peace be his – that drooping weary sire
Or theirs, that offspring round their feeble fire,
Or hers, that matron pale, whose trembling hand
180   Turns on the wretched hearth the expiring brand.

Nor yet can time itself obtain for these
Life's latest comforts, due respect and ease;
For yonder see that hoary swain, whose age
Can with no cares except its own engage;
Who, propped on that rude staff, looks up to see
The bare arms broken from the withering tree;
On which, a boy, he climbed the loftiest bough,
Then his first joy, but his sad emblem now.

190   He once was chief in all the rustic trade,
His steady hand the straightest furrow made;
Full many a prize he won, and still is proud
To find the triumphs of his youth allowed;
A transient pleasure sparkles in his eyes,
He hears and smiles, then thinks again and sighs:
For now he journeys to his grave in pain;
The rich disdain him; nay, the poor disdain;
Alternate masters now their slave command,
And urge the efforts of his feeble hand;
200   Who, when his age attempts its task in vain,
With ruthless taunts of lazy poor complain.

Oft may you see him when he tends the sheep,
His winter charge, beneath the hillock weep;
Oft hear him murmur to the winds that blow

O'er his white locks, and bury them in snow;
When roused by rage and muttering in the morn,
He mends the broken hedge with icy thorn.

'Why do I live, when I desire to be
At once from life and life's long labour free?
Like leaves in spring, the young are blown away,   210
Without the sorrows of a slow decay;
I, like yon withered leaf, remain behind,
Nipped by the frost and shivering in the wind;
There it abides till younger buds come on,
As I, now all my fellow swains are gone;
Then, from the rising generation thrust,
It falls, like me, unnoticed to the dust.

'These fruitful fields, these numerous flocks I see,
Are others' gain, but killing cares to me;
To me the children of my youth are lords,   220
Slow in their gifts but hasty in their words;
Wants of their own demand their care, and who
Feels his own want and succours others too?
A lonely, wretched man, in pain I go,
None need my help and none relieve my woe;
Then let my bones beneath the turf be laid,
And men forget the wretch they would not aid.'

Thus groan the old, till by disease oppressed,
They taste a final woe, and then they rest.

Theirs is yon house that holds the parish poor,   230
Whose walls of mud scarce bear the broken door;
There, where the putrid vapours flagging, play,
And the dull wheel hums doleful through the day;
There children dwell who know no parents' care,
Parents, who know no children's love, dwell there;
Heart-broken matrons on their joyless bed,
Forsaken wives and mothers never wed;
Dejected widows with unheeded tears,

And crippled age with more than childhood-fears;
240   The lame, the blind, and, far the happiest they!
The moping idiot and the madman gay.

Here too the sick their final doom receive,
Here brought amid the scenes of grief, to grieve;
Where the loud groans from some sad chamber flow,
Mixed with the clamours of the crowd below;
Here sorrowing, they each kindred sorrow scan,
And the cold charities of man to man.
Whose laws indeed for ruined age provide,
And strong compulsion plucks the scrap from pride;
250   But still that scrap is bought with many a sigh,
And pride embitters what it can't deny.

Say ye, oppressed by some fantastic woes,
Some jarring nerve that baffles your repose;
Who press the downy couch, while slaves advance
With timid eye, to read the distant glance;
Who with sad prayers the weary doctor tease
To name the nameless ever-new disease;
Who with mock patience dire complaints endure,
Which real pain, and that alone can cure;
260   How would ye bear in real pain to lie,
Despised, neglected, left alone to die?
How would ye bear to draw your latest breath,
Where all that's wretched paves the way for death?

Such is that room which one rude beam divides,
And naked rafters form the sloping sides;
Where the vile bands that bind the thatch are seen,
And lath and mud is all that lie between;
Save one dull pane, that, coarsely patched, gives way
To the rude tempest, yet excludes the day:
270   Here, on a matted flock, with dust o'erspread,
The drooping wretch reclines his languid head;
For him no hand the cordial cup applies,
Nor wipes the tear that stagnates in his eyes;

No friends with soft discourse his pain beguile,
Nor promise hope till sickness wears a smile.

But soon a loud and hasty summons calls,
Shakes the thin roof, and echoes round the walls;
Anon, a figure enters, quaintly neat,
All pride and business, bustle and conceit;
With looks unaltered by these scenes of woe,   280
With speed that entering, speaks his haste to go;
He bids the gazing throng around him fly,
And carries fate and physic in his eye;
A potent quack, long versed in human ills,
Who first insults the victim whom he kills;
Whose murderous hand a drowsy bench protect,
And whose most tender mercy is neglect.

Paid by the parish for attendance here,
He wears contempt upon his sapient sneer;
In haste he seeks the bed where misery lies,   290
Impatience marked in his averted eyes;
And, some habitual queries hurried o'er,
Without reply, he rushes on the door;
His drooping patient, long inured to pain,
And long unheeded, knows remonstrance vain;
He ceases now the feeble help to crave
Of man, and mutely hastens to the grave.

But ere his death some pious doubts arise,
Some simple fears which 'bold bad' men despise;
Fain would he ask the parish priest to prove   300
His title certain to the joys above;
For this he sends the murmuring nurse, who calls
The holy stranger to these dismal walls;
And doth not he, the pious man, appear,
He, 'passing rich with forty pounds a year?'
Ah! no, a shepherd of a different stock,
And far unlike him, feeds this little flock;
A jovial youth, who thinks his Sunday's task

As much as God or man can fairly ask;
The rest he gives to loves and labours light,
To fields the morning and to feasts the night;
None better skilled, the noisy pack to guide,
To urge their chase, to cheer them or to chide;
Sure in his shot, his game he seldom missed,
And seldom failed to win his game at whist;
Then, while such honours bloom around his head,
Shall he sit sadly by the sick man's bed
To raise the hope he feels not, or with zeal
To combat fears that even the pious feel?

Now once again the gloomy scene explore,
Less gloomy now; the bitter hour is o'er,
The man of many sorrows sighs no more.

Up yonder hill, behold how sadly slow
The bier moves winding from the vale below;
There lie the happy dead, from trouble free,
And the glad parish pays the frugal fee;
No more, oh! Death, thy victim starts to hear
Churchwarden stern, or kingly overseer;
No more the farmer gets his humble bow,
Thou art his lord, the best of tyrants thou!

Now to the church behold the mourners come,
Sedately torpid and devoutly dumb;
The village children now their games suspend,
To see the bier that bears their ancient friend;
For he was one in all their idle sport,
And like a monarch ruled their little court;
The pliant bow he formed, the flying ball,
The bat, the wicket, were his labours all;
Him now they follow to his grave, and stand
Silent and sad, and gazing, hand in hand;
While bending low, their eager eyes explore
The mingled relics of the parish poor:

The bell tolls late, the moping owl flies round,
Fear marks the flight and magnifies the sound;
The busy priest, detained by weightier care,
Defers his duty till the day of prayer;
And waiting long, the crowd retire distressed,
To think a poor man's bones should lie unblessed.

BOOK II

No longer truth, though shown in verse, disdain,
But own the village life a life of pain;
I too must yield, that oft amid these woes
Are gleams of transient mirth and hours of sweet repose.
Such as you find on yonder sportive Green,
The 'Squire's tall gate and churchway-walk between;
Where loitering stray a little tribe of friends,
On a fair Sunday when the sermon ends:
Then rural beaux their best attire put on,
To win their nymphs, as other nymphs are won;   10
While those long wed go plain, and by degrees,
Like other husbands, quit their care to please.
Some of the sermon talk, a sober crowd,
And loudly praise, if it were preached aloud;
Some on the labours of the week look round,
Feel their own worth, and think their toil renowned;
While some, whose hopes to no renown extend,
Are only pleased to find their labours end.

Thus, as their hours glide on with pleasure fraught,
Their careful masters brood the painful thought;   20
Much in their mind they murmur and lament,
That one fair day should be so idly spent;
And think that Heaven deals hard, to tythe their store
And tax their time for preachers and the poor.

Yet still, ye humbler friends, enjoy your hour,
This is your portion, yet unclaimed of power;

This is Heaven's gift to weary men oppressed,
And seems the type of their expected rest:
But yours, alas! are joys that soon decay;
Frail joys, began and ended with the day;
Or yet, while day permits those joys to reign,
The village vices drive them from the plain.

See the stout churl, in drunken fury great,
Strike the bare bosom of his teeming mate!
His naked vices, rude and unrefined,
Exert their open empire o'er the mind;
But can we less the senseless rage despise,
Because the savage acts without disguise?

Yet here Disguise, the city's vice, is seen,
And Slander steals along and taints the Green.
At her approach domestic peace is gone,
Domestic broils at her approach come on;
She to the wife the husband's crime conveys,
She tells the husband when his consort strays;
Her busy tongue, through all the little state,
Diffuses doubt, suspicion, and debate;
Peace, timorous goddess! quits her old domain,
In sentiment and song content to reign.

Nor are the nymphs that breathe the rural air
So fair as Cynthia's, nor so chaste as fair;
These to the town afford each fresher face,
And the Clown's trull receives the Lord's embrace;
From whom, should chance again convey her down,
The Peer's disease in turn attacks the Clown.

Hear too the 'Squire, or 'squire-like farmer, talk,
How round their regions nightly pilferers walk;
How from their ponds the fish are borne, and all
The ripening treasures from their lofty wall;
How their maids languish, while their men run loose,
And leave them scarce a damsel to seduce.

And hark! the riots of the Green begin,
That sprang at first from yonder noisy inn;
What time the weekly pay was vanished all,
And the slow hostess scored the threatening wall;
What time they asked, their friendly feast to close,
One cup, and that just serves to make them foes;
When blows ensue that break the arm of Toil,
And battered faces end the boobies' broil.

Save when to yonder hall they bend their way,
Where the grave Justice ends the grievous fray;   70
He who recites, to keep the poor in awe,
The law's vast volume – for he knows the law. –
To him with anger or with shame repair
The injured peasant and deluded fair.

Lo! at his throne the silent nymph appears,
Frail by her shape, but modest in her tears;
And while she stands abashed, with conscious eye,
Some favourite female of her judge glides by;
Who views with scornful glance the strumpet's fate,
And thanks the stars that made her keeper great: 80
Near her the swain, about to bear for life
One certain evil, doubts 'twixt war and wife;
But, while the faltering damsel takes her oath,
Consents to wed, and so secures them both.

Yet why, you ask, these humble crimes relate,
Why make the poor as guilty as the great?
    To show the great, those mightier sons of Pride,
    How near in vice the lowest are allied;
    Such are their natures, and their passions such,
    But these disguise too little, those too much: 90
    So shall the man of power and pleasure see
    In his own slave as vile a wretch as he;
    In his luxurious lord the servant find
    His own low pleasures and degenerate mind;
    And each in all the kindred vices trace

Of a poor, blind, bewildered, erring race;
Who, a short time in varied fortune passed,
Die, and are equal in the dust at last.

And you, ye poor, who still lament your fate,
Forbear to envy those you reckon great;
And know, amid those blessings they possess,
They are, like you, the victims of distress;
While Sloth with many a pang torments her slave,
Fear waits on guilt, and Danger shakes the brave.

Oh! if in life one noble chief appears,
Great in his name, while blooming in his years;
Born to enjoy whate'er delights mankind,
And yet to all you feel or fear resigned;
Who gave up pleasures you could never share,
For pain which you are seldom doomed to bear;
If such there be, then let your murmurs cease,
Think, think of him, and take your lot in peace.

And such there was: — Oh! grief, that checks our pride,
Weeping we say there was, for MANNERS died; —
Belov'd of Heaven! these humble lines forgive,
That sing of thee, and thus aspire to live.
As the tall oak, whose vigorous branches form
An ample shade and brave the wildest storm,
High o'er the subject wood is seen to grow,
The guard and glory of the trees below;
Till on its head the fiery bolt descends,
And o'er the plain the shattered trunk extends;
Yet then it lies, all wonderous as before,
And still the glory, though the guard no more.

So THOU, when every virtue, every grace,
Rose in thy soul, or shone within thy face;
When, though the Son of GRANBY, thou wert known
Less by thy father's glory than thy own;
When Honour loved, and gave thee every charm,

Fire to thy eye and vigour to thy arm; 130
Then from our lofty hopes and longing eyes
Fate and thy virtues called thee to the skies;
Yet still we wonder at thy towering fame,
And losing thee, still dwell upon thy name.

Oh! ever honoured, ever valued! say
What verse can praise thee, or what work repay?
Yet Verse (in all we can) thy worth repays,
Nor trusts the tardy zeal of future days; —
Honours for thee thy Country shall prepare,
Thee in their hearts, the Good, the Brave shall bear; 140
To deeds like thine shall noblest chiefs aspire,
The Muse shall mourn thee, and the world admire.

In future times, when smit with glory's charms,
The untried youth first quits a father's arms;
'Oh be like him,' the weeping sire shall say,
'Like MANNERS walk, who walked in honour's way;
In danger foremost, yet in death sedate,
Oh! be like him in all things, but his fate!'

If for that fate such public tears be shed,
That victory seems to die now THOU art dead; 150
How shall a friend his nearer hope resign,
That friend a brother, and whose soul was thine?
By what bold lines shall we his grief express,
Or by what soothing numbers make it less?

'Tis not, I know, the chiming of a song,
Nor all the powers that to the Muse belong;
Words aptly culled, and meanings well expressed,
Can calm the sorrows of a wounded breast:
But RUTLAND'S virtues shall his griefs restrain,
And join to heal the bosom where they reign. 160

Yet hard the task to heal the bleeding heart,
To bid the still-recurring thoughts depart;
Hush the loud grief, and stem the rising sigh,

And curb rebellious passion with reply;
Calmly to dwell on all that pleased before,
And yet to know that all can please no more –
Oh! glorious labour of the soul, to save
Her captive powers, and bravely mourn the brave!

To such, these thoughts will lasting comfort give: –
Life is not valued by the time we live;
'Tis not an even course of threescore years,
A life of narrow views and paltry fears;
Grey hairs and wrinkles, and the cares they bring,
That take from death the terror or the sting:
But 'tis the spirit that is mounting high
Above the world; a native of the sky;
The noble spirit, that, in dangers brave,
Calmly looks on, or looks beyond the grave.
Such MANNERS was, so he resign'd his breath!
If in a glorious, then a timely death.

Cease then that grief, and let those tears subside:
If Passion rule us, be that passion Pride;
If Reason, Reason bids us strive to raise
Our sinking hearts, and be like him we praise;
Or if Affection still the soul subdue,
Bring all his virtues, all his worth in view,
And let Affection find its comfort too;
For how can grief so deeply wound the heart,
Where admiration claims so large a part?

Grief is a foe, expel him then thy soul;
Let nobler thoughts the nearer woes control;
Oh! make the age to come thy better care,
See other RUTLANDS, other GRANBYS there;
And as thy thoughts through streaming ages glide,
See other heroes die as MANNERS died;
Victims victorious, who with him shall stand
In Fame's fair book the guardians of the land;

And from their fate thy race shall nobler grow,
As trees shoot upward that are pruned below:
Or, as old Thames, borne down with decent pride,   200
Sees his young streams go murmuring by his side;
Though some, by art cut off, no longer run,
And some are lost beneath the summer's sun;
Yet the strong stream moves on, and as it moves,
Its power increases, and its use improves;
While plenty round its spacious waves bestow,
Still it flows on, and shall for ever flow.

THE HALL OF JUSTICE

PART THE FIRST

Confiteor facere hoc annos; sed et altera causa est,
Anxietas animi, continuusque dolor.

OVID

MAGISTRATE, VAGRANT, CONSTABLE, ETC

VAGRANT

Take, take away thy barbarous Hand,
    And let me to thy Master speak;
Remit awhile the harsh Command,
    And hear me, or my Heart will break.

MAGISTRATE

Fond Wretch! and what canst thou relate,
    But Deeds of Sorrow, Shame, and Sin?
Thy Crime is proved, thou know'st thy Fate;
    But come, thy Tale! begin, begin! –

VAGRANT

'My Crime! – This sickening Child to feed,
    I seized the Food, your Witness saw;
I knew your Laws forbad the Deed,
    But yielded to a stronger Law.

Know'st thou, to Nature's great Command,
    All human Laws are frail and weak?
Nay! frown not – stay his eager Hand,
    And hear me, or my Heart will break.

In this, the adopted Babe I hold,
    With anxious Fondness to my Breast,
My Heart's sole Comfort, I behold,
    More dear than Life, when Life was blessed,

I saw her pining, fainting, cold,
 I begged – but vain was my Request.

I saw the tempting Food, and seized –
 My Infant-Sufferer found Relief;
And, in the pilfered Treasure pleased,
 Smiled on my Guilt and hushed my Grief.

But I have Griefs of other Kind,
 Troubles and Sorrows more severe;
Give me to ease my tortured Mind,
 Lend to my Woes, a patient Ear;   30
And let me – if I may not find
 A Friend to help – find one to hear.

Yet nameless let me plead – my Name
 Would only wake the Cry of Scorn;
A Child of Sin, conceived in Shame,
 Brought forth in Woe, to Misery born.

My Mother dead, my Father lost,
 I wandered with a vagrant Crew;
A common Care, a common Cost,
 Their Sorrows and their Sins I knew;   40
With them, on Want and Error forced,
 Like them, I base and guilty grew.

Few are my Years, not so my Crimes;
 The Age, which these sad Looks declare,
Is Sorrow's Work, it is not Time's,
 And I am old in Shame and Care.

Taught to believe the World a place,
 Where every Stranger was a Foe,
Trained in the Arts that mark our Race,
 To what new People could I go?   50
Could I a better Life embrace,
 Or live as Virtue dictates? No! –

So through the Land, I wandering went,
 And little found of Grief or Joy;

But lost my Bosom's sweet Content,
    When first I loved, the Gipsy-Boy.

A sturdy Youth he was and tall,
    His Looks would all his Soul declare,
His piercing Eyes were deep and small,
60   And strongly curled his Raven-Hair.

Yes, Aaron had each manly Charm,
    All in the May of youthful Pride,
He scarcely feared his Father's Arm,
    And every other Arm defied. –
Oft when they grew in Anger warm,
    (Whom will not Love and Power divide?)
I rose, their wrathful Souls to calm,
    Not yet in sinful Combat tried.

His Father was our Party's Chief,
70   And dark and dreadful was his Look,
His Presence filled my Heart with Grief,
    Although to me, he kindly spoke.

With Aaron I delighted went,
    His Favour was my Bliss and Pride;
In growing Hope our Days we spent,
    Love, growing Charms in either spied,
It saw them, all which Nature lent,
    It lent them, all which she denied.

Could I the Father's Kindness prize,
80   Or grateful Looks on him bestow;
Whom I beheld in wrath arise,
    When Aaron sank beneath his Blow?

He drove him down with wicked Hand,
    It was a dreadful Sight to see;
Then vexed him, till he left the Land,
    And told his cruel Love to me; –
The Clan were all at his Command,
    Whatever his Command might be.

The Night was dark, the Lanes were deep, 90
    And one by one, they took their way;
He bade me lay me down and sleep,
    I only wept and wished for Day.

Accursèd be the Love he bore, –
    Accursèd was the Force he used,
So let him of his GOD implore
    For Mercy, and be so refused!

You frown again, – to show my Wrong,
    Can I in gentle Language speak?
My Woes are deep, my Words are strong, –
    And hear me; or my Heart will break. 100

MAGISTRATE

I hear thy Words, I feel thy Pain;
    Forbear awhile to speak thy Woes;
Receive our Aid, and then again,
    The Story of thy Life disclose.

For, though seduced and led astray,
    Thou'st travelled far and wandered long
Thy GOD hath seen thee all the way,
    And all the Turns that led thee wrong.

PART THE SECOND

Quondam ridentes oculi, nunc fonte perenni
Deplorant poenas nocte dieque suas.
                CORN. *Galli Eleg.*

MAGISTRATE

Come, now again thy Woes impart,
    Tell all thy Sorrows, all thy Sin;
We cannot heal the throbbing Heart,
    Till we discern the Wounds within.

Compunction weeps our Guilt away,
    The Sinner's Safety is his Pain;
Such Pangs for our Offences pay,
    And these severer Griefs are Gain.

VAGRANT

The Son came back – he found us wed,
    Then dreadful was the Oath he swore; –
His Way through *Blackburn* Forest led, –
    His Father we beheld no more.

Of all our daring Clan, not one,
    Would on the doubtful Subject dwell;
For all esteemed the injured Son,
    And feared the Tale, which he could tell.

But I had mightier Cause for Fear,
    For slow and mournful round my Bed,
I saw a dreadful Form appear, –
    It came when I and Aaron wed.

(Yes! we were wed, I know my Crime, –
    We slept beneath the Elmin Tree;
But I was grieving all the time,
    And Aaron frowned my Tears to see.

For he not yet had felt the Pain,
    That rankles in a wounded Breast;
He waked to Sin, then slept again,
    Forsook his GOD, yet took his Rest. –

But I was forced to feign Delight,
    And Joy in Mirth and Music sought, –
And Memory now recalls the Night,
    With such Surprise and Horror fraught,
That Reason felt a moment's Flight,
    And left a Mind, to Madness wrought.)

When waking, on my heaving Breast,
    I felt a Hand as cold as Death;

A sudden Fear my Voice suppressed,
  A chilling Terror stopped my Breath. –

I seemed – no Words can utter how!
  For there my Father-Husband stood, –   40
And thus he said: – 'Will GOD allow,
  The great Avenger, just and good,
A Wife, to break her Marriage Vow?
  A Son, to shed his Father's Blood?'

I trembled at the dismal Sounds,
  But vainly strove a Word to say;
So, pointing to his bleeding Wounds,
  * The threatening Spectre stalked away.

I brought a lovely Daughter forth,
  His Father's Child, in Aaron's Bed;   50
He took her from me in his wrath,
  'Where is my Child?' – 'Thy Child is dead.'

'Twas false – we wandered far and wide,
  Through Town and Country, Field and Fen,
Till Aaron fighting, fell and died,
  And I became a Wife again.

I then was young: – my Husband sold
  My fancied Charms, for wicked Price;
He gave me oft, for sinful Gold,
  The Slave, but not the Friend of Vice: –   60
Behold me Heaven! my Pains behold,
  And let them for my Sins suffice!

The Wretch who lent me thus for Gain,
  Despised me when my Youth was fled;
Then came Disease and brought me Pain: –
  Come, Death, and bear me to the Dead!
For though I grieve, my Grief is vain,
  And fruitless all the Tears I shed.

* The state of mind here described, will account for a vision of this nature, without
  having recourse to any supernatural appearance.

True, I was not to Virtue trained,
    Yet well I knew my Deeds were ill;
By each Offence my Heart was pained,
    I wept, but I offended still;
My better Thoughts my life disdained,
    But yet the viler led my Will.

My Husband died, and now no more,
    My Smile was sought or asked my Hand,
A widowed Vagrant, vile and poor,
    Beneath a Vagrant's vile command.

Ceaseless I roved the Country round,
    To win my Bread by fraudful Arts,
And long a poor Subsistence found,
    By spreading Nets for simple Hearts.

Though poor, and abject, and despised,
    Their Fortunes to the Crowd I told;
I gave the Young the Love they prized,
    And promised Wealth to bless the Old;
Schemes for the Doubtful I devised,
    And Charms for the Forsaken sold.

At length for Arts like these confined,
    In Prison with a lawless Crew;
I soon perceived a kindred Mind,
    And there my long-lost Daughter knew.

His Father's Child, whom Aaron gave
    To wander with a distant Clan,
The Miseries of the World to brave,
    And be the Slave of Vice and Man.

She knew my Name — we met in Pain,
    Our parting Pangs, can I express?
She sailed a Convict o'er the Main,
    And left an Heir to her Distress.

This is that Heir to Shame and Pain,
    For whom I only could descry

A World of Trouble and Disdain:
　　Yet, could I bear to see her die,
Or stretch her feeble Hands in vain,
　　And weeping, beg of me Supply?

No! though the Fate thy Mother knew,
　　Was shameful! shameful though thy Race
Have wandered all, a lawless Crew,
　　Outcasts, despised in every Place; —.　　　　110

Yet as the dark and muddy Tide,
　　When far from its polluted Source,
Becomes more pure, and purified,
　　Flows in a clear and happy Course; —
In thee, dear Infant! so may end,
　　Our Shame, in thee our Sorrows cease!
And thy pure Course will then extend,
　　In Floods of Joy, o'er Vales of Peace.

Oh! by the GOD who loves to spare,
　　Deny me not the Boon I crave;　　　　120
Let this loved Child your Mercy share,
　　And let me find a peaceful Grave;
Make her yet spotless Soul your Care,
　　And let my Sins their Portion have,
Her for a better Fate prepare,
　　And punish whom 'twere Sin to save!

MAGISTRATE

Recall the Word, renounce the Thought,
　　Command thy Heart and bend thy Knee,
There is to all a Pardon brought,
　　A Ransom rich, assured and free;　　　　130
'Tis full when found, 'tis found if sought,
　　Oh! seek it, till 'tis sealed to Thee.

VAGRANT

But how my Pardon shall I know?

MAGISTRATE

By feeling Dread that 'tis not sent,
  By Tears for Sin that freely flow,
By Grief, that all thy Tears are spent,
  By Thoughts on that great Debt we owe,
With all the Mercy GOD has lent,
  By suffering what thou canst not show,
Yet showing how thine Heart is rent,
  Till thou canst feel thy Bosom glow,
And say, 'MY SAVIOUR, I REPENT!'

140

SIR EUSTACE GREY

Scene. – A MADHOUSE

Persons: VISITOR, PHYSICIAN, AND PATIENT

Veris miscens falsa. –
SENECA in *Herc. furente*

VISITOR
I'll know no more; – the Heart is torn
   By Views of Woe, we cannot heal;
Long shall I see these Things forlorn,
   And oft again their Griefs shall feel;
   As each upon the Mind, shall steal;
That wan Projector's mystic Style,
   That lumpish Idiot leering by,
That peevish Idler's ceaseless Wile,
   And that poor Maiden's half-formed Smile,
While struggling for the full-drawn Sigh! . . .   10
   I'll know no more.

PHYSICIAN
       . . . Yes, turn again;
Then speed to happier Scenes thy Way,
   When thou hast viewed, what yet remain,
The Ruins of Sir *Eustace Grey*,
   The Sport of Madness, Misery's Prey:
But he will no Historian need,
   His Cares, his Crimes will he display,
And show (as one from Frenzy freed)
   The proud-lost Mind, the rash-done Deed.

That Cell, to him is *Greyling Hall:* –
    Approach; he'll bid thee welcome there;
Will sometimes for his Servant call,
    And sometimes point the vacant Chair:
He can, with free and easy air,
    Appear attentive and polite;
Can veil his Woes in Manners fair,
    And Pity with Respect excite.

PATIENT

Who comes? – Approach! – 'Tis kindly done: –
    My learn'd Physician, and a Friend,
Their Pleasures quit, to visit One,
    Who cannot to their Ease attend
Nor Joys bestow, nor Comforts lend,
    As when I lived so blessed, so well,
And dreamed not, I must soon contend
    With those malignant Powers of Hell.

PHYSICIAN

Less warmth, Sir Eustace, or we go. –

PATIENT

    See! I am calm as Infant-Love,
A very Child, but one of Woe,
    Whom you should pity, not reprove: –
But Men at ease, who never strove
    With Passions wild, will calmly show,
How soon we may their Ills remove,
    And Masters of their Madness grow.

Some twenty Years I think are gone, –
    (Time flies, I know not how, away,)
The Sun upon no happier shone,
    Nor prouder Man, than *Eustace Grey*.
Ask where you would, and all would say,
    The Man admired and praised of all,

By Rich and Poor, by Grave and Gay,   50
   Was the young Lord of *Greyling Hall*.

Yes! I had Youth and rosy Health;
   Was nobly formed, as Man might be;
For Sickness then, of all my Wealth,
   I never gave a single Fee:
The Ladies fair, the Maidens free,
   Were all accustomed then to say,
Who would an handsome Figure see,
   Should look upon Sir *Eustace Grey*.

He had a frank and pleasant Look,   60
   A cheerful Eye and Accent bland;
His very Speech and Manner spoke
   The generous Heart, the open Hand;
About him all was gay or grand,
   He had the Praise of Great and Small;
He bought, improved, projected, planned,
   And reigned a Prince at *Greyling Hall*.

My Lady! – she was all we love;
   All Praise (to speak her Worth) is faint;
Her Manners showed the yielding Dove,   70
   Her Morals, the seraphic Saint;
She never breathed nor looked Complaint,
   No Equal upon Earth had she: . . .
Now, what is this fair Thing I paint?
   Alas! as all that live, shall be.

There was beside, a gallant Youth,
   And him my Bosom's Friend, I had: . . .
Oh! I was rich – in very truth,
   It made me proud – it made me mad! –
Yes I was lost – but there was Cause! . . .   80
   Where stood my Tale? – I cannot find –
But I had all Mankind's Applause,
   And all the Smiles of Womankind.

There were two Cherub-things beside,
    A gracious Girl, a glorious Boy;
Yet more to swell my full-blown Pride,
    To varnish higher my fading Joy,
Pleasures were ours without alloy,
    Nay Paradise, . . . till my frail Eve
Our Bliss was tempted to destroy;
    Deceived and fated to deceive.

But I deserved; for all that time,
    When I was loved, admired, caressed,
There was within, each secret Crime,
    Unfelt, uncancelled, unconfessed;
I never then my GOD addressed,
    In grateful Praise or humble Prayer;
And if His Word was not my Jest!
    (Dread thought!) it never was my Care.

I doubted: — Fool I was to doubt!
    If that all-piercing Eye could see, —
If He who looks all Worlds throughout,
    Would so minute and careful be,
As to perceive and punish me: —
    With Man I would be great and high,
But with my GOD so lost, that He,
    In his large View, should pass me by.

Thus blessed with Children, Friend, and Wife,
    Blessed far beyond the vulgar Lot;
Of all that gladdens human Life,
    Where was the Good, that I had not?
But my vile Heart had sinful Spot,
    And Heaven beheld its deepening Stain,
Eternal Justice I forgot,
    And Mercy, sought not to obtain.

Come near, . . . I'll softly speak the rest! —
    Alas! 'tis known to all the Crowd,
Her guilty Love was all confessed;

And his, who so much Truth avowed,
My faithless Friends. – In Pleasure proud   120
   I sat, when these cursed Tidings came;
Their Guilt, their Flight was told aloud,
   And Envy smiled to hear my Shame!

I called on Vengeance; at the Word
   She came: – Can I the Deed forget?
I held the Sword, the accursèd Sword,
   The Blood of his false Heart made wet;
And that fair Victim paid her Debt,
   She pined, she died, she loathed to live; . . .
I saw her dying – see her yet: 130
   Fair fallen Thing! my Rage forgive!

Those Cherubs still, my Life to bless,
   Were left: Could I my Fears remove,
Sad Fears that checked each fond Caress,
   And poisoned all parental Love;
Yet that, with jealous Feelings strove,
   And would at last have won my Will,
Had I not, Wretch! been doomed to prove
   The Extremes of mortal Good and Ill.

In Youth! Health! Joy! in Beauty's Pride!   140
   They drooped: as Flowers when blighted bow,
The dire Infection came: – They died,
   And I was cursed – as I am now –
Nay frown not, angry Friend. – allow,
   That I was deeply, sorely tried;
Hear then, and you must wonder how
   I could such Storms and Strifes abide.

Storms! – not that Clouds embattled make,
   When they afflict this earthly Globe;
But such as with their Terrors shake   150
   Man's Breast, and to the bottom probe;
They make the Hypocrite disrobe,
   They try us all, if false or true;

For this, one Devil had power on *Job*;
   And I was long the Slave of two.

PHYSICIAN

Peace, peace, my Friend; these Subjects fly;
   Collect thy Thoughts – go calmly on. –

PATIENT

And shall I then the Fact deny?
   I was, – thou knowest, – I was begone,
160   Like him who filled the Eastern Throne,
   To whom the WATCHER* cried aloud;
That royal Wretch of *Babylon*,
   Who was so guilty and so proud.

Like him with haughty, stubborn Mind,
   I, in my State, my Comforts sought;
Delight and Praise I hoped to find,
   In what I builded, planted, bought!
Oh! Arrogance! by Misery taught –
   Soon came a Voice! I felt it come;
170   'Full be his Cup, with Evil fraught,
   Demons his Guides, and Death his Doom!'

Then was I cast from out my State;
   Two Fiends of Darkness led my Way;
They waked me early, watched me late,
   My Dread by Night, my Plague by Day!
Oh! I was made their Sport, their Play,
   Through many a stormy troubled Year,
And how they used their passive Prey,
   Is sad to tell: but you shall hear.

180   And first, before they sent me forth,
   Through this unpitying World to run,
They robbed *Sir Eustace* of his Worth,
   Lands, Manors, Lordships, every one;

* Prophecy of Daniel, chap. iv. 22.

So was that gracious Man undone,
    Was spurned as vile, was scorned as poor,
Whom every former Friend would shun,
    And Menials drove from every Door.

Then those ill-favoured Ones*, whom none
    But my unhappy Eyes could view,
Led me, with wild Emotion on,   190
    And, with resistless Terror, drew.
Through Lands we fled, o'er Seas we flew,
    And halted on a boundless Plain;
Where nothing fed, nor breathed nor grew,
    But Silence ruled the still Domain.

Upon that boundless Plain, below,
    The setting Sun's last Rays were shed,
And gave a mild and sober Glow,
    Where all were still, asleep or dead;
Vast Ruins in the midst were spread,   200
    Pillars and Pediments sublime,
Where the grey Moss had formed a Bed,
    And clothed the crumbling Spoils of Time.

There was I fixed, I know not how,
    Condemned for untold Years to stay;
Yet Years were not; – one dreadful *Now*,
    Endured no Change of Night or Day;
The same mild Evening's sleeping Ray,
    Shone softly-solemn and serene,
And all that time, I gazed away,   210
    The setting Sun's sad Rays were seen.

At length a Moment's Sleep stole on, –
    Again came my commissioned Foes;
Again through Sea and Land we're gone,
    No Peace, no Respite, no Repose;
Above the dark broad Sea we rose,

* Vide Bunyan's *Pilgrim's Progress*.

We ran through bleak and frozen Land;
  I had no Strength, their Strength to oppose,
    An Infant in a Giant's hand.

They placed me where those Streamers play,
    Those nimble Beams of brilliant Light;
It would the stoutest Heart dismay,
    To see, to feel, that dreadful Sight:
So swift, so pure, so cold, so bright,
    They pierced my Frame with icy Wound,
And all that half-year's polar Night,
    Those dancing Streamers wrapped me round.

Slowly that Darkness passed away,
    When down upon the Earth I fell, –
Some hurried Sleep, was mine by day;
    But soon as tolled the Evening Bell,
They forced me on, where ever dwell
    Far-distant Men in Cities fair,
Cities of whom no Travellers tell,
    Nor Feet but mine were Wanderers there.

Their Watchmen stare, and stand aghast,
    As on we hurry through the dark;
The Watch-light blinks, as we go past,
    The Watch-dog shrinks and fears to bark;
The Watch-tower's Bell sounds shrill; and, hark
    The free Wind blows – we've left the Town –
A wide Sepulchral Ground I mark,
    And on a Tomb-stone place me down.

What Monuments of mighty Dead!
    What Tombs of various kinds are found!
And Stones erect, their Shadows shed,
    On humble Graves, with Wickers bound;
Some risen fresh, above the Ground,
    Some level with the native Clay,
What sleeping Millions wait the Sound,
    'Arise, ye Dead, and come away!'

Alas! they stay not for that Call;
　　Spare me this Woe! ye Demons, spare! –
They come! the shrouded Shadows all, –
　　'Tis more than mortal Brain can bear:
Rustling they rise, they sternly glare
　　At Man upheld by vital Breath!
Who led by wicked Fiends should dare
　　To join the shadowy Troops of Death!

Yes! I have felt all Man can feel,   260
　　Till he shall pay his Nature's Debt;
Ills that no Hope has Strength to heal,
　　No Mind the Comfort to forget:
Whatever Cares the Heart can fret,
　　The Spirits wear, the Temper gall;
Woe, Want, Dread, Anguish, all beset
　　My sinful Soul! – together all!

Those Fiends, upon a shaking Fen,
　　Fixed me, in dark tempestuous Night;
There never trod the Foot of Men,   270
　　There flocked the Fowl in wintry Flight;
There danced the Moor's deceitful Light,
　　Above the Pool where Sedges grow;
And when the Morning-Sun shone bright,
　　It shone upon a Field of Snow.

They hung me on a Bough, so small,
　　The Rook could build her nest no higher;
They fixed me on the trembling Ball,
　　That crowns the Steeple's quivering Spire;
They set me where the Seas retire,   280
　　But drown with their returning Tide,
And made me flee the Mountain's Fire,
　　When rolling from its burning Side.

I've hung upon the ridgy Steep
　　Of Cliffs, and held the rambling Briar;
I've plunged below the billowy Deep,

Where Air was sent me to respire;
  I've been where hungry Wolves retire;
    And (to complete my Woes) I've ran,
Where Bedlam's crazy Crew conspire
    Against the Life of reasoning Man.

I've furled in Storms the flapping Sail,
  By hanging from the Top-mast-head;
I've served the vilest Slaves in Jail,
  And picked the Dunghill's Spoil for Bread;
I've made the Badger's Hole my Bed,
  I've wandered with a Gipsy Crew,
I've dreaded all the Guilty dread,
  And done what they would fear to do.

On Sand where ebbs and flows the Food,
  Midway they placed and bade me die,
Propped on my Staff, I stoutly stood
  When the swift Waves came rolling by;
And high they rose, and still more high,
  Till my Lips drank the bitter Brine;
I sobbed convulsed, then cast mine Eye
  And saw the Tide's reflowing sign.

And then, my Dreams were such as nought
  Could yield but my unhappy Case;
I've been of thousand Devils caught,
  And thrust into that horrid Place,
Where reign Dismay, Despair, Disgrace;
  Furies with iron Fangs were there,
To torture that accursèd Race,
  Doomed to Dismay, Disgrace, Despair.

Harmless I was; yet hunted down
  For Treasons, to my Soul unfit;
I've been pursued through many a Town,
  For Crimes that petty Knaves commit:
I've been adjudged to have lost my Wit,
  Because I preached so loud and well,

And thrown into the Dungeon's Pit,
   For trampling on the Pit of Hell.

Such were the Evils, Man of Sin,
   That I was fated to sustain;
And add to all, without – within,
   A Soul defiled with every Stain,
That Man's reflecting Mind can pain;
   That Pride, Wrong, Rage, Despair can make;
In fact, they'd nearly touched my Brain,   330
   And Reason on her Throne would shake.

But Pity will the vilest seek,
   If punished Guilt will not repine, –
I heard an heavenly Teacher speak,
   And felt the SUN of MERCY shine:
I hailed the Light! the Birth divine!
   And then was sealed among the few;
Those angry Fiends beheld the Sign;
   And from me in an instant flew.

Come hear how thus, the Charmers cry,   340
   To wandering Sheep the Strays of Sin;
While some the Wicket-gate pass by,
   And some will knock and enter in,
Full joyful 'tis a Soul to win,
   For he that winneth Souls is wise;
Now hark! the holy Strains begin,
   And thus the sainted Preacher cries *: –

'Pilgrim burdened with thy Sin,
Come the way to Zion's Gate,

---

* It has been suggested to me, that this change from restlessness to repose, in the mind of Sir EUSTACE, is wrought by a methodistic call; and it is admitted to be such: a sober and rational conversion, could not have happened while the disorder of the brain continued: yet the verses which follow, in a different measure, are not intended to make any religious Persuasion appear ridiculous; they are to be supposed as the effect of memory in the disordered mind of the speaker, and though evidently enthusiastic, in respect to language, are not meant to convey any impropriety of sentiment.

350 There, till Mercy lets thee in,
Knock and weep and watch and wait.
   Knock! – He knows the Sinner's Cry;
   Weep! – He loves the Mourner's Tears:
   Watch! – for saving grace is nigh:
   Wait, – till heavenly Light appears.

'Hark! it is the Bridegroom's Voice:
Welcome, Pilgrim, to thy Rest;
Now within the Gate rejoice,
Safe and sealed and bought and blessed!
360   Safe – from all the Lures of Vice,
   Sealed – by Signs the Chosen know,
   Bought by Love and Life the Price,
   Blessed – the mighty Debt to owe.

'Holy Pilgrim! what for thee,
In a World like this remain?
From thy guarded Breast shall flee,
Fear and Shame, and Doubt and Pain.
   Fear – the Hope of Heaven shall fly,
   Shame – from Glory's View retire,
370   Doubt – in certain Rapture die,
   Pain – in endless Bliss expire.'

But though my Day of Grace was come,
   Yet still my Days of Grief I find;
The former Clouds' collected gloom,
   Still sadden the reflecting Mind;
The Soul to evil Things consigned
   Will of their Evil some retain;
The Man will seem to Earth inclined,
   And will not look erect again.

380 Thus, though elect, I feel it hard,
   To lose what I possessed before,
To be from all my Wealth debarred –
   The brave *Sir Eustace* is no more;
But old I wax and passing poor,

Stern, rugged Men my Conduct view;
They chide my Wish, they bar my Door,
　'Tis hard – I weep – you see I do. –

Must you, my Friends, no longer stay?
　Thus quickly all my Pleasures end?
But I'll remember, when I pray,   390
　My kind Physician and his Friend;
And those sad Hours, you deign to spend
　With me, I shall requite them all;
Sir Eustace for his Friends shall send,
　And thank their Love at *Greyling Hall*.

———

VISITOR

The poor Sir Eustace! – yet his Hope.
　Leads him to think of Joys again;
And when his Earthly Visions droop,
　His Views of Heavenly Kind remain: –
But whence that meek and humbled Strain,   400
　That Spirit wounded, lost, resigned;
Would not so proud a Soul disdain
　The Madness of the poorest Mind.

PHYSICIAN

No! for the more he swelled with Pride,
　The more he felt Misfortune's Blow;
Disgrace and Grief he could not hide,
　And Poverty had laid him low:
Thus Shame and Sorrow working slow,
　At length this humble Spirit gave;
Madness on these began to grow,   410
　And bound him to his Fiends a Slave.

Though the wild Thoughts had touched his Brain,
　Then was he free: – So, forth he ran;
To soothe or threat, alike were vain;
　He spake of Fiends; looked wild and wan;

Year after year, the hurried Man
  Obeyed those Fiends from place to place;
Till his religious Change began
  To form a frenzied Child of Grace.

For, as the Fury lost its Strength,
  The Mind reposed; by slow Degrees,
Came lingering Hope, and brought at length,
  To the tormented Spirit, Ease:
This Slave of Sin, whom Fiends could seize;
  Felt or believed their Power had end;
''Tis faith,' he cried, 'my Bosom frees,
  And now my SAVIOUR is my Friend.'

But ah! though Time can yield Relief,
  And soften Woes it cannot cure;
Would we not suffer Pain and Grief,
  To have our Reason sound and sure?
Then let us keep our Bosoms pure,
  Our Fancy's favourite Flights suppress;
Prepare the Body to endure,
  And bend the Mind to meet Distress;
And then His guardian Care implore,
Whom Demons dread and Men adore.

THE BOROUGH

LETTER XIX

THE POOR OF THE BOROUGH

THE PARISH-CLERK

Nam dives qui fieri vult,
Et citò vult fieri; sed quae reverentia legum,
Quis metus, aut pudor est unquam properantis avari?
JUVENAL. *Sat.* 14.

Nocte brevem si fortè indulsit cura soporem,
Et toto versata thoro jam membra quiescunt,
Continuò templum et violati Numinis aras,
Et quod praecipuis mentem sudoribus urget,
Te videt in somnis; tua sacra et major imago
Humanâ turbat pavidum, cogitque fateri.
JUVENAL. *Sat.* 13.

Began his Duties with the late Vicar, a grave and austere Man;
one fully orthodox; a Detecter and Opposer of the Wiles of
Satan. – His Opinion of his own Fortitude. – The more Frail
offended by these Professions. – His good Advice gives further
Provocation. – They invent Stratagems to overcome his Virtue.
– His Triumph. – He is yet not invulnerable: is assaulted by
Fear of Want, and Avarice. – He gradually yields to the
Seduction. – He reasons with himself and is persuaded. – He
offends, but with Terror; repeats his Offence; grows familiar
with Crime; is detected. – His sufferings and Death.

With our late Vicar, and his Age the same,
His Clerk, hight *Jachin*, to his Office came;
The like slow Speech was his, the like tall slender Frame:

But *Jachin* was the gravest Man on ground,
And heard his Master's Jokes with look profound;
For worldly Wealth this Man of Letters sighed,
And had a sprinkling of the Spirit's Pride:
But he was sober, chaste, devout, and just,
One whom his Neighbours could believe and trust:
Of none suspected, neither Man nor Maid
By him were wronged, or were of him afraid.

There was indeed a frown, a trick of State
In *Jachin*; – formal was his Air and Gait;
But if he seemed more solemn and less kind,
Than some light Men to light Affairs confined,
Still 'twas allowed that he should so behave
As in high Seat, and be severely grave.

This book-taught Man to Man's first foe professed
Defiance stern, and Hate that knew not rest;
He held that *Satan*, since the World began,
In every act, had Strife with every Man;
That never evil Deed on Earth was done,
But of the acting Parties he was one;
The flattering Guide to make ill Prospects clear;
To smooth rough Ways, the constant Pioneer;
The ever-tempting, soothing, softening Power,
Ready to cheat, seduce, deceive, devour.

'Me has the sly Seducer oft withstood,'
Said pious *Jachin*, – 'but he gets no good;
I pass the House where swings the tempting Sign,
And pointing, tell him, "*Satan*, that is thine:"
I pass the Damsels pacing down the Street,
And look more grave and solemn when we meet;
Nor doth it irk me to rebuke their Smiles,
Their wanton Ambling and their watchful Wiles:
Nay, like the good *John Bunyan*, when I view
Those forms, I'm angry at the Ills they do;

That I could pinch and spoil, in Sin's despite,
Beauties! which frail and evil Thoughts excite.*

'At Feasts and Banquets seldom am I found,   40
And (save at Church) abhor a tuneful Sound;
To Plays and Shows I run not to and fro,
And where my Master goes, forbear to go.'

No wonder *Satan* took the thing amiss,
To be opposed by such a Man as this —
A Man so grave, important, cautious, wise,
Who dared not trust his Feeling or his Eyes;
No wonder he should lurk and lie in wait,
Should fit his Hooks and ponder on his Bait,
Should on his Movements keep a watchful eye,   50
For he pursued a Fish who led the Fry.

With his own Peace our Clerk was not content,
He tried, good Man! to make his Friends repent.

'Nay, nay, my Friends, from Inns and Taverns fly,
You may suppress your thirst, but not supply:
A foolish Proverb says, *the Devil's at home*;
But he is there, and tempts in every Room:
Men feel, they know not why, such places please;
His are the Spells — they're Idleness and Ease;
Magic of fatal kind he throws around,   60
Where Care is banished but the Heart is bound.

'Think not of Beauty; — when a Maid you meet,
Turn from her view and step across the Street:
Dread all the Sex; their Looks create a Charm,
A Smile should fright you and a Word alarm:
E'en I myself, with all my watchful care,
Have for an instant felt the insidious snare,
And caught my sinful eyes at the endangering stare;
Till I was forced to smite my bounding breast
With forceful blow and bid the bold-one rest.   70

---

* *John Bunyan*, in one of the many productions of his zeal, has ventured to make
public this extraordinary sentiment, which the frigid piety of our Clerk so readily
adopted.

'Go not with Crowds when they to Pleasure run,
But public Joy in private Safety shun;
When Bells, diverted from their true intent,
Ring loud for some deluded Mortal sent
To hear or make long Speech in Parliament;
What time, the Many, that unruly beast,
Roars its rough Joy and shares the final Feast;
Then heed my Counsel, shut thine ears and eyes,
A few will hear me – for the Few are wise.'

Not *Satan*'s Friends, nor *Satan*'s self could bear
The cautious Man who took of Souls such care;
An Interloper, – one who, out of place,
Had volunteered upon the side of Grace:
There was his Master ready once a week
To give Advice; what further need he seek?
'Amen, so be it:' – what had he to do
With more than this? – 'twas insolent and new;
And some determined on a way to see
How frail he was, that so it might not be.

First they essayed to tempt our Saint to sin,
By points of Doctrine argued at an Inn;
Where he might warmly reason, deeply drink,
Then lose all power to argue and to think.

In vain they tried; he took the Question up,
Cleared every Doubt, and barely touched the Cup:
By many a Text he proved his Doctrine sound,
And looked in triumph on the Tempters round.

Next 'twas their care an artful Lass to find,
Who might consult him, as perplexed in Mind;
She they conceived might put her Case with fears,
With tender tremblings and seducing tears;
She might such Charms of various kind display,
That he would feel their force and melt away:
For why of Nymphs such caution and such dread,
Unless he felt, and feared to be misled.

She came, she spake: he calmly heard her Case,
And plainly told her 'twas a want of Grace,
Bade her 'such Fancies and Affections check,
And wear a thicker Muslin on her Neck.'
Abashed, his human Foes the Combat fled,   110
And the stern Clerk yet higher held his Head.
They were indeed a weak, impatient Set,
But their shrewd Prompter had his Engines yet;
Had various means to make a Mortal trip,
Who shunned a flowing Bowl and rosy Lip;
And knew a thousand ways his Heart to move,
Who flies from Banquets and who laughs at Love.

Thus far the playful Muse has lent her aid,
But now departs, of graver theme afraid;
Her may we seek in more appropriate time, —   120
There is no jesting with Distress and Crime.

Our worthy Clerk had now arrived at Fame,
Such as but few in his degree might claim;
But he was poor, and wanted not the sense
That lowly rates the Praise without the Pence:
He saw the common Herd with reverence treat
The weakest Burgess whom they chanced to meet;
While few respected his exalted Views,
And all beheld his Doublet and his Shoes:
None, when they meet, would to his Parts allow   130
(Save his poor Boys) an hearing or a bow:
To this false Judgement of the vulgar Mind,
He was not fully, as a Saint, resigned;
He found it much his jealous Soul affect,
To fear Derision and to find Neglect.

The Year was bad, the Christening-Fees were small,
The Weddings few, the Parties Paupers all:
Desire of Gain with fear of Want combined,
Raised sad Commotion in his wounded Mind;
Wealth was in all his Thoughts, his Views, his Dreams,   140
And prompted base Desires and baseless Schemes.

Alas! how often erring Mortals keep
The strongest Watch against the Foes who sleep;
While the more wakeful, bold and artful Foe
Is suffered, guardless and unmarked, to go.

Once in a month the Sacramental Bread
Our Clerk with Wine upon the Table spread;
The Custom this, that, as the Vicar reads,
He for our Offerings round the Church proceeds:
150   Tall spacious Seats the wealthier People hid,
And none had view of what his Neighbour did;
Laid on the Box and mingled when they fell,
Who should the worth of each Oblation tell?
Now as poor *Jachin* took the usual round,
And saw the Alms and heard the Metal sound,
He had a thought; — at first it was no more
Than 'these have Cash and give it to the Poor:'
A second thought from this to work began —
'And can they give it to a poorer Man?'
160   Proceeding thus, — 'My Merit could they know,
And knew my Need, how freely they'd bestow;
But though they know not, these remain the same,
And are a strong, although a secret claim:
To me, alas! the Want and Worth are known,
Why then, in fact, 'tis but to take my own.'

Thought after thought poured in, a tempting train, —
'Suppose it done, — who is it could complain?
How could the Poor? for they such Trifles share,
As add no Comfort, as suppress no Care;
170   But many a Pittance makes a worthy Heap, —
What says the Law? that Silence puts to sleep: —
Nought then forbids, the danger could we shun,
And sure the business may be safely done.

'But am I earnest? — earnest? No. — I say,
If such my Mind, that I could plan a way,
Let me reflect; — I've not allowed me time

To purse the Pieces, and if dropped they'd chime:'
Fertile is Evil in the soul of Man, –
He paused, – said *Jachin*, 'They may drop on Bran.
Why then 'tis safe and (all considered) just,   180
The Poor receive it, – 'tis no breach of Trust;
The Old and Widows may their Trifles miss,
There must be Evil in a Good like this:
But I'll be kind, – the Sick I'll visit twice,
When now but once, and freely give Advice.
Yet let me think again:' – Again he tried,
For stronger Reasons on his Passion's side,
And quickly these were found, yet slowly he complied.

The Morning came: the common Service done, –
Shut every Door, – the solemn Rite begun, –   190
And, as the Priest the sacred Sayings read,
The Clerk went forward, trembling as he tread;
O'er the tall Pew he held the Box, and heard
The offered Piece, rejoicing as he feared:
Just by the Pillar, as he cautious tripped,
And turned the Aisle, he then a Portion slipped
From the full Store, and to the Pocket sent,
But held a moment – and then down it went.

The Priest read on, on walked the Man afraid,
Till a gold Offering in the Plate was laid;   200
Trembling he took it, for a moment stopped,
Then down it fell and sounded as it dropped:
Amazed he started, for the affrighted Man,
Lost and bewildered, thought not of the Bran;
But all were silent, all on things intent
Of high concern, none ear to Money lent;
So on he walked, more cautious than before,
And gained the purposed Sum and one Piece more.

Practice makes perfect, – when the Month came round,
He dropped the Cash nor listened for a Sound;   210
But yet, when last of all the assembled Flock,

He ate and drank, – it gave the electric Shock:
Oft was he forced his Reasons to repeat,
Ere he could kneel in quiet at his Seat;
But Custom soothed him – ere a single Year
All this was done without Restraint or Fear:
Cool and collected, easy and composed,
He was correct till all the Service closed;
Then to his Home, without a groan or sigh,
220   Gravely he went and laid his Treasure by.

     Want will complain: some Widows had expressed
A doubt if they were favoured like the rest;
The rest described with like regret their Dole,
And thus from parts they reasoned to the whole;
When all agreed some Evil must be done,
Or rich Men's Hearts grew harder than a Stone.

     Our easy Vicar cut the matter short,
He would not listen to such vile Report.

     All were not thus – there governed in that Year
230   A stern stout Churl, an angry Overseer;
A Tyrant fond of Power, loud, lewd, and most severe:
Him the mild Vicar, him the graver Clerk,
Advised, reproved, but nothing would he mark,
Save the Disgrace, 'and that, my Friends,' said he,
'Will I avenge, whenever time may be.'
And now, alas! 'twas time; – from Man to Man
Doubt and Alarm and shrewd Suspicions ran.

     With angry spirit and with sly intent,
This Parish Ruler to the Altar went;
240   A private Mark he fixed on Shillings three,
And but one Mark could in the Money see;
Besides, in peering round, he chanced to note
A sprinkling slight on *Jachin*'s Sunday-Coat:
All doubt was over: – when the Flock were blessed,
In wrath he rose, and thus his Mind expressed.

'Foul Deeds are here!' and saying this, he took
The Clerk, whose Conscience, in her cold-fit, shook;
His Pocket then was emptied on the place;
All saw his Guilt; all witnessed his Disgrace:
He fell, he fainted, not a groan, a look   250
Escaped the Culprit; 'twas a final stroke –
A death-wound never to be healed – a fall
That all had witnessed, and amazed were all.

As he recovered, to his Mind it came,
'I owe to *Satan* this Disgrace and Shame:'
All the Seduction now appeared in view,
'Let me withdraw,' he said, and he withdrew;
No one withheld him, all in union cried,
E'en the Avenger, – 'We are satisfied:'
For what has Death in any form to give,   260
Equal to that Man's Terrors, if he live?

He lived in freedom, but he hourly saw
How much more fatal Justice is than Law;
He saw another in his office reign,
And his mild Master treat him with disdain;
He saw that all Men shunned him, some reviled,
The harsh passed frowning, and the simple smiled;
The Town maintained him, but with some Reproof,
And Clerks and Scholars proudly kept aloof.

In each lone place, dejected and dismayed,   270
Shrinking from view, his wasting Form he laid;
Or to the restless Sea and roaring Wind,
Gave the strong yearnings of a ruined Mind:
On the broad Beach, the silent Summer-day,
Stretched on some Wreck, he wore his Life away;
Or where the River mingles with the Sea,
Or on the Mud-bank by the Elder-tree,
Or by the bounding Marsh-dyke, there was he:
And when unable to forsake the Town,
In the blind Courts he sate desponding down –   280

Always alone; then feebly would he crawl
The Church-way Walk, and lean upon the Wall:
Too ill for this, he laid beside the Door,
Compelled to hear the reasoning of the Poor:
He looked so pale, so weak, the pitying Crowd
Their firm belief of his Repentance vowed;
They saw him then so ghastly and so thin,
That they exclaimed, 'Is this the work of Sin?'

    'Yes,' in his better moments, he replied,
290 'Of sinful Avarice and the Spirit's Pride; –
While yet untempted, I was safe and well;
Temptation came; I reasoned, and I fell:
To be Man's Guide and Glory I designed,
A rare Example for our sinful kind;
But now my Weakness and my Guilt I see,
And am a Warning – Man, be warned by me!'

    He said, and saw no more the human Face;
To a lone Loft he went, his dying-place,
And, as the Vicar of his state enquired,
300 Turned to the wall and silently expired!

THE POOR OF THE BOROUGH

ELLEN ORFORD

> Patience and sorrow strove
> Who should express her goodliest.
> SHAKESPEARE. *Lear*.

'No charms she now can boast,' – 'tis true,
But other charmers wither too:
'And she is old,' – the fact I know,
And old will other heroines grow;
But not like them has she been laid,
In ruin'd castle, sore dismay'd;
Where naughty man and ghostly sprite
   Fill'd her pure mind with awe and dread,
Stalk'd round the room, put out the light,
   And shook the curtains round her bed.
No cruel uncle kept her land,
No tyrant father forced her hand;
   She had no vixen virgin-aunt,
Without whose aid she could not eat,
And yet who poison'd all her meat,
   With gibe and sneer and taunt.
Yet of the heroine she'd a share,
She saved a lover from despair,
And granted all his wish, in spite
Of what she knew and felt was right:
   But heroine then no more,
She own'd the fault, and wept and pray'd,
And humbly took the parish aid,
   And dwelt among the poor.

The Widow's Cottage. – Blind *Ellen* one. – Hers not the
Sorrows or Adventures of Heroines. – What these are, first
described. – Deserted Wives; rash Lovers; courageous
Damsels: in desolated Mansions; in grievous Perplexity. –
These Evils, however severe, of short Duration. – *Ellen*'s
Story. – Her Employment in Childhood. – First Love; first
Adventure; its miserable termination. – An idiot Daughter. –
An Husband. – Care in Business without Success. – The
Man's Despondency, and its Effect. – Their Children: how
disposed of. – One particularly unfortunate. – Fate of the
Daughter. – *Ellen* keeps a School and is happy. – Becomes
blind: loses her School. – Her Consolations.

    Observe yon Tenement, apart and small,
    Where the wet Pebbles shine upon the Wall;
    Where the low Benches lean beside the Door,
    And the red Paling bounds the Space before;
    Where *Thrift* and *Lavender*, and *Lad's-love** bloom, –
    That humble Dwelling is the Widow's Home:
    There live a Pair, for various Fortunes known,
    But the blind *Ellen* will relate her own; –
    Yet ere we hear the Story she can tell,
10   On prouder Sorrows let us briefly dwell.

    I've often marvelled, when by night, by day,
    I've marked the Manners moving in my way,
    And heard the Language and beheld the Lives
    Of Lass and Lover, Goddesses and Wives,
    That Books, which promise much of Life to give,
    Should show so little how we truly live.

    To me it seems their Females and their Men
    Are but the Creatures of the Author's Pen;
    Nay, Creatures borrowed and again conveyed

---

* The lad's or boy's love of some counties is the plant Southernwood, the *Artemisia abrotanum* of Botanists.

From Book to Book – the Shadows of a Shade: 20
Life, if they'd search, would show them many a change;
The Ruin sudden and the Misery strange!
With more of grievous, base, and dreadful things,
Than Novelists relate or Poet sings:
But they, who ought to look the World around,
Spy out a single Spot in Fairy-Ground;
Where all, in turn, ideal Forms behold,
And Plots are laid and Histories are told.

Time have I lent – I would their Debt were less –
To flowery Pages of sublime Distress;   30
And to the Heroine's soul-distracting Fears
I early gave my Sixpences and Tears:
Oft have I travelled in these tender Tales,
To *Darnley-Cottages* and *Maple-Vales*,
And watched the Fair-one from the first-born sigh,
When *Henry* passed and gazed in passing by;
Till I beheld them pacing in the Park,
Close by a Coppice where 'twas cold and dark;
When such Affection with such Fate appeared,
Want and a Father to be shunned and feared,   40
Without Employment, Prospect, Cot, or Cash,
That I have judged the heroic Souls were rash.

Now shifts the Scene, – the Fair in Tower confined,
In all things suffers but in change of Mind;
Now wooed by Greatness to a Bed of State,
Now deeply threatened with a Dungeon's Grate;
Till suffering much and being tried enough,
She shines, triumphant Maid! – temptation-proof.

Then was I led to vengeful Monks, who mix
With Nymphs and Swains, and play unpriestly tricks;   50
Then viewed *Banditti*, who in Forest wide,
And Cavern vast, indignant Virgins hide;
Who, hemmed with bands of sturdiest Rogues about,
Find some strange Succour, and come Virgins out.

I've watched a wintry Night on Castle-Walls,
I've stalked by Moonlight through deserted Halls,
And when the weary World was sunk to rest,
I've had such Sights as – may not be expressed.

Lo! that Chateau, the western Tower decayed,
The Peasants shun it, – they are all afraid;
For there was done a Deed! could Walls reveal,
Or Timbers tell it, how the Heart would feel!
Most horrid was it: – for, behold, the Floor
Has stain of Blood, and will be clean no more:
Hark to the Winds! which through the wide Saloon
And the long Passage send a dismal Tune, –
Music that Ghosts delight in; – and now heed
Yon beauteous Nymph, who must unmask the Deed;
See! with majestic Sweep she swims alone
Through Rooms all dreary, guided by a Groan:
Though Windows rattle, and though Tapestries shake,
And the Feet falter every step they take,
'Mid Moans and gibing Sprites she silent goes,
To find a something, which will soon expose
The villainies and wiles of her determined Foes:
And, having thus adventured, thus endured,
Fame, Wealth, and Lover, are for Life secured.

Much have I feared, but am no more afraid,
When some chaste Beauty, by some Wretch betrayed,
Is drawn away with such distracted speed,
That she anticipates a dreadful Deed:
Not so do I – Let solid Walls impound
The captive Fair, and dig a Moat around;
Let there be brazen Locks and Bars of steel,
And Keepers cruel, such as never feel;
With not a single Note the Purse supply,
And when she begs, let Men and Maids deny;
Be Windows those from which she dares not fall,
And Help so distant, 'tis in vain to call;

Still means of Freedom will some power devise,   90
And from the baffled Ruffian snatch his prize.

To Northern Wales, in some sequestered Spot,
I've followed fair *Louisa* to her Cot;
Where, then a wretched and deserted Bride,
The injured Fair-one wished from Man to hide;
Till by her fond repenting *Belville* found,
By some kind chance – the straying of an Hound,
He at her Feet craved Mercy, nor in vain,
For the relenting Dove flew back again.

There's something rapturous in Distress, or, oh!   100
Could *Clementina* bear her lot of Woe?
Or what she underwent, could Maiden undergo?
The Day was fixed; for so the Lover sighed,
So knelt and craved, he couldn't be denied;
When, Tale most dreadful! every Hope adieu; –
For the fond Lover is the Brother too:
All other Griefs abate; this monstrous Grief
Has no Remission, Comfort, or Relief;
Four ample Volumes, through each page disclose,
Good Heaven protect us! only Woes on Woes;   110
Till some strange Means afford a sudden view
Of some vile Plot, and every Woe adieu! *

Now should we grant these Beauties all endure
Severest Pangs, they've still the speediest Cure;
Before one Charm be withered from the Face,

* As this incident points out the work alluded to, I wish it to be remembered, that the gloomy tenor, the querulous melancholy of the story, is all I censure. The language of the writer is often animated, and is, I believe, correct; the characters well drawn, and the manners described from real life; but the perpetual occurrence of sad events, the protracted list of teasing and perplexing mischances, joined with much waspish invective, unallayed by pleasantry or sprightliness, and these continued through many hundred pages, render publications, intended for amusement and executed with ability, heavy and displeasing: – You find your favourite persons happy in the end; but they have teased you so much with their perplexities by the way, that you were frequently disposed to quit them in their distresses.

Except the Bloom, which shall again have place,
In Wedlock ends each Wish, in Triumph all Disgrace;
And Life to come, we fairly may suppose,
One light, bright Contrast to these wild dark Woes.

120   These let us leave and at her Sorrows look,
Too often seen, but seldom in a Book;
Let her who felt, relate them: – on her chair
The Heroine sits – in former Years, the Fair,
Now ag'd and poor; but *Ellen Orford* knows,
That we should humbly take what Heaven bestows.

'My Father died – again my Mother wed,
And found the Comforts of her Life were fled;
Her angry Husband, vexed through half his Years
By Loss and Troubles, filled her Soul with fears:
130   Their Children many, and 'twas my poor place
To nurse and wait on all the Infant Race;
Labour and Hunger were indeed my part,
And should have strengthened an erroneous Heart.

'Sore was the Grief to see him angry come,
And, teased with Business, make Distress at home:
The Father's Fury and the Children's Cries
I soon could bear, but not my Mother's Sighs;
For she looked back on Comforts and would say
"I wronged thee, *Ellen*," and then turn away.
140   Thus, for my Age's good, my Youth was tried,
And this my Fortune till my Mother died.

'So, amid Sorrow much and little Cheer –
A common case, I passed my twentieth Year;
For these are frequent Evils; thousands share
An equal Grief – the like domestic Care.

'Then in my days of Bloom, of Health and Youth,
One, much above me, vowed his Love and Truth:
We often met, he dreading to be seen,
And much I questioned what such dread might mean;

Yet I believed him true; my simple Heart 150
And undirected Reason took his part.

'Can he who loves me, whom I love, deceive?
Can I such Wrong of one so kind believe,
Who lives but in my Smile, who trembles when I grieve?

'He dared not marry, but we met to prove
What sad Encroachments and Deceits has Love:
Weak that I was, when he, rebuked withdrew,
I let him see that I was wretched too;
When less my Caution, I had still the Pain
Of his or mine own Weakness to complain. 160

'Happy the Lovers, classed alike in Life,
Or happier yet the rich endowing Wife;
But most aggrieved the fond believing Maid,
Of her rich Lover tenderly afraid:
You judge the Event; for grievous was my Fate,
Painful to feel and shameful to relate:
Ah! sad it was my Burden to sustain,
When the least Misery was the dread of Pain;
When I have grieving told him my Disgrace,
And plainly marked Indifference in his Face. 170

'Hard! with these Fears and Terrors to behold
The cause of all, the faithless Lover cold;
Impatient grown at every wish denied,
And barely civil, soothed and gratified;
Peevish when urged to think of Vows so strong,
And angry when I spake of Crime and Wrong.
All this I felt, and still the Sorrow grew,
Because I felt that I deserved it too,
And begged my infant Stranger to forgive
The Mother's Shame, which in herself must live. 180

'When known that Shame, I, soon expelled from Home,
With a frail Sister shared an Hovel's gloom;

There barely fed – (what could I more request?)
My infant Slumberer sleeping at my breast.
I from my window saw his blooming Bride,
And my Seducer smiling at her side:
Hope lived till then; I sank upon the Floor,
And Grief and Thought and Feeling were no more:
Although revived, I judged that Life would close,
190 And went to rest, to wonder that I rose:
My Dreams were dismal, – wheresoe'er I strayed,
I seemed ashamed, alarmed, despised, betrayed;
Always in grief, in guilt, disgraced, forlorn,
Mourning that one so weak, so vile was born;
The Earth a Desert, Tumult in the Sea,
The Birds affrighted fled from Tree to Tree,
Obscured the setting Sun, and every thing like me:
But Heaven had Mercy, and my Need at length
Urged me to labour and renewed my Strength.

200 'I strove for Patience as a Sinner must,
Yet felt the Opinion of the World unjust;
There was my Lover, in his Joy, esteemed,
And I, in my Distress, as guilty deemed;
Yet sure, not all the Guilt and Shame belong
To her who feels and suffers for the Wrong:
The Cheat at play may use the Wealth he's won,
But is not honoured for the Mischief done;
The Cheat in Love may use each Villain-art,
And boast the Deed that breaks the Victim's Heart.

210 'Four Years were past; I might again have found
Some erring Wish, but for another Wound:
Lovely my Daughter grew, her Face was fair,
But no Expression ever brightened there;
I doubted long, and vainly strove to make
Some certain Meaning of the Words she spake;
But Meaning there was none, and I surveyed
With dread the Beauties of my Idiot-Maid.

'Still I submitted; – Oh! 'tis meet and fit
In all we feel to make the Heart submit;
Gloomy and calm my Days, but I had then,   220
It seemed, Attractions for the Eyes of Men;
The sober Master of a decent Trade
O'erlooked my Errors and his Offer made;
Reason assented: – true, my Heart denied,
"But thou," I said, "shalt be no more my Guide."

'We wed, our Toil and Trouble, Pains and Care,
Of Means to live procured us humble Share;
Five were our Sons, and we, though careful, found
Our Hopes declining as the Year came round;
For I perceived, yet would not soon perceive,   230
My Husband stealing from my view to grieve;
Silent he grew, and when he spoke he sighed,
And surly looked and peevishly replied:
Pensive by Nature, he had gone of late
To those who preached of Destiny and Fate,
Of things fore-doomed, and of Election-grace,
And how in vain we strive to run our race;
That all by Works and moral Worth we gain,
Is to perceive our Care and Labour vain;
That still the more we pay, our Debts the more remain;   240
That he who feels not the mysterious Call,
Lies bound in Sin, still grovelling from the Fall.
My Husband felt not: – our Persuasion, Prayer,
And our best Reason, darkened his Despair;
His very Nature changed; he now reviled
My former Conduct, – he reproached my Child:
He talked of Bastard Slips, and cursed his Bed,
And from our Kindness to Concealment fled;
For ever to some evil Change inclined,
To every gloomy thought he lent his Mind,   250
Nor Rest would give to us, nor Rest himself could find; –
His Son suspended saw him, long bereft
Of Life, nor prospect of Revival left.

'With him died all our Prospects, and once more
I shared the Allotments of the Parish Poor;
They took my Children too, and this I know
Was just and lawful, but I felt the Blow:
My Idiot-Maid and one unhealthy Boy
Were left, a Mother's Misery and her Joy.

260   'Three Sons I followed to the Grave, and one –
Oh! can I speak of that unhappy Son?
Would all the Memory of that time were fled,
And all those Horrors, with my Child, were dead!
Before the World seduced him, what a Grace
And smile of Gladness shone upon his Face!
Then he had Knowledge; finely would he write,
Study to him was Pleasure and Delight;
Great was his Courage, and but few could stand
Against the Slight and Vigour of his Hand:
270   The Maidens loved him; – when he came to die,
No, not the coldest could suppress a Sigh:
Here I must cease – how can I say, my Child
Was by the bad of either Sex beguiled?
Worst of the Bad – they taught him that the Laws
Made Wrong and Right; there was no other Cause;
That all Religion was the Trade of Priests,
And Men, when dead, must perish like the Beasts: –
And he, so lively and so gay before, . . .
Ah! spare a Mother – I can tell no more.

280   'Interest was made that they should not destroy
The comely Form of my deluded Boy –
But Pardon came not; damp the Place and deep
Where he was kept, as they'd a Tyger keep;
For he, unhappy! had before them all
Vowed he'd escape, whatever might befall.

'He'd means of Dress, and dressed beyond his Means,
And so to see him, in such dismal Scenes,

I cannot speak it – cannot bear to tell
Of that sad Hour – I heard the Passing-bell.

'Slowly they went; he smiled and looked so smart,   290
Yet sure he shuddered when he saw the Cart,
And gave a Look – until my dying-Day,
That Look will never from my Mind away;
Oft as I sit, and ever in my Dreams,
I see that Look and they have heard my Screams.

'Now let me speak no more – yet all declared
That one so young in pity should be spared,
And one so manly; – on his graceful Neck,
That Chains of Jewels might be proud to deck,
To a small Mole a Mother's Lips have pressed, –   300
And there the Cord . . . my Breath is sore oppressed.

'I now can speak again; my elder Boy
Was that Year drowned, – a Seaman in an Hoy:
He left a numerous Race; of these would some
In their young Troubles to my Cottage come,
And these I taught – an humble Teacher I –
Upon their Heavenly Parent to rely.

'Alas! I needed such Reliance more: –
My Idiot-Girl, so simply gay before,
Now wept in pain; some Wretch had found a time,   310
Depraved and wicked, for that Coward-crime;
I had indeed my doubt, but I suppressed
The thought that day and night disturbed my rest;
She and that sick-pale Brother . . . but why strive
To keep the Terrors of that time alive?

'The Hour arrived, the new, the undreaded Pain,
That came with violence and yet came in vain.
I saw her die: her Brother too is dead;
Nor owned such Crime – what is it that I dread?

'The Parish-Aid withdrawn, I looked around,   320
And in my School a bless'd Subsistence found –

My Winter-calm of Life: to be of use
Would pleasant Thoughts and heavenly Hopes produce;
I loved them all; – it soothed me to presage
The various Trials of their riper Age,
Then dwell on mine, and bless the Power who gave
Pains to correct us, and Remorse to save.

   'Yes! these were Days of Peace, but they are past, –
A Trial came, I will believe, a last;
330   I lost my Sight, and my Employment gone,
Useless I live, but to the Day live on;
Those Eyes which long the Light of Heaven enjoyed,
Were not by Pain, by Agony destroyed:
My Senses fail not all; I speak, I pray,
By Night my Rest, my Food I take by Day;
And as my Mind looks cheerful to my End,
I love Mankind and call my God my Friend.'

THE POOR OF THE BOROUGH

ABEL KEENE

Coepis meliùs quàm desines: ultima primis
Cedunt. Dissimiles: hic vir et ille puer.
OVID. *Deïanira Hereuli.*

Now the Spirit speaketh expressly, that, in the latter times, some shall
depart from the faith, giving heed to seducing spirits and doctrines of devils.
Epistle to Timothy.

Abel, a poor Man, Teacher of a School of the lower Order; is
placed in the Office of a Merchant; is alarmed by Discourses
of the Clerks; unable to reply; becomes a Convert; dresses,
drinks, and ridicules his former Conduct. – The Remonstrance
of his Sister, a devout Maiden. – Its Effect. – The Merchant
dies. – *Abel* returns to Poverty unpitied; but relieved. – His
abject Condition. – His Melancholy. – He wanders about: is
found. – His own Account of himself and the Revolutions in
his Mind.

A quiet simple Man was *Abel Keene*,
He meant no harm, nor did he often *mean*;
He kept a School of loud rebellious Boys,
And growing old, grew nervous with the Noise,
When a kind Merchant hired his useful Pen,
And made him happiest of Accompting Men;
With glee he rose to every easy Day,
When half the Labour brought him twice the Pay.

There were young Clerks, and there the Merchant's Son,
10   Choice Spirits all, who wished him to be one;
It must, no question, give them lively Joy,
Hopes long indulged, to combat and destroy;
At these they levelled all their Skill and Strength,
He fell not quickly, but he fell at length:
They quoted Books, to him both bold and new,
And scorned as Fables all he held as true;
'Such Monkish Stories and such Nursery Lies,'
That he was struck with Terror and Surprise.

'What! all his Life had he the Laws obeyed,
20   Which they broke through and were not once afraid?
Had he so long his evil Passions checked,
And yet at last had nothing to expect?
While they their Lives in Joy and Pleasure led,
And then had nothing, at the end, to dread?
Was all his Priest with so much zeal conveyed,
A *Part!* a *Speech!* for which the Man was paid?
And were his pious Books, his solemn Prayers,
Not worth one Tale of the admired *Voltaire's*?
Then was it time, while yet some Years remained,
30   To drink untroubled and to think unchained,
And on all Pleasures, which his Purse could give,
Freely to seize, and, while he lived, to live.'

Much time he passed in this important Strife,
The Bliss or Bane of his remaining Life;
For Converts all are made with Care and Grief,
And Pangs attend the Birth of Unbelief;
Nor pass they soon; – with Awe and Fear he took
The flowery way, and cast back many a look.

The Youths applauded much his wise Design,
40   With weighty Reasoning o'er their Evening Wine;
And much in private 'twould their Mirth improve,
To hear how *Abel* spake of Life and Love;
To hear him own what grievous Pains it cost,

Ere the old Saint was in the Sinner lost,
Ere his poor Mind, with every Deed alarmed,
By Wit was settled and by Vice was charmed.

For *Abel* entered in his bold Career,
Like Boys on Ice, with Pleasure and with Fear;
Lingering, yet longing for the Joy, he went,
Repenting now, now dreading to repent;   50
With awkward Pace, and with himself at war,
Far gone, yet frightened that he went so far;
Oft for his Efforts he'd solicit Praise,
And then proceed with Blunders and Delays:
The Young more aptly Passion's Calls pursue,
But Age and Weakness start at Scenes so new,
And tremble when they've done, for all they dared to do.

At length Example *Abel*'s dread removed,
With small concern he sought the Joys he loved;
Not resting here, he claimed his share of Fame,   60
And first their Votary, then their Wit became:
His Jest was bitter and his Satire bold,
When he his Tales of formal Brethren told;
What time with pious Neighbours he discussed
Their boasted Treasure and their boundless Trust:
'Such were our Dreams,' the jovial Elder cried;
'Awake and live,' his youthful Friends replied.

Now the gay Clerk a modest Drab despised,
And clad him smartly as his Friends advised;
So fine a coat upon his Back he threw,   70
That not an Alley-Boy Old *Abel* knew;
Broad polished Buttons blazed that Coat upon,
And just beneath the Watch's Trinkets shone –
A splendid Watch, that pointed out the Time,
To fly from Business and make free with Crime:
The crimson Waistcoat and the silken Hose
Ranked the lean Man among the Borough Beaux;
His raven Hair he cropped with fierce disdain,

And light elastic Locks encased his Brain:
80   More pliant Pupil who could hope to find,
So decked in Person and so changed in Mind?

When *Abel* walked the Streets, with pleasant mien
He met his Friends, delighted to be seen;
And when he rode along the public Way,
No Beau so gaudy and no Youth so gay.

His pious Sister, now an ancient Maid,
For *Abel* fearing, first in secret prayed;
Then thus in Love and Scorn her Notions she conveyed:

'Alas! my Brother! can I see thee pace
90   Hood-winked to Hell, and not lament thy Case,
Nor stretch my feeble Hand to stop thy headlong Race?
Lo! thou art bound; a Slave in *Satan*'s Chain,
The righteous *Abel* turned the wretched *Cain*;
His Brother's Blood against the Murderer cried,
Against thee thine, unhappy Suicide!
Are all our pious Nights and peaceful Days,
Our Evening Readings and our Morning Praise,
Our Spirits' Comfort in the Trials sent,
Our Hearts' Rejoicings in the Blessings lent,
100   All that o'er Grief a cheering Influence shed,
Are these for ever and for ever fled?

'When in the Years gone by, the trying Years
When Faith and Hope had Strife with Wants and Fears,
Thy Nerves have trembled till thou couldst not eat
(Dressed by this Hand) thy Mess of simple Meat;
When, grieved by Fastings, galled by Fates severe,
Slow passed the Days of the successless Year;
Still in these gloomy Hours, my Brother then
Had glorious Views, unseen by prosperous Men:
110   And when thine Heart has felt its Wish denied,
What gracious Texts hast thou to Grief applied;
Till thou hast entered in thine humble Bed,
By lofty Hopes and heavenly Musings fed!

Then I have seen thy lively Looks express
The Spirit's Comforts in the Man's Distress.

   'Then didst thou cry, exulting, "Yes, 'tis fit,
'Tis meet and right, my Heart! that we submit:"
And wilt thou, *Abel*, thy new Pleasures weigh
Against such Triumphs? – Oh! repent and pray.

   'What are thy Pleasures? – with the Gay to sit,   120
And thy poor Brain torment for awkward Wit;
All thy good Thoughts (thou hat'st them) to restrain,
And give a wicked Pleasure to the Vain;
Thy long lean Frame by Fashion to attire,
That Lads may laugh and Wantons may admire;
To raise the mirth of Boys, and not to see,
Unhappy Maniac! that they laugh at thee.

   'These boyish Follies, which alone the Boy
Can idly act or gracefully enjoy,
Add new reproaches to thy fallen state,   130
And make Men scorn what they would only hate.

   'What Pains, my Brother, dost thou take to prove
A taste for Follies which thou canst not love?
Why do thy stiffening Limbs the Steed bestride –
That Lads may laugh to see thou canst not ride?
And why (I feel the crimson tinge my cheek)
Dost thou by night in Diamond-Alley sneak?

   'Farewell! the Parish will thy Sister keep,
Where she in peace shall pray and sing and sleep,
Save when for thee she mourns, thou wicked, wandering sheep!   140
When Youth is fallen, there's hope the Young may rise,
But fallen Age for ever hopeless lies:
Torn up by Storms and placed in Earth once more,
The younger Tree may Sun and Soil restore;
But when the old and sapless Trunk likes low,
No Care or Soil can former Life bestow;
Reserved for burning is the worthless Tree,
And what – O *Abel!* – is reserved for thee?'

These angry words our Hero deeply felt,
150   Though hard his Heart and indisposed to melt!
To gain Relief he took a Glass the more,
And then went on as careless as before:
Henceforth, unchecked, Amusements he partook,
And (save his Ledger) saw no decent Book;
Him found the Merchant punctual at his task,
And that performed, he'd nothing more to ask;
He cared not how Old *Abel* played the fool,
No Master he, beyond the hours of School:
Thus they proceeding, had their Wine and Joke,
160   Till Merchant *Dixon* felt a warning stroke,
And, after struggling half a gloomy week,
Left his poor Clerk another Friend to seek.

Alas! the Son, who led the Saint astray,
Forgot the Man whose Follies made him gay;
He cared no more for *Abel* in his need,
Than *Abel* cared about his hackney Steed;
He now, alas! had all his Earnings spent,
And thus was left to languish and repent;
No School nor Clerkship found he in the place,
170   Now lost to Fortune, as before to Grace.

For Town-relief the grieving Man applied,
And begged with tears, what some with scorn denied;
Others looked down upon the glowing Vest,
And frowning, asked him at what Price he dressed?
Happy for him his Country's Laws are mild,
They must support him, though they still reviled;
Grieved, abject, scorned, insulted, and betrayed,
Of God unmindful, and of Man afraid, –
No more he talked; 'twas pain, 'twas shame to speak,
180   His Heart was sinking, and his Frame was weak.
His Sister died with such serene delight,
He once again began to think her right;
Poor like himself, the happy Spinster laid,

And sweet Assurance blessed the dying Maid:
Poor like the Spinster, he, when Death was nigh,
Assured of nothing, felt afraid to die.
The cheerful Clerk who sometimes passed the door,
Just mentioned '*Abel!*' and then thought no more.
So *Abel* pondering on his state forlorn,
Looked round for Comfort, and was chased by Scorn.   190
And now we saw him on the Beach reclined,
Or causeless walking in the wintry Wind;
And when it raised a loud and angry Sea,
He stood and gazed, in wretched reverie:
He heeded not the Frost, the Rain, the Snow,
Close by the Sea he walked alone and slow:
Sometimes his Frame through many an hour he spread
Upon a Tomb-stone, moveless as the dead;
And was there found a sad and silent place,
There would he creep with slow and measured pace: 200
Then would he wander by the River's side,
And fix his eyes upon the falling Tide;
The deep dry Ditch, the Rushes in the Fen,
And mossy Crag-pits were his Lodgings then:
There, to his discontented Thoughts a prey,
The melancholy Mortal pined away.

   The neighbouring Poor at length began to speak
Of *Abel*'s Ramblings – he'd been gone a week;
They knew not where, and little care they took
For one so friendless and so poor to look: 210
At last a Stranger, in a Pedlar's Shed,
Beheld him hanging – he had long been dead.
He left a Paper, penned at sundry times,
Intitled thus – 'My Groanings and my Crimes!

   'I was a Christian Man, and none could lay
Aught to my charge; I walked the narrow Way:
All then was simple Faith, serene and pure,
My Hope was steadfast and my Prospects sure;
Then was I tried by Want and Sickness sore,

220 But these I clapped my Shield of Faith before,
And Cares and Wants and Man's Rebukes I bore:
Alas! new Foes assailed me, I was vain,
They stung my Pride and they confused my Brain;
Oh! these Deluders! with what glee they saw
Their simple Dupe transgress the righteous Law;
'Twas joy to them to view that dreadful Strife,
When Faith and Frailty warred for more than Life:
So with their Pleasures they beguiled the Heart,
Then with their Logic they allayed the smart;
230 They proved (so thought I then) with Reasons strong,
That no Man's Feelings ever lead him wrong:
And thus I went, as on the varnished Ice,
The smooth Career of Unbelief and Vice.
Oft would the Youths, with sprightly Speech and bold,
Their witty Tales of naughty Priests unfold;
" 'Twas all a Craft," they said, "a cunning Trade,
Not she the Priests, but Priests Religion made:"
So I believed:' – No, *Abel*! to thy grief,
So thou relinquished all that was Belief: –
240 'I grew as very Flint, and when the rest
Laughed at Devotion, I enjoyed the jest;
But this all vanished like the Morning-dew,
When unemployed, and poor again I grew;
Yea! I was doubly poor, for I was wicked too.

'The Mouse, that trespassed and the Treasure stole
Found his lean Body fitted to the Hole;
Till having fatted, he was forced to stay,
And, fasting, starve his stolen Bulk away:
Ah! worse for me – grown poor, I yet remain
250 In sinful Bonds, and pray and fast in vain.

'At length I thought, although these Friends of Sin
Have spread their Net and caught their Prey therein;
Though my hard Heart could not for Mercy call,
Because, though great my Grief, my Faith was small;

Yet, as the Sick on skilful Men rely,
The Soul, diseased, may to a Doctor fly.

'A famous one there was, whose Skill had wrought
Cures past belief, and him the Sinners sought;
Numbers there were defiled by Mire and Filth,
Whom he recovered by his goodly Tilth; –   260
"Come then," I said, "let me the Man behold,
And tell my case" – I saw him and I told.

'With trembling voice, "Oh! reverend Sir," I said,
"I once believed, and I was then misled;
And now such Doubts my sinful Soul beset,
I dare not say that I'm a Christian yet:
Canst thou, good Sir, by thy superior Skill,
Inform my Judgement and direct my Will?
Ah! give thy Cordial; let my Soul have rest,
And be the outward Man alone distressed,   270
For at my state I tremble" – "Tremble more,"
Said the good Man, "and then rejoice therefore;
'Tis good to tremble; Prospects then are fair,
When the lost Soul is plunged in deep Despair:
Once thou wert simply honest, just and pure,
Whole, as thou thought'st, and never wished a Cure;
Now thou hast plunged in Folly, Shame, Disgrace;
Now! thou'rt an Object meet for healing Grace:
No Merit thine, no Virtue, Hope, Belief,
Nothing hast thou, but Misery, Sin, and Grief,   280
The best, the only titles to Relief."

'"What must I do," I said, "my Soul to free?"
– "Do nothing, Man; it will be done for thee." –
"But must I not, my reverend Guide, believe?"
– "If thou art called, thou wilt the Faith receive:" –
"But I repent not." – Angry he replied,
"If thou art called, thou needest nought beside:
Attend on us, and if 'tis Heaven's Decree,
The Call will come, – if not, ah! woe for thee."

290   'There then I waited, ever on the watch,
A spark of Hope, a ray of Light to catch;
His Words fell softly like the flakes of Snow,
But I could never find mine Heart o'erflow;
He cried aloud, till in the Flock began
The Sigh, the Tear, as caught from Man to Man:
They wept and they rejoiced, and there was I
Hard as a Flint, and as the Desert dry:
To me no Tokens of the Call would come,
I felt my Sentence and received my Doom;
300 But I complained: – "Let thy Repinings cease,
Oh! Man of Sin, for they thy Guilt increase;
It bloweth where it listeth; – die in peace." –
– "In peace, and perish?" I replied; "impart
Some better Comfort to a burdened Heart." –
"Alas!" the Priest returned, "can I direct
The heavenly Call? – Do I proclaim the Elect?
Raise not thy Voice against the Eternal Will,
But take thy part with Sinners and be still."

    'Alas for me, no more the times of Peace
310 Are mine on Earth – in Death my Pains may cease.

    'Foes to my Soul! ye young Seducers, know,
What serious Ills from your Amusements flow;
Opinions, you with so much ease profess,
O'erwhelm the Simple and their Minds oppress:
Let such be happy, nor with Reasons strong,
That make them wretched, prove their Notions wrong:
Let them proceed in that they deem the way,
Fast when they will, and at their pleasure pray:
Yes, I have Pity for my Brethren's Lot,
320 And so had *Dives*, but it helped him not:
And is it thus? – I'm full of Doubts: – Adieu!
Perhaps his Reverence is mistaken too.'

THE POOR OF THE BOROUGH

PETER GRIMES

———————Was a sordid soul,
Such as does murder for a meed:
Who but for fear knows no control,
Because his conscience, sear'd and foul,
Feels not the import of the deed;
One whose brute feeling ne'er aspires
Beyond his own more brute desires.
                                    SCOTT. *Marmion*

Methought the souls of all that I had murder'd
Came to my tent, and every one did threat———
                                    SHAKESPEARE. *Richard III.*

The times have been,
That when the brains were out, the man would die,
And there an end; but now they rise again,
With twenty mortal murders on their crowns,
And push us from our stools.
                                    Macbeth.

The Father of *Peter* a Fisherman. – *Peter*'s early Conduct. –
His Grief for the old Man. – He takes an Apprentice. – The
Boy's Suffering and Fate. – A second Boy: how he died. –
Peter acquitted. – A third Apprentice. – A Voyage by Sea: the
Boy does not return. – Evil Report on *Peter*: he is tried and
threatened. – Lives alone. – His Melancholy and incipient
Madness. – Is observed and visited. – He escapes and is taken;
is lodged in a Parish-House: Women attend and watch him. –

He speaks in a Delirium: grows more collected. – His Account
of his Feelings and visionary Terrors previous to his Death.

Old *Peter Grimes* made Fishing his employ,
His Wife he cabined with him and his Boy,
And seemed that Life laborious to enjoy:
To Town came quiet *Peter* with his Fish,
And had of all a civil word and wish.
He left his Trade upon the Sabbath-Day,
And took young *Peter* in his hand to pray;
But soon the stubborn Boy from care broke loose,
At first refused, then added his abuse:
His Father's Love he scorned, his Power defied,
But being drunk, wept sorely when he died.

Yes! then he wept, and to his Mind there came
Much of his Conduct, and he felt the Shame, –
How he had oft the good Old Man reviled,
And never paid the Duty of a Child:
How, when the Father in his Bible read,
He in contempt and anger left the Shed:
'It is the Word of Life,' the Parent cried;
– 'This is the Life itself,' the Boy replied;
And while Old *Peter* in amazement stood,
Gave the hot Spirit to his boiling Blood: –
How he, with Oath and furious Speech, began
To prove his Freedom and assert the Man;
And when the Parent checked his impious Rage,
How he had cursed the Tyranny of Age, –
Nay, once had dealt the sacrilegious Blow
On his bare Head and laid his Parent low:
The Father groaned – 'If thou art old,' said he,
'And hast a Son – thou wilt remember me:
Thy Mother left me in an happy Time,
Thou kill'dst not her – Heaven spares the double Crime.'

On an Inn-settle, in his maudlin Grief,
This he revolved and drank for his Relief.

Now lived the Youth in freedom, but debarred
From constant Pleasure, and he thought it hard;
Hard that he could not every Wish obey,
But must awhile relinquish Ale and Play;
Hard! that he could not to his Cards attend,
But must acquire the Money he would spend.

With greedy eye he looked on all he saw,   40
He knew not Justice, and he laughed at Law;
On all he marked, he stretched his ready Hand;
He fished by Water and he filched by Land:
Oft in the Night has *Peter* dropped his Oar,
Fled from his Boat and sought for Prey on shore;
Oft up the Hedge-row glided, on his Back
Bearing the Orchard's Produce in a Sack,
Or Farm-yard Load, tugged fiercely from the Stack;
And as these Wrongs to greater numbers rose,
The more he looked on all Men as his Foes.   50

He built a mud-walled Hovel, where he kept
His various Wealth, and there he oft-times slept;
But no Success could please his cruel Soul,
He wished for One to trouble and control;
He wanted some obedient Boy to stand
And bear the blow of his outrageous hand;
And hoped to find in some propitious hour
A feeling Creature subject to his Power.

Peter had heard there were in London then, –
Still have they being? – Workhouse-clearing Men,   60
Who, undisturbed by Feelings just or kind,
Would Parish-Boys to needy Tradesmen bind:
They in their want a trifling Sum would take,
And toiling Slaves of piteous Orphans make.

Such *Peter* sought, and when a Lad was found,
The Sum was dealt him and the Slave was bound.

Some few in Town observed in *Peter*'s Trap
A Boy, with Jacket blue and woollen Cap;
But none inquired how *Peter* used the Rope,
70   Or what the Bruise, that made the Stripling stoop;
None could the Ridges on his Back behold,
None sought him shivering in the Winter's Cold;
None put the question, – '*Peter*, dost thou give
The Boy his Food? – What, Man! the Lad must live:
Consider, *Peter*, let the Child have Bread,
He'll serve thee better if he's stroked and fed.'
None reasoned thus – and some, on hearing Cries,
Said calmly, '*Grimes* is at his Exercise.'

Pinned, beaten, cold, pinched, threatened, and abused, –
80   His Efforts punished and his Food refused, –
Awake tormented, – soon aroused from sleep, –
Struck if he wept, and yet compelled to weep,
The trembling Boy dropped down and strove to pray,
Received a Blow and trembling turned away,
Or sobbed and hid his piteous face; – while he,
The savage Master, grinned in horrid glee;
He'd now the power he ever loved to show,
A feeling Being subject to his Blow.

Thus lived the Lad in Hunger, Peril, Pain,
90   His Tears despised, his Supplications vain:
Compelled by fear to lie, by need to steal,
His Bed uneasy and unblessed his Meal,
For three sad Years the Boy his Tortures bore,
And then his Pains and Trials were no more.

'How died he, *Peter*?' when the People said,
He growled – 'I found him lifeless in his Bed;'
Then tried for softer tone, and sighed, 'Poor *Sam* is dead.'
Yet murmurs were there and some questions asked, –
How he was fed, how punished, and how tasked?
100   Much they suspected, but they little proved,
And *Peter* passed untroubled and unmoved.

Another Boy with equal ease was found,
The Money granted and the Victim bound;
And what his Fate? – One night it chanced he fell
From the Boat's Mast and perished in her Well,
Where Fish were living kept, and where the Boy
(So reasoned Men) could not himself destroy: –

'Yes! so it was,' said *Peter*, 'in his play,
For he was idle both by night and day;
He climbed the Main-mast and then fell below;' –   110
Then showed his Corpse and pointed to the Blow:
'What said the Jury?' – they were long in doubt,
But sturdy *Peter* faced the matter out:
So they dismissed him, saying at the time,
'Keep fast your Hatchway when you've Boys who climb.'
This hit the Conscience, and he coloured more
Than for the closest questions put before.

Thus all his fears the Verdict set aside,
And at the Slave-shop *Peter* still applied.

Then came a Boy, of Manners soft and mild, –   120
Our Seamen's Wives with grief beheld the Child;
All thought (the Poor themselves) that he was one
Of gentle Blood, some noble Sinner's Son,
Who had, belike, deceived some humble Maid,
Whom he had first seduced and then betrayed: –
However this, he seemed a gracious Lad,
In Grief submissive and with Patience sad.

Passive he laboured, till his slender Frame
Bent with his Loads, and he at length was lame:
Strange that a Frame so weak could bear so long   130
The grossest Insult and the foulest Wrong;
But there were causes – in the Town they gave
Fire, Food, and Comfort, to the gentle Slave;
And though stern *Peter*, with a cruel Hand,
And knotted Rope, enforced the rude Command,

Yet he considered what he'd lately felt,
And his vile Blows with selfish Pity dealt.

One day such Draughts the cruel Fisher made,
He could not vend them in his Borough-Trade,
140   But sailed for London-Mart: the Boy was ill,
But ever humbled to his Master's will;
And on the River, where they smoothly sailed,
He strove with terror and awhile prevailed;
But new to Danger on the angry Sea,
He clung affrighted to his Master's knee:
The Boat grew leaky and the Wind was strong,
Rough was the passage and the Time was long;
His Liquor failed, and *Peter*'s Wrath arose, . . . :
No more is known – the rest we must suppose,
150   Or learn of *Peter*; – *Peter*, says he, 'spied
The Stripling's danger and for Harbour tried;
Meantime the Fish and then the Apprentice died.'

The pitying Women raised a Clamour round,
And weeping said, 'Thou hast thy 'Prentice drowned.'

Now the stern Man was summoned to the Hall,
To tell his Tale before the Burghers all:
He gave the Account; professed, the Lad he loved,
And kept his brazen Features all unmoved.
The Mayor himself with tone severe replied,
160   'Henceforth with thee shall never Boy abide;
Hire thee a Freeman, whom thou durst not beat,
But who, in thy despite, will sleep and eat:
Free thou art now! – again shouldst thou appear,
Thou'lt find thy Sentence, like thy Soul, severe.'

Alas, for *Peter* not an helping Hand,
So was he hated, could he now command;
Alone he rowed his Boat, alone he cast
His Nets beside, or made his Anchor fast;
To hold a Rope or hear a Curse was none, –
170   He toiled and railed; he groaned and swore alone.

Thus by himself compelled to live each day,
To wait for certain hours the Tide's delay;
At the same times the same dull views to see,
The bounding Marsh-bank and the blighted Tree;
The Water only, when the Tides were high,
When low, the Mud half-covered and half-dry;
The Sun-burnt Tar that blisters on the Planks,
And Bank-side Stakes in their uneven ranks;
Heaps of entangled Weeds that slowly float,
As the Tide rolls by the impeded Boat. 180

When Tides were neap, and, in the sultry day,
Through the tall-bounding Mud-banks made their way,
Which on each side rose swelling, and below
The dark warm Flood ran silently and slow;
There anchoring, *Peter* chose from Man to hide,
There hang his Head, and view the lazy Tide
In its hot slimy Channel slowly glide;
Where the small Eels that left the deeper way
For the warm Shore, within the Shallows play;
Where gaping Mussels, left upon the Mud, 190
Slope their slow passage to the fallen Flood; –
Here dull and hopeless he'll lie down and trace
How sidelong Crabs had scrawled their crooked race;
Or sadly listen to the tuneless cry
Of fishing *Gull* or clanging *Golden-eye*;
What time the Sea-birds to the Marsh would come,
And the loud *Bittern*, from the Bull-rush home,
Gave the Salt-ditch side the bellowing Boom:
He nursed the Feelings these dull Scenes produce,
And loved to stop beside the opening Sluice; 200
Where the small Stream, confined in narrow bound,
Ran with a dull, unvaried, saddening sound;
Where all presented to the Eye or Ear,
Oppressed the Soul! with Misery, Grief, and Fear.

Besides these objects, there were places three,
Which *Peter* seemed with certain dread to see;

When he drew near them he would turn from each,
And loudly whistle till he passed the *Reach*.*

A change of Scene to him brought no relief,
In Town, 'twas plain, Men took him for a Thief:
The Sailors' Wives would stop him in the Street,
And say, 'Now, *Peter*, thou'st no Boy to beat:'
Infants at play, when they perceived him, ran,
Warning each other – 'That's the wicked Man:'
He growled an oath, and in an angry tone
Cursed the whole Place and wished to be alone.

Alone he was, the same dull Scenes in view,
And still more gloomy in his sight they grew:
Though Man he hated, yet employed alone
At bootless labour, he would swear and groan,
Cursing the Shoals that glided by the spot,
And *Gulls* that caught them when his arts could not.

Cold nervous Tremblings shook his sturdy Frame,
And strange Disease – he couldn't say the name;
Wild were his Dreams, and oft he rose in fright,
Waked by his view of Horrors in the Night, –
Horrors that would the sternest Minds amaze,
Horrors that Demons might be proud to raise:
And though he felt forsaken, grieved at heart,
To think he lived from all Mankind apart;
Yet, if a Man approached, in terrors he would start.

A Winter passed since *Peter* saw the Town,
And Summer Lodgers were again come down;
These, idly-curious, with their glasses spied
The Ships in Bay as anchored for the Tide, –
The River's Craft, – the Bustle of the Quay, –
And Sea-port Views, which Landmen love to see.

One, up the River, had a Man and Boat

210

220

230

* The reaches in a river are those parts which extend from point to point. *Johnson* has
not the word precisely in this sense, but it is very common, and I believe used
wheresoever a navigable river can be found in this country.

Seen day by day, now anchored, now afloat;
Fisher he seemed, yet used no Net nor Hook,   240
Of Sea-fowl swimming by, no heed he took,
But on the gliding Waves still fixed his lazy look:
At certain stations he would view the Stream,
As if he stood bewildered in a Dream,
Or that some Power had chained him for a time,
To feel a Curse or meditate on Crime.

This known, some curious, some in pity went,
And others questioned – 'Wretch, dost thou repent?'
He heard, he trembled, and in fear resigned
His Boat: new terror filled his restless Mind: 250
Furious he grew and up the Country ran,
And there they seized him – a distempered Man: –
Him we received, and to a Parish-bed,
Followed and cursed, the groaning Man was led.

Here when they saw him, whom they used to shun,
A lost, lone Man, so harassed and undone;
Our gentle Females, ever prompt to feel,
Perceived Compassion on their Anger steal;
His Crimes they could not from their Memories blot,
But they were grieved and trembled at his Lot.   260

A Priest too came, to whom his words are told,
And all the signs they shuddered to behold.

'Look! look!' they cried; 'his Limbs with horror shake,
And as he grinds his Teeth, what noise they make!
How glare his angry Eyes, and yet he's not awake:
See! what cold drops upon his Forehead stand,
And how he clenches that broad bony Hand.'

The Priest attending, found he spoke at times
As one alluding to his Fears and Crimes:
'It was the fall,' he muttered, 'I can show   270
The manner how – I never struck a blow:' –
And then aloud – 'Unhand me, free my Chain;
On Oath, he fell – it struck him to the Brain: . . .

Why ask my Father? – that old Man will swear
Against my Life; besides, he wasn't there: . . .
What, all agreed? – Am I to die to-day? –
My Lord, in mercy, give me time to pray.'

Then as they watched him, calmer he became,
And grew so weak he couldn't move his Frame,
280　But murmuring spake, – while they could see and hear
The start of Terror and the groan of Fear;
See the large Dew-beads on his Forehead rise,
And the cold Death-drop glaze his sunken Eyes;
Nor yet he died, but with unwonted force,
Seemed with some fancied Being to discourse:
He knew not us, or with accustomed art
He hid the knowledge, yet exposed his Heart;
'Twas part Confession and the rest Defence,
A Madman's Tale, with gleams of waking Sense.

290　'I'll tell you all,' he said, 'the very day
When the old Man first placed them in my way:
My Father's Spirit – he who always tried
To give me trouble, when he lived and died –
When he was gone, he could not be content
To see my Days in painful Labour spent,
But would appoint his Meetings, and he made
Me watch at these, and so neglect my Trade.

''Twas one hot Noon, all silent, still, serene,
No living Being had I lately seen;
300　I paddled up and down and dipped my Net,
'But (such his pleasure) I could nothing get, –
A Father's pleasure! when his Toil was done,
To plague and torture thus an only Son;
And so I sat and looked upon the Stream,
How it ran on; and felt as in a Dream:
But Dream it was not; No! – I fixed my Eyes
On the mid Stream and saw the Spirits rise;
I saw my Father on the Water stand,

And hold a thin pale Boy in either hand;
And there they glided ghastly on the top   310
Of the salt Flood and never touched a drop:
I would have struck them, but they knew the intent,
And smiled upon the Oar, and down they went.

  'Now, from that day, whenever I began
To dip my Net, there stood the hard Old Man –
He and those Boys: I humbled me and prayed
They would be gone; – they heeded not, but stayed:
Nor could I turn, nor would the Boat go by,
But gazing on the Spirits, there was I;
They bade me leap to death, but I was loth to die: 320
'And every day, as sure as day arose,
Would these three spirits meet me ere the close;
To hear and mark them daily was my doom,
And "Come," they said, with weak, sad voices, "come."
To row away with all my strength I tried,
But there were they, hard by me in the Tide,
  The three unbodied Forms – and "Come," still "come" they
    cried.

  'Fathers should pity – but this old Man shook
His hoary Locks and froze me by a Look:
Thrice, when I struck them, through the water came   320
An hollow Groan, that weakened all my Frame:
"Father!" said I, "have Mercy:" – He replied,
I know not what – the angry Spirit lied, –
"Didst thou not draw thy Knife?" said he: – 'Twas true,
But I had Pity and my Arm withdrew:
He cried for Mercy, which I kindly gave,
But he has no Compassion in his Grave.

  'There were three places, where they ever rose, –
The whole long River has not such as those, –
Places accursed, where, if a Man remain,   340
He'll see the things which strike him to the Brain;
And there they made me on my Paddle lean,

And look at them for hours; – accursèd Scene!
When they would glide to that smooth Eddy-space,
Then bid me leap and join them in the place;
And at my Groans each little villain Sprite
Enjoyed my Pains and vanished in delight.

    'In one fierce Summer-day, when my poor Brain
Was burning-hot and cruel was my Pain,
350   Then came this Father-foe, and there he stood
With his two Boys again upon the Flood;
There was more Mischief in their Eyes, more Glee
In their pale Faces when they glared at me:
Still did they force me on the Oar to rest,
And when they saw me fainting and oppressed,
He, with his Hand, the old Man, scooped the Flood,
And there came Flame about him mixed with Blood;
He bade me stoop and look upon the place,
Then flung the hot-red Liquor in my Face;
360   Burning it blazed, and then I roared for Pain,
I thought the Demons would have turned my Brain.

    'Still there they stood, and forced me to behold
A place of Horrors – they cannot be told –
Where the Flood opened, there I heard the Shriek
Of tortured Guilt – no earthly Tongue can speak:
"All Days alike! for ever!" did they say,
"And unremitted Torments every Day." –
Yes, so they said:' – But here he ceased and gazed
On all around, affrightened and amazed;
370   And still he tried to speak and looked in dread
Of frightened Females gathering round his Bed;
Then dropped exhausted and appeared at rest,
Till the strong Foe the vital Powers possessed;
Then with an inward, broken voice he cried,
'Again they come,' and muttered as he died.

TALES

TALE I

THE DUMB ORATORS;
OR,
THE BENEFIT OF SOCIETY

With fair round belly with good capon lin'd,
With eyes severe ——
Full of wise saws and modern instances.
As You Like It, Act II. Scene 7.

Deep shame hath struck me dumb.
King John, Act IV. Scene 2.

He gives the bastinado with his tongue,
Our ears are cudgell'd.
King John, Act II. Scene 2.

Let's kill all the lawyers;
Now show yourselves men: 'tis for liberty:
We will not leave one lord or gentleman.
2 Henry VI, Act II. Scene 7.

And thus the whirligig of time brings in his revenges.
Twelfth Night, Act V. Scene Last.

That all Men would be cowards if they dare,
Some men we know have courage to declare;
And this the life of many an hero shows,
That like the tide, man's courage ebbs and flows:
With friends and gay companions round them, then
Men boldly speak and have the hearts of Men;
Who, with opponents seated, miss the aid
Of kind applauding looks, and grow afraid;

Like timid travellers in the night, they fear
The assault of foes, when not a friend is near.

In contest mighty and of conquest proud,
Was *Justice Bolt*, impetuous, warm, and loud;
His fame, his prowess all the country knew,
And disputants, with one so fierce, were few:
He was a younger son, for law designed,
With dauntless look and persevering mind;
While yet a clerk for disputation famed,
No efforts tired him, and no conflicts tamed.

Scarcely he bade his master's desk adieu,
When both his brothers from the world withdrew:
An ample fortune he from them possessed,
And was with saving care and prudence blessed.
Now would he go and to the country give
Example how an *English* Squire should live;
How bounteous, yet how frugal man may be,
By a well-ordered hospitality;
He would the rights of all so well maintain,
That none should idle be, and none complain.

All this and more he purposed – and what man
Could do, he did to realise his plan:
But time convinced him that we cannot keep
A breed of Reasoners like a flock of sheep;
For they, so far from following as we lead,
Make that a cause why they will not proceed.
Man will not follow where a rule is shown,
But loves to take a method of his own;
Explain the way with all your care and skill,
This will he quit, if but to prove he will. –
Yet had our Justice honour – and the crowd,
Awed by his presence, their respect avowed.

In later years he found his heart incline,
More than in youth, to generous food and wine;

But no indulgence checked the powerful love
He felt to teach, to argue, and reprove.

   Meetings, or public calls, he never missed, –
To dictate often, always to assist:
Oft he the Clergy joined, and not a cause
Pertained to them but he could quote the laws;
He, upon tithes and residence displayed
A fund of knowledge for the hearer's aid;   50
And could on glebe and farming, wool and grain,
A long discourse, without a pause, maintain.

   To his experience and his native sense,
He joined a bold imperious eloquence;
The grave, stern look of men informed and wise,
A full command of feature, heart, and eyes,
An awe-compelling frown, and fear-inspiring size.
When at the table, not a guest was seen
With appetite so lingering, or so keen;
But when the outer man no more required,   60
The inner waked and he was man inspired.
His subjects then were those, a subject true
Presents in fairest form to public view;
Of Church and State, of Law, with mighty strength
Of words he spoke, in speech of mighty length:
And now, into the vale of years declined,
He hides too little of the monarch-mind:
He kindles anger by untimely jokes,
And opposition by contempt provokes;
Mirth he suppresses by his awful frown,   70
And humble spirits, by disdain keeps down;
Blamed by the mild, approved by the severe,
The prudent fly him, and the valiant fear.

   For overbearing is his proud discourse,
And overwhelming of his voice the force;
And overpowering is he when he shows
What floats upon a mind that always overflows.

This ready Man at every meeting rose,
Something to hint, determine, or propose;
80   And grew so fond of teaching, that he taught
Those who instruction needed not or sought:
Happy our Hero, when he could excite
Some thoughtless talker to the wordy fight:
Let him a subject at his pleasure choose,
Physic or Law, Religion, or the Muse;
On all such themes he was prepared to shine,
Physician, poet, lawyer, and divine.
Hemmed in by some tough argument, borne down
By press of language and the awful frown,
90   In vain for mercy shall the culprit plead;
His crime is past, and sentence must proceed;
Ah! suffering man, have patience, bear thy woes, –
For lo! the clock, – at ten the Justice goes.

This powerful Man, on business or to please
A curious taste, or weary grown of ease;
On a long journey travelled many a mile
Westward, and halted midway in our isle;
Content to view a city large and fair,
Though none had notice, – what a man was there!

100   Silent two days, he then began to long
Again to try a voice so loud and strong;
To give his favourite topics some new grace,
And gain some glory in such distant place;
To reap some present pleasure, and to sow
Seeds of fair fame, in after-time to grow:
Here will men say, 'We heard, at such an hour,
The best of speakers – wonderful his power.'

Inquiry made, he found that day would meet
A learnèd Club, and in the very street:
110   Knowledge to gain and give, was the design;
To speak, to hearken, to debate, and dine:

This pleased our Traveller, for he felt his force
In either way, to eat or to discourse.

  Nothing more easy than to gain access
To men like these, with his polite address:
So he succeeded, and first looked around,
To view his objects and to take his ground;
And therefore silent chose awhile to sit,
Then enter boldly by some lucky hit;
Some observation keen or stroke severe,   120
To cause some wonder or excite some fear.

  Now, dinner past, no longer he suppressed
His strong dislike to be a silent guest;
Subjects and words were now at his command, –
When disappointment frowned on all he planned;
For, hark! – he heard amazed, on every side,
His Church insulted and her Priests belied;
The Laws reviled, the Ruling Power abused,
The Land derided, and its Foes excused: –
He heard and pondered. – What, to men so vile,   130
Should be his language? For his threatening style
They were too many; – if his speech were meek,
They would despise such poor attempts to speak;
At other times with every word at will,
He now sat lost, perplexed, astonished, still.

  Here were Socinians, Deists, and indeed
All who, as foes to England's Church, agreed;
But still with creeds unlike, and some without a creed:
Here, too, fierce friends of Liberty he saw,
Who owned no prince and who obey no law;   140
There were Reformers of each different sort,
Foes to the Laws, the Priesthood, and the Court;
Some on their favourite plans alone intent,
Some purely angry and malevolent:
The rash were proud to blame their Country's laws;
The vain, to seem supporters of a cause;

One called for change, that he would dread to see;
Another sighed for Gallic Liberty!
And numbers joining with the forward crew,
150   For no one reason – but that numbers do.

 'How,' said the Justice, 'can this trouble rise,
This shame and pain, from creatures I despise?'
And Conscience answered, – 'The prevailing cause
Is, thy delight in listening to applause;
Here, thou art seated with a tribe, who spurn
Thy favourite themes, and into laughter turn
Thy fears and wishes; silent and obscure
Thyself, shalt thou the long harangue endure;
And learn, by feeling, what it is to force
160   On thy unwilling friends the long discourse:
What though thy thoughts be just, and these, it seems,
Are traitors' projects, idiots' empty schemes;
Yet minds like bodies crammed, reject their food,
Nor will be forced and tortured for their good!'

 At length, a sharp, shrewd, sallow Man arose;
And begged he briefly might his mind disclose;
'It was his duty, in these worst of times,
To inform the governed of their Rulers' crimes:'
This pleasant subject to attend, they each
170   Prepared to listen, and forbore to teach.

 Then voluble and fierce the wordy Man
Through a long chain of favourite horrors ran: –
First, of the Church, from whose enslaving power
He was delivered, and he blessed the hour;
'Bishops and deans, and prebendaries all,'
He said, 'were cattle fattening in the stall;
Slothful and pursy, insolent and mean,
Were every bishop, prebendary, dean,
And wealthy rector: curates poorly paid,
180   Were only dull; – he would not them upbraid.'

 From priests he turned to canons, creeds, and prayers,

Rubrics and rules, and all our Church affairs;
Churches themselves, desk, pulpit, altar, all
The Justice reverenced – and pronounced their fall.

Then from Religion *Hammond* turned his view,
To give our Rulers the correction due;
Not one wise action had these triflers planned;
There was, it seemed, no wisdom in the land;
Save in this Patriot tribe, who meet at times
To show the statesman's errors and his crimes.   190

Now here was *Justice Bolt* compelled to sit,
To hear the Deist's scorn, the Rebel's wit:
The fact mis-stated, the envenomed lie,
And staring spell-bound made not one reply.

Then were our Laws abused – and with the laws,
All who prepare, defend, or judge a cause:
'We have no lawyer whom a man can trust,'
Proceeded *Hammond*, – 'if the laws were just;
But they are evil; 'tis the savage state
Is only good, and ours sophisticate!   200
See! the free creatures in their woods and plains,
Where without laws each happy monarch reigns,
King of himself, – while we a number dread,
By slaves commanded and by dunces led;
Oh, let the name with either state agree –
Savage our own we'll name, and civil theirs shall be.'

The silent Justice still astonished sate,
And wondered much whom he was gazing at;
Twice he essayed to speak – but in a cough,
The faint, indignant, dying speech went off;
'But who is this?' thought he, – 'a demon vile,
With wicked meaning and a vulgar style;
Hammond they call him; they can give the name
Of man to devils. – Why am I so tame?
Why crush I not the viper?' – Fear replied,
'Watch him awhile and let his strength be tried;

He will be foiled, if man; but if his aid
Be from beneath, 'tis well to be afraid.'

'We are called free!' said *Hammond* – 'doleful times,
When Rulers add their insult to their crimes;
For should our scorn expose each powerful vice,
It would be libel, and we pay the price.'

Thus with licentious words the man went on,
Proving that liberty of speech was gone;
That all were slaves – nor had we better chance,
For better times, than as allies to *France*.

Loud groaned the Stranger – Why, he must relate;
And owned, 'In sorrow for his Country's fate;'
'Nay she were safe,' the ready Man replied,
'Might Patriots rule her, and could Reasoners guide;
When all to vote, to speak, to teach are free,
Whate'er their creeds or their opinions be;
When books of statutes are consumed in flames,
And courts and copyholds are empty names:
Then will be times of joy, – but ere they come,
Havock, and war, and blood must be our doom.'

The Man here paused – then loudly for Reform
He called, and hailed the prospect of the storm;
The wholesome blast, the fertilizing flood –
Peace gained by tumult, plenty bought with blood:
Sharp means, he owned; but when the land's disease
Asks cure complete, no medicines are like these.

Our Justice now, more led by fear than rage,
Saw it in vain with madness to engage;
With imps of darkness no man seeks to fight,
Knaves to instruct, or set deceivers right:
Then as the daring speech denounced these woes,
Sick at the soul, the grieving Guest arose;
Quick on the board his ready cash he threw,
And from the demons to his closet flew:

There when secured, he prayed with earnest zeal,
That all they wished, these patriot-souls might feel;
'Let them to *France*, their darling country, haste,
And all the comforts of a Frenchman taste;
Let them his safety, freedom, pleasure know,
Feel all their rulers on the land bestow;
And be at length dismissed by one unerring blow;
Not hacked and hewed by one afraid to strike,
But shorn by that which shears all men alike;
Nor, as in *Britain*, let them curse delay
Of law, but borne without a form away –
Suspected, tried, condemned, and carted in a day;
Oh! let them taste what they so much approve,
These strong fierce freedoms of the land they love.'*

   Home came our Hero, to forget no more
The fear he felt and ever must deplore:
For though he quickly joined his friends again,
And could with decent force his themes maintain;
Still it occurred that in a luckless time,
He failed to fight with Heresy and Crime;   270
It was observed his words were not so strong,
His tones so powerful, his harangues so long,
As in old times – for he would often drop
The lofty look, and of a sudden stop;
When Conscience whispered, that he once was still,
And let the wicked triumph at their will;
And therefore now, when not a foe was near;
He had no right so valiant to appear.

   Some years had passed, and he perceived his fears
Yield to the spirit of his earlier years, –   280
When at a meeting, with his friends beside,
He saw an object that awaked his pride;

* The reader will perceive in these and the preceding verses, allusions to the state of *France*, as that country was circumstanced some years since, rather than as it appears to be in the present date; several years elapsing between the alarm of the loyal Magistrate on the occasion now related, and a subsequent event that farther illustrates the remark with which the narrative commences.

His shame, wrath, vengeance, indignation – all
Man's harsher feelings did that sight recall.

For lo! beneath him fixed, our Man of Law,
That lawless man the Foe of Order, saw;
Once feared, now scorned; once dreaded, now abhorred;
A wordy man, and evil every word;
Again he gazed, – 'It is,' said he, 'the same:
290 Caught and secure: his master owes him shame:'
So thought our Hero, who each instant found
His courage rising, from the numbers round.

As when a felon has escaped and fled,
So long, that law conceives the culprit dead;
And back recalled her myrmidons, intent
On some new game, and with a stronger scent;
Till she beholds him in a place, where none
Could have conceived the culprit would have gone;
There he sits upright in his seat, secure,
300 As one whose conscience is correct and pure:
This rouses anger for the old offence,
And scorn for all such seeming and pretence:
So on this *Hammond* looked our Hero bold,
Remembering well that vile offence of old:
And now he saw the rebel dared to intrude
Among the pure, the loyal, and the good;
The crime provoked his wrath, the folly stirred his blood:
Nor wonder was it, if so strange a sight
Caused joy with vengeance, terror with delight;
310 Terror like this a tiger might create,
A joy like that to see his captive state,
At once to know his force and then decree his fate.

Hammond, much praised by numerous friends, was come
To read his lectures, so admired at home;
Historic lectures, where he loved to mix
His free plain hints on modern politics:
Here, he had heard, that numbers had design,

Their business finished, to sit down and dine;
This gave him pleasure, for he judged it right
To show by day, that he could speak at night. 320
Rash the design – for he perceived, too late,
Not one approving friend beside him sate;
The greater number, whom he traced around,
Were men in black, and he conceived they frowned.
'I will not speak,' he thought; 'no pearls of mine
Shall be presented to this herd of swine;'
Not this availed him, when he cast his eye
On *Justice Bolt*; he could not fight, nor fly:
He saw a man to whom he gave the pain,
Which now he felt must be returned again; 330
His conscience told him, with what keen delight,
He, at that time enjoyed a stranger's fright;
That stranger now befriended – he alone,
For all his insult, friendless, to atone;
Now he could feel it cruel that a heart
Should be distressed and none to take its part;
'Though one by one,' said Pride, 'I would defy
Much greater men, yet meeting every eye,
I do confess a fear, – but he will pass me by.'

Vain hope! the *Justice* saw the foe's distress, 340
With exultation he could not suppress;
He felt the fish was hooked – and so forbore,
In playful spite, to draw it to the shore.
Hammond looked round again, but none were near,
With friendly smile to still his growing fear;
But all above him seemed a solemn row
Of priests and deacons, so they seemed below;
He wondered who his right-hand man might be –
Vicar of *Holt cum Uppingham*, was he;
And who the man of that dark frown possessed – 350
Rector of *Bradley* and of *Barton-west*;
'A pluralist,' he growled – but checked the word,
That warfare might not, by his zeal, be stirred.

But now began the man above, to show
Fierce looks and threatenings to the man below;
Who had some thoughts, his peace, by flight to seek –
But how then lecture, if he dared not speak? –

Now as the Justice for the war prepared,
He seemed just then to question if he dared;
'He may resist, although his power be small,
And growing desperate may defy us all;
One dog attack, and he prepares for flight –
Resist another, and he strives to bite;
Nor can I say, if this rebellious cur
Will fly for safety, or will scorn to stir.'
Alarmed by this, he lashed his soul to rage,
Burned with strong shame and hurried to engage.

As a male turkey straggling on the green,
When by fierce harriers, terriers, mongrels seen,
He feels the insult of the noisy train,
And skulks aside though moved by much disdain;
But when that turkey at his own barn-door,
Sees one poor straying puppy and no more;
(A foolish puppy who had left the pack,
Thoughtless what foe was threatening at his back,)
He moves about as ship prepared to sail,
He hoists his proud rotundity of tail,
The half-sealed eyes and changeful neck he shows,
Where, in its quickening colours, vengeance glows;
From red to blue the pendant wattles turn,
Blue mixed with red as matches when they burn;
And thus the intruding snarler to oppose,
Urged by enkindling wrath, he gobbling goes.

So looked our Hero in his wrath, his cheeks
Flushed with fresh fires and glowed in tingling streaks;
His breath by passion's force awhile restrained,
Like a stopped current greater force regained;

360

370

380

So spoke, so looked he; every eye and ear
Were fixed to view him or were turned to hear.

'My friends, you know me, you can witness all, 390
How, urged by passion, I restrain my gall;
And every motive to revenge withstand
Save, when I hear abused my native land.

'Is it not known, agreed, confirmed, confessed,
That of all people, we are governed best?
We have the force of Monarchies; are free,
As the most proud Republicans can be;
And have those prudent counsels that arise
In grave and cautious Aristocracies:
And live there those, in such all-glorious state, 400
Traitors protected in the land they hate?
Rebels, still warring with the laws that give
To them subsistence? – Yes, such wretches live.

'Ours, is a Church reformed, and now no more
Is aught for man to mend or to restore;
'Tis pure in doctrines, 'tis correct in creeds,
Has nought redundant, and it nothing needs;
No evil is therein, – no wrinkle, spot,
Stain, blame, or blemish; – I affirm, there's not.

'All this you know – now mark what once befell, 410
With grief I bore it and with shame I tell;
I was entrapped, – yes, so it came to pass,
'Mid heathen rebels, a tumultuous class;
Each to his country bore a hellish mind,
Each like his neighbour was of cursèd kind;
The Land that nursed them, they blasphemed; the laws,
Their Sovereign's glory, and their Country's cause;
And who their mouth, their master-fiend, and who
Rebellion's Oracle? – You, caitiff, you!'

He spoke, and standing stretched his mighty arm, 420
And fixed the Man of Words, as by a charm.

'How raved that Railer! Sure some hellish power
Restrained my tongue in that delirious hour,
Or I had hurled the shame and vengeance due,
On him, the guide of that infuriate crew;
But to mine eyes, such dreadful looks appeared,
Such mingled yell of lying words I heard,
That I conceived around were demons all,
And till I fled the house, I feared its fall.

430   'Oh! could our Country from our coasts expel
Such foes! to nourish those who wish her well:
This her mild laws forbid, but we may still
From us eject them by our sovereign will;
This let us do.' – He said, and then began
A gentler feeling for the Silent Man;
Even in our Hero's mighty soul arose,
A touch of pity for experienced woes;
But this was transient, and with angry eye
He sternly looked, and paused for a reply.

440   'Twas then the Man of many Words would speak –
But in his trial, had them all to seek;
To find a friend he looked the circle round,
But joy or scorn in every feature found:
He sipped his wine, but in those times of dread
Wine only adds confusion to the head;
In doubt he reasoned with himself, – 'And how
Harangue at night, if I be silent now?'
From pride and praise received, he sought to draw
Courage to speak, but still remained the awe;
450   One moment rose he with a forced disdain,
And then abashed, sunk sadly down again;
While in our Hero's glance he seemed to read,
'Slave and insurgent! what hast thou to plead?' –

By desperation urged, he now began: –
'I seek no favour – I – the Rights of Man!
Claim; and I, – nay! – but give me leave – and I

Insist – a man – that is – and in reply,
I speak.' – Alas! each new attempt was vain:
Confused he stood, he sate, he rose again;
At length he growled defiance, sought the door,   460
Cursed the whole synod, and was seen no more.

'Laud we,' said Justice *Bolt*, 'the Powers above;
Thus could our speech the sturdiest foe remove.'
Exulting now he gained new strength of fame,
And lost all feelings of defeat and shame.

'He dared not strive, you witnessed – dared not lift
His voice, nor drive at his accursèd drift:
So all shall tremble, wretches who oppose
Our Church or State – thus be it to our foes.'

He spoke, and, seated with his former air,   470
Looked his full self, and filled his ample chair;
Took one full bumper to each favourite cause,
And dwelt all night on politics and laws,
With high applauding voice, that gained him high applause.

TALE II
THE PARTING HOUR

<hr>

> I did not take my leave of him, but had
> Most pretty things to say: ere I could tell him
> How I would think of him, at certain hours,
> Such thoughts and such; – or ere I could
> Give him that parting kiss, which I had set
> Betwixt two charming words – comes forth my father. –
>> *Cymbeline*, Act I. Scene 4.

> Grief hath chang'd me since you saw me last,
> And careful hours with Time's deformed hand
> Hath written strange defeatures o'er my face.
>> *Comedy of Errors*, Act V. Scene 1.

> Oh! if thou be the same Egean, speak,
> And speak unto the same Emilia.
>> *Comedy of Errors*, Act V. Scene 5.

> I ran it through, ev'n from my boyish years,
> To the very moment when she bad me tell it,
> Wherein I spake of most disasterous chances,
> Of moving accident by fire and flood,
> Of being taken by th' insolent foe
> And sold to slavery.
>> *Othello*, Act I. Scene 3.

> An old man, broken with the storms of fate,
> Is come to lay his weary bones among you;
> Give him a little earth, for charity.
>> *Henry VIII*, Act IV. Scene 2.

Minutely trace man's life; year after year,
Through all his days let all his deeds appear,
And then, though some may in that life be strange,
Yet there appears no vast nor sudden change:
The links that bind those various deeds are seen,
And no mysterious void is left between.

But let these binding links be all destroyed,
All that through years he suffered or enjoyed;
Let that vast gap be made, and then behold —
This was the youth, and he is thus when old;   10
Then we at once the work of Time survey,
And in an instant see a life's decay;
Pain mixed with pity in our bosoms rise,
And sorrow takes new sadness from surprise.

Beneath yon tree, observe an ancient Pair —
A sleeping man; a woman, in her chair,
Watching his looks, with kind and pensive air:
No wife, nor sister she, nor is the name
Nor kindred of this friendly Pair the same;
Yet so allied are they, that few can feel   20
Her constant, warm, unwearied, anxious zeal:
Their years and woes, although they long have loved,
Keep their good name and conduct unreproved;
Thus life's small comforts they together share,
And while life lingers, for the grave prepare.

No other subjects on their spirits press,
Nor gain such interest as the past distress;
Grievous events, that from the memory drive
Life's common cares, and those alone survive,
Mix with each thought, in every action share,   30
Darken each dream and blend with every prayer.

To *David Booth*, his fourth and last-born boy,
Allen his name, was more than common joy;
And as the child grew up, there seemed in him
A more than common life in every limb;

A strong and handsome stripling he became,
And the gay spirit answered to the frame;
A lighter, happier lad was never seen,
For ever easy, cheerful, or serene;
His early love he fixed upon a fair
And gentle Maid – they were a handsome pair.

They at an infant-school together played,
Where the foundation of their love was laid;
The boyish champion would his choice attend
In every sport, in every fray defend.
As prospects opened and as life advanced,
They walked together, they together danced;
On all occasions, from their early years,
They mixed their joys and sorrows, hopes and fears;
Each heart was anxious, till it could impart
Its daily feelings to its kindred heart;
As years increased, unnumbered petty wars
Broke out between them; jealousies and jars;
Causeless indeed, and followed by a peace,
That gave to love – growth, vigour and increase.
Whilst yet a boy, when other minds are void,
Domestic thoughts young *Allen*'s hours employed;
Judith in gaining hearts had no concern,
Rather intent the Matron's part to learn;
Thus early prudent and sedate they grew,
While lovers, thoughtful – and though children, true.
To either parents not a day appeared,
When with this love they might have interfered:
Childish at first, they cared not to restrain;
And strong at last, they saw restriction vain;
Nor knew they when that passion to reprove –
Now idle fondness, now resistless love.

So while the waters rise, the children tread
On the broad *Estuary*'s sandy bed;
But soon the channel fills, from side to side
Comes danger rolling with the deepening tide;

Yet none who saw the rapid current flow,
Could the first instant of that danger know.

The Lovers waited till the time should come,
When they together could possess a home:
In either house were men and maids unwed,
Hopes to be soothed, and tempers to be led.
Then *Allen*'s mother, of his favourite maid
Spoke from the feelings of a mind afraid:
'Dress and amusements were her sole employ,'   80
She said, – 'entangling her deluded boy;'
And yet, in truth, a mother's jealous love
Had much imagined and could little prove;
Judith had beauty – and if vain, was kind,
Discreet, and mild, and had a serious mind.

Dull was their prospect – when the Lovers met,
They said, we must not – dare not venture yet:
'Oh! could I labour for thee,' *Allen* cried,
'Why should our friends be thus dissatisfied?
On my own arm I could depend, but they
Still urge obedience, – must I yet obey?'   90
Poor *Judith* felt the grief, but grieving begged delay.

At length a prospect came that seemed to smile,
And faintly woo them, from a Western Isle;
A kinsman there a widow's hand had gained,
'Was old, was rich, and childless yet remained;
Would some young *Booth* to his affairs attend,
And wait awhile, he might expect a friend.'
The elder brothers, who were not in love,
Feared the false seas, unwilling to remove;   100
But the young *Allen*, an enamoured boy,
Eager an independence to enjoy,
Would through all perils seek it, – by the sea, –
Through labour, danger, pain or slavery.
The faithful *Judith* his design approved,
For both were sanguine, they were young and loved.
The mother's slow consent was then obtained;

The time arrived, to part alone remained:
All things prepared, on the expected day
Was seen the vessel anchored in the bay.
From her would seamen in the evening come,
To take the adventurous *Allen* from his home;
With his own friends the final day he passed,
And every painful hour, except the last.
The grieving Father urged the cheerful glass,
To make the moments with less sorrow pass;
Intent the Mother looked upon her son,
And wished the assent withdrawn, the deed undone;
The younger Sister, as he took his way,
Hung on his coat, and begged for more delay:
But his own *Judith* called him to the shore,
Whom he must meet, for they might meet no more; –
And there he found her – faithful, mournful, true,
Weeping and waiting for a last adieu!
The ebbing tide had left the sand, and there
Moved with slow steps the melancholy Pair:
Sweet were the painful moments, – but how sweet,
And without pain, when they again should meet!
Now either spoke, as hope and fear impressed
Each their alternate triumph in the breast.

Distance alarmed the Maid – she cried, ' 'Tis far!'
And danger too – 'it is a time of war:
Then in those countries are diseases strange,
And women gay, and men are prone to change;
What then may happen in a year, when things
Of vast importance every moment brings!
But hark! an oar!' she cried, yet none appeared –
'Twas love's mistake, who fancied what it feared:
And she continued, – 'Do, my *Allen*, keep
Thy heart from evil, let thy passions sleep;
Believe it good, nay glorious, to prevail,
And stand in safety where so many fail;
And do not, *Allen*, or for shame, or pride,
Thy faith abjure, or thy profession hide:

Can I believe *his* love will lasting prove,
Who has no reverence for the God I love?
I know thee well! how good thou art and kind;
But strong the passions that invade thy mind. –
Now, what to me has *Allen* to commend?' –
'Upon my Mother,' said the Youth, 'attend;   150
Forget her spleen, and in my place appear,
Her love to me will make my *Judith* dear;
Oft I shall think, (such comfort lovers seek,)
Who speaks of me, and fancy what they speak;
Then write on all occasions, always dwell
On Hope's fair prospects, and be kind and well,
And ever choose the fondest, tenderest style.'
She answered, 'No,' but answered with a smile.
'And now, my *Judith*, at so sad a time,
Forgive my fear, and call it not my crime;   160
When with our youthful neighbours 'tis thy chance
To meet in walks, the visit or the dance,
When every lad would on my lass attend,
Choose not a smooth designer for a friend;
That fawning *Philip* – nay, be not severe,
A rival's hope must cause a lover's fear.'

   Displeased she felt, and might in her reply
Have mixed some anger, but the boat was nigh,
Now truly heard! – it soon was full in sight! –
Now the sad farewell, and the long good-night;   170
For see! – his friends come hastening to the beach,
And now the gunwale is within the reach:
'Adieu! – farewell! – remember!' – and what more
Affection taught, was uttered from the shore!
But *Judith* left them with a heavy heart,
Took a last view, and went to weep apart!
And now his friends went slowly from the place,
Where she stood still, the dashing oar to trace;
Till all were silent! – for the Youth she prayed,
And softly then returned the weeping Maid.   180

They parted, thus by hope and fortune led,
And *Judith*'s hours in pensive pleasure fled:
But when returned the Youth? – the Youth no more
Returned exulting to his native shore;
But forty years were passed, and then there came
A worn-out man, with withered limbs and lame;
His mind oppressed with woes, and bent with age his frame.
Yes! old and grieved, and trembling with decay,
Was *Allen*, landing in his native bay,
190   Willing his breathless form should blend with kindred clay.
In an autumnal eve he left the beach,
In such an eve he chanced the port to reach:
He was alone; he pressed the very place
Of the sad parting, of the last embrace:
There stood his parents, there retired the Maid,
So fond, so tender, and so much afraid;
And on that spot, through many a year, his mind
Turned mournful back, half sinking, half resigned.

No one was present; of its crew bereft,
200   A single boat was in the billows left;
Sent from some anchored vessel in the bay,
At the returning tide to sail away:
O'er the black stern the moon-light softly played,
The loosened foresail flapping in the shade:
All silent else on shore: but from the town
A drowsy peal of distant bells came down:
From the tall houses here and there, a light
Served some confused remembrance to excite:
'There,' he observed, and new emotions felt,
210   'Was my first home – and yonder *Judith* dwelt: –
Dead! dead are all! I long – I fear to know,'
He said, and walked impatient, and yet slow.

Sudden there broke upon his grief a noise
Of merry tumult and of vulgar joys:

Seamen returning to their ship, were come,
With idle numbers straying from their home;
Allen among them mixed, and in the old
Strove some familiar features to behold;
While fancy aided memory: – 'Man! what cheer?'
A sailor cried; 'Art thou at anchor here?'   220
Faintly he answered, and then tried to trace
Some youthful features in some agèd face:
A swarthy matron he beheld, and thought
She might unfold the very truths he sought;
Confused and trembling, he the dame addressed: –
'The *Booths*! yet live they?' pausing and oppressed:
Then spake again: – 'Is there no ancient man,
David his name? – assist me, if you can. –
Flemmings there were – and *Judith*, doth she live?'
The woman gazed, nor could an answer give;   230
Yet wondering stood, and all were silent by,
Feeling a strange and solemn sympathy.
The woman musing, said: 'She knew full well
Where the old people came at last to dwell;
They had a married daughter, and a son;
But they were dead, and now remained not one.'

'Yes,' said an elder, who had paused intent
On days long past, 'there was a sad event; –
One of these *Booths* – it was my mother's tale –
Here left his lass, I know not where to sail: 240
She saw their parting, and observed the pain;
But never came the unhappy man again:'
'The ship was captured' – *Allen* meekly said:
'And what became of the forsaken Maid?'
The woman answered: 'I remember now,
She used to tell the lasses of her vow,
And of her lover's loss, and I have seen
The gayest hearts grow sad where she has been:
Yet in her grief she married, and was made
Slave to a wretch, whom meekly she obeyed,   250

And early buried – but I know no more.
And hark! our friends are hastening to the shore.'

    Allen soon found a lodging in the town,
And walked a man unnoticed up and down.
This house, and this, he knew, and thought a face
He sometimes could among a number trace:
Of names remembered there remained a few,
But they no favourites, and the rest were new:
A merchant's wealth, when *Allen* went to sea,
Was reckoned boundless. – Could he living be?
Or lived his son? for one he had, the heir
To a vast business, and a fortune fair. –
No! but that heir's poor widow, from her shed,
With crutches went to take her dole of bread:
There was a friend whom he had left a boy,
With hope to sail the master of a hoy;
Him, after many a stormy day, he found
With his great wish, his life's whole purpose, crowned:
This hoy's proud Captain looked in *Allen*'s face, –
'Yours is, my friend,' said he, 'a woeful case;
We cannot all succeed; I now command
The *Betsey* sloop, and am not much at land:
But when we meet, you shall your story tell
Of foreign parts – I bid you now farewell!'

    Allen so long had left his native shore,
He saw but few whom he had seen before;
The older people, as they met him, cast
A pitying look, oft speaking as they past –
'The Man is *Allen Booth*, and it appears
He dwelt among us in his early years;
We see the name engraved upon the stones,
Where this poor wanderer means to lay his bones.'
Thus where he lived and loved, – unhappy change! –
He seems a stranger, and finds all are strange.

    But now a Widow, in a village near,

260

270

280

Chanced of the melancholy man to hear:
Old as she was, to *Judith*'s bosom came
Some strong emotions at the well-known name;
He was her much-loved *Allen*, she had stayed
Ten troubled years, a sad afflicted maid: 290
Then was she wedded, of his death assured,
And much of misery in her lot endured;
Her husband died; her children sought their bread
In various places, and to her were dead.
The once-fond Lovers met; not grief nor age,
Sickness or pain, their hearts could disengage:
Each had immediate confidence; a friend
Both now beheld, on whom they might depend:
'Now is there one to whom I can express
My nature's weakness, and my soul's distress.'   300
Allen looked up, and with impatient heart –
'Let me not lose thee – never let us part:
So Heaven this comfort to my sufferings give,
'Tis not such bitter pain, to think and live.'
Thus *Allen* spoke; for time had not removed
The charms attached to one so fondly loved;
Who, with more health, the mistress of their cot,
Labours to soothe the evils of his lot.
To her, to her alone, his various fate,
At various times, 'tis comfort to relate;   310
And yet is sorrow – she too loves to hear
What wrings her bosom, and compels the tear.

    First he related – How he left the shore,
Alarmed with fears that they should meet no more;
Then, ere the ship had reached her purposed course,
They met and yielded to the Spanish force;
Then 'cross the Atlantic seas they bore their prey,
Who grieving landed from their sultry bay;
And marching many a burning league, he found
Himself a slave upon a miner's ground: 320
There a good priest his native language spoke,

And gave some ease to his tormenting yoke;
Kindly advanced him in his master's grace,
And he was stationed in an easier place:
There, hopeless ever to escape the land,
He to a Spanish maiden gave his hand;
In cottage sheltered from the blaze of day,
He saw his happy infants round him play;
Where summer shadows, made by lofty trees,
330   Waved o'er his seat, and soothed his reveries;
E'en then he thought of *England*, nor could sigh,
But his fond *Isabel* demanded, 'Why?'
Grieved by the story, she the sigh repaid,
And wept in pity for the English Maid:
Thus twenty years were passed, and passed his views
Of further bliss, for he had wealth to lose:
His friend now dead, some foe had dared to paint
'His faith is tainted: he his spouse would taint;
Make all his children Infidels, and found
340   An *English* Heresy on Christian ground.'

'Whilst I was poor,' said *Allen*, 'none would care
What my poor notions of religion were;
None asked me whom I worshipped, how I prayed,
If due obedience to the laws were paid;
My good adviser taught me to be still,
Nor to make converts had I power or will.
I preached no foreign doctrine to my wife,
And never mentioned *Luther* in my life;
I, all they said, say what they would, allowed,
350   And when the Fathers bade me bow, I bowed:
Their forms I followed, whether well or sick,
And was a most obedient Catholic.
But I had money, and these pastors found
My notions vague, heretical, unsound:
A wicked book they seized; the very Turk
Could not have read a more pernicious work;
To me pernicious, who if it were good

Or evil questioned not, nor understood;
Oh! had I little but the book possessed,
I might have read it, and enjoyed my rest.'   360

   Alas! poor *Allen*, through his wealth was seen
Crimes that by poverty concealed had been:
Faults, that in dusty pictures rest unknown,
Are in an instant through the varnish shown.

   He told their cruel mercy; how at last,
In Christian kindness for the merits past,
They spared his forfeit life, but bade him fly,
Or for his crime and contumacy die;
Fly from all scenes, all objects of delight;
His wife, his children weeping in his sight,   370
All urging him to flee, he fled, and cursed his flight.

   He next related how he found a way,
Guideless and grieving, to Campeachy-Bay:
There in the woods he wrought, and there, among
Some labouring seamen, heard his native tongue:
The sound, one moment, broke upon his pain
With joyful force; he longed to hear again:
Again he heard; he seized an offered hand,
'And when beheld you last our native land?'
He cried, 'and in what county? quickly say' –   380
The seamen answered – strangers all were they;
One only at his native port had been;
He, landing once, the quay and church had seen,
For that esteemed; but nothing more he knew.
Still more to know, would *Allen* join the crew,
Sail where they sailed, and, many a peril past,
They at his kinsman's isle their anchor cast;
But him they found not, nor could one relate
Aught of his will, his wish, or his estate.
This grieved not *Allen*; – then again he sailed   390
For *England*'s coast, again his fate prevailed:
War raged, and he, an active man and strong,

Was soon impressed, and served his country long.
By various shores he passed, on various seas,
Never so happy as when void of ease. –
And then he told how in a calm distressed,
Day after day his soul was sick of rest;
When, as a log upon the deep they stood,
Then roved his spirit to the inland wood;
400 Till, while awake, he dreamed, that on the seas
Were his loved home, the hill, the stream, the trees:
He gazed, he pointed to the scenes: – 'There stand
My wife, my children, 'tis my lovely land;
See! there my dwelling – oh! delicious scene
Of my best life – unhand me – are ye men?'

And thus the frenzy ruled him, till the wind
Brushed the fond pictures from the stagnant mind.

He told of bloody fights, and how at length
The rage of battle gave his spirits strength;
410 'Twas in the Indian seas his limb he lost,
And he was left half-dead upon the coast:
But living gained, 'mid rich aspiring men,
A fair subsistence by his ready pen.
'Thus,' he continued, 'passed unvaried years,
Without events producing hopes or fears.'
Augmented pay procured him decent wealth,
But years advancing undermined his health:
Then oft-times in delightful dream he flew
To *England*'s shore, and scenes his childhood knew:
420 He his parents, saw his favourite Maid,
No feature wrinkled, not a charm decayed;
And thus excited, in his bosom rose
A wish so strong, it baffled his repose;
Anxious he felt on *English* earth to lie;
To view the native soil, and there to die.

He then described the gloom, the dread he found,
When first he landed on the chosen ground,

Where undefined was all he hoped and feared,
And how confused and troubled all appeared;
His thoughts in past and present scenes employed,   430
All views in future blighted and destroyed:
His were a medley of bewildering themes,
Sad as realities, and wild as dreams.

Here his relation closes, but his mind
Flees back again some resting-place to find;
Thus silent, musing through the day, he sees
His children sporting by those lofty trees,
Their mother singing in the shady scene,
Where the fresh springs burst o'er the lively green;
So strong his eager fancy, he affrights   440
The faithful widow by its powerful flights;
For what disturbs him he aloud will tell,
And cry – ' 'Tis she, my wife! my *Isabel*!
Where are my children?' – *Judith* grieves to hear
How the soul works in sorrows so severe; –
Assiduous all his wishes to attend,
Deprived of much, he yet may boast a friend;
Watched by her care, in sleep, his spirit takes
Its flight, and watchful finds her when he wakes.

'Tis now her office; her attention see!   450
While her friend sleeps beneath that shading tree,
Careful, she guards him from the glowing heat,
And pensive muses at her *Allen*'s feet.

And where is he? Ah! doubtless, in those scenes
Of his best days, amid the vivid greens,
Fresh with unnumbered rills, where every gale
Breathes the rich fragrance of the neighbouring vale;
Smiles not his wife, and listens as there comes
The night-bird's music from the thickening glooms?
And as he sits with all these treasures nigh,   460
Blaze not with fairy-light the phosphor-fly,
When like a sparkling gem it wheels illumined by?

This is the joy that now so plainly speaks
In the warm transient flushing of his cheeks;
For he is listening to the fancied noise
Of his own children, eager in their joys: –
All this he feels, a dream's delusive bliss
Gives the expression, and the glow like this.
And now his *Judith* lays her knitting by,
470   These strong emotions in her friend to spy;
For she can fully of their nature deem –
But see! he breaks the long-protracted theme,
And wakes and cries – 'My God! 'twas but a dream!'

THE GENTLEMAN FARMER

═══════════════

> Pause then,
> And weigh thy value with an even hand,
> If thou beest rated by thy estimation,
> Thou dost deserve enough.
>
> *Merchant of Venice*, Act II. Scene 7.

> Because I will not do them wrong to mistrust any, I will do myself the right to trust none; and the fine is (for which I may go the finer), I will live a bachelor.
>
> *Much Ado about Nothing*, Act I. Scene 3.

> Throw physic to the dogs; I'll none of it.
>
> *Macbeth*, Act V. Scene 3.

> His promises are, as he then was, mighty;
> And his performance, as he now is, nothing.
>
> *Henry Eighth*, Act IV. Scene 2.

Gwyn was a Farmer, whom the farmers all,
Who dwelt around, the *Gentleman* would call;
Whether in pure humility or pride,
They only knew, and they would not decide.
  Far different he from that poor tasteless tribe,
Whom it was his amusement to describe;
Creatures no more enlivened than the clod,
But treading still as their dull fathers trod;
Who lived in times when not a man had seen
Corn sown by Drill, or threshed by a Machine: 10
He was of those whose skill assigns the prize
For creatures fed in Pens, and Stalls, and Sties;

And who, in places where Improvers meet,
To fill the land with fatness, had a seat;
Who in large mansions live like petty kings,
And speak of Farms but as amusing things;
Who plans encourage, and who journals keep,
And talk with lords about a breed of sheep.

    Two are the species in this genus known;
20 One, who is rich in his profession grown,
Who yearly finds his ample stores increase,
From fortune's favours and a favouring lease;
Who rides his hunter, who his house adorns;
Who drinks his wine, and his disbursements scorns;
Who freely lives, and loves to show he can –
This is the Farmer made the Gentleman.

    The second species from the world is sent,
Tired with its strife, or with his wealth content;
In books and men beyond the former read,
30 To Farming solely by a passion led,
Or by a fashion; curious in his land;
Now planning much, now changing what he planned;
Pleased by each trial, not by failures vexed,
And ever certain to succeed the next;
Quick to resolve, and easy to persuade –
This is the Gentleman, a Farmer made.

    Gwyn was of these; he from the world withdrew
Early in life, his reasons known to few:
Some disappointment said, some pure good sense,
40 The love of land, the press of indolence:
Wealthy he seemed, and wishing to retire,
Would be the Farmer, and be called the Squire.

    Forty and five his years, no child or wife
Crossed the still tenor of his chosen life:
Much land he purchased, planted far around,
And let some portions of superfluous ground

To farmers near him, not displeased to say,
'My tenants,' nor 'our worthy landlord' they.

    Fixed in his Farm, he soon displayed his skill
In small-boned Lambs, the Horse-hoe, and the Drill;   50
From these he rose to themes of nobler kind,
And showed the riches of a fertile mind:
To all around their visits he repaid,
And thus his mansion and himself displayed.
His rooms were stately, rather fine than neat,
And guests politely called his house a Seat:
At much expense was each apartment graced.
His taste was gorgeous, but it still was taste;
In full festoons the crimson curtains fell,
The sofas rose in bold elastic swell;   60
Mirrors in gilded frames displayed the tints
Of glowing carpets and of coloured prints:
The weary eye saw every object shine,
And all was costly, fanciful, and fine.

    As with his friends he passed the social hours,
His generous spirit scorned to hide its powers;
Powers unexpected, for his eye and air
Gave no sure signs that eloquence was there:
Oft he began with sudden fire and force,
As loth to lose occasion for discourse: 70
Some, 'tis observed, who feel a wish to speak,
Will a due place for introduction seek;
On to their purpose step by step they steal,
And all their way, by certain signals, feel;
Others plunge in at once, and never heed
Whose turn they take, whose purpose they impede:
Resolved to shine, they hasten to begin,
Of ending thoughtless – and of these was *Gwyn*.
And thus he spake –
                – 'It grieves me to the soul,
To see how Man submits to Man's control;

How overpowered and shackled minds are led
In vulgar tracks, and to submission bred:
The coward never on himself relies,
But to an equal for assistance flies;
Man yields to custom, as he bows to fate,
In all things ruled – mind, body, and estate:
In pain, in sickness, we for cure apply
To them we know not, and we know not why;
But that the creature has some jargon read,
And got some *Scotchman*'s system in his head;
Some grave impostor, who will health ensure,
Long as your patience or your wealth endure.
But mark them well, the pale and sickly crew,
They have not health, and can they give it you?
These solemn cheats their various methods choose;
A system fires them, as a bard his muse:
Hence wordy wars arise; the learn'd divide,
And groaning patients curse each erring guide.

'Next, our affairs are governed, – buy or sell,
Upon the deed the Law must fix its spell;
Whether we hire or let, we must have still
The dubious aid of an Attorney's skill;
They take a part in every man's affairs,
And in all business, some concern is theirs:
Because mankind in ways prescribed are found,
Like flocks that follow on a beaten ground,
Each abject nature in the way proceeds,
That now to shearing, now to slaughter leads.

'Should you offend, though meaning no offence,
You have no safety in your innocence;
The statute broken then is placed in view,
And men must pay for crimes they never knew.
Who would by Law regain his plundered store,
Would pick up fallen mercury from the floor:
If he pursue it, here and there it slides;
He would collect it, but it more divides;

This part and this he stops, but still in vain,
It slips aside, and breaks in parts again;
Till, after time and pains, and care and cost,
He finds his labour and his object lost.   120

'But most it grieves me, (friends alone are round,)
To see a man in Priestly fetters bound;
Guides to the Soul, these Friends of Heaven contrive,
Long as man lives, to keep his fears alive;
Soon as an infant breathes, their rites begin;
Who knows not sinning, must be freed from sin;
Who needs no bond, must yet engage in vows;
Who has no judgement, must a creed espouse:
Advanced in life, our boys are bound by rules,
Are catechised in churches, cloisters, schools,   130
And trained in thraldom to be fit for tools:
The youth grown up, he now a partner needs,
And lo! a Priest, as soon as he succeeds.
What man of sense can marriage-rites approve?
What man of spirit can be bound to love?
Forced to be kind! compelled to be sincere!
Do chains and fetters make companions dear?
Prisoners indeed we bind; but though the bond
May keep them safe, it does not make them fond:
The ring, the vow, the witness, licence, prayers,   140
All parties known! made public all affairs!
Such forms men suffer, and from these they date
A deed of love begun with all they hate:
Absurd! that none the beaten road should shun,
But love to do what other dupes have done.

'Well, now your Priest has made you one of twain,
Look you for rest? alas! you look in vain.
If sick, he comes; you cannot die in peace,
Till he attends to witness your release;
To vex your soul, and urge you to confess   150
The sins you feel, remember, or can guess:
Nay, when departed, to your grave he goes –
But there indeed he hurts not your repose.

'Such are our burdens; part we must sustain,
But need not link new grievance to the chain:
Yet men like idiots will their frames surround
With these vile shackles, nor confess they're bound;
In all that most confines them they confide,
Their slavery boast, and make their bonds their pride;
E'en as the pressure galls them, they declare,
(Good souls!) how happy and how free they are!
As madmen, pointing round their wretched cells,
Cry, "Lo! the palace where our honour dwells."

'Such is our state: but I resolve to live
By rules my reason and my feelings give;
No legal guards shall keep enthralled my mind,
No slaves command me, and no teachers blind.

'Tempted by sins, let me their strength defy,
But have no second in a surplice by;
No bottle-holder with officious aid,
To comfort conscience, weakened and afraid:
Then if I yield, my frailty is not known;
And if I stand, the glory is my own.

'When Truth and Reason are our friends, we seem
Alive! awake! – the superstitious dream.

'Oh! then, fair Truth, for thee alone I seek,
Friend to the wise, supporter of the weak;
From thee we learn whate'er is right and just;
Forms to despise, professions to distrust;
Creeds to reject, pretensions to deride,
And following thee, to follow none beside.'

Such was the speech; it struck upon the ear
Like sudden thunder, none expect to hear.
He saw men's wonder with a manly pride,
And gravely smiled at guest electrified;
'A farmer, this,' they said, 'oh! let him seek
That place where he may for his country speak;

On some great question to harangue for hours,
While speakers hearing, envy nobler powers!'

    Wisdom like this, as all things rich and rare,   190
Must be acquired with pains, and kept with care.
In books he sought it, which his friends might view
When their kind host the guarding curtain drew.
There were historic works for graver hours,
And lighter verse, to spur the languid powers;
There metaphysics, logic there had place,
But of devotion not a single trace –
Save what is taught in *Gibbon*'s florid page,
And other guides of this inquiring age;
There *Hume* appeared, and near, a splendid book   200
Composed by *Gay*'s good Lord of *Bolingbroke*:
With these were mixed the light, the free, the vain,
And from a corner peeped the sage *Tom Paine*:
Here four neat volumes *Chesterfield* were named,
For manners much and easy morals famed;
With chaste Memoirs of Females, to be read
When deeper studies had confused the head.

    Such his resources, treasures where he sought
For daily knowledge till his mind was fraught;
Then when his friends were present, for their use   210
He would the riches he had stored produce;
He found his lamp burn clearer, when each day
He drew for all he purposed to display:
For these occasions, forth his knowledge sprung,
As mustard quickens on a bed of dung;
All was prepared, and guests allowed the praise
For what they saw he could so quickly raise.

    Such this new friend; and when the year came round,
The same impressive, reasoning sage was found:
Then, too, was seen the pleasant mansion graced   220
With a fair Damsel – his no vulgar taste;
The neat *Rebecca*, sly, observant, still;

Watching his eye, and waiting on his will;
Simple yet smart her dress, her manners meek,
Her smiles spoke for her, she would seldom speak;
But watched each look, each meaning to detect,
And (pleased with notice) felt for all neglect.

With her lived *Gwyn* a sweet harmonious life,
Who, forms excepted, was a charming wife:
230 The wives indeed, so made by vulgar law,
Affected scorn, and censured what they saw,
And what they saw not, fancied; said 'twas sin,
And took no notice of the Wife of *Gwyn*:
But he despised their rudeness, and would prove
Theirs was compulsion and distrust, not love;
'Fools as they were ! could they conceive that rings
And parsons' blessings were substantial things?'
They answered 'Yes,' while he contemptuous spoke
Of the low notions held by simple folk;
240 Yet strange, that anger in a man so wise,
Should from the notions of those fools arise:
Can they so vex us, whom we so despise?

Brave as he was, our hero felt a dread,
Lest those who saw him kind should think him led;
If to his bosom fear a visit paid,
It was lest he should be supposed afraid:
Hence sprang his orders; not that he desired
The things when done, obedience he required;
And thus, to prove his absolute command
250 Ruled every heart, and moved each subject hand,
Assent he asked for every word and whim,
To prove that *he alone was king of him*.

The still *Rebecca*, who her station knew,
With ease resigned the honours not her due;
Well pleased, she saw that men her board would grace,
And wished not there to see a female face;
When by her lover she his spouse was styled,
Polite she thought it and demurely smiled!

But when he wanted wives and maidens round,
So to regard her, she grew grave and frowned;   260
And sometimes whispered – 'Why should you respect
These people's notions, yet their forms reject?'

    Gwyn, though from marriage bond and fetter free,
Still felt abridgment in his liberty;
Something of hesitation he betrayed,
And in her presence thought of what he said.
Thus fair *Rebecca*, though she walked astray,
His creed rejecting, judged it right to pray;
To be at church, to sit with serious looks,
To read her Bible and her Sunday-books: 270
She hated all those new and daring themes,
And called his free conjectures 'Devil's Dreams.'
She honoured still the Priesthood in her fall,
And claimed respect and reverence for them all;
Called them 'Of sin's destructive power the foes,
And not such blockheads as he might suppose.'
Gwyn to his friends would smile, and sometimes say,
' 'Tis a kind fool, why vex her in her way?'
Her way she took, and still had more in view,
For she contrived that he should take it too.   280
The daring freedom of his soul, 'twas plain,
In part was lost in a divided reign;
A king and queen, who yet in prudence swayed
Their peaceful state, and were in turn obeyed.

    Yet such our fate, that when we plan the best,
Something arises to disturb our rest:
For though in spirits high, in body strong,
Gwyn something felt – he knew not what – was wrong;
He wished to know, for he believed the thing,
If unremoved, would other evil bring: 290
'She must perceive, of late he could not eat,
And when he walked, he trembled on his feet;
He had forebodings, and he seemed as one
Stopped on the road, or threatened by a dun;

He could not live, and yet, should he apply
To those physicians – he must sooner die.'

    The mild *Rebecca* heard with some disdain,
And some distress, her friend and lord complain:
His death she feared not, but had painful doubt
What his distempered nerves might bring about;
With power like hers she dreaded an ally,
And yet there was a person in her eye; –
She thought, debated, fixed – 'Alas!' she said,
'A case like yours must be no more delayed:
You hate these doctors; well! but were a Friend
And Doctor one, your fears would have an end;
My cousin *Mollet* – Scotland holds him now –
Is above all men skilful, all allow;
Of late a Doctor, and within a while
He means to settle in this favoured isle;
Should he attend you, with his skill profound,
You must be safe, and shortly would be sound.'

    When men in health against Physicians rail,
They should consider that their nerves may fail;
Who calls a Lawyer rogue, may find, too late,
On one of these depends his whole estate;
Nay, when the world can nothing more produce,
The Priest, the insulted Priest, may have his use:
Ease, health, and comfort, lift a man so high,
These powers are dwarfs that he can scarcely spy:
Pain, sickness, languor, keep a man so low,
That these neglected dwarfs to giants grow.
Happy is he, who through the medium sees
Of clear good sense – but *Gwyn* was not of these.

    He heard and he rejoiced: 'Ah! let him come,
And till he fixes, make my house his home.'
Home came the Doctor – he was much admired;
He told the patient what his case required;
His hours for sleep, his time to eat and drink,

300

310

320

When he should ride, read, rest, compose, or think. 330
Thus joined peculiar skill and art profound,
To make the fancy-sick no more than fancy-sound.

   With such attention, who could long be ill?
Returning health proclaimed the Doctor's skill.
Presents and praises from a grateful heart,
Were freely offered on the patient's part;
In high repute the Doctor seemed to stand,
But still had got no footing on the land;
And as he saw the seat was rich and fair,
He felt disposed to fix his station there: 340
To gain his purpose, he performed the part
Of a good actor, and prepared to start;
Not like a traveller in a day serene,
When the sun shone and when the roads were clean;
Not like the pilgrim, whom the morning grey,
The ruddy eve succeeding, sends his way;
But in a season when the sharp East wind
Had all its influence on a nervous mind;
When past the parlour's front it fiercely blew,
And *Gwyn* sat pitying every bird that flew, 350
This strange Physician said – 'Adieu! adieu!
Farewell! – Heaven bless you! – if you should – but no,
You need not fear – farewell! 'tis time to go.'

   The Doctor spoke; and as the patient heard,
His old disorders (dreadful train!) appeared;
He felt the tingling tremor, and the stress
Upon his nerves, that he could not express.
'Should his good friend forsake him, he perhaps
Might meet his death, and surely a relapse.'
So as the Doctor seemed intent to part,
He cried in terror – 'Oh! be where thou art:
Come, thou art young and unengaged; oh! come,
Make me thy friend, give comfort to mine home.
I have now symptoms that require thine aid;
Do, Doctor, stay' – the obliging Doctor stayed.

Thus *Gwyn* was happy; he had now a friend,
And a meek spouse, on whom he could depend;
But now possessed of male and female guide,
Divided power he then must subdivide:
370   In earlier days he rode, or sat at ease
Reclined, and having but himself to please;
Now if he would a favourite nag bestride,
He sought permission – 'Doctor, may I ride?'
(*Rebecca*'s eye her sovereign pleasure told) –
'I think you may, but guarded from the cold,
Ride forty minutes.' – Free and happy soul!
He scorned submission, and a man's control;
But where such friends in every care unite,
All for his good, obedience is delight.

380   Now *Gwyn* a Sultan bade affairs adieu,
Led and assisted by the faithful two;
The favourite fair, *Rebecca*, near him sat,
And whispered whom to love, assist, or hate;
While the chief Vizier eased his lord of cares,
And bore himself the burden of affairs:
No dangers could from such alliance flow,
But from that law, that changes all below.

When wintry winds with leaves bestrewed the ground,
And men were coughing all the village round;
390   When public papers of invasion told,
Diseases, famines, perils new and old;
When philosophic writers failed to clear
The mind of gloom, and lighter works to cheer;
Then came fresh terrors on our hero's mind –
Fears unforeseen, and feelings undefined.

'In outward ills,' he cried, 'I'll rest assured
Of my friend's aid; they will in time be cured;
But can his art subdue, resist, control
These inward griefs and troubles of the soul?

Oh, my *Rebecca*! my disorderd mind,   400
No help in study, nor in thought can find:
What must I do, *Rebecca*?' She proposed
The Parish Guide; but what could be disclosed
To a proud Priest? – 'No! him I have defied,
Insulted, slighted – shall he be my guide?
But one there is, and if report be just,
A wise good man, whom I may safely trust;
Who goes from house to house, from ear to ear,
To make his truths, his Gospel-truths appear;
True if indeed they be, 'tis time that I should hear: 410
Send for that man; and if report be just,
I, like *Cornelius* will the teacher trust;
But if deceiver, I the vile deceit
Shall soon discover, and discharge the cheat.'

    To Doctor *Mollet* was the grief confessed,
While *Gwyn* the freedom of his mind expressed;
Yet owned it was to ills and errors prone,
And he for guilt and frailty must atone.
'My books, perhaps,' the wavering mortal cried,
'Like men, deceive – I would be satisfied;   420
And to my soul the pious man may bring
Comfort and light – do let me try the thing.'

    The cousins met, what passed with *Gwyn* was told:
'Alas!' the Doctor said, 'how hard to hold
These easy minds! where all impressions made
At first sink deeply, and then quickly fade;
For while so strong these new-born fancies reign,
We must divert them, to oppose is vain:
You see him valiant now, he scorns to heed
The bigot's threatenings, or the zealot's creed;   430
Shook by a dream, he next for truth receives
What frenzy teaches, and what fear believes;
And this will place him in the power of one
Whom we must seek, because we cannot shun.'

Wisp had been ostler at a busy inn,
Where he beheld and grew in dread of sin;
Then to a Baptists' Meeting found his way,
Became a convert, and was taught to pray;
Then preached; and being earnest and sincere,
Brought other sinners to religious fear:
Together grew his influence and his fame,
Till our dejected hero heard his name:
His little failings were a grain of pride,
Raised by the numbers he presumed to guide;
A love of presents, and of lofty praise
For his meek spirit and his humble ways;
But though this spirit would on flattery feed,
No praise could blind him, and no arts mislead: –
To him the Doctor made the wishes known
Of his good Patron, but concealed his own;
He of all teachers had distrust and doubt,
And was reserved in what he came about:
Though on a plain and simple message sent,
He had a secret and a bold intent:
Their minds at first were deeply veiled; disguise
Formed the slow speech, and oped the eager eyes;
Till by degrees sufficient light was thrown
On every view, and all the business shown.
Wisp, as a skilful guide who led the blind,
Had powers to rule and awe the vapourish mind;
But not the changeful will, the wavering fear to bind:
And should his conscience give him leave to dwell
With *Gwyn*, and every rival power expel,
(A dubious point,) yet he, with every care,
Might soon the lot of the rejected share,
And other *Wisps* be found like him to reign,
And then be thrown upon the world again:
He thought it prudent then, and felt it just,
The present guides of his new Friend to trust;
True he conceived, to touch the harder heart
Of the cool Doctor, was beyond his art;

440

450

460

470

But mild *Rebecca* he could surely sway,
While *Gwyn* would follow where she led the way:
So to do good, (and why a duty shun,
Because rewarded for the good when done?)
He with his Friends would join in all they planned,
Save when his faith or feelings should withstand;
There he must rest, sole judge of his affairs,
While they might rule exclusively in theirs.

When *Gwyn* his message to the Teacher sent, 480
He feared his Friends would show their discontent;
And prudent seemed it to the attendant pair,
Not all at once to show an aspect fair:
On *Wisp* they seemed to look with jealous eye,
And fair *Rebecca* was demure and shy;
But by degrees the Teacher's worth they knew,
And were so kind, they seemed converted too.

Wisp took occasion to the Nymph to say,
'You must be married; will you name the day?'
She smiled, – ''Tis well; but should he not comply, 490
Is it quite safe the experiment to try?' –
'My child,' the Teacher said, 'who feels remorse,
And feels not he? must wish relief of course;
And can he find it, while he fears the crime? –
You must be married; will you name the time?'

Glad was the Patron as a man could be,
Yet marvelled too, to find his guides agree:
'But what the cause?' he cried; ' 'tis genuine love for me.'

Each found his part, and let one act describe
The powers and honours of the accordant tribe: – 500
A man for favour to the mansion speeds,
And conns his threefold task as he proceeds;
To Teacher *Wisp* he bows with humble air,
And begs his interest for a barn's repair;
Then for the Doctor he inquires, who loves
To hear applause for what his skill improves,

And gives for praise, assent, – and to the Fair,
He brings of pullets a delicious pair;
Thus sees a peasant with discernment nice,
510   A love of power, conceit, and avarice.

Lo! now the change complete; the convert *Gwyn*
Has sold his books, and has renounced his sin;
Mollet his body orders, *Wisp* his soul;
And o'er his purse, the Lady takes control:
No friends beside he needs, and none attend –
Soul, Body, and Estate, has each a friend;
And fair *Rebecca* leads a virtuous life –
She rules a Mistress, and she reigns a Wife.

TALE IV

PROCRASTINATION

Heaven witness
I have been to you ever true and humble.
Henry VIII, Act II. Scene 4.

Gentle lady,
When first I did impart my love to you,
I freely told you all the wealth I had.
Merchant of Venice, Act III. Scene 2.

The fatal time
Cuts off all ceremonies and vows of love,
And ample interchange of sweet discourse,
Which so long sunder'd friends should dwell upon.
Richard III, Act V. Scene 3.

I know thee not, old Man, fall to thy prayers.
2 Henry IV, Act V. Scene 5.

Farewell,
Thou pure impiety, thou impious purity,
For thee I'll lock up all the gates of love.
Much Ado About Nothing, Act IV. Scene 2.

Love will expire; the gay, the happy dream
Will turn to scorn, indifference, or esteem:
Some favoured pairs, in this exchange, are blessed,
Nor sigh for raptures in a state of rest:
Others, ill matched, with minds unpaired, repent
At once the deed, and know no more content;
From joy to anguish they, in haste, decline,
And with their fondness, their esteem resign:

More luckless still their fate, who are the prey
Of long-protracted hope and dull delay;
'Mid plans of bliss, the heavy hours pass on,
Till love is withered, and till joy is gone.

This gentle flame two youthful hearts possessed,
The sweet disturber of unenvied rest:
The prudent *Dinah* was the maid beloved,
And the kind *Rupert* was the swain approved:
A wealthy Aunt her gentle Niece sustained,
He, with a father, at his desk remained;
The youthful couple, to their vows sincere,
Thus loved expectant! year succeeding year,
With pleasant views and hopes, but not a prospect near.
Rupert some comfort in his station saw,
But the poor Virgin lived in dread and awe;
Upon her anxious looks the Widow smiled,
And bade her wait, 'for she was yet a child.'
She for her neighbour had a due respect,
Nor would his son encourage or reject;
And thus the pair, with expectations vain,
Beheld the seasons change and change again:
Meantime the Nymph her tender tales perused,
Where cruel aunts impatient girls refused;
While hers, though teasing, boasted to be kind,
And she, resenting, to be all resigned.

The Dame was sick, and when the Youth applied
For her consent, she groaned, and coughed, and cried;
Talked of departing, and again her breath
Drew hard, and coughed, and talked again of death:
'Here you may live, my *Dinah!* here the boy
And you together my estate enjoy;'
Thus to the lovers was her mind expressed,
Till they forbore to urge the fond request.

Servant, and nurse, and comforter, and friend,
Dinah had still some duty to attend;
But yet their walk, when *Rupert*'s evening call

Obtained an hour, made sweet amends for all:
So long they now each other's thoughts had known,
That nothing seemed exclusively their own;
But with the common wish, the mutual fear,
They now had travelled to their thirtieth year.

At length a prospect opened, – but, alas!   50
Long time must yet, before the union, pass;
Rupert was called in other clime, to increase
Another's wealth and toil for future peace:
Loth were the Lovers; but the Aunt declared
'Twas fortune's call, and they must be prepared;
'You now are young, and for this brief delay,
And *Dinah*'s care, what I bequeath will pay;
All will be yours; nay, love, suppress that sigh,
The kind must suffer, and the best must die:'
Then came the cough, and strong the signs it gave   60
Of holding long contention with the grave.

The Lovers parted with a gloomy view,
And little comfort, but that both were true;
He for uncertain duties doomed to steer,
While hers remained too certain and severe.

Letters arrived, and *Rupert* fairly told
'His cares were many, and his hopes were cold;
The view more clouded, that was never fair,
And Love alone preserved him from despair:
In other letters brighter hopes he drew,   70
His friends were kind, and he believed them true.'

When the sage Widow *Dinah*'s grief descried,
She wondered much why one so happy sighed;
Then bade her see how her poor Aunt sustained
The ills of life, nor murmured nor complained.
To vary pleasures, from the Lady's chest
Were drawn the pearly string and tabby-vest;
Beads, jewels, laces, – all their value shown,
With the kind notice – 'They will be your own.'

80   This hope, these comforts cherished day by day,
         To *Dinah*'s bosom made a gradual way;
         Till love of treasure had as large a part,
         As love of *Rupert*, in the Virgin's heart.
         Whether it be that tender passions fail,
         From their own nature, while the strong prevail;
         Or whether Avarice, like the poison-tree,*
         Kills all beside it, and alone will be;
         Whatever cause prevailed, the pleasure grew
         In *Dinah*'s soul, – she loved the hoards to view;
90   With lively joy those comforts she surveyed,
         And love grew languid in the careful Maid.

         Now the grave Niece partook the Widow's cares,
         Looked to the great, and ruled the small affairs;
         Saw cleaned the plate, arranged the china-show,
         And felt her passion for a shilling grow:
         The indulgent Aunt increased the Maid's delight,
         By placing tokens of her wealth in sight;
         She loved the value of her bonds to tell,
         And spake of stocks, and how they rose and fell.

100   This passion grew, and gained at length such sway,
         That other passions shrank to make it way;
         Romantic notions now the heart forsook,
         She read but seldom, and she changed her book;
         And for the verses she was wont to send,
         Short was her prose, and 'she was *Rupert*'s Friend.'
         Seldom she wrote, and then the Widow's cough,
         And constant call, excused her breaking off;
         Who, now oppressed, no longer took the air,
         But sate and dozed upon an easy chair.
110   The cautious Doctor saw the case was clear,
         But judged it best to have companions near;
         They came, they reasoned, they prescribed – at last,

* Allusion is here made, not to the well-known species of *Sumach*, called the Poison
Oak, or *Toxicodendron*, but to the *Upas*, or Poison-tree of *Java*: whether it be real or
imaginary, this is no proper place for inquiry.

Like honest men, they said their hopes were past:
Then came a Priest – 'tis comfort to reflect,
When all is over, there was no neglect:
And all was over – by her Husband's bones,
The Widow rests beneath the sculptured stones;
That yet record their fondness and their fame,
While all they left, the Virgin's care became;
Stock, bonds, and buildings; – it disturbed her rest,   120
To think what load of troubles she possessed:
Yet, if a trouble, she resolved to take
The important duty, for the donor's sake;
She too was heiress to the Widow's taste,
Her love of hoarding, and her dread of waste.

Sometimes the past would on her mind intrude,
And then a conflict full of care ensued,
The thoughts of *Rupert* on her mind would press,
His worth she knew, but doubted his success:
Of old she saw him heedless; what the boy   130
Forbore to save, the man would not enjoy;
Oft had he lost the chance that care would seize,
Willing to live, but more to live at ease:
Yet could she not a broken vow defend,
And Heaven, perhaps, might yet enrich her friend.

Month after month was passed, and all were spent
In quiet comfort and in rich content:
Miseries there were, and woes, the world around,
But these had not her pleasant dwelling found;
She knew that mothers grieved, and widows wept,   140
And she was sorry, said her prayers, and slept:
Thus passed the seasons, and to *Dinah*'s board
Gave what the seasons to the rich afford;
For she indulged, nor was her heart so small,
That one strong passion should engross it all.

A love of splendour now with avarice strove,
And oft appeared to be the stronger love:

A secret pleasure filled the Widow's breast,
When she reflected on the hoards possessed;
150   But livelier joys inspired the ambitious Maid,
When she the purchase of those hoards displayed:
In small but splendid room she loved to see
That all was placed in view and harmony;
There as with eager glance she looked around,
She much delight in every object found;
While books devout were near her – to destroy,
Should it arise, an overflow of joy.

Within that fair apartment, guests might see
The comforts culled for wealth by vanity:
160   Around the room an Indian paper blazed,
With lively tint and figures boldly raised;
Silky and soft upon the floor below,
The elastic carpet rose with crimson glow;
All things around implied both cost and care,
What met the eye, was elegant or rare:
Some curious trifles round the room were laid,
By Hope presented to the wealthy Maid:
Within a costly case of varnished wood,
In level rows, her polished volumes stood;
170   Shown as a favour to a chosen few,
To prove what beauty for a book could do:
A silver urn with curious work was fraught;
A silver lamp from Grecian pattern wrought:
Above her head, all gorgeous to behold,
A time-piece stood on feet of burnished gold;
A stag's-head crest adorned the pictured case,
Through the pure crystal shone the enamelled face;
And, while on brilliants moved the hands of steel,
It clicked from prayer to prayer, from meal to meal.

180   Here as the Lady sate, a friendly pair
Stepped in to admire the view, and took their chair:
They then related how the young and gay
Were thoughtless wandering in the broad high-way;

How tender damsels sailed in tilted boats,
And laughed with wicked men in scarlet coats;
And how we live in such degenerate times,
That men conceal their wants, and show their crimes;
While vicious deeds are screened by fashion's name,
And what was once our pride is now our shame.

Dinah was musing, as her friends discoursed,   190
When these last words a sudden entrance forced
Upon her mind, and what was once her pride
And now her shame, some painful views supplied;
Thoughts of the past within her bosom pressed,
And there a change was felt, and was confessed:
While thus the Virgin strove with secret pain,
Her mind was wandering o'er the troubled main;
Still she was silent, nothing seemed to see,
But sate and sighed in pensive reverie.

The friends prepared new subjects to begin,   200
When tall *Susannah*, maiden starch, stalked in;
Not in her ancient mode, sedate and slow,
As when she came, the mind she knew, to know;
Nor as, when listening half an hour before,
She twice or thrice tapped gently at the door;
But, all decorum cast in wrath aside,
'I think the devil's in the man!' she cried;
'A huge tall Sailor, with his tawny cheek
And pitted face, will with my Lady speak;
He grinned an ugly smile, and said he knew,   210
Please you, my Lady, 'twould be joy to you;
What must I answer?' Trembling and distressed
Sank the pale *Dinah*, by her fears oppressed;
When thus alarmed, and brooking no delay,
Swift to her room the stranger made his way.

'Revive, my love,' said he, 'I've done thee harm,
Give me thy pardon,' and he looked alarm:
Meantime the prudent *Dinah* had contrived
Her soul to question, and she then revived.

220   'See! my good friend,' and then she raised her head,
'The bloom of life, the strength of youth is fled;
Living we die; to us the world is dead;
We parted blessed with health, and I am now
Age-struck and feeble, so I find art thou;
Thine eye is sunken, furrowed is thy face,
And downward look'st thou – so we run our race:
And happier they, whose race is nearly run,
Their troubles over, and their duties done.'

    'True, Lady, true, we are not girl and boy;
230   But time has left us something to enjoy.'

    'What! thou hast learned my fortune? – yes, I live
To feel how poor the comforts wealth can give.
Thou too perhaps art wealthy; but our fate
Still mocks our wishes, wealth is come too late.'

    'To me nor late nor early; I am come
Poor as I left thee to my native home:
Nor yet,' said *Rupert*, 'will I grieve; 'tis mine
To share thy comforts, and the glory thine;
For thou wilt gladly take that generous part
240   That both exalts and gratifies the heart;
While mine rejoices.' – 'Heavens!' returned the Maid,
'This talk to one so withered and decayed?
No! all my care is now to fit my mind
For other spousal, and to die resigned:
As friend and neighbour, I shall hope to see
These noble views, this pious love in thee;
That we together may the change await,
Guides and spectators in each other's fate;
When, fellow-pilgrims, we shall daily crave
250   The mutual prayer that arms us for the grave.'

    Half angry, half in doubt, the Lover gazed
On the meek Maiden, by her speech amazed:
'*Dinah*,' said he, 'dost thou respect thy vows?

What spousal mean'st thou? – thou art *Rupert*'s spouse;
The chance is mine to take, and thine to give;
But, trifling this, if we together live:
Can I believe, that, after all the past,
Our vows, our loves, thou wilt be false at last?
Something thou hast – I know not what – in view;
I find thee pious – let me find thee true.'   260

   'Ah! cruel this; but do, my friend, depart,
And to its feelings leave my wounded heart.'

   'Nay, speak at once; and *Dinah*, let me know,
Mean'st thou to take me, now I'm wrecked, in tow?
Be fair, nor longer keep me in the dark;
Am I forsaken for a trimmer spark?
Heaven's spouse thou art not; nor can I believe
That God accepts her, who will Man deceive:
True I am shattered, I have service seen,
And service done, and have in trouble been;   270
My cheek – it shames me not – has lost its red,
And the brown buff is o'er my features spread;
Perchance my speech is rude, for I among
The untamed have been, in temper and in tongue;
Have been trepanned, have lived in toil and care,
And wrought for wealth I was not doomed to share:
It touched me deeply, for I felt a pride
In gaining riches for my destined bride:
Speak then my fate; for these my sorrows past,
Time lost, youth fled, hope wearied, and at last   280
This doubt of thee – a childish thing to tell,
But certain truth – my very throat they swell;
They stop the breath, and but for shame could I
Give way to weakness, and with passion cry;
These are unmanly struggles, but I feel
This hour must end them, and perhaps will heal,' –

   Here *Dinah* sighed as if afraid to speak –
And then repeated, – 'They were frail and weak;

His soul she loved, and hoped he had the grace
290   To fix his thoughts upon a better place.'

She ceased; – with steady glance, as if to see
The very root of this hypocrisy, –
He her small fingers moulded in his hard
And bronzed broad hand; then told her his regard,
His best respect were gone, but Love had still
Hold in his heart, and governed yet the will –
Or he would curse her: – saying this, he threw
The hand in scorn away, and bade adieu
To every lingering hope, with every care in view.

300   Proud and indignant, suffering, sick, and poor,
He grieved unseen, and spoke of Love no more –
Till all he felt in Indignation died,
As hers had sunk in Avarice and Pride.

In health declining as in mind distressed,
To some in power his troubles he confessed,
And shares a parish-gift; – at prayers he sees
The pious *Dinah* dropped upon her knees;
Thence as she walks the street with stately air,
As chance directs, oft meet the parted pair:
310   When he, with thickset coat of Badge-man's blue,
Moves near her shaded silk of changeful hue;
When his thin locks of grey approach her braid,
A costly purchase, made in beauty's aid;
When his frank air, and his unstudied pace,
Are seen with her soft manner, air, and grace,
And his plain artless look with her sharp meaning face;
It might some wonder in a stranger move,
How these together could have talked of love.

Behold them now! see there a Tradesman stands,
320   And humbly hearkens to some fresh commands;
He moves to speak – she interrupts him – 'Stay!'
Her air expresses, – 'Hark! to what I say:' –

Ten paces off, poor *Rupert* on a seat
Has taken refuge from the noon-day heat,
His eyes on her intent, as if to find
What were the movements of that subtle mind:
How still! – how earnest is he! – it appears
His thoughts are wandering through his earlier years;
Through years of fruitless labour, to the day
When all his earthly prospects died away;   330
'Had I,' he thinks, 'been wealthier of the two,
Would she have found me so unkind, untrue?
Or knows not man when poor, what man when rich will do?
Yes, yes! I feel that I had faithful proved,
And should have soothed and raised her, blessed and loved.'

But *Dinah* moves – she had observed before,
The pensive *Rupert* at an humble door:
Some thoughts of pity raised by his distress,
Some feeling touch of ancient tenderness;
Religion, duty urged the Maid to speak   340
In terms of kindness to a man so weak:
But pride forbad, and to return would prove
She felt the shame of his neglected love;
Nor wrapped in silence could she pass, afraid
Each eye should see her, and each heart upbraid;
One way remained – the way the Levite took,
Who without mercy could on misery look;
(A way perceived by Craft, approved by Pride,)
She crossed and passed him on the other side.

THE PATRON

———————

It were all one,
That I should love a bright peculiar star,
And think to wed it; she is so much above me;
In her bright radiance and collateral heat.
Must I be comforted, not in her sphere.
All's Well that Ends Well, Act I. Scene 1.

Poor wretches, that depend
On greatness' favours, dream as I have done, –
Wake and find nothing.
Cymbeline, Act V. Scene 4.

And since ——
Th' affliction of my mind amends, with which
I fear a madness held me.
Tempest, Act V.

A Borough-Bailiff, who to law was trained,
A wife and sons in decent state maintained;
He had his way in life's rough ocean steered;
And many a rock and coast of danger cleared;
He saw where others failed, and care had he,
Others in him should not such failings see:
His sons in various busy states were placed,
And all began the sweets of gain to taste;
Save *John*, the younger; *who*, of sprightly parts,
Felt not a love for money-making arts:
In childhood feeble, he, for country air,
Had long resided with a rustic pair;
All round whose room were doleful ballads, songs,

10

Of lovers' sufferings, and of ladies' wrongs;
Of peevish ghosts, who came at dark midnight,
For breach of promise, guilty men to fright;
Love, marriage, murder, were the themes, with these,
All that on idle, ardent spirits seize;
Robbers at land and pirates on the main;
Enchanters foiled, spells broken, giants slain;   20
Legends of love, with tales of halls and bowers,
Choice of rare songs, and garlands of choice flowers,
And all the hungry mind without a choice devours.

From village-children kept apart by pride,
With such enjoyments, and without a guide;
Inspired by feelings all such works infused,
John snatched a pen, and wrote as he perused:
With the like fancy, he could make his knight
Slay half an host, and put the rest to flight;
With the like knowledge, he could make him ride   30
From isle to isle at *Parthenissa*'s side;
And with a heart yet free, no busy brain
Formed wilder notions of delight and pain,
The raptures smiles create, the anguish of disdain.

Such were the fruits of *John*'s poetic toil;
Weeds, but still proofs of vigour in the soil:
He nothing purposed but with vast delight,
Let Fancy loose, and wondered at her flight:
His notions of poetic worth were high,
And of his own still-hoarded poetry;   40
These to his father's house he bore with pride,
A miser's treasure, in his room to hide;
Till spurred by glory, to a reading friend
He kindly showed the Sonnets he had penned:
With erring judgement, though with heart sincere,
That friend exclaimed, 'These beauties must appear.'
In Magazines they claimed their share of fame,
Though undistinguished by their Author's name;
And with delight the young Enthusiast found
The muse of *Marcus* with applauses crowned.   50

This heard the Father, and with some alarm;
'The boy,' said he, 'will neither trade nor farm;
He for both Law and Physic is unfit;
Wit he may have, but cannot live on wit:
Let him his talents then to learning give,
Where verse is honoured, and where poets live.'

John kept his terms at College unreproved.
Took his degree, and left the life he loved:
Not yet ordained, his leisure he employed
In the light labours he so much enjoyed;
His favourite notions and his daring views
Were cherished still, and he adored the Muse.

'A little time, and he should burst to light,
And admiration of the world excite;
And every friend, now cool, and apt to blame
His fond pursuit, would wonder at his fame.'
When led by fancy, and from view retired,
He called before him all his heart desired;
'Fame shall be mine, then wealth shall I possess,
And beauty next an ardent lover bless;
For me the maid shall leave her nobler state,
Happy to raise and share her poet's fate.'
He saw each day his Father's frugal board,
With simple fare by cautious prudence stored;
Where each indulgence was foreweighed with care,
And the grand maxims were, to save and spare:
Yet in his walks, his closet, and his bed,
All frugal cares and prudent counsels fled;
And bounteous Fancy, for his glowing mind
Wrought various scenes, and all of glorious kind:
Slaves of the *ring* and *lamp*! what need of you,
When Fancy's self such magic deeds can do?

Though rapt in visions of no vulgar kind,
To common subjects stooped our Poet's mind;
And oft, when wearied with more ardent flight,
He felt a spur satiric song to write:

60

70

80

A rival burgess his bold Muse attacked,
And whipped severely for a well-known fact;
For while he seemed to all demure and shy,
Our Poet gazed at what was passing by;   90
And e'en his Father smiled when playful wit,
From his young Bard, some haughty object hit.

From ancient times, the Borough where they dwelt
Had mighty contest at elections felt:
Sir Godfrey Ball, 'tis true, had held in pay
Electors many for the trying day;
But in such golden chains to bind them all,
Required too much for e'en Sir Godfrey Ball.
A member died, and to supply his place,
Two heroes entered for the important race;   100
Sir Godfrey's friend and Earl Fitzdonnel's son,
Lord Frederick Damer, both prepared to run;
And partial numbers saw with vast delight
Their good young Lord oppose the proud old Knight.

Our poet's Father, at a first request,
Gave the young Lord his vote and interest;
And what he could our Poet, for he stung
The foe by verse satiric said and sung:
Lord Frederick heard of all this youthful zeal,
And felt as Lords upon a canvass feel;   110
He read the satire, and he saw the use
That such cool insult and such keen abuse
Might on the wavering minds of voting men produce:
Then too his praises were in contrast seen,
'A Lord as noble as the Knight was mean.'

'I much rejoice,' he said, 'such worth to find;
To this the world must be no longer blind;
His glory will descend from sire to son,
The Burns of English race, the happier Chatterton.' –
Our Poet's mind, now hurried and elate,   120
Alarmed the anxious Parent for his fate;

Who saw with sorrow, should their friend succeed,
That much discretion would the Poet need.

    Their Friend succeeded, and repaid the zeal
The Poet felt, and made opposers feel,
By praise, (from Lords how soothing and how sweet!)
And invitation to his noble seat.
The Father pondered, doubtful if the brain
Of his proud Boy such honour could sustain;
Pleased with the favours offered to a son,
But seeing dangers few so ardent shun.

    Thus, when they parted, to the youthful breast
The Father's fears were by his love impressed:
'There will you find, my Son, the courteous ease
That must subdue the soul it means to please;
That soft attention which e'en beauty pays
To wake our passions, or provoke our praise:
There all the eye beholds will give delight,
Where every sense is flattered like the sight:
This is your peril; can you from such scene
Of splendour part and feel your mind serene,
And in the father's humble state resume
The frugal diet, and the narrow room?'
To this the Youth with cheerful heart replied,
Pleased with the trial, but as yet untried;
And while professing patience, should he fail,
He suffered hope o'er reason to prevail.

    Impatient, by the morning mail conveyed,
The happy guest his promised visit paid;
And now arriving at the Hall, he tried
For air composed, serene, and satisfied;
As he had practised in his room alone,
And there acquired a free and easy tone:
There he had said, 'Whatever the degree
A man obtains, what more than man is he?'
And when arrived, – 'This room is but a room;

130

140

150

Can aught we see the steady soul o'ercome?
Let me in all a manly firmness show,
Upheld by talents, and their value know.'

This Reason urged; but it surpassed his skill   160
To be in act as manly as in will:
When he his Lordship and the Lady saw,
Brave as he was, he felt oppressed with awe;
And spite of verse, that so much praise had won,
The Poet found he was the Bailiff's son.

But dinner came, and the succeeding hours
Fixed his weak nerves, and raised his failing powers;
Praised and assured, he ventured once or twice
On some remark, and bravely broke the ice;
So that at night, reflecting on his words,   170
He found, in time, he might converse with Lords.

Now was the Sister of his Patron seen, –
A lovely creature, with majestic mien;
Who, softly smiling while she looked so fair,
Praised the young Poet with such friendly air;
Such winning frankness in her looks expressed,
And such attention to her Brother's guest;
That so much beauty, joined with speech so kind,
Raised strong emotions in the Poet's mind;
Till reason failed his bosom to defend,   180
From the sweet power of this enchanting Friend. –
Rash boy! what hope thy frantic mind invades?
What love confuses, and what pride persuades?
Awake to Truth! should'st thou deluded feed
On hopes so groundless – thou art mad indeed.

What say'st thou, wise-one? 'that all-powerful love
Can fortune's strong impediments remove;
Nor is it strange that worth should wed to worth,
The pride of Genius with the pride of Birth.'
While thou art dreaming thus, the Beauty spies   190
Love in thy tremor, passion in thine eyes;

And with the amusement pleased, of conquest vain,
She seeks her pleasure, careless of thy pain;
She gives thee praise to humble and confound,
Smiles to ensnare, and flatters thee to wound.

Why has she said, that in the lowest state,
The noble mind insures a noble fate?
And why thy daring mind to glory call?
That thou may'st dare and suffer, soar and fall.
Beauties are tyrants, and if they can reign,
They have no feeling for their subject's pain;
Their victim's anguish gives their charms applause,
And their chief glory is the woe they cause:
Something of this was felt, in spite of love,
Which hope, in spite of reason, would remove.

Thus lived our Youth, with conversation, books,
And *Lady Emma*'s soul-subduing looks;
Lost in delight, astonished at his lot,
All prudence banished, all advice forgot, –
Hopes, fears, and every thought, were fixed upon the spot.

'Twas autumn yet, and many a day must frown
On *Brandon-Hall*, ere went my Lord to town;
Meantime the Father, who had heard his boy
Lived in a round of luxury and joy;
And justly thinking that the youth was one
Who, meeting danger, was unskilled to shun;
Knowing his temper, virtue, spirit, zeal,
How prone to hope and trust, believe and feel;
These on the Parent's soul their weight impressed,
And thus he wrote the counsels of his breast.

'*John*, thou'rt a genius, thou hast some pretence,
I think, to wit, but hast thou sterling sense?
That which, like gold, may through the world go forth,
And always pass for what 'tis truly worth;
Whereas this genius, like a bill, must take
Only the value our opinions make.

'Men famed for wit, of dangerous talents vain,
Treat those of common parts with proud disdain;
The powers that wisdom would, improving, hide,
They blaze abroad with inconsiderate pride;　　　　　230
While yet but mere probationers for fame,
They seize the honour they should then disclaim:
Honour so hurried to the light must fade,
The lasting laurels flourish in the shade.

'Genius is jealous; I have heard of some
Who, if unnoticed, grew perversely dumb;
Nay, different talents would their envy raise,
Poets have sickened at a dancer's praise;
And one, the happiest writer of his time,
Grew pale at hearing *Reynolds* was sublime;　　　　　240
That *Rutland's Duchess* wore a heavenly smile –
And I, said he, neglected all the while!

'A waspish tribe are these, on gilded wings,
Humming their lays, and brandishing their stings;
And thus they move their friends and foes among,
Prepared for soothing or satiric song.

'Hear me, my Boy, thou hast a virtuous mind –
But be thy virtues of the sober kind;
Be not a *Quixote*, ever up in arms
To give the guilty and the great alarms:　　　　　250
If never heeded, thy attack is vain;
And if they heed thee, they'll attack again;
Then too in striking at that heedless rate,
Thou in an instant may'st decide thy fate.

'Leave admonition – let the Vicar give
Rules how the Nobles of his flock should live;
Nor take that simple fancy to thy brain,
That thou canst cure the wicked and the vain.

'Our *Pope*, they say, once entertained the whim,
Who feared not God should be afraid of him;　　　　　260
But grant they feared him, was it further said,

That he reformed the hearts he made afraid?
Did *Chartres* mend? *Ward*, *Waters*, and a score
Of flagrant felons, with his floggings sore?
Was *Cibber* silenced? No, with vigour blessed,
And brazen front, half earnest, half in jest,
He dared the Bard to battle, and was seen
In all his glory matched with *Pope* and spleen;
Himself he stripped, the harder blow to hit,
270   Then boldly matched his ribaldry with wit;
The Poet's conquest Truth and Time proclaim,
But yet the battle hurt his peace and fame.

'Strive not too much for favour, seem at ease,
And rather pleased thyself, than bent to please:
Upon thy Lord with decent care attend,
But not too near; thou canst not be a friend;
And favourite be not, 'tis a dangerous post, —
Is gained by labour, and by fortune lost:
Talents like thine may make a man approved,
280   But other talents trusted and beloved.
Look round, my Son, and thou wilt early see
The kind of man thou art not formed to be.

'The real favourites of the Great are they,
Who to their views and wants attention pay,
And pay it ever; who, with all their skill,
Dive to the heart, and learn the secret Will;
If that be vicious, soon can they provide
The favourite ill, and o'er the soul preside;
For vice is weakness, and the artful know
290   Their power increases as the passions grow:
If indolent the pupil, hard their task;
Such minds will ever for amusement ask;
And great the labour! for a man to choose,
Objects for one whom nothing can amuse;
For ere those objects can the soul delight,
They must to joy the soul herself excite;
Therefore it is, this patient, watchful kind

With gentle friction stir the drowsy mind:
Fixed on their end, with caution they proceed,
And sometimes give, and sometimes take the lead;   300
Will now a hint convey, and then retire,
And let the spark awake the lingering fire;
Or seek new joys, and livelier pleasures bring,
To give the jaded sense a quickening spring.

'These arts, indeed, my Son must not pursue;
Nor must he quarrel with the tribe that do:
It is not safe another's crimes to know,
Nor is it wise our proper worth to show: –
"My Lord," you say, "engaged me for that worth;" –
True, and preserve it ready to come forth;   310
If questioned, fairly answer, – and that done,
Shrink back, be silent, and thy Father's son;
For they who doubt thy talents scorn thy boast,
But they who grant them will dislike thee most:
Observe the Prudent; they in silence sit,
Display no learning and affect no wit;
They hazard nothing, nothing they assume,
But know the useful art of *acting dumb*.
Yet to their eyes each varying look appears,
And every word finds entrance at their ears.   320

'Thou art Religion's advocate – take heed,
Hurt not the cause, thy pleasure 'tis to plead;
With wine before thee, and with wits beside,
Do not in strength of reasoning powers confide;
What seems to thee convincing, certain, plain,
They will deny, and dare thee to maintain;
And thus will triumph o'er thy eager youth,
While thou wilt grieve for so disgracing Truth.

'With pain I've seen, these wrangling wits among,
Faith's weak defenders, passionate and young;
Weak thou art not, yet not enough on guard,
Where Wit and Humour keep their watch and ward: 330

Men gay and noisy will o'erwhelm thy sense,
Then loudly laugh at Truth's and thy expense;
While the kind Ladies will do all they can
To check their mirth, and cry, "*The good young man!*"

'Prudence, my Boy, forbids thee to commend
The cause or party of thy Noble Friend;
What are his praises worth, who must be known
To take a Patron's maxims for his own?
When ladies sing, or in thy presence play,
Do not, dear *John*, in rapture melt away;
'Tis not thy part, there will be listeners round,
To cry *Divine!* and dote upon the sound;
Remember too, that though the poor have ears,
They take not in the music of the spheres;
They must not feel the warble and the thrill,
Or be dissolved in ecstasy at will;
Beside, 'tis freedom in a youth like thee,
To drop his awe, and deal in ecstasy!

'In silent ease, at least in silence, dine,
Nor one opinion start of food or wine:
Thou know'st that all the science thou canst boast,
Is of thy father's simple boiled and roast;
Nor always these; he sometimes saved his cash,
By interlinear days of frugal hash:
Wine hadst thou seldom; wilt thou be so vain
As to decide on claret or champagne?
Dost thou from me derive this taste sublime,
Who order port the dozen at a time?
When (every glass held precious in our eyes)
We judged the value by the bottle's size:
Then never merit for thy praise assume,
Its worth well knows each servant in the room.

'Hard, Boy, thy task, to steer thy way among
That servile, supple, shrewd, insidious throng;
Who look upon thee as of doubtful race,
An interloper, one who wants a place:

Freedom with these let thy free soul condemn,
Nor with thy heart's concerns associate them.   370

   'Of all be cautious – but be most afraid
Of the pale charms that grace My Lady's Maid;
Of those sweet dimples, of that fraudful eye,
The frequent glance designed for thee to spy;
The soft bewitching look, the fond bewailing sigh:
Let others frown and envy; she the while
(Insidious siren!) will demurely smile;
And for her gentle purpose, every day
Inquire thy wants, and meet thee in thy way;
She has her blandishments, and, though so weak,   380
Her person pleases, and her actions speak:
At first her folly may her aim defeat;
But kindness shown, at length will kindness meet:
Have some offended? them will she disdain,
And, for thy sake, contempt and pity feign;
She hates the vulgar, she admires to look
On woods and groves, and dotes upon a book:
Let her once see thee on her features dwell,
And hear one sigh, then liberty farewell.

   'But *John!* remember we cannot maintain   390
A poor, proud girl, extravagant and vain.

   'Doubt much of friendship: shouldst thou find a friend
Pleased to advise thee, anxious to commend;
Should he, the praises he has heard, report,
And confidence (in thee confiding) court;
Much of neglectful Patrons should he say,
And then exclaim – "How long must merit stay!"
Then show how high thy modest hopes may stretch,
And point to stations far beyond thy reach; –
Let such designer, by thy conduct, see   400
(Civil and cool) he makes no dupe of thee;
And he will quit thee, as a man too wise
For him to ruin first, and then despise.

'Such are thy dangers: – yet, if thou canst steer
Past all the perils, all the quicksands clear,
Then may'st thou profit; but if storms prevail,
If foes beset thee, if thy spirits fail, –
No more of winds or waters be the sport,
But in thy Father's mansion find a port.'

410   Our Poet read. – 'It is in truth,' said he,
'Correct in part, but what is *this* to me?
I love a foolish *Abigail!* in base
And sordid office! fear not such disgrace;
Am I so blind?' 'Or thou wouldst surely see
That Lady's fall, if she should stoop to thee!'
'The cases differ,' 'True! for what surprise
Could from thy marriage with the Maid arise?
But through the island would the shame be spread,
Should the fair Mistress deign with thee to wed.'

420   *John* saw not this; and many a week had passed,
While the vain Beauty held her victim fast;
The Noble Friend still condescension showed,
And, as before, with praises overflowed;
But his grave Lady took a silent view
Of all that passed, and smiling, pitied too.

Cold grew the foggy morn, the day was brief,
Loose on the cherry hung the crimson leaf;
The dew dwelt ever on the herb; the woods
Roared with strong blasts, with mighty showers the floods;
430   All green was vanished, save of pine and yew,
That still displayed their melancholy hue;
Save the green holly with its berries red,
And the green moss that o'er the gravel spread.

To public views my Lord must soon attend;
And soon the Ladies – would they leave their friend?
The time was fixed – approached – was near – was come;
The trying time that filled his soul with gloom;

Thoughtful our Poet in the morning rose,
And cried, 'One hour my fortune will disclose;
Terrific hour! from thee have I to date 440
Life's loftier views, or my degraded state;
For now to be what I have been before,
Is so to fall, that I can rise no more.'

   The morning meal was past; and all around
The mansion rang with each discordant sound;
Haste was in every foot, and every look
The traveller's joy for London-journey spoke:
Not so our Youth; whose feelings, at the noise
Of preparation, had no touch of joys;
He pensive stood, and saw each carriage drawn, 450
With lackies mounted, ready on the lawn:
The Ladies came; and *John* in terror threw
One painful glance, and then his eyes withdrew;
Not with such speed, but he in other eyes
With anguish read, – 'I pity but despise –
Unhappy boy! presumptuous scribbler! – you
To dream such dreams – be sober, and adieu!'

   Then came the Noble Friend – 'And will my Lord
Vouchsafe no comfort? drop no soothing word?
Yes, he must speak:' he speaks, 'My good young friend, 460
You know my views; upon my care depend;
My hearty thanks to your good Father pay,
And be a student. – *Harry*, drive away.'

   Stillness reigned all around; of late so full
The busy scene, deserted now and full:
Stern is his nature who forbears to feel
Gloom o'er his spirits on such trials steal;
Most keenly felt our Poet as he went
From room to room without a fixed intent;
'And here,' he thought, 'I was caressed, admired 470
Were here my songs; she smiled, and I aspired:

The change how grievous!' As he mused, a dame
Busy and peevish to her duties came;
Aside the tables and the chairs she drew,
And sang and muttered in the Poet's view:
'This was her fortune; here they leave the poor;
Enjoy themselves, and think of us no more;
I had a promise –' here his pride and shame
Urged him to fly from this familiar dame;
480 He gave one farewell look, and by a coach
Reached his own mansion at the night's approach.

His Father met him with an anxious air,
Heard his sad tale, and checked what seemed despair:
Hope was in him corrected, but alive;
My Lord would something for a friend contrive;
His word was pledged: our Hero's feverish mind
Admitted this, and half his grief resigned:
But, when three months had fled, and every day
Drew from the sickening hopes their strength away,
490 The Youth became abstracted, pensive, dull;
He uttered nothing, though his heart was full;
Teased by inquiring words, and anxious looks,
And all forgetful of his Muse and books;
Awake he mourned, but in his sleep perceived
A lovely vision that his pain relieved: –
His soul transported, hailed the happy seat,
Where once his pleasure was so pure and sweet;
Where joys departed came in blissful view,
Till reason waked, and not a joy he knew.

500 Questions now vexed his spirit, most from those
Who are called friends because they are not foes;
'John!' they would say; he starting turned around;
'John!' there was something shocking in the sound;
Ill brooked he then the pert familiar phrase,
The untaught freedom, and the inquiring gaze;
Much was his temper touched, his spleen provoked,
When asked how Ladies talked, or walked, or looked?

'What said my Lord of politics? how spent
He there his time? and was he glad he went?'

At length a letter came both cool and brief,   510
But still it gave the burdened heart relief;
Though not inspired by lofty hopes, the Youth
Placed much reliance on *Lord Frederick*'s truth;
Summoned to town, he thought the visit one
Where something fair and friendly would be done;
Although he judged not as before his fall,
When all was love and promise at the Hall.

Arrived in town, he early sought to know
The fate such dubious friendship would bestow;
At a tall building trembling he appeared,   520
And his low rap was indistinctly heard;
A well-known servant came – 'A while,' said he,
'Be pleased to wait; my Lord has company.'

Alone our Hero sate, the news in hand,
Which though he read, he could not understand:
Cold was the day; in days so cold as these
There needs a fire, where minds and bodies freeze;
The vast and echoing room, the polished grate,
The crimson chairs, the sideboard with its plate;
The splendid sofa, which, though made for rest,   530
He then had thought it freedom to have pressed;
The shining tables, curiously inlaid,
Were all in comfortless proud style displayed;
And to the troubled feelings terror gave,
That made the once-dear friend, the sickening slave.

'Was he forgotten?' Thrice upon his ear
Struck the loud clock, yet no relief was near:
Each rattling carriage and each thundering stroke
On the loud door, the dream of Fancy broke;
Oft as a servant chanced the way to come,   540
'Brings he a message?' no! he passed the room:

At length 'tis certain; 'Sir, you will attend
At twelve on Thursday.' Thus the day had end.

Vexed by these tedious hours of needless pain,
John left the noble mansion with disdain;
For there was something in that still, cold place,
That seemed to threaten and portend disgrace.

Punctual again the modest rap declared
The Youth attended; then was all prepared;
For the same servant, by his Lord's command,
A paper offered to his trembling hand:
'No more!' he cried, 'disdains he to afford
One kind expression, one consoling word?'

With troubled spirit he began to read
That 'In the Church my Lord could not succeed;'
Who had 'to Peers of either kind applied,
And was with dignity and grace denied;
While his own livings were by men possessed,
Not likely in their chancels yet to rest;
And therefore, all things weighed, (as he, my Lord,
Had done maturely, and he pledged his word),
Wisdom it seemed for *John* to turn his view
To busier scenes, and bid the Church adieu.'

Here grieved the Youth; he felt his father's pride
Must with his own be shocked and mortified;
But, when he found his future comforts placed,
Where he, alas! conceived himself disgraced –
In some appointment on the London Quays,
He bade farewell to honour and to ease;
His spirit fell, and, from that hour assured
How vain his dreams, he suffered and was cured.

Our Poet hurried on, with wish to fly
From all mankind, to be concealed, and die.
Alas! what hopes, what high romantic views
Did that one visit to the soul infuse,
Which cherished with such love, 'twas worse than death to lose!

550

560

570

Still he would strive, though painful was the strife,
To walk in this appointed road of life;
On these low duties, duteous he would wait,
And patient bear the anguish of his fate. 580
Thanks to the Patron, but of coldest kind,
Expressed the sadness of the Poet's mind;
Whose heavy hours were passed with busy men,
In the dull practice of the official pen;
Who to Superiors must in time impart
(The custom this) his progress in their art:
But, so had grief on his perception wrought,
That all unheeded were the duties taught;
No answers gave he when his trial came,
Silent he stood, but suffering without shame; 590
And they observed that words severe or kind
Made no impression on his wounded mind;
For all perceived from whence his failure rose,
Some grief whose cause he deigned not to disclose.
A soul averse from scenes and works so new,
Fear ever shrinking from the vulgar crew;
Distaste for each mechanic law and rule,
Thoughts of past honour, and a patron cool;
A grieving parent, and a feeling mind,
Timid and ardent, tender and refined; 600
These all with mighty force the Youth assailed,
Till his soul fainted, and his reason failed:
When this was known, and some debate arose,
How they who saw it should the fact disclose;
He found their purpose, and in terror fled,
From unseen kindness, with mistaken dread.

Meantime the Parent was distressed to find
His Son no longer for a Priest designed:
But still he gained some comfort by the news
Of *John*'s promotion, though with humbler views; 610
For he conceived that in no distant time
The Boy would learn to scramble and to climb:

He little thought a Son, his hope and pride,
His favoured Boy, was now a home denied;
Yes! while the Parent was intent to trace
How men in office climb from place to place;
From place to place, o'er moor, and heath, and hill
Roved the sad Youth, with ever-changing will,
Of every aid bereft, exposed to every ill.

Thus as he sate, absorbed in all the care
And all the hope that anxious fathers share,
A Friend abruptly to his presence brought,
With trembling hand, the subject of his thought;
Whom he had found afflicted and subdued
By hunger, sorrow, cold, and solitude.

Silent he entered the forgotten room,
As ghostly forms may be conceived to come;
With sorrow-shrunken face and hair upright,
He looked dismay, neglect, despair, affright;
But, dead to comfort, and on misery thrown,
His Parent's loss he felt not, nor his own.

The good Man, struck with horror, cried aloud,
And drew around him an astonished crowd;
The sons and servants to the Father ran,
To share the feelings of the grieved old man:

'Our Brother, speak!' they all exclaimed; 'explain
Thy grief, thy suffering:' but they asked in vain:
The Friend told all he knew; and all was known,
Save the sad causes whence the ills had grown;
But, if obscure the cause, they all agreed
From rest and kindness must the cure proceed:
And he was cured; for quiet, love, and care,
Strove with the gloom, and broke on the despair;
Yet slow their progress, and as vapours move
Dense and reluctant from the wintry grove
All is confusion till the morning light

Gives the dim scene obscurely to the sight;
More and yet more defined the trunks appear,
Till the wild prospect stands distinct and clear; –
So the dark mind of our young Poet grew   650
Clear and sedate, the dreadful mist withdrew;
And he resembled that bleak wintry scene –
Sad, though unclouded, dismal, though serene.

At times he uttered, 'What a dream was mine!
And what a prospect! glorious and divine!
Oh! in that room, and on that night to see
These looks, that sweetness beaming all on me;
That siren-flattery – and to send me then
Hope-raised and softened to those heartless men;
That dark-browed stern Director, pleased to show   660
Knowledge of subjects, I disdained to know;
Cold and controlling – but 'tis gone, 'tis past,
I had my trial, and have peace at last.'

Now grew the Youth resigned; he bade adieu
To all that Hope, to all that Fancy drew;
His frame was languid, and the hectic heat
Flushed on his pallid face, and countless beat
The quickening pulse, and faint the limbs that bore
The slender form that soon would breathe no more.

Then hope of holy kind the soul sustained,   670
And not a lingering thought of earth remained;
Now Heaven had all, and he could smile at love,
And the wild sallies of his youth reprove;
Then could he dwell upon the tempting days,
The proud aspiring thought, the partial praise;
Victorious now, his worldly views were closed,
And on the bed of death the Youth reposed.

The Father grieved – but as the Poet's heart
Was all unfitted for his earthly part;
As, he conceived, some other haughty Fair   680
Would, had he lived, have led him to despair;

As, with this fear, the silent grave shut out
All feverish hope and all tormenting doubt;
While the strong faith the pious Youth possessed,
His hope enlivening, gave his sorrows rest;
Soothed by these thoughts, he felt a mournful joy
For his aspiring and devoted Boy.

Meantime the news through various channels spread,
The Youth, once favoured with such praise, was dead;
690   '*Emma*,' the Lady cried, 'my words attend,
Your siren-smiles have killed your humble friend;
The hope you raised can now delude no more,
Nor charms, that once inspired, can now restore.'

   Faint was the flush of anger and of shame,
That o'er the cheek of conscious beauty came;
'You censure not,' said she, 'the Sun's bright rays,
When fools imprudent dare the dangerous gaze;
And should a stripling look till he were blind,
You would not justly call the light unkind;
700   But is he dead? and am I to suppose
The power of poison in such looks as those;' –
She spoke, and, pointing to the mirror, cast
A pleased gay glance, and curtsied as she passed.

   My Lord, to whom the Poet's fate was told,
Was much affected, for a man so cold;
'Dead!' said his Lordship, 'run distracted, mad!
Upon my soul I'm sorry for the lad;
And now, no doubt, the obliging world will say,
That my harsh usage helped him on his way;
What! I suppose I should have nursed his muse,
And with champagne have brightened up his views;
Then had he made me famed my whole life long,
And stunned my ears with gratitude and song.
Still should the Father hear that I regret
Our joint misfortune – Yes! I'll not forget. –'

   Thus they: – The Father to his grave conveyed
The Son he loved, and his last duties paid.

'There lies my Boy,' he cried, 'of care bereft,
And, Heaven be praised, I've not a genius left:
No one among ye, Sons! is doomed to live   720
On high-raised hopes of what the Great may give;
None, with exalted views and fortunes mean,
To die in anguish, or to live in spleen:
Your pious Brother soon escaped the strife
Of such contention, but it cost his life;
You then, my Sons, upon yourselves depend,
And in your own exertions find the friend.'

TALE VI
THE FRANK COURTSHIP

Yes, faith, it is my Cousin's duty to make a curtsy, and say, 'Father, as it please you;' but for all that, Cousin, let him be a handsome fellow, or else make another curtsy and say, 'Father, as it pleases me.'

Much Ado About Nothing, Act II. Scene 1.

He cannot flatter, he!
As honest mind and plain – he must speak truth,
King Lear, Act II. Scene 2.

God hath given you one face, and you make yourselves another; you jig, you amble, you nick-name God's creatures, and make your wantonness your ignorance.

Hamlet, Act III. Scene 1.

What fire is in mine ears? Can this be true?
Am I contemn'd for pride and scorn so much?
Much Ado About Nothing, Act II. Scene 1.

Grave *Jonas Kindred*, *Sybil Kindred*'s sire,
Was six feet high, and looked six inches higher;
Erect, morose, determined, solemn, slow,
Who knew the man, could never cease to know;
His faithful Spouse, when *Jonas* was not by,
Had a firm presence and a steady eye;
But with her husband dropped her look and tone,
And *Jonas* ruled unquestioned and alone.

He read, and oft would quote the sacred words,
How pious husbands of their wives were lords;
Sarah called *Abraham* Lord! and who could be,

So *Jonas* thought, a greater man than he?
Himself he viewed with undisguised respect,
And never pardoned freedom or neglect.

They had one daughter, and this favourite child
Had oft the father of his spleen beguiled;
Soothed by attention from her early years,
She gained all wishes by her smiles or tears:
But *Sybil* then was in that playful time,
When contradiction is not held a crime;   20
When parents yield their children idle praise,
For faults corrected in their after days.

Peace in the sober house of *Jonas* dwelt,
Where each his duty and his station felt:
Yet not that peace some favoured mortals find,
In equal views and harmony of mind;
Not the soft peace that blesses those who love,
Where all with one consent in union move;
But it was that which one superior will
Commands, by making all inferiors still;   30
Who bids all murmurs, all objections cease,
And with imperious voice, announces – Peace!

They were, to wit, a remnant of that crew,
Who, as their foes maintain, their Sovereign slew;
An independent race, precise, correct,
Who ever married in the kindred sect;
No son or daughter of their order wed,
A friend to *England*'s King who lost his head;
Cromwell was still their Saint, and when they met,
They mourned that Saints* were not our Rulers yet.   40

Fixed were their habits; they arose betimes,
Then prayed their hour, and sang their party-rhymes;
Their meals were plenteous, regular, and plain,
The trade of *Jonas* brought him constant gain;

* This appellation is here used not ironically nor with malignity; but it is taken
merely to designate a morosely devout people, with peculiar austerity of manners.

Vender of Hops and Malt, of Coals and Corn –
And, like his father, he was Merchant born:
Neat was their house; each table, chair, and stool,
Stood in its place, or moving moved by rule;
No lively print or picture graced the room;
50   A plain brown paper lent its decent gloom;
But here the eye, in glancing round, surveyed,
A small Recess that seemed for china made;
Such pleasing pictures seemed this pencilled ware,
That few would search for nobler objects there –
Yet, turned by chosen friends, and there appeared
His stern, strong features, whom they all revered;
For there in lofty air was seen to stand,
The bold Protector of the conquered land;
Drawn in that look with which he wept and swore,
60   Turned out the Members and made fast the door,
Ridding the House of every knave and drone,
Forced, though it grieved his soul, to rule alone.
The stern still smile each Friend approving gave,
Then turned the view, and all again were grave.

There stood a clock, though small the owner's need,
For habit told when all things should proceed;
Few their amusements, but when Friends appeared,
They with the world's distress their spirits cheered;
The nation's guilt, that would not long endure
70   The reign of men so modest and so pure:
Their town was large, and seldom passed a day
But some had failed, and others gone astray;
Clerks had absconded, wives eloped, girls flown
To Gretna-Green, or sons rebellious grown;
Quarrels and fires arose! – and it was plain
The times were bad; the Saints had ceased to reign!
A few yet lived to languish and to mourn
For good old manners never to return.

Jonas had Sisters, and of these was one
80   Who lost a husband and an only son:

Twelve months her sables she in sorrow wore,
And mourned so long that she could mourn no more.
Distant from *Jonas*, and from all her race,
She now resided in a lively place;
There, by the sect unseen, at whist she played,
Nor was of Churchmen, or their Church afraid:
If much of this the graver Brother heard,
He something censured, but he little feared;
He knew her rich and frugal; for the rest
He felt no care, or if he felt, suppressed: 90
Nor for companion when she asked her Niece,
Had he suspicions that disturbed his peace;
Frugal and rich, these virtues as a charm
Preserved the thoughtful man from all alarm;
An infant yet, she soon would home return,
Nor stay the manners of the world to learn;
Meantime his Boys would all his care engross,
And be his comforts if he felt the loss.

  The sprightly *Sybil*, pleased and unconfined,
Felt the pure pleasure of the opening mind: 100
All here was gay and cheerful – all at home
Unvaried quiet and unruffled gloom;
There were no changes, and amusements few –
Here, all was varied, wonderful, and new;
There were plain meals, plain dresses, and grave looks –
Here, gay companions and amusing books;
And the young Beauty soon began to taste
The light vocations of the scene she graced.

  A man of business feels it as a crime,
On calls domestic to consume his time;   100
Yet this grave Man had not so cold a heart,
But with his Daughter he was grieved to part;
And he demanded that in every year
The Aunt and Niece should at his house appear.
'Yes! we must go, my Child, and by our dress
A grave conformity of mind express;

Must sing at Meeting, and from cards refrain,
The more to enjoy when we return again.'

Thus spake the Aunt, and the discerning Child
Was pleased to learn how fathers are beguiled.
Her artful part the young dissembler took,
And from the Matron caught the approving look:
When thrice the Friends had met, excuse was sent
For more delay, and *Jonas* was content;
Till a tall maiden by her Sire was seen
In all the bloom and beauty of sixteen:
He gazed admiring; – she, with visage prim,
Glanced an arch look of gravity on him;
For she was gay at heart, and wore disguise,
And stood a Vestal in her Father's eyes;
Pure, pensive, simple, sad: the Damsel's heart,
When *Jonas* praised, reproved her for the part;
For *Sybil*, fond of pleasure, gay and light,
Had still a secret bias to the right,
Vain as she was – and flattery made her vain –
Her simulation gave her bosom pain.

Again returned, the Matron and the Niece
Found the late quiet gave their joy increase;
The Aunt infirm, no more her visits paid,
But still with her sojourned the favourite Maid.
Letters were sent when franks could be procured,
And, when they could not, silence was endured;
All were in health, and if they older grew,
It seemed a fact that none among them knew;
The Aunt and Niece still led a pleasant life,
And quiet days had *Jonas* and his Wife.

Near him a Widow dwelt of worthy fame,
Like his her manners, and her creed the same;
The wealth her husband left, her care retained
For one tall Youth, and widow she remained;
His love respectful all her care repaid,
Her wishes watched, and her commands obeyed.

120

130

140

150

Sober he was and grave from early youth,
Mindful of forms, but more intent on truth;
In a light drab he uniformly dressed,
And looks serene the unruffled mind expressed;
A hat with ample verge his brows o'erspread,
And his brown locks curled graceful on his head:
Yet might observers in his speaking eye   160
Some observation, some acuteness spy;
The friendly thought it keen, the treacherous deemed it sly;
Yet not a crime could foe or friend detect, –
His actions all were, like his speech, correct;
And they who jested on a mind so sound,
Upon his virtues must their laughter found;
Chaste, sober, solemn, and devout they named
Him who was thus, and not of *this* ashamed.

Such were the virtues *Jonas* found in one
In whom he warmly wished to find a Son: 170
Three years had passed since he had *Sybil* seen;
But she was doubtless what she once had been,
Lovely and mild, obedient and discreet;
The pair must love whenever they should meet;
Then ere the Widow or her Son should choose
Some happier Maid, he would explain his views:
Now she, like him, was politic and shrewd,
With strong desire of lawful gain embued;
To all he said, she bowed with much respect,
Pleased to comply, yet seeming to reject;   180
Cool and yet eager, each admired the strength
Of the opponent, and agreed at length:
As a drawn battle shows to each a force
Powerful as his, he honours it of course;
So in these neighbours, each the power discerned,
And gave the praise that was to each returned.

Jonas now asked his Daughter – and the Aunt,
Though loth to lose her, was obliged to grant:
But would not *Sybil* to the Matron cling,

190 And fear to leave the shelter of her wing?
No! in the young there lives a love of change,
And to the easy they prefer the strange!
Then too the joys she once pursued with zeal,
From whist and visits sprung, she ceased to feel:
When with the matrons *Sybil* first sat down,
To cut for partners and to stake her crown,
This to the youthful maid preferment seemed,
Who thought what woman she was then esteemed;
But in few years, when she perceived, indeed,
200 The real woman to the girl succeed,
No longer tricks and honours filled her mind,
But other feelings, not so well defined;
She then reluctant grew, and thought it hard
To sit and ponder o'er an ugly card;
Rather the nut-tree shade the Nymph preferred,
Pleased with the pensive gloom and evening bird;
Thither, from company retired, she took
The silent walk, or read the favourite book.

The Father's letter, sudden, short, and kind,
210 Awaked her wonder, and disturbed her mind;
She found new dreams upon her fancy seize,
Wild roving thoughts and endless reveries:
The parting came; – and when the Aunt perceived
The tears of *Sybil*, and how much she grieved,–
To love for her that tender grief she laid,
That various, soft, contending passions made.

When *Sybil* rested in her Father's arms,
His pride exulted in a daughter's charms;
A maid accomplished he was pleased to find,
220 Nor seemed the form more lovely than the mind:
But when the fit of pride and fondness fled,
He saw his judgement by his hopes misled;
High were the Lady's spirits, far more free
Her mode of speaking than a maid's should be;
Too much, as *Jonas* thought, she seemed to know,

And all her knowledge was disposed to show;
'Too gay her dress, like theirs who idly dote
On a young coxcomb, or a coxcomb's coat;
In foolish spirits when our friends appear,
And vainly grave when not a man is near.'   230

Thus *Jonas!* adding to his sorrow blame,
And terms disdainful to his Sister's name: –
'The sinful wretch has by her arts defiled
The ductile spirit of my darling Child.'

'The Maid is virtuous,' said the Dame. – Quoth he,
'Let her give proof, by acting virtuously:
Is it in gaping when the Elders pray,
In reading nonsense half a summer's day?
In those mock forms that she delights to trace,
Or her loud laughs in *Hezekiah*'s face?   240
She – O Susannah! – to the world belongs;
She loves the follies of its idle throngs,
And reads soft tales of love, and sings love's softening songs.
But, as our friend is yet delayed in town,
We must prepare her till the Youth comes down:
You shall advise the Maiden; I will threat;
Her fears and hopes may yield us comfort yet.'

Now the grave Father took the Lass aside,
Demanding sternly, 'Wilt thou be a bride?'
She answered, calling up an air sedate,   250
'I have not vowed against the holy state.'

'No folly, *Sybil*,' said the Parent, 'know
What to their Parents virtuous maidens owe;
A worthy, wealthy Youth, whom I approve,
Must thou prepare to honour and to love.
Formal to thee his air and dress may seem,
But the good youth is worthy of esteem:
Shouldst thou with rudeness treat him; of disdain,
Should he with justice or of slight complain,

260   Or of one taunting speech give certain proof,
       Girl! I reject thee from my sober roof'

       'My Aunt,' said *Sybil*, 'will with pride protect
       One whom a Father can for this reject;
       Nor shall a formal, rigid, soul-less boy
       My manners alter, or my views destroy.'

       Jonas then lifted up his hands on high,
       And, uttering something 'twixt a groan and sigh,
       Left the determined Maid, her doubtful Mother by.

       'Hear me,' she said, 'incline thy heart, my child,
270   And fix thy fancy on a man so mild;
       Thy Father, *Sybil*, never could be moved
       By one who loved him, or by one he loved.
       Union like ours is but a bargain made
       By slave and tyrant – he will be obeyed;
       Then calls the quiet, comfort – but thy Youth
       Is mild by nature, and as frank as truth.'

       'But will he love?' said *Sybil*, 'I am told
       That these mild creatures are by nature cold.'

       'Alas!' the Matron answered, 'much I dread
280   That dangerous love by which the young are led!
       That love is earthy; you the creature prize,
       And trust your feelings and believe your eyes:
       Can eyes and feelings inward worth descry?
       No! my fair Daughter, on our choice rely!
       Your love, like that displayed upon the stage,
       Indulged is folly, and opposed is rage; –
       More prudent love our sober couples show,
       All that to mortal beings, mortals owe;
       All flesh is grass – before you give a heart,
290   Remember, *Sybil*, that in death you part;
       And should your husband die before your love,
       What needless anguish must a Widow prove!
       No! My fair Child, let all such visions cease;

Yield but esteem, and only try for peace.'

'I must be loved,' said *Sybil*, 'I must see
The man in terrors who aspires to me;
At my forbidding frown, his heart must ache,
His tongue must falter, and his frame must shake;
And if I grant him at my feet to kneel,
What trembling, fearful pleasure must he feel;   300
Nay, such the raptures that my smiles inspire,
That Reason's self must for a time retire.'

'Alas! for good *Josiah*,' said the Dame,
These wicked thoughts would fill his soul with shame;
He kneel and tremble at a thing of dust!
He cannot, Child;' – the Child replied, 'He must.'

They ceased: the Matron left her with a frown;
So *Jonas* met her when the Youth came down:
'Behold,' said he, 'thy future Spouse attends,
Receive him, Daughter, as the best of friends;   310
Observe, respect him – humble be each word,
That welcomes home thy Husband and thy Lord.'

Forewarned, thought *Sybil*, with a bitter smile.
I shall prepare my manner and my style.

Ere yet *Josiah* entered on his task,
The Father met him – 'Deign to wear a mask
A few dull days, *Josiah*, – but a few, –
It is our duty, and the sex's due;
I wore it once, and every grateful wife
Repays it with obedience through her life: 320
Have no regard to *Sybil*'s dress, have none
To her pert language, to her flippant tone;
Henceforward thou shalt rule unquestioned and alone;
And she thy pleasure in thy looks shall seek –
How she shall dress, and whether she may speak.'

A sober smile returned the Youth, and said,
'Can I cause fear, who am myself afraid?'

Sybil, meantime, sat thoughtful in her room,
And often wondered – 'Will the creature come?
Nothing shall tempt, shall force me to bestow
My hand upon him, – yet I wish to know.'

The door unclosed, and she beheld her Sire
Lead in the Youth, then hasten to retire;
'Daughter, my Friend – my Daughter, Friend,' he cried,
And gave a meaning look, and stepped aside;
That look contained a mingled threat and prayer,
'Do take him, Child – offend him, if you dare.'

The couple gazed – were silent, and the Maid
Looked in his face, to make the Man afraid;
The Man, unmoved, upon the Maiden cast
A steady view – so salutation passed:
But in this instant *Sybil*'s eye had seen
The tall fair person and the still staid mien;
The glow that temperance o'er the cheek had spread,
Where the soft down half-veiled the purest red;
And the serene deportment that proclaimed
A heart unspotted, and a life unblamed:
But then with these she saw attire too plain,
The pale brown coat though worn without a stain;
The formal air, and something of the pride
That indicates the wealth it seems to hide;
And looks that were not, she conceived, exempt
From a proud pity, or a sly contempt.

Josiah's eyes had their employment too,
Engaged and softened by so bright a view;
A fair and meaning face, an eye of fire,
That checked the bold, and made the free retire:
But then with these he marked the studied dress
And lofty air, that scorn or pride express;
With that insidious look, that seemed to hide
In an affected smile the scorn and pride;
And if his mind the Virgin's meaning caught,

He saw a foe with treacherous purpose fraught –
Captive the heart to take, and to reject it, caught.

Silent they sate – thought *Sybil*, that he seeks
Something, no doubt; I wonder if he speaks;
Scarcely she wondered, when these accents fell
Slow in her ear – 'Fair Maiden, art thou well?' –
'Art thou Physician?' she replied; 'my hand,
My pulse at least shall be at thy command.'   370

She said, and saw, surprised, *Josiah* kneel,
And gave his lips the offered pulse to feel;
The rosy colour rising in her cheek,
Seemed that surprise unmixed with wrath to speak;
Then sternness she assumed, and – 'Doctor, tell,
Thy words cannot alarm me, – am I well?'

'Thou art,' said he, 'and yet thy dress so light,
I do conceive, some danger must excite:'
'In whom?' said *Sybil*, with a look demure;
'In more,' said he, 'than I expect to cure. –   380
I, in thy light luxuriant robe, behold
Want and excess, abounding and yet cold!
Here needed, there displayed in many a wanton fold;
Both health and beauty, learnèd authors show,
From a just medium in our clothing flow.'

'Proceed, good Doctor; if so great my need,
What is thy fee? Good Doctor, pray proceed.'

'Large is my fee, fair Lady, but I take
None till some progress in my cure I make:
Thou hast disease, fair Maiden; thou art vain;   390
Within that face, sit insult and disdain;
Thou art enamoured of thyself; my art
Can see the naughty malice of thy heart:
With a strong pleasure would thy bosom move,
Were I to own thy power and ask thy love;
And such thy beauty, Damsel, that I might,

But for thy pride, feel danger in thy sight,
And lose my present peace in dreams of vain delight.'
'And can thy patients,' said the Nymph, 'endure
400   Physic like this? and will it work a cure?'

     'Such is my hope, fair Damsel; thou, I find,
Hast the true tokens of a noble mind;
But the world wins thee, *Sybil*, and thy joys
Are placed in trifles, fashions, follies, toys;
Thou has sought pleasure in the world around,
That in thine own pure bosom should be found:
Did all that world admire thee, praise and love,
Could it the least of Nature's pains remove?
Could it for errors, follies, sins atone,
410   Or give thee comfort, thoughful and alone?
It has, believe me, Maid, no power to charm
Thy soul from sorrow, or thy flesh from harm:
Turn then, fair creature, from a world of sin,
And seek the jewel happiness within.'

     'Speak'st thou at Meeting?' said the Nymph: 'thy speech
Is that of mortal very prone to teach;
But wouldst thou, Doctor, from the Patient learn
Thine own disease? – The cure is thy concern.'

     'Yea, with good will.' – 'Then know 'tis thy complaint,
420   That for a sinner, thou'rt too much a saint;
Hast too much show of the sedate and pure,
And without cause art formal and demure:
This makes a man unsocial, unpolite;
Odious when wrong, and insolent if right.
Thou may'st be good, but why should goodness be
Wrapped in a garb of such formality?
Thy person well might please a damsel's eye,
In decent habit with a scarlet dye.
But, jest apart, – what virtue canst thou trace
430   In that broad brim that hides thy sober face?
Does that long-skirted drab, that over-nice

And formal clothing prove a scorn of vice?
Then for thine accent, – what in sound can be
So void of grace as dull monotony?
Love has a thousand varied notes to move
The human heart; – thou may'st not speak of love,
Till thou hast cast thy formal ways aside,
And those becoming youth and nature tried;
Not till exterior freedom, spirit, ease,
Prove it thy study and delight to please;   440
Not till these follies meet thy just disdain,
While yet thy virtues and thy worth remain.'

'This is severe! – Oh! Maiden, wilt not thou
Something for habits, manners, modes, allow?' –
'Yes! but allowing much, I much require,
In my behalf, for manners, modes, attire!'

'True, lovely *Sybil*; and, this point agreed,
Let me to those of greater weight proceed;
'Thy Father' – 'Nay,' she quickly interposed,
'Good Doctor, here our conference is closed!'   450

Then left the Youth, who, lost in his retreat,
Passed the good Matron on her garden-seat;
His looks were troubled, and his air, once mild
And calm, was hurried: – 'My audacious child!'
Exclaimed the Dame, 'I read what she has done
In thy displeasure – Ah! the thoughtless one;
But yet, *Josiah*, to my stern good man
Speak of the Maid as mildly as you can;
Can you not seem to woo a little while
The Daughter's will, the Father to beguile?   460
So that his wrath in time may wear away:
Will you preserve our peace, *Josiah?* say.'

'Yes! my good neighbour,' said the gentle Youth,
'Rely securely on my care and truth;
And should thy comfort with my efforts cease,

And only then, – perpetual is thy peace.'

The Dame had doubts: she well his virtues knew,
His deeds were friendly, and his words were true;
'But to address this vixen, is a task
470   He is ashamed to take, and I to ask.'
Soon as the Father from *Josiah* learned
What passed with *Sybil*, he the truth discerned.
'He loves,' the man exclaimed, 'He loves, 'tis plain,
The thoughtless girl, – and shall he love in vain?
She may be stubborn, but she shall be tried,
Born as she is of wilfulness and pride.'

With anger fraught, but willing to persuade,
The wrathful Father met the smiling Maid:
480   '*Sybil*,' said he, 'I long, and yet I dread
To know thy conduct – hath *Josiah* fled?
And, grieved and fretted by thy scornful air,
For his lost peace, betaken him to prayer?
Couldst thou his pure and modest mind distress,
By vile remarks upon his speech, address,
Attire, and voice,' – 'All this I must confess' –
'Unhappy Child! what labour will it cost
To win him back!' – 'I do not think him lost.' –
'Courts he then (trifler!) insult and disdain?'
'No: but from these he courts me to refrain.' –
490   'Then hear me, *Sybil* – should *Josiah* leave
Thy Father's house?' 'My Father's Child would grieve;'
'That is of grace, and if he come again
To speak of love?' 'I might from grief refrain.' –
'Then wilt thou, Daughter, our design embrace?' –
'Can I resist it, if it be of grace?' –
'Dear Child! in three plain words they mind express –
Wilt thou have this good Youth?' 'Dear Father! yes.'

THE WIDOW'S TALE

Ah me! for aught that I could ever read,
Or ever hear by tale or history,
The course of true Love never did run smooth;
But either it was different in blood,
Or else misgrafted in respect of years,
Or else it stood upon the choice of friends,
Or if there were a sympathy in choice,
War, death, or sickness did lay siege to it.
Midsummer Night's Dream, Act I. Scene 1.

Oh! thou didst then ne'er love so heartily,
If thou rememberest not the slightest folly
That ever Love did make thee run into.
As You Like It, Act II. Scene 4.

Cry the man mercy; love him, take his offer.
As You Like It, Act III. Scene 5.

To Farmer *Moss* in Langar Vale, came down
His only Daughter, from her school in town;
A tender, timid maid! who knew not how
To pass a pig-sty, or to face a cow:
Smiling she came, with petty talents graced,
A fair complexion, and a slender waist.

Used to spare meals, disposed in manner pure,
Her Father's kitchen she could ill endure;
Where by the steaming beef he hungry sat,

10 And laid at once a pound upon his plate;
Hot from the field, her eager Brother seized
An equal part, and hunger's rage appeased;
The air surcharged with moisture, flagged around,
And the offended Damsel sighed and frowned;
The swelling fat in lumps conglomerate laid,
And fancy's sickness seized the loathing Maid:
But when the men beside their station took,
The maidens with them, and with these the cook;
When one huge wooden bowl before them stood,
20 Filled with huge balls of farinaceous food;
With bacon, mass saline, where never lean
Beneath the brown and bristly rind was seen;
When from a single horn the party drew
Their copious draughts of heavy ale and new;
When the coarse cloth she saw, with many a stain,
Soiled by rude hinds who cut and came again, –
She could not breathe; but, with a heavy sigh,
Reined the fair neck, and shut the offended eye;
She minced the sanguine flesh in frustums fine,
30 And wondered much to see the creatures dine;
When she resolved her Father's heart to move,
If hearts of farmers were alive to love.

She now intreated, by herself to sit
In the small parlour, if papa thought fit,
And there to dine, to read, to work alone –
'No!' said the Farmer, in an angry tone;
'These are your school-taught airs; your mother's pride
Would send you there; but I am now your guide. –
Arise betimes, our early meal prepare,
40 And this dispatched, let business be your care;
Look to the lasses, let there not be one
Who lacks attention, till her tasks be done;
In every household work your portion take,
And what you make not, see that others make;
At leisure times attend the wheel, and see

The whitening web besprinkled on the lea;
When thus employed, should our young neighbour view
An useful lass – you might have more to do.'

Dreadful were these commands; but worse than these
The parting hint – a Farmer could not please: 50
'Tis true she had without abhorrence seen
Young *Harry Carr*, when he was smart and clean;
But, to be married – be a Farmer's wife,
A slave! a drudge! – she could not, for her life.

With swimming eyes the fretful Nymph withdrew,
And, deeply sighing, to her chamber flew;
There on her knees, to Heaven she grieving prayed
For change of prospect to a tortured maid.

Harry, a youth whose late-departed Sire
Had left him all industrious men require, 60
Saw the pale Beauty, – and her shape and air
Engaged him much, and yet he must forbear;
'For my small farm, what can the Damsel do?'
He said, – then stopped to take another view:
'Pity so sweet a lass will nothing learn
Of household cares, for what can beauty earn
By those small arts which they at school attain,
To keep them useless, and yet make them vain?'

This luckless Damsel looked the village round,
To find a friend, and one was quickly found; 70
A pensive Widow, – whose mild air and dress
Pleased the sad Nymph, who wished her soul's distress,
To one so seeming kind, confiding, to confess.

'What Lady that?' the anxious Lass inquired,
Who then beheld the one she most admired;
'Here,' said the Brother, 'are no Ladies seen, –
That is a Widow dwelling on the Green;
A dainty Dame, who can but barely live
On her poor pittance, yet contrives to give;

80 She happier days has known, but seems at ease,
 And you may call her Lady, if you please.
 But if you wish, good Sister, to improve,
 You shall see twenty better worth your love.'

 These *Nancy* met; but, spite of all they taught,
 This useless Widow was the one she sought:
 The Father growled; but said he knew no harm
 In such connexion that could give alarm;
 'And if we thwart the Trifler in her course,
 'Tis odds against us, she will take a worse.'

90 Then met the friends; the Widow heard the sigh
 That asked at once compassion and reply: –
 'Would you, my Child, converse with one so poor,
 Yours were the kindness – yonder is my door;
 And, save the time that we in public pray,
 From that poor cottage I but rarely stray.'

 There went the Nymph, and made her strong complaints,
 Painting her woe as injured feeling paints.

 'Oh, dearest friend! do think how one must feel,
 Shocked all day long and sickened every meal;
100 Could you behold our kitchen, (and to you
 A scene so shocking must indeed be new,)
 A mind like yours, with true refinement graced,
 Would let no vulgar scenes pollute your taste;
 And yet, in truth, from such a polished mind
 All base ideas must resistance find,
 And sordid pictures from the fancy pass,
 As the breath startles from the polished glass.

 'Here you enjoy a sweet romantic scene,
110 Without so pleasant, and within so clean:
 These twining jess'mines, what delicious gloom
 And soothing fragrance yield they to the room!
 What lovely garden! there you oft retire,
 And tales of woe and tenderness admire:

In that neat case your books, in order placed,
Soothe the full soul and charm the cultured taste;
And thus, while all about you wears a charm,
How must you scorn the Farmer and the Farm!'

The Widow smiled, and 'Know you not,' said she,
'How much these farmers scorn or pity me;
Who see what you admire and laugh at all they see?   120
True, their opinion alters not my fate,
By falsely judging of an humble state:
This garden you with such delight behold,
Tempts not a feeble dame who dreads the cold;
These plants, which please so well your livelier sense,
To mine but little of their sweets dispense;
Books soon are painful to my failing sight,
And oftener read from duty than delight;
(Yet let me own, that I can sometimes find
Both joy and duty in the act combined;)   130
But view me rightly, you will see no more
Than a poor female, willing to be poor;
Happy indeed, but not in books nor flowers,
Not in fair dreams, indulged in earlier hours,
Of never-tasted joys; – such visions shun,
My youthful Friend, nor scorn the Farmer's Son'

'Nay,' said the Damsel, nothing pleased to see
A Friend's advice could like a Father's be,
'Blessed in your cottage, you must surely smile
At those who live in our detested style: 140
To my *Lucinda*'s sympathizing heart,
Could I my prospects and my griefs impart,
She would console me; but I dare not show
Ills that would wound her tender soul to know:
And I confess it hurts my pride to tell
The secrets of the prison where I dwell;
For that dear Maiden would be shocked to feel
The secrets I should shudder to reveal;
When told her friend was by a parent asked,

150   Fed you the swine? – Good heaven! how I am tasked! –
       What! can you smile? ah! smile not at the grief
       That woos your pity and demands relief.'

       'Trifles, my love; you take a false alarm;
       Think, I beseech you, better of the Farm:
       Duties in every state demand your care,
       And light are those that will require it there;
       Fix on the Youth a favouring eye, and these,
       To him pertaining, or as his, will please.'

       'What words,' the Lass replied, 'offend my ear!
160   Try you my patience? Can you be sincere?
       And am I told, a willing hand to give
       To a rude Farmer, and with rustics live?
       Far other fate was yours: – some gentle youth
       Admired your beauty, and avowed his truth;
       The power of love prevailed, and freely both
       Gave the fond heart, and pledged the binding oath;
       And then the rivals' plot, the parent's power,
       And jealous fears, drew on the happy hour:
       Ah! let not memory lose the blissful view,
170   But fairly show what Love has done for you.'

       'Agreed, my daughter; what my heart has known
       Of Love's strange power, shall be with frankness shown;
       But let me warn you, that Experience finds
       Few of the scenes that lively Hope designs.' –

       'Mysterious all,' said *Nancy;* 'you, I know,
       Have suffered much; now deign the grief to show; –
       I am your friend, and so prepare my heart,
       In all your sorrows to receive a part!'

       The Widow answered: 'I had once, like you,
180   Such thoughts of Love; no dream is more untrue:
       You judge it fated and decreed to dwell
       In youthful hearts, which nothing can expel,
       A passion doomed to reign, and irresistible.
       The struggling mind, when once subdued, in vain

Rejects the fury or defies the pain,
The strongest reason fails the flame to allay,
And resolution droops and faints away:
Hence, when the destined lovers meet, they prove
At once the force of this all-powerful love;
Each from that period feels the mutual smart,   190
Nor seek to cure it, – Heart is changed for Heart;
Nor is there peace till they delighted stand,
And, at the Altar, – Hand is joined to Hand.

  'Alas! my child, there are who, dreaming so,
Waste their fresh youth, and waking feel the woe;
There is no spirit sent the heart to move
With such prevailing and alarming love;
Passion to Reason will submit – or why
Should wealthy maids the poorest swains deny?
Or how could classes and degrees create   200
The slightest bar to such resistless fate?
Yet high and low, you see, forbear to mix;
No Beggars' eyes the hearts of Kings transfix;
And who but amorous Peers or Nobles sigh,
When titled beauties pass triumphant by?
For Reason wakes, proud wishes to reprove;
You cannot hope, and therefore dare not love:
All would be safe, did we at first require –
"Does Reason sanction what our hearts desire?"
But, quitting precept, let example show   210
What joys from Love unchecked by Prudence flow.

  'A Youth, my Father in his office placed,
Of humble fortune, but with sense and taste;
But he was thin and pale, had downcast looks;
He studied much, and pored upon his books!
Confused he was when seen, and when he saw
Me or my sisters, would in haste withdraw;
And had this Youth departed with the year,
His loss had cost us neither sigh nor tear.

220   'But with my Father still the Youth remained,
        And more reward and kinder notice gained:
        He often, reading, to the garden strayed,
        Where I by books or musing was delayed;
        This to discourse in summer evenings led,
        Of these same evenings, or of what we read;
        On such occasions we were much alone;
        But, save the look, the manner, and the tone,
        (These might have meaning,) all that we discussed
        We could with pleasure to a parent trust.

230   'At length 'twas friendship – and my Friend and I
        Said we were happy, and began to sigh:
        My Sisters first, and then my Father found,
        That we were wandering o'er enchanted ground:
        But he had troubles in his own affairs,
        And would not bear addition to his cares:
        With pity moved, yet angry, "Child," said he,
        "Will you embrace contempt and beggary?
        Can you endure to see each other cursed
        By want, of every human woe the worst?
240   Warring for ever with distress, in dread
        Either of begging or of wanting bread;
        While poverty, with unrelenting force,
        Will your own offspring from your love divorce;
        They, through your folly, must be doomed to pine,
        And you deplore your passion, or resign;
        For if it die, what good will then remain?
        And if it live, it doubles every pain"'

250   'But you were true,' exclaimed the Lass, 'and fled
        The tyrant's power who filled your soul with dread?'
        'But,' said the smiling Friend, 'he filled my mouth with bread:
        And in what other place that bread to gain,
        We long considered, and we sought in vain;
        This was my twentieth year, – at thirty-five
        Our hope was fainter, yet our love alive;
        So many years in anxious doubt had passed.'

'Then,' said the Damsel, 'you were blessed at last?'
A smile again adorned the Widow's face,
But soon a starting tear usurped its place.

'Slow passed the heavy years, and each had more
Pains and vexations than the years before.
My Father failed; his family was rent,   260
And to new states his grieving Daughters sent;
Each to more thriving *Kindred* found a way,
Guests without welcome – Servants without pay;
Our parting hour was grievous; still I feel
The sad, sweet converse at our final meal;
Our Father then revealed his former fears,
Cause of his sternness, and then joined our tears;
Kindly he strove our feelings to repress,
But died, and left us heirs to his distress.   270
The Rich as humble friends my Sisters chose,
I with a wealthy widow sought repose;
Who with a chilling frown her friend received,
Bade me rejoice, and wondered that I grieved:
In vain my anxious Lover tried his skill
To rise in life, he was dependent still;
We met in grief, nor can I paint the fears
Of these unhappy, troubled, trying years:
Our dying hopes and stronger fears between,
We felt no season peaceful or serene;   280
Our fleeting joys, like meteors in the night,
Shone on our gloom with inauspicious light;
Add then domestic sorrows, till the mind,
Worn with distresses, to despair inclined;
Add too the ill that from the passion flows,
When its contemptuous frown the world bestows,
The peevish spirit caused by long delay,
When being gloomy we contemn the gay,
When, being wretched, we incline to hate
And censure others in a happier state: 290
Yet loving still, and still compelled to move

In the sad labyrinth of lingering love:
While you, exempt from want, despair, alarm,
May wed – oh! take the Farmer and the Farm.'

  'Nay,' said the Nymph, 'Joy smiled on you at last?'
'Smiled for a moment,' she replied, 'and passed:
My Lover still the same dull means pursued,
Assistant called, but kept in servitude;
His spirits wearied in the prime of life,
By fears and wishes in eternal strife;
At length he urged impatient – "Now consent;
With thee united, Fortune may relent."
I paused, consenting; but a Friend arose,
Pleased a fair view, though distant, to disclose;
From the rough Ocean we beheld a gleam
Of joy, as transient as the joys we dream;
By lying hopes deceived, my Friend retired,
And sailed, – was wounded – reached us – and expired!
You shall behold his grave, and when I die,
There! – but 'tis folly, – I request to lie.'

  'Thus,' said the Lass, 'to joy you bade adieu!
But how a widow? – that cannot be true:
Or was it force, in some unhappy hour,
That placed you, grieving, in a tyrant's power?'

  'Force, my young friend, when forty years are fled,
Is what a woman seldom has to dread;
She needs no brazen locks nor guarding walls,
And seldom comes a lover though she calls:
Yet, moved by fancy, one approved my face,
Though time and tears has wrought it much disgrace.

  'The man I married was sedate and meek,
And spoke of love as men in earnest speak;
Poor as I was, he ceaseless sought, for years,
A heart in sorrow and a face in tears:
That heart I gave not; and 'twas long before
I gave attention, and then nothing more;

But, in my breast some grateful feeling rose,
For one whose love so sad a subject chose;
Till long delaying, fearing to repent,
But grateful still, I gave a cold assent. 330

'Thus we were wed; no fault had I to find,
And he but one; my heart could not be kind:
Alas! of every early hope bereft,
There was no fondness in my bosom left;
So had I told him, but had told in vain,
He lived but to indulge me and complain:
His was this cottage, he enclosed this ground,
And planted all these blooming shrubs around;
He to my room these curious trifles brought,
And with assiduous love my pleasure sought; 340
He lived to please me, and I ofttimes strove,
Smiling, to thank his unrequited love:
"Teach me," he cried, "that pensive mind to ease,
For all my pleasure is the hope to please."

'Serene, though heavy, were the days we spent,
Yet kind each word and generous each intent;
But his dejection lessened every day,
And to a placid kindness died away:
In tranquil ease we passed our latter years,
By griefs untroubled, unassailed by fears. 350

'Let not romantic views your bosom sway,
Yield to your duties and their call obey:
Fly not a Youth, frank, honest, and sincere;
Observe his merits, and his passion hear!
'Tis true, no hero, but a Farmer sues –
Slow in his speech, but worthy in his views;
With him you cannot that affliction prove,
That rends the bosom of the poor, in love:
Health, comfort, competence, and cheerful days,
Your Friends' approval, and your Father's praise, 360

Will crown the deed, and you escape *their* fate
Who plan so wildly and are wise too late.'

The Damsel heard; at first the advice was strange,
Yet wrought a happy, nay a speedy change:
'I have no care,' she said, when next they met,
'But one may wonder, he is silent yet;
He looks around him with his usual stare,
And utters nothing – not that I shall care.'

This pettish humour pleased the experienced Friend –
370 None need despair, whose silence can offend;
'Should I,' resumed the thoughtful Lass, 'consent
To hear the Man, the Man may now repent:
Think you my sighs shall call him from the plough,
Or give one hint, that "You may woo me now?"'

'Persist, my love,' replied the Friend, 'and gain
A Parent's praise, *that* cannot be in vain.'

The Father saw the change, but not the cause,
And gave the altered Maid his fond applause:
The coarser manners she in part removed,
380 In part endured, improving and improved;
She spoke of household works, she rose betimes,
And said neglect and indolence were crimes;
The various duties of their life she weighed,
And strict attention to her dairy paid;
The names of servants now familiar grew,
And fair *Lucinda*'s from her mind withdrew:
As prudent travellers for their ease assume
Their modes and language to whose lands they come;
So to the Farmer this fair Lass inclined,
390 Gave to the business of the Farm her mind;
To useful arts she turned her hand and eye,
And by her manners told him – 'You may try.'

The observing Lover more attention paid,
With growing pleasure, to the altered Maid;

He feared to lose her, and began to see
That a slim beauty might a helpmate be:
'Twixt hope and fear he now the Lass addressed,
And in his Sunday robe his love expressed:
She felt no chilling dread, no thrilling joy,
Nor was too quickly kind, too slowly coy;   400
But still she lent an unreluctant ear
To all the rural business of the year;
Till Love's strong hopes endured no more delay,
And *Harry* asked, and *Nancy* named the day.

'A Happy change! my Boy,' the Father cried:
'How lost your Sister all her school-day pride?'
The Youth replied, 'it is the Widow's deed;
The cure is perfect, and was wrought with speed;'
'And comes there, Boy, this benefit of books,
Of that smart dress, and of those dainty looks?   410
We must be kind – some offerings from the Farm
To the White Cot will speak our feelings warm;
Will show that people, when they know the fact,
Where they have judged severely, can retract.
Oft have I smiled, when I beheld her pass
With cautious step, as if she hurt the grass;
Where, if a Snail's retreat she chanced to storm,
She looked as begging pardon of the Worm;
And what, said I, still laughing at the view,
Have these weak creatures in the world to do?   420
But some are made for action, some to speak,
And, while she looks so pitiful and meek,
Her words are weighty, though her nerves are weak.'

Soon told the village-bells the rite was done,
That joined the school-bred Miss and Farmer's Son;
Her former habits some slight scandal raised,
But real worth was soon perceived and praised;
She, her neat taste imparted to the Farm,
And he, the improving skill and vigorous arm.

THE MOTHER

> What though you have beauty,
> Must you be therefore proud and pityless?
>
> *As You Like It*, Act IV. Scene 4.

I would not marry her, though she were endow'd with all that *Adam* had left him before he transgress'd.

As You Like it.

Wilt thou love such a woman? What! to make thee an instrument and play false strains upon thee! – Not to be endured.

As You Like It.

> Your son,
> As mad in folly, lack'd the sense to know
> Her estimation hence.
>
> *All's Well that Ends Well*, Act IV. Scene 3.

> Be this sweet *Helen*'s knell;
> He left a wife whose words all ears took captive,
> Whose dear perfections hearts that scorn'd to serve
> Humbly call'd Mistress.
>
> *All's Well that Ends Well*, Act V. Scene 3.

There was a worthy, but a simple Pair,
Who nursed a Daughter, fairest of the fair:
Sons they had lost, and she alone remained,
Heir to the kindness they had all obtained;
Heir to the fortune they designed for all,
Nor had the allotted portion then been small;
But now, by Fate enriched with beauty rare,
They watched their treasure with peculiar care:

The fairest features they could early trace,
And, blind with love, saw merit in her face –   10
Saw virtue, wisdom, dignity, and grace;
And *Dorothea*, from her infant years,
Gained all her wishes from their pride or fears:
She wrote a Billet, and a Novel read,
And with her fame her vanity was fed;
Each word, each look, each action was a cause
For flattering wonder, and for fond applause;
She rode or danced, and ever glanced around,
Seeking for praise, and smiling when she found.
The yielding Pair to her petitions gave   20
An humble friend to be a civil slave;
Who for a poor support herself resigned
To the base toil of a dependent mind:
By nature cold, our Heiress stooped to art,
To gain the credit of a tender heart,
Hence at her door, must suppliant paupers stand,
To bless the bounty of her beauteous hand:
And now, her education all complete,
She talked of virtuous love and union sweet;
She was indeed by no soft passion moved,   30
But wished, with all her soul, to be beloved.
Here, on the favoured beauty, Fortune smiled;
Her chosen Husband was a man so mild,
So humbly tempered, so intent to please,
It quite distressed her to remain at ease,
Without a cause to sigh, without pretence to tease;
She tried his patience in a thousand modes,
And tired it not upon the roughest roads.
Pleasure she sought, and, disappointed, sighed
For joys, she said, 'to her alone denied;'   40
And she was 'sure her Parents, if alive,
Would many comforts for their Child contrive:'
The gentle Husband bade her name him one;
'No – that,' she answered, 'should for her be done;
How could she say what pleasures were around?

But she was certain many might be found:' –
'Would she some Sea-port, *Weymouth, Scarborough*, grace?' –
'He knew she hated every watering-place:'
'The Town?' – 'What! now 'twas empty, joyless, dull?'
50   'In winter?' 'No! she liked it worse when full.'
She talked of building – 'Would she plan a room?' –
'No! she could live, as he desired, in gloom:'
'Call then our friends and neighbours;' 'He might call,
And they might come and fill his ugly hall;
A noisy vulgar set, he knew she scorned them all:' –
'Then might their two dear girls the time employ,
And their improvement yield a solid joy;' –
'Solid indeed! and heavy – oh! the bliss
Of teaching letters to a lisping Miss!' –
60   'My dear, my gentle *Dorothea*, say,
Can I oblige you?' – 'You may go away.'

    Twelve heavy years this patient soul sustained
This wasp's attack, and then her praise obtained,
Graved on a marble tomb, where he at peace remained.

    Two daughters wept their loss; the one a child
With a plain face, strong sense, and temper mild;
Who keenly felt the Mother's angry taunt,
'Thou art the image of thy pious Aunt:'
Long time had *Lucy* wept her slighted face,
70   And then began to smile at her disgrace.
Her Father's Sister, who the world had seen
Near sixty years when *Lucy* saw sixteen,
Begged the plain girl: the gracious Mother smiled,
And freely gave her grieved but passive child;
And with her elder-born, the beauty, blessed,
This parent rested, if such minds can rest:
No Miss her waxen babe could so admire,
 Nurse with such care, or with such pride attire;
They were companions meet, with equal mind,
80   Blessed with one love, and to one point inclined;
Beauty to keep, adorn, increase, and guard,

Was their sole care, and had its full reward:
In rising splendour with the one it reigned,
And in the other was by care sustained,
The Daughter's charms increased, the Parent's yet remained.
Leave we these ladies to their daily care,
To see how meekness and discretion fare: –
A Village-maid unvexed by want or love,
Could not with more delight than *Lucy* move;
The village-lark, high mounted in the spring,   90
Could not with purer joy than *Lucy* sing;
Her cares all light, her pleasures all sincere,
Her duty joy, and her companion dear;
In tender friendship and in true respect,
Lived Aunt and Niece, no flattery, no neglect –
They read, walked, visited, – together prayed,
Together slept the Matron and the Maid:
There was such goodness, such pure nature seen
In *Lucy*'s looks, a manner so serene;
Such harmony in motion, speech, and air,   100
That without fairness, she was more than fair;
Had more than beauty in each speaking grace,
That lent their cloudless glory to the face;
Where mild good sense in placid looks were shown,
And felt in every bosom but her own.
The one presiding feature in her mind,
Was the pure meekness of a will resigned;
A tender spirit, freed from all pretence
Of wit, and pleased in mild benevolence;
Blessed in protecting fondness she reposed,   110
With every wish indulged though undisclosed;
But Love, like Zephyr on the limpid lake,
Was now the bosom of the Maid to shake,
And in that gentle mind a gentle strife to make.

    Among their chosen friends, a favoured few,
The Aunt and Niece a youthful Rector knew;
Who, though a younger Brother, might address

A younger Sister, fearless of success:
His friends, a lofty race, their native pride
At first displayed, and their assent denied;
But, pleased such virtues and such love to trace,
They owned she would adorn the loftiest race.
The Aunt, a Mother's caution to supply,
Had watched the youthful Priest with jealous eye;
And, anxious for her charge, had viewed unseen
The cautious life that keeps the conscience clean:
In all she found him all she wished to find,
With slight exception of a lofty mind;
A certain manner that expressed desire,
To be received as brother to the 'Squire.
Lucy's meek eye had beamed with many a tear,
Lucy's soft heart had beat with many a fear,
Before he told (although his looks, she thought,
Had oft confessed) that he her favour sought:
But when he kneeled, (she wished him not to kneel)
And spoke the fears and hopes that lovers feel;
When too the prudent Aunt herself confessed
Her wishes on the gentle Youth would rest;
The Maiden's eye with tender passion beamed,
She dwelt with fondness on the life she schemed;
The household cares, the soft and lasting ties
Of Love, with all his binding charities;
Their Village taught, consoled, assisted, fed,
Till the young Zealot, tears of pleasure shed.

But would her Mother? Ah! she feared it wrong
To have indulged these forward hopes so long;
Her Mother loved, but was not used to grant
Favours so freely as her gentle Aunt. –
Her gentle Aunt, with smiles that angels wear,
Dispelled her *Lucy*'s apprehensive tear:
Her prudent foresight the request had made
To one whom none could govern, few persuade;
She doubted much if one in earnest wooed

120
130
140
150

A girl with not a single charm endued:
The Sister's nobler views she then declared,
And what small sum for *Lucy* could be spared;
'If more than this the foolish Priest requires,
Tell him,' she wrote, 'to check his vain desires.'
At length, with many a cold expression mixed,
With many a sneer on girls so fondly fixed,   160
There came a promise, – should they not repent,
But take with grateful minds the portion meant,
And wait the Sister's day – the Mother might consent.

And here might pitying Hope o'er Truth prevail,
Or Love o'er Fortune, we would end our Tale;
For, who more blessed than youthful pair removed
From fear of want – by mutual friends approved, –
Short time to wait, and in that time to live,
With all the pleasures Hope and Fancy give;
Their equal passion raised on just esteem,   170
When Reason sanctions all that Love can dream?

Yes! Reason sanctions what stern Fate denies;
The early prospect in the glory dies,
As the soft smiles on dying infants play
In their mild features, and then pass away.

The *Beauty* died, ere she could yield her hand
In the high marriage by the *Mother* planned;
Who grieved indeed, but found a vast relief
In a cold heart, that ever warred with grief.

Lucy was present when her Sister died,   180
Heiress to duties that she ill supplied:
There were no mutual feelings, sister arts,
No kindred taste, nor intercourse of hearts;
When in the mirror played the Matron's smile,
The Maiden's thoughts were travelling all the while;
And when desired to speak, she sighed to find
Her pause offended; 'Envy made her blind:'
Tasteless she was, nor had a claim in life

Above the station of a Rector's Wife;
190   Yet as an heiress, she must shun disgrace,
Although no heiress to her mother's face:
'It is your duty,' said the imperious Dame,
'(Advanced your fortune) to advance your name,
And with superior rank, superior offers claim;
Your Sister's Lover, when his sorrows die,
May look upon you and for favour sigh;
Nor can you offer a reluctant hand,
His birth is noble and his seat is grand.'

Alarmed was *Lucy*, was in tears – 'a fool!
200   Was she a Child in Love? – a Miss at School?
Doubts any mortal, if a change of state
Dissolves all claims and ties of earlier date?'

The Rector doubted, for he came to mourn
A Sister dead, and with a Wife return:
Lucy with heart unchanged received the Youth,
True in herself, confiding in his truth;
But owned her Mother's change; the haughty dame
Poured strong contempt upon the youthful flame;
She firmly vowed her purpose to pursue,
210   Judged her own cause, and bade the Youth adieu!
The Lover begged, insisted, urged his pain,
His Brother wrote to threaten and complain,
Her Sister reasoning, proved the promise made,
Lucy appealing to a parent prayed;
But all opposed the event that she designed,
And all in vain – she never changed her mind;
But coldly answered in her wonted way,
That she 'would rule, and *Lucy* must obey.'

With peevish fear, she saw her health decline,
220   And cried, 'Oh! monstrous, for a man to pine:
But if your foolish heart must yield to love,
Let him possess it whom I now approve;
This is my pleasure:' – Still the Rector came

With larger offers and with bolder claim:
But the stern Lady would attend no more –
She frowned, and rudely pointed to the door;
Whate'er he wrote, he saw unread returned,
And he, indignant, the dishonour spurned;
Nay, fixed suspicion where he might confide,
And sacrificed his passion to his pride.   230

   Lucy, meantime, though threatened and distressed,
Against her marriage made a strong protest:
All was domestic war; the Aunt rebelled
Against the sovereign will, and was expelled;
And every power was tried, and every art,
To bend to falsehood one determined heart;
Assailed, in patience it received the shock,
Soft as the wave, unshaken as the rock:
But while the unconquered soul endures the storm
Of angry Fate, it preys upon the form: 240
With conscious virtue she resisted still,
And conscious love gave vigour to her will:
But *Lucy*'s trial was at hand; with joy
The Mother cried, – 'Behold your constant Boy –
Thursday – was married: – take the Paper, sweet,
And read the conduct of your Reverend cheat;
See with what pomp of coaches, in what crowd
The creature married, – of his falsehood proud!
False did I say? – at least no whining fool;
And thus will hopeless passions ever cool: 250
But shall his Bride your single state reproach?
No! give him crowd for crowd, and coach for coach.
Oh! you retire; reflect, then, gentle Miss,
And gain some spirit in a cause like this.'

   Some spirit *Lucy* gained; a steady soul,
Defying all persuasion, all control:
In vain reproach, derision, threats were tried;
The constant mind all outward force defied,

By vengeance vainly urged, in vain assailed by pride:
260   Fixed in her purpose, perfect in her part,
She felt the courage of a wounded heart;
The world receded from her rising view,
When Heaven approached as earthly things withdrew;
Not strange before, for in the days of love,
Joy, hope, and pleasure, she had thoughts above;
Pious when most of worldly prospects fond,
When they best pleased her she could look beyond:
Had the young Priest a faithful lover died,
Something had been her bosom to divide;
270   Now Heaven had all, for in her holiest views,
She saw the Matron whom she feared to lose;
While from her Parent, the dejected Maid
Forced the unpleasant thought, or thinking prayed.

Surprised, the Mother saw the languid frame,
And felt indignant, yet forbore to blame;
Once with a frown she cried, 'And do you mean
To die of Love – the folly of fifteen?'
But as her anger met with no reply,
She let the gentle girl in quiet die;
280   And to her Sister wrote, impelled by pain,
'Come quickly, *Martha*, or you come in vain.'
Lucy meantime professed with joy sincere,
That nothing held, employed, engaged her here.

'I am an humble actor, doomed to play
A part obscure, and then to glide away;
Incurious how the great or happy shine,
Or who have parts obscure and sad as mine:
In its best prospect I but wished, for life,
To be the assiduous, gentle, useful wife;
290   That lost, with wearied mind, and spirit poor,
I drop my efforts, and can act no more;
With growing joy I feel my spirits tend
To that last scene where all my duties end.'

Hope, ease, delight, the thoughts of dying gave,
Till *Lucy* spoke with fondness of the grave;
She smiled with wasted form but spirit firm,
And said, 'She left but little for the worm;'
As tolled the bell, 'There's one,' she said, 'hath pressed
Awhile before me to the bed of rest;'
And she beside her with attention spread   300
The decorations of the Maiden – dead.

While quickly thus the mortal part declined,
The happiest visions filled the active mind;
A soft, religious melancholy gained
Entire possession, and for ever reigned:
On Holy Writ her mind reposing dwelt,
She saw the wonders, she the mercies felt;
Till in a blessed and glorious reverie,
She seemed the Saviour as on earth to see,
And, filled with Love Divine, the attending friend to be;   310
Or she who trembling, yet confiding, stole
Near to the garment, touched it, and was whole;
When, such the intenseness of the working thought,
On her it seemed the very deed was wrought;
She the glad patient's fear and rapture found,
The holy transport, and the healing wound;
This was so fixed, so grafted in the heart,
That she adopted, nay became the part;
But one chief scene was present to her sight,
Her Saviour resting in the Tomb by night;   320
Her fever rose, and still her wedded mind
Was to that scene, that hallowed cave, confined, –
Where in the shade of death the body laid,
There watched the spirit of the wandering Maid;
Her looks were fixed, intranced, illumed, serene,
In the still glory of the midnight scene;
There, at her Saviour's feet, in visions blessed,
The enraptured Maid a sacred joy possessed;
In patience waiting for the first-born ray

330   Of that all-glorious and triumphant day:
To this idea all her soul she gave,
Her mind reposing by the sacred grave;
Then sleep would seal the eye, the vision close,
And steep the solemn thoughts in brief repose.

Then grew the soul serene, and all its powers
Again restored illumed the dying hours;
But Reason dwelt where Fancy strayed before,
And the mind wandered from its views no more;
Till Death approached, when every look expressed
340   A sense of bliss, till every sense had rest.

The Mother lives, and has enough to buy
The attentive ear and the submissive eye
Of abject natures – these are daily told,
How triumphed beauty in the days of old;
How, by her window seated, crowds have cast
Admiring glances, wondering as they passed;
How from her carriage as she stepped to pray,
Divided ranks would humbly make her way;
And how each voice in the astonished throng
350   Pronounced her peerless as she moved along.

Her picture then the greedy Dame displays;
Touched by no shame, she now demands its praise;
In her tall mirror then she shows her face,
Still coldly fair with unaffecting grace;
These she compares, 'It has the form,' she cries,
'But wants the air, the spirit, and the eyes;
This as a likeness is correct and true,
But there alone the living grace we view.'
This said, the applauding voice the Dame required,
360   And, gazing, slowly from the glass retired.

ARABELLA

Thrice blessed they that master so their blood –
But earthly happier is the rose distill'd,
Than that which, withering on the virgin thorn,
Grows, lives, and dies in single blessedness.
>> *Midsummer Night's Dream*, Act I. Scene 1.

I sometimes do excuse the thing I hate,
For his advantage whom I dearly love.
>> *Measure for Measure*, Act II. Scene 4.

Contempt, farewell! and maiden pride, adieu!
>> *Measure for Measure*, Act II. Scene 4.

Of a fair town where Doctor *Rack* was guide,
His only daughter was the boast and pride;
Wise *Arabella*, yet not wise alone,
She like a bright and polished brilliant shone;
Her father owned her for his prop and stay,
Able to guide yet willing to obey;
Pleased with her learning while discourse could please,
And with her love in languor and disease:
To every mother were her virtues known,
And to their daughters as a pattern shown; 10
Who in her youth had all that age requires,
And with her prudence, all that youth admires;
These odious praises made the damsels try
Not to obtain such merits, but deny;
For, whatsoever wise mammas might say,
To guide a daughter, this was not the way;

From such applause disdain and anger rise,
And envy lives where emulation dies:
In all his strength, contends the noble Horse,
With one who just precedes him on the course;
But when the rival flies too far before,
His spirit fails, and he attempts no more.

This reasoning Maid, above her sex's dread,
Had dared to read, and dared to say she read;
Not the last novel, not the new-born play;
Not the mere trash and scandal of the day;
But (though her young companions felt the shock)
She studied *Berkeley*, *Bacon*, *Hobbes*, and *Locke*;
Her mind within the maze of History dwelt,
And of the Moral Muse the beauty felt;
The merits of the Roman page she knew,
And could converse with *Moore* and *Montague*:
Thus she became the wonder of the town,
From that she reaped, to that she gave renown;
And strangers coming, all were taught to admire
The learned Lady, and the lofty Spire.

Thus Fame in public fixed the Maid, where all
Might throw their darts, and see the idol fall;
A hundred arrows came with vengeance keen,
From tongues envenomed, and from arms unseen;
A thousand eyes were fixed upon the place,
That, if she fell, she might not fly disgrace:
But malice vainly throws the poisoned dart,
Unless our frailty shows the peccant part;
And *Arabella* still preserved her name
Untouched, and shone with undisputed fame;
Her very notice some respect would cause,
And her esteem was honour and applause.

Men she avoided; not in childish fear,
As if she thought some savage foe was near;
Not as a prude, who hides that Man should seek,

Or who by silence hints that they should speak;
But with discretion all the sex she viewed,
Ere yet engaged pursuing or pursued;
Ere love had made her to his vices blind,
Or hid the favourite's failings from her mind.

Thus was the picture of the man portrayed,
By merit destined for so rare a maid;
At whose request she might exchange her state,
Or still be happy in a virgin's fate.

He must be one with manners like her own,
His life unquestioned, his opinions known;
His stainless virtue must all tests endure,
His honour spotless, and his bosom pure:
She no allowance made for sex or times,
Of lax opinion – crimes were ever crimes;
No wretch forsaken must his frailty curse,
No spurious offspring drain his private purse;
He at all times his passions must command,
And yet possess – or be refused her hand.   70

All this without reserve the Maiden told,
And some began to weigh the Rector's gold;
To ask what sum a prudent man might gain,
Who had such store of virtues to maintain?

A Doctor *Campbell*, north of *Tweed*, came forth,
Declared his passion, and proclaimed his worth;
Not unapproved, for he had much to say
On every cause, and in a pleasant way;
Not all his trust was in a pliant tongue,
His form was good, and ruddy he, and young;   80
But though the Doctor was a man of parts,
He read not deeply male or female hearts;
But judged that all whom he esteemed as wise,
Must think alike, though some assumed disguise;
That every reasoning *Brahmin*, *Christian*, *Jew*,
Of all religions took their liberal view;

And of her own, no doubt, this learnèd Maid
Denied the substance, and the forms obeyed;
And thus persuaded, he his thoughts expressed
90 Of her opinions, and his own professed:
'All states demand this aid, the vulgar need
Their priests and prayers, their sermons and their creed;
And those of stronger minds should never speak
(In his opinion) what might hurt the weak;
A man may smile, but still he should attend
His hour at church, and be the Church's friend,
What there he thinks conceal, and what he hears commend.'

Frank was the speech, but heard with high disdain,
Nor had the Doctor leave to speak again;
100 A man who owned, nay gloried in deceit,
'He might despise her, but he should not cheat.'

Then Vicar *Holmes* appeared; he heard it said
That ancient men best pleased the prudent Maid;
And, true it was her ancient friends she loved,
Servants when old she favoured and approved;
Age in her pious Parent she revered,
And neighbours were by length of days endeared;
But, if her husband too must ancient be,
The good old Vicar found it was not he.

110 On Captain *Bligh* her mind in balance hung –
Though valiant, modest; and reserved, tho' young:
Against these merits must defects be set –
Though poor, imprudent; and though proud, in debt:
In vain the Captain close attention paid,
She found him wanting, whom she fairly weighed.

Then came a youth, and all their friends agreed,
That *Edward Huntly* was the man indeed:
Respectful duty he had paid awhile,
Then asked her hand, and had a gracious smile;
A lover now declared, he led the Fair
To woods and fields, to visits, and to prayer;

Then whispered softly – 'Will you name the day?'
She softly whispered 'If you love me, stay:' –
'Oh! try me not beyond my strength,' he cried;
'Oh! be not weak,' the prudent Maid replied;
But by some trial your affection prove,
Respect and not impatience argues love:
And Love no more is by impatience known,
Than Ocean's depth is by its tempests shown;
He whom a weak and fond impatience sways,   130
But for himself with all his fervour prays,
And not the maid he wooes, but his own will obeys;
And will she love the being who prefers,
With so much ardour, his desire to hers?'

Young *Edward* grieved, but let not grief be seen;
He knew obedience pleased his fancy's queen;
Awhile he waited, and then cried – 'Behold!
The year advancing, be no longer cold!'
For she had promised, 'Let the flowers appear,
And I will pass with thee the smiling year:'   140
Then pressing grew the Youth; the more he pressed,
The less inclined the Maid to his request;
'Let *June* arrive.' – Alas! when *April* came,
It brought a stranger, and the stranger, shame;
Nor could the Lover from his house persuade
A stubborn lass whom he had mournful made;
Angry and weak, by thoughtless vengeance moved,
She told her story to the Fair belov'd;
In strongest terms the unwelcome truth was shown,
To blight his prospects, careless of her own.   150

Our Heroine grieved, but had too firm a heart
For him to soften, when she swore to part;
In vain his seeming penitence and prayer,
His vows, his tears; she left him in despair;
His mother fondly laid her grief aside,
And to the reason of the Nymph applied –

'It well becomes thee, Lady, to appear,
But not to be, in very truth severe;
Although the crime be odious in thy sight,
160   That daring sex is taught such things to slight;
His heart is thine, although it once was frail;
Think of his grief, and let his love prevail! –'

'Plead thou no more,' the lofty Lass returned,
'Forgiving woman is deceived and spurned;
Say that the crime is common – shall I take
A common man my wedded lord to make?
See! a weak woman by his arts betrayed
An infant born his father to upbraid;
Shall I forgive his vileness, take his name,
170   Sanction his error, and partake his shame?
No! this assent would kindred frailty prove,
A love for him would be a vicious love;
Can a chaste maiden secret counsel hold
With one whose crime by every mouth is told?
Forbid it spirit, prudence, virtuous pride;
He must despise me, were he not denied;
The way from Vice the erring mind to win,
Is with presuming sinners to begin,
And show, by scorning them, a just contempt for Sin.'

180   The Youth repulsed, to one more mild conveyed
His heart, and smiled on the remorseless Maid;
The Maid, remorseless in her pride, the while
Despised the insult, and returned the smile.

First to admire, to praise her, and defend,
Was (now in years advanced) a Virgin-Friend:
Much she preferred, she cried, the single state,
'It was her choice,' – it surely was her fate;
And, much it pleased her in the train to view
A maiden-votress wise and lovely too.

190   Time to the yielding mind his change imparts,
He varies notions, and he alters hearts;

'Tis right, 'tis just to feel contempt for Vice,
But he that shows it may be over-nice:
There are who feel, when young, the false sublime,
And proudly love to show disdain for Crime;
To whom the future will new thoughts supply,
The pride will soften, and the scorn will die;
Nay, where they still the vice itself condemn,
They bear the vicious and consort with them.
Young Captain *Grove*, when one had changed his side,   200
Despised the venal turn-coat, and defied;
Old Colonel *Grove* now shakes him by the hand,
Though he who bribes may still his vote command;
Why would not *Ellen* to *Belinda* speak,
When she had flown to *London* for a week;
And then returned, to every friend's surprise,
With twice the spirit, and with half the size?
She spoke not then – but, after years had flown,
A better friend had *Ellen* never known;
Was it the lady her mistake had seen?   210
Or had she also such a journey been?
No: 'twas the gradual change in human hearts,
That time, in commerce with the world, imparts;
That on the roughest temper throws disguise,
And steals from Virtue her asperities.
The young and ardent, who with glowing zeal
Felt wrath for trifles, and were proud to feel;
Now find those trifles all the mind engage,
To soothe dull hours, and cheat the cares of age:
As young *Zelinda*, in her quaker-dress,   220
Disdained each varying fashion's vile excess,
And now her friends on old *Zelinda* gaze,
Pleased in rich silks and orient gems to blaze;
Changes like these 'tis folly to condemn,
So Virtue yields not, nor is changed with them.

   Let us proceed: – Twelve brilliant years were past,
Yet each with less of glory than the last;

Whether these years to this fair Virgin gave
A softer mind – effect they often have;
230   Whether the Virgin-state was not so blessed
As that good Maiden in her zeal professed;
Or whether lovers falling from her train,
Gave greater price to those she could retain,
Is all unknown; – but *Arabella* now
Was kindly listening to a Merchant's vow;
Who offered terms so fair, against his love
To strive was folly, so she never strove. –
Man in his earlier days we often find
With a too easy and unguarded mind;
240   But by increasing years and prudence taught,
He grows reserved, and locks up every thought:
Not thus the Maiden, for in blooming youth
She hides her thought, and guards the tender truth;
This, when no longer young, no more she hides,
But frankly in the favoured swain confides:
Man, stubborn Man, is like the growing tree,
That longer standing, still will harder be;
And like its fruit, the Virgin, first austere,
Then kindly softening with the ripening year.

250   Now was the Lover urgent, and the kind
And yielding Lady to his suit inclined;
'A little time, my friend, is just, is right;
We must be decent in our neighbour's sight;'
Still she allowed him of his hopes to speak,
And in compassion took off week by week;
Till few remained, when, wearied with delay,
She kindly meant to take off day by day.

That female Friend who gave our Virgin praise
For flying man and all his treacherous ways,
260   Now heard with mingled anger, shame and fear,
Of one accepted, and a wedding near;
But she resolved again with friendly zeal,
To make the Maid her scorn of wedlock feel;

For she was grieved to find her work undone,
And like a Sister mourned the failing Nun.

  Why are these gentle Maidens prone to make
Their sister-doves the tempting world forsake?
Why all their triumph, when a maid disdains
The tyrant-sex and scorns to wear its chains?
Is it pure joy to see a Sister flown   270
From the false pleasures they themselves have known?
Or do they, as the call-birds in the cage,
Try, in pure envy, others to engage?
And therefore paint their native woods and groves,
As scenes of dangerous joys and naughty loves?

  Strong was the Maiden's hope; her Friend was proud,
And had her notions to the world avowed;
And, could she find the Merchant weak and frail,
With power to prove it, then she must prevail;
For she aloud would publish his disgrace,   280
And save his victim from a man so base.

  When all inquiries had been duly made,
Came the kind Friend her burden to unlade –
'Alas! my dear! not all our care and art
Can tread the maze of man's deceitful heart;
Look not surprise – nor let resentment swell
Those lovely features, all will yet be well;
And thou, from Love's and Man's deceptions free,
Wilt dwell in virgin-state, and walk to Heaven with me.'

The Maiden frowned, and then conceived 'that wives   290
Could walk as well, and lead as holy lives
As angry prudes who scorned the marriage-chain,
Or luckless maids who sought it still in vain.'

The Friend was vexed – she paused, at length she cried:
'Know your own danger, then your lot decide;
That traitor *Beswell*, while he seeks your hand,
Has, I affirm, a wanton at command;

A slave, a creature from a foreign place,
The nurse and mother of a spurious race;
300   Brown, ugly bastards – (Heaven the word forgive,
And the deed punish!) – in his cottage live;
To town if business calls him, there he stays
In sinful pleasures wasting countless days;
Nor doubt the facts, for I can witness call
For every crime, and prove them one and all.'

Here ceased the informer; *Arabella's* look
Was like a school-boy's puzzled by his book;
Intent she cast her eyes upon the floor,
Paused – then replied –
                                    – 'I wish to know no more:
310   I question not your motive, zeal or love,
But must decline such dubious points to prove –
All is not true, I judge, for who can guess
Those deeds of darkness men with care suppress?
He brought a slave perhaps to England's coast,
And made her free; it is our country's boast!
And she perchance too grateful – good and ill
Were sown at first, and grow together still;
The coloured infants on the village-green,
What are they more than we have often seen?
320   Children half-clothed, who round their village stray,
In sun or rain, now starved, now beaten, they
Will the dark colour of their fate betray:
Let us in Christian love for all account,
And then behold to what such tales amount.'

'His heart is evil,' said the impatient Friend:
'My duty bids me try that heart to mend,'
Replied the Virgin – 'We may be too nice,
And lose a soul in our contempt of Vice;
If false the charge, I then shall show regard
330   For a good man, and be his just reward;
And what for Virtue can I better do,
Than to reclaim him, if the charge be true?'

She spoke; nor more her holy work delayed,
'Twas time to lend an erring mortal aid;
'The noblest way,' she judged, 'a soul to win,
Was with an act of kindness to begin,
To make the sinner sure, and then to attack the sin.'*

---

* As the Author's purpose in this Tale may be mistaken, he wishes to observe, that conduct like that of the Lady's here described must be meritorious or censurable just as the motives to it are pure or selfish; that these motives may in a great measure be concealed from the mind of the agent; and that we often take credit to our virtue, for actions which spring originally from our tempers, inclinations, or our indifference. It cannot therefore be improper, much less immoral, to give an instance of such self-deception.

THE LOVER'S JOURNEY

The Sun is in the heavens, and the proud day,
Attended with the pleasures of the world,
Is all too wanton.
King John, Act III. Scene 3.

The Lunatic, the Lover, and the Poet,
Are of imagination all compact.
Midsummer Night's Dream.

Oh! how this spring of Love resembleth
   Th' uncertain glory of an April day,
Which now shows all her beauty to the Sun,
   And by and by a cloud bears all away.

And happily I have arriv'd at last
Unto the wish'd haven of my bliss.
Taming of the Shrew, Act V. Scene 1.

It is the Soul that sees; the outward eyes
Present the object, but the Mind descries;
And thence delight, disgust, or cool indifference rise:
When minds are joyful, then we look around,
And what is seen is all on fairy ground;
Again they sicken, and on every view
Cast their own dull and melancholy hue;
Or, if absorbed by their peculiar cares,
The vacant eye on viewless matter glares;
Our feelings still upon our views attend,
And their own natures to the objects lend;
Sorrow and joy are in their influence sure,

Long as the passion reigns the effects endure;
But Love in minds his various changes makes,
And clothes each object with the change he takes;
His light and shade on every view he throws,
And on each object, what he feels, bestows.

Fair was the morning, and the month was June,
When rose a Lover; Love awakens soon;
Brief his repose, yet much he dreamt the while   20
Of that day's meeting, and his *Laura*'s smile;
Fancy and Love that name assigned to her,
Called *Susan* in the parish-register;
And he no more was *John* – his *Laura* gave
The name *Orlando* to her faithful slave.

Bright shone the glory of the rising day,
When the fond traveller took his favourite way;
He mounted gaily, felt his bosom light,
And all he saw was pleasing in his sight.

'Ye hours of expectation, quickly fly,   30
And bring on hours of blessed reality;
When I shall *Laura* see, beside her stand,
Hear her sweet voice, and press her yielded hand.'

First o'er a barren heath beside the coast
Orlando rode, and joy began to boast.

'This neat low gorse,' said he, 'with golden bloom,
Delights each sense, is beauty, is perfume;
And this gay ling, with all its purple flowers,
A man at leisure might admire for hours;
This green-fringed cup-moss has a scarlet tip,   40
That yields to nothing but my *Laura*'s lip;
And then how fine this herbage! men may say
A heath is barren, nothing is so gay;
Barren or bare to call such charming scene,
Argues a mind possessed by care and spleen.'

Onward he went and fiercer grew the heat,

Dust rose in clouds before the horse's feet;
For now he passed through lanes of burning sand,
Bounds to thin crops or yet uncultured land;
50   Where the dark poppy flourished on the dry
And sterile soil, and mocked the thin-set rye.

'How lovely this!' the rapt *Orlando* said,
'With what delight is labouring man repaid!
The very lane has sweets that all admire,
The rambling suckling and the vigorous briar;
See! wholesome wormwood grows beside the way,
Where, dew-pressed yet, the dog-rose bends the spray;
Fresh herbs the fields, fair shrubs the banks adorn,
And snow-white bloom falls flaky from the thorn;
60   No fostering hand they need, no sheltering wall,
They spring uncultured and they bloom for all.'

The Lover rode as hasty lovers ride,
And reached a common pasture wild and wide;
Small black-legged sheep devour with hunger keen
The meagre herbage, fleshless, lank and lean;
Such o'er thy level turf, *Newmarket!* stray,
And there, with other *Black-legs*, find their prey:
He saw some scattered hovels; turf was piled
In square brown stacks; a prospect bleak and wild!
70   A mill, indeed, was in the centre found,
With short sear herbage withering all around;
A smith's black shed opposed a wright's long shop,
And joined an inn where humble travellers stop.

'Aye, this is Nature,' said the gentle 'Squire;
'This ease, peace, pleasure – who would not admire?
With what delight these sturdy children play,
And joyful rustics at the close of day;
Sport follows labour, on this even space
Will soon commence the wrestling and the race;
80   Then will the Village-Maidens leave their home,

And to the dance with buoyant spirits come;
No affectation in their looks is seen,
Nor know they what disguise or flattery mean;
Nor aught to move an envious pang they see,
Easy their service, and their love is free;
Hence early springs that love, it long endures,
And life's first comfort, while they live, ensures:
They the low roof and rustic comforts prize,
Nor cast on prouder mansions envying eyes:
Sometimes the news at yonder town they hear,   90
And learn what busier mortals feel and fear,
Secure themselves, although by tales amazed,
Of towns bombarded and of cities razed;
As if they doubted, in their still retreat,
The very news that makes their quiet sweet,
And their days happy – happier only knows
He on whom *Laura* her regard bestows.'

On rode *Orlando*, counting all the while
The miles he passed and every coming mile;
Like all attracted things, he quicker flies,   100
The place approaching where the attraction lies;
When next appeared a *dam*, – so call the place, –
Where lies a road confined in narrow space;
A work of labour, for on either side
Is level fen, a prospect wild and wide,
With dykes on either hand by Ocean's self supplied:
Far on the right, the distant sea is seen,
And salt the springs that feed the marsh between;
Beneath an ancient bridge, the straitened flood
Rolls through its sloping banks of slimy mud;   110
Near it a sunken boat resists the tide,
That frets and hurries to the opposing side;
The rushes sharp, that on the borders grow,
Bend their brown florets to the stream below,
Impure in all its course, in all its progress slow:

Here a grave* *Flora* scarcely deigns to bloom,
Nor wears a rosy blush, nor sheds perfume;
The few dull flowers that o'er the place are spread,
Partake the nature of their fenny bed;
120   Here on its wiry stem, in rigid bloom,
Grows the salt lavender that lacks perfume;
Here the dwarf sallows creep, the septfoil harsh,
And the soft slimy mallow of the marsh;
Low on the ear the distant billows sound,
And just in view appears their stony bound;
No hedge nor tree conceals the glowing sun,
Birds, save a watery tribe, the district shun,
Nor chirp among the reeds where bitter waters run.

'Various as beauteous, Nature, is thy face,'
130   Exclaimed *Orlando*; 'all that grows has grace;
All are appropriate – bog, and marsh, and fen,
Are only poor to undiscerning men;
Here may the nice and curious eye explore,
How Nature's hand adorns the rushy moor;
Here the rare moss in secret shade is found,
Here the sweet myrtle of the shaking ground;
Beauties are these that from the view retire,
But well repay the attention they require;
For these, my *Laura* will her home forsake,
140   And all the pleasures they afford partake.'

* The ditches of a Fen so near the Ocean are lined with irregular patches of a coarse and stained Laver; a muddy sediment rests on the Horse-tail, and other perennial herbs, which in part conceal the shallowness of the stream; a fat-leaved pale-flowering Scurvy-grass appears early in the year, and the razor-edged Bull-rush in the summer and autumn. The Fen itself has a dark and saline herbage; there are Rushes and *Arrow-head*, and in a few patches the flakes of the Cotton-grass are seen, but more commonly the *Sea-aster*, the dullest of that numerous and hardy genus: a *Thrift*, blue in flower, but withering and remaining withered till the winter scatters it; the *Saltwort*, both simple and shrubby; a few kinds of grass changed by their soil and atmosphere, and low plants of two or three denominations undistinguished in a general view of the scenery: – such is the vegetation of the Fen when it is at a small distance from the Ocean; and in this case there arise from it effluvia strong and peculiar, half-saline, half-putrid, which would be considered by most people as offensive, and by some as dangerous; but there are others to whom singularity of taste or association of ideas has rendered it agreeable and pleasant.

Again, the country was enclosed, a wide
And sandy road has banks on either side;
Where, lo! a hollow on the left appeared,
And there a Gipsy-tribe their tent had reared;
'Twas open spread, to catch the morning sun,
And they had now their early meal begun,
When two brown Boys just left their grassy seat,
The early Traveller with their prayers to greet:
While yet *Orlando* held his pence in hand,
He saw their Sister on her duty stand;   150
Some twelve years old, demure, affected, sly,
Prepared the force of early powers to try;
Sudden a look of languor he descries,
And well-feigned apprehension in her eyes;
Trained but yet savage, in her speaking face,
He marked the features of her vagrant race;
When a light laugh and roguish leer expressed
The vice implanted in her youthful breast:
Forth from the tent her elder Brother came,
Who seemed offended, yet forbore to blame   160
The young designer, but could only trace
The looks of pity in the Traveller's face:
Within, the Father, who from fences nigh
Had brought the fuel for the fire's supply,
Watched now the feeble blaze, and stood dejected by:
On ragged rug, just borrowed from the bed,
And by the hand of coarse indulgence fed,
In dirty patchwork negligently dressed,
Reclined the Wife, an infant at her breast:
In her wild face some touch of grace remained,   170
Of vigour palsied and of beauty stained;
Her blood-shot eyes on her unheeding mate
Were wrathful turned, and seemed her wants to state,
Cursing his tardy aid – her Mother there
With Gipsy-state engrossed the only chair;
Solemn and dull her look; with such she stands,
And reads the Milk-maid's fortune in her hands,

Tracing the lines of life; assumed through years,
Each feature now the steady falsehood wears;
180   With hard and savage eye she views the food,
And grudging pinches their intruding brood:
Last in the group, the worn-out Grandsire sits
Neglected, lost, and living but by fits;
Useless, despised, his worthless labours done,
And half protected by the vicious Son,
Who half supports him; he with heavy glance,
Views the young ruffians who around him dance;
And, by the sadness in his face, appears
To trace the progress of their future years;
190   Through what strange course of misery, vice, deceit,
Must wildly wander each unpractised cheat;
What shame and grief, what punishment and pain,
Sport of fierce passions, must each child sustain –
Ere they like him approach their latter end,
Without a hope, a comfort, or a friend!

But this *Orlando* felt not; 'Rogues,' said he,
'Doubtless they are, but merry rogues they be;
They wander round the land, and be it true,
They break the laws – then let the laws pursue
200   The wanton idlers; for the life they live,
Acquit I cannot, but I can forgive.'
This said, a portion from his purse was thrown,
And every heart seemed happy like his own.

He hurried forth, for now the town was nigh –
'The happiest man of mortal men am I.'
Thou art! but change in every state is near,
(So while the wretched hope, the blessed may fear;)
'Say where is *Laura?*' – 'That her words must show,'
A lass replied; 'read this and thou shalt know!'

210   'What, gone!' – her friend insisted – forced to go: –
'Is vexed, was teased, could not refuse her! – No?'
'But you can follow;' 'Yes;' 'the miles are few,
The way is pleasant; will you come? – Adieu!

Thy *Laura!* 'No! I feel I must resign
The pleasing hope, thou hadst been here, if mine:
A lady was it? – Was no Brother there?
But why should I afflict me, if there were?'
'The way is pleasant:' 'What to me the way?
I cannot reach her till the close of day.
My dumb companion! is it thus we speed?   220
Not I from grief nor thou from toil art freed;
Still art thou doomed to travel and to pine,
For my vexation – What a fate is mine!

  'Gone to a friend, she tells me; I commend
Her purpose; means she to a female friend?
By Heaven, I wish she suffered half the pain
Of hope protracted through the day in vain:
Shall I persist to see the ungrateful Maid?
Yes, I will see her, slight her and upbraid;
What! in the very hour? She knew the time,   230
And doubtless chose it to increase her crime.'

  Forth rode *Orlando* by a river's side,
Inland and winding, smooth and full and wide,
That rolled majestic on, in one soft-flowing tide;
The bottom gravel, flowery were the banks,
Tall willows waving in their broken ranks;
The road, now near, now distant, winding led
By lovely meadows which the waters fed;
He passed the way-side inn, the village spire,
Nor stopped to gaze, to question, or admire;   240
On either side the rural mansions stood,
With hedge-row trees and hills high-crowned with wood,
And many a devious stream that reached the nobler flood.

  'I hate these scenes,' *Orlando* angry cried,
'And these proud farmers! yes, I hate their pride;
See! that sleek fellow, how he strides along,
Strong as an ox, and ignorant as strong;
Can yon close crops a single eye detain,
But his who counts the profits of the grain?

250 And these vile beans with deleterious smell,
Where is their beauty? can a mortal tell?
These deep fat meadows I detest; it shocks
One's feelings there to see the grazing ox; –
For slaughter fatted, as a lady's smile
Rejoices man and means his death the while.
Lo! now the sons of labour! every day
Employed in toil, and vexed in every way;
Theirs is but mirth assumed, and they conceal,
In their affected joys, the ills they feel;
260 I hate these long green lanes; there's nothing seen
In this vile country but eternal green;
Woods! waters! meadows! will they never end?
'Tis a vile prospect: – Gone to see a friend! –'

    Still on he rode! – a mansion fair and tall
Rose on his view, – the pride of *Loddon-Hall*;
Spread o'er the park he saw the grazing steer,
The full-fed steed, and herds of bounding deer:
On a clear stream the vivid sun-beams played,
Through noble elms, and on the surface made
270 That moving picture, chequered light and shade;
The attended children, there indulged to stray,
Enjoyed and gave new beauty to the day;
Whose happy parents from their room were seen
Pleased with the sportive idlers on the green.

    'Well!' said *Orlando*, 'and for one so blessed,
A thousand reasoning wretches are distressed;
Nay, these so seeming glad, are grieving like the rest:
Man is a cheat – and all but strive to hide
Their inward misery by their outward pride.
280 What do yon lofty gates and walls contain,
But fruitless means to soothe unconquered pain?
The parents read each infant daughter's smile,
Formed to seduce, encouraged to beguile;
They view the boys unconscious of their fate,
Sure to be tempted, sure to take the bait;

These will be *Lauras*, sad *Orlandos* these –
There's guilt and grief in all one hears and sees.'

 Our Traveller, labouring up a hill, looked down
Upon a lively, busy, pleasant town;
All he beheld were there alert, alive,
The busiest bees that ever stocked a hive;   290
A pair were married, and the bells aloud
Proclaimed their joy, and joyful seemed the crowd;
And now proceeding on his way, he spied,
Bound by strong ties, the Bridegroom and the Bride;
Each by some friends attended, near they drew,
And Spleen beheld them with prophetic view.

 'Married! nay, mad!' *Orlando* cried in scorn;
'Another wretch on this unlucky morn;
What are this foolish mirth, these idle joys?   300
Attempts to stifle doubt and fear by noise:
To me these robes, expressive of delight,
Foreshow distress, and only grief excite;
And for these cheerful friends, will they behold
Their wailing brood in sickness, want, and cold;
And his proud look, and her soft languid air
Will – but I spare you – go, unhappy pair!'

 And now approaching to the journey's end,
His anger fails, his thoughts to kindness tend,
He less offended feels! and rather fears to offend: 310
Now gently rising, Hope contends with Doubt,
And casts a sun-shine on the views without;
And still reviving Joy and lingering Gloom,
Alternate empire o'er his soul assume;
Till, long perplexed, he now began to find
The softer thoughts engross the settling mind:
He saw the mansion, and should quickly see
His *Laura*'s self – and angry could he be?
No! the resentment melted all away –
'For this my grief a single smile will pay,'   320

Our Traveller cried; – 'And why should it offend,
That one so good should have a pressing friend?
Grieve not, my heart! to find a favourite guest
Thy pride and boast – ye selfish sorrows, rest;
She will be kind, and I again be blessed.

While gentler passions thus his bosom swayed,
He reached the mansion, and he saw the Maid;
'My *Laura!*' – 'My *Orlando!* – this is kind;
In truth I came persuaded, not inclined;
330   Our friends' amusement let us now pursue,
And I tomorrow will return with you.'

Like man entranced, the happy Lover stood –
'As *Laura* wills, for she is kind and good;
Ever the truest, gentlest, fairest, best –
As *Laura* wills, I see her and am blessed.'

Home went the Lovers through that busy place,
By *Loddon-Hall*, the country's pride and grace;
By the rich meadows where the oxen fed,
Through the green vale that formed the river's bed;
340   And by unnumbered cottages and farms,
That have for musing minds unnumbered charms;
And how affected by the view of these
Was then *Orlando* – did they pain or please?

Nor pain nor pleasure could they yield – and why?
The mind was filled, was happy, and the eye
Roved o'er the fleeting views, that but appeared to die.

Alone *Orlando* on the morrow paced
The well-known road; the Gipsy-tent he traced;
The dam high-raised, the reedy dykes between,
350   The scattered hovels on the barren green,
The burning sand, the fields of thin-set rye,
Mocked by the useless *Flora*, blooming by;
And last the heath with all its various bloom,
And the close lanes that led the Traveller home.

Then could these scenes the former joys renew?
Or was there now dejection in the view? –
Nor one nor other would they yield – and why?
The mind was absent, and the vacant eye
Wandered o'er viewless scenes, that but appeared to die.

TALE XI
EDWARD SHORE

Seem they grave or learned?
Why, so didst thou – Seem they religious?
Why, so didst thou; or are they spare in diet,
Free from gross passion, or of mirth or anger,
Constant in spirit, not swerving with the blood,
Garnish'd and deck'd in modest compliment,
Not working with the eye without the ear,
And but with purged judgment trusting neither?
Such and so finely bolted didst thou seem.
Henry V, Act II. Scene 2.

Better I were distract,
So should my thoughts be sever'd from my griefs,
And woes by strong imagination lose
The knowledge of themselves.
Lear, Act IV. Scene 6.

Genius! thou gift of Heaven! thou light divine!
Amid what dangers art thou doomed to shine!
Oft will the body's weakness check thy force,
Oft damp thy vigour, and impede thy course;
And trembling nerves compel thee to restrain
Thy nobler efforts, to contend with pain;
Or Want (sad guest!) will in thy presence come,
And breathe around her melancholy gloom;
To life's low cares will thy proud thought confine,
And make her sufferings, her impatience, thine.

Evil and strong, seducing passions prey
On soaring minds, and win them from their way;

Who then to Vice the subject spirits give,
And in the service of the conqueror live;
Like captive *Sampson* making sport for all,
Who feared their strength, and glory in their fall.

Genius, with virtue, still may lack the aid
Implored by humble minds and hearts afraid;
May leave to timid souls the shield and sword
Of the tried Faith, and the resistless Word;   20
Amid a world of dangers venturing forth,
Frail, but yet fearless, proud in conscious worth,
Till strong temptation, in some fatal time,
Assails the heart, and wins the soul to Crime;
When left by Honour, and by Sorrow spent,
Unused to pray, unable to repent;
The nobler powers, that once exalted high
The aspiring man, shall then degraded lie;
Reason, through anguish, shall her throne forsake,
And strength of mind but stronger madness make.   30

When *Edward Shore* had reached his twentieth year,
He felt his bosom light, his conscience clear;
Applause at school the youthful hero gained
And trials there with manly strength sustained:
With prospects bright upon the world he came,
Pure love of virtue, strong desire of fame;
Men watched the way his lofty mind would take,
And all foretold the progress he would make.

Boast of these friends, to older men a guide,
Proud of his parts, but gracious in his pride;   40
He bore a gay good-nature in his face,
And in his air was dignity and grace;
Dress that became his state and years he wore,
And sense and spirit shone in *Edward Shore*.

Thus while admiring friends the Youth beheld,
His own disgust their forward hopes repelled;
For he unfixed, unfixing looked around,

And no employment but in seeking found;
He gave his restless thoughts to views refined,
And shrank from worldly cares with wounded mind.

Rejecting trade; awhile he dwelt on laws,
'But who could plead, if unapproved the cause?'
A doubting, dismal tribe physicians seemed,
Divines o'er texts and disputations dreamed;
War and its glory he perhaps could love,
But there again he must the cause approve.

Our Hero thought no deed should gain applause,
Where timid virtue found support in laws;
He to all good would soar, would fly all sin,
By the pure prompting of the will within;
'Who needs a law that binds him not to steal,'
Asked the young teacher, 'can he rightly feel?
To curb the will, or arm in honour's cause,
Or aid the weak – are these enforced by laws?
Should we a foul, ungenerous action dread,
Because a law condemns the adulterous bed?
Or fly pollution, not for fear of stain,
But that some statute tells us to refrain?
The grosser herd in ties like these we bind,
In virtue's freedom moves the enlightened mind.'

'Man's heart deceives him,' said a friend: 'Of course,'
Replied the Youth, 'but, has it power to force?
Unless it forces, call it as you will,
It is but wish, and proneness to the ill.'

'Art thou not tempted?' 'Do I fall?' said *Shore;*
'The pure have fallen,' – 'Then are pure no more;
While reason guides me, I shall walk aright,
Nor need a steadier hand, or stronger light;
Nor this in dread of awful threats, designed
For the weak spirit and the grovelling mind;
But that, engaged by thoughts and views sublime,

I wage free war with grossness and with crime.'
Thus looked he proudly on the vulgar crew,
Whom statutes govern, and whom fears subdue.

Faith, with his virtue, he indeed professed,
But doubts deprived his ardent mind of rest;
Reason, his sovereign mistress, failed to show
Light through the mazes of the world below;
Questions arose, and they surpassed the skill
Of his sole aid, and would be dubious still;   90
These to discuss he sought no common guide,
But to the doubters in his doubts applied;
When all together might in freedom speak,
And their loved truth with mutual ardour seek.
Alas! though men who feel their eyes decay
Take more than common pains to find their way,
Yet, when for this they ask each other's aid,
Their mutual purpose is the more delayed:
Of all their doubts, their reasoning cleared not one,
Still the same spots were present in the sun;   100
Still the same scruples haunted *Edward*'s mind,
Who found no rest, nor took the means to find.

But though with shaken faith, and slave to fame,
Vain and aspiring on the world he came;
Yet was he studious, serious, moral, grave,
No passion's victim, and no system's slave;
Vice he opposed, indulgence he disdained,
And o'er each sense in conscious triumph reigned.

Who often reads, will sometimes wish to write,
And *Shore* would yield instruction and delight;   110
A serious drama he designed, but found
'Twas tedious travelling in that gloomy ground;
A deep and solemn story he would try,
But grew ashamed of ghosts, and laid it by;
Sermons he wrote, but they who knew his creed,
Or knew it not, were ill disposed to read;

And he would lastly be the nation's guide,
But, studying, failed to fix upon a side;
Fame he desired, and talents he possessed,
120 But loved not labour, though he could not rest,
Nor firmly fix the vacillating mind,
That, ever working, could no centre find.

   'Tis thus a sanguine Reader loves to trace
The *Nile* forth rushing on his glorious race;
Calm and secure the fancied Traveller goes
Through sterile deserts and by threatening foes:
He thinks not then of *Africk*'s scorching sands,
The Arabian sea, the Abyssinian bands;
*Fasils** and *Michaels*, and the robbers all,
130 Whom we politely chiefs and heroes call;
He of success alone delights to think,
He views that fount, he stands upon the brink,
And drinks a fancied draught, exulting so to drink.

   In his own room, and with his books around,
His lively mind its chief employment found;
Then idly busy, quietly employed,
And, lost to life, his visions were enjoyed:
Yet still he took a keen inquiring view,
Of all that crowds neglect, desire, pursue;
140 And thus abstracted, curious, still, serene,
He, unemployed, beheld life's shifting scene;
Still more averse from vulgar joys and cares,
Still more unfitted for the world's affairs.

   There was a house where *Edward* ofttimes went,
And social hours in pleasant trifling spent;
He read, conversed and reasoned, sang and played,

---

* *Fasil* was a Rebel Chief, and *Michael* the General of the Royal army in *Abyssinia*, when Mr. Bruce visited that country. In all other respects their characters were nearly similar. They are both represented as cruel and treacherous; and even the apparently strong distinction of *loyal* and *rebellious* is in a great measure set aside, when we are informed that *Fasil* was an open enemy, and *Michael* an insolent and ambitious controller of the Royal person and family.

And all were happy while the idler stayed;
Too happy one, for thence arose the pain,
Till this engaging trifler came again.

But did he love? We answer, day by day,   150
The loving feet would take the accustomed way;
The amorous eye would rove as if in quest
Of something rare, and on the mansion rest;
The same soft passion touched the gentle tongue,
And *Anna*'s charms in tender notes were sung;
The ear too seemed to feel the common flame,
Soothed and delighted with the fair-one's name;
And thus as love each other part possessed,
The heart, no doubt, its sovereign power confessed.

Pleased in her sight, the Youth required no more;   160
Not rich himself, he saw the Damsel poor;
And he too wisely, nay, too kindly loved,
To pain the being whom his soul approved.

A serious Friend our cautious Youth possessed,
And at his table sat a welcome guest;
Both unemployed, it was their chief delight
To read what free and daring authors write;
Authors who loved from common views to soar,
And seek the fountains never traced before;
Truth they professed, yet often left the true   170
And beaten prospect, for the wild and new.
His chosen Friend his fiftieth year had seen,
His fortune easy, and his air serene;
Deist and Atheist called; for few agreed
What were his notions, principles, or creed;
His mind reposed not, for he hated rest,
But all things made a query or a jest;
Perplexed himself, he ever sought to prove
That man is doomed in endless doubt to rove;
Himself in darkness he professed to be,   180
And would maintain that not a man could see.

The youthful Friend, dissentient, reasoned still

Of the soul's prowess, and the subject-will;
Of virtue's beauty, and of honour's force,
And a warm zeal gave life to his discourse:
Since from his feelings all his fire arose,
And he had interest in the themes he chose.

The Friend, indulging a sarcastic smile,
Said – 'Dear Enthusiast! thou wilt change thy style,
190   When Man's delusions, errors, crimes, deceit,
No more distress thee, and no longer cheat.'

Yet lo! this cautious Man, so coolly wise,
On a young beauty fixed unguarded eyes;
And her he married: *Edward* at the view
Bade to his cheerful visits long adieu;
But haply erred, for this engaging Bride
No mirth suppressed, but rather cause supplied:
And when she saw the friends, by reasoning long,
Confused if right, and positive if wrong;
200   With playful speech and smile, that spoke delight,
She made them careless both of wrong and right.

This gentle Damsel gave consent to wed,
With school and school-day dinners in her head:
She now was promised choice of daintiest food,
And costly dress, that made her sovereign good;
With walks on hilly heath to banish spleen,
And summer-visits when the roads were clean.
All these she loved, to these she gave consent,
And she was married to her heart's content.

210   Their manner this – the Friends together read,
Till books a cause for disputation bred;
Debate then followed, and the vapoured Child
Declared they argued till her head was wild;
And strange to her it was that mortal brain
Could seek the trial, or endure the pain.

Then as the Friend reposed, the younger Pair

Sat down to cards, and played beside his chair;
Till he awaking, to his books applied,
Or heard the music of the obedient Bride:
If mild the evening, in the fields they strayed,   220
And their own flock with partial eye surveyed;
But oft the Husband, to indulgence prone,
Resumed his book, and bade them walk alone.

'Do, my kind *Edward!* I must take mine ease,
Name the dear girl the planets and the trees;
Tell her what warblers pour their evening song,
What insects flutter, as you walk along;
Teach her to fix the roving thoughts, to bind
The wandering sense, and methodize the mind.'

This was obeyed; and oft when this was done   230
They calmly gazed on the declining sun;
In silence saw the glowing landscape fade,
Or, sitting, sang beneath the arbor's shade:
Till rose the moon, and on each youthful face,
Shed a soft beauty, and a dangerous grace.

When the young Wife beheld in long debate
The Friends, all careless as she seeming sate;
It soon appeared, there was in one combined
The nobler person, and the richer mind:
He wore no wig, no grisly beard was seen,   240
And none beheld him careless or unclean;
Or watched him sleeping: – we indeed have heard
Of sleeping beauty, and it has appeared;
'Tis seen in infants, there indeed we find
The features softened by the slumbering mind;
But other beauties, when disposed to sleep,
Should from the eye of keen inspector keep:
The lovely nymph who would her swain surprise,
May close her mouth, but not conceal her eyes;
Sleep from the fairest face some beauty takes,   250
And all the homely features, homelier makes;

So thought our Wife, beholding with a sigh
Her sleeping Spouse, and *Edward* smiling by.

A sick Relation for the Husband sent,
Without delay the friendly Sceptic went;
Nor feared the youthful Pair, for he had seen
The Wife untroubled, and the Friend serene;
No selfish purpose in his roving eyes,
No vile deception in her fond replies:
So judged the Husband, and with judgement true,
For neither yet the guilt or danger knew.

What now remained? but they again should play
The accustomed game, and walk the accustomed way;
With careless freedom should converse or read,
And the Friend's absence neither fear nor heed:
But rather now they seemed confused, constrained;
Within their room still restless they remained,
And painfully they felt, and knew each other pained. —
Ah! foolish men! how could ye thus depend
One on himself, the other on his friend?

The Youth with troubled eye the Lady saw,
Yet felt too brave, too daring to withdraw;
While she, with tuneless hand the jarring keys
Touching, was not one moment at her ease;
Now would she walk, and call her friendly Guide,
Now speak of rain, and cast her cloak aside;
Seize on a book, unconscious what she read,
And restless still to new resources fled;
Then laughed aloud, then tried to look serene,
And ever changed, and every change was seen.

Painful it is to dwell on deeds of shame —
The trying day was past, another came;
The third was all remorse, confusion, dread,
And (all too late!) the fallen Hero fled.

Then felt the Youth, in that seducing time,
How feebly Honour guards the heart from crime:
Small is his native strength; man needs the stay,
The strength imparted in the trying day;
For all that Honour brings against the force
Of headlong passion, aids its rapid course; 290
Its slight resistance but provokes the fire,
As wood-work stops the flame, and then conveys it higher.

The Husband came; a Wife by guilt made bold
Had, meeting, soothed him, as in days of old;
But soon this fact transpired; her strong distress,
And his Friend's absence, left him nought to guess.

Still cool, though grieved, thus prudence bade him write –
'I cannot pardon, and I will not fight;
Thou art too poor a culprit for the laws,
And I too faulty to support my cause: 300
All must be punished; I must sigh alone,
At home thy victim for her guilt atone;
And thou, unhappy! virtuous now no more,
Must loss of fame, peace, purity deplore;
Sinners with praise will pierce thee to the heart,
And Saints, deriding, tell thee what thou art.'

Such was his fall; and *Edward*, from that time,
Felt in full force the censure and the crime –
Despised, ashamed; his noble views before,
And his proud thoughts, degraded him the more: 310
Should he repent – would that conceal his shame?
Could peace be his? It perished with his fame:
Himself he scorned, nor could his crime forgive, –
He feared to die, yet felt ashamed to live:
Grieved, but not contrite was his heart; oppressed,
Not broken; not converted, but distressed;
He wanted will to bend the stubborn knee,
He wanted light the cause of ill to see,
To learn how frail is man, how humble then should be;

320 For faith he had not, or a faith too weak
To gain the help that humbled sinners seek;
Else had he prayed – to an offended God
His tears had flown a penitential flood;
Though far astray, he would have heard the call
Of mercy – 'Come! return thou prodigal;'
Then, though confused, distressed, ashamed, afraid,
Still had the trembling penitent obeyed;
Though faith had fainted, when assailed by fear,
Hope to the soul had whispered, 'Persevere!'
330 Till in his Father's house an humbled guest,
He would have found forgiveness, comfort, rest.

 But all this joy was to our Youth denied,
By his fierce passions and his daring pride;
And shame and doubt impelled him in a course
Once so abhorred, with unresisted force.
Proud minds and guilty, whom their crimes oppress,
Fly to new crimes for comfort and redress;
So found our fallen Youth a short relief
In wine, the opiate Guilt applies to Grief, –
340 From fleeting mirth that o'er the bottle lives,
From the false joy its inspiration gives;
And from associates pleased to find a friend,
With powers to lead them, gladden, and defend,
In all those scenes where transient ease is found,
For minds whom sins oppress, and sorrows wound.

 Wine is like anger; for it makes us strong,
Blind and impatient, and it leads us wrong;
The strength is quickly lost, we feel the error long;
Thus led, thus strengthened in an evil cause,
350 For folly pleading, sought the Youth applause;
Sad for a time, then eloquently wild,
He gaily spoke, as his companions smiled;
Lightly he rose, and with his former grace
Proposed some doubt, and argued on the case;
Fate and fore-knowledge were his favourite themes –

How vain man's purpose, how absurd his schemes:
'Whatever is, was ere our birth decreed;
We think our actions from ourselves proceed,
And idly we lament the inevitable deed;
It seems our own, but there's a power above   360
Directs the motion, nay, that makes us move;
Nor good nor evil can you beings name,
Who are but Rooks and Castles in the game;
Superior natures with their puppets play,
Till, bagged or buried, all are swept away.'

Such were the notions of a mind to ill
Now prone, but ardent and determined still;
Of joy now eager, as before of fame,
And screened by folly when assailed by shame,
Deeply he sank; obeyed each passion's call,   370
And used his reason to defend them all.

Shall I proceed, and step by step relate
The odious progress of a Sinner's fate?
No — let me rather hasten to the time
(Sure to arrive) when misery waits on crime.

With Virtue, Prudence fled; what *Shore* possessed
Was sold, was spent, and he was now distressed;
And Want, unwelcome stranger, pale and wan
Met with her haggard looks the hurried Man;
His pride felt keenly what he must expect   380
From useless pity and from cold neglect.

Struck by new terrors, from his friends he fled,
And wept his woes upon a restless bed;
Retiring late, at early hour to rise,
With shrunken features, and with bloodshot eyes;
If sleep one moment closed the dismal view,
Fancy her terrors built upon the true;
And night and day had their alternate woes,
That baffled pleasure, and that mocked repose;

390   Till to despair and anguish was consigned,
The wreck and ruin of a noble mind.

   Now seized for debt, and lodged within a jail,
He tried his friendships, and he found them fail;
Then failed his spirits, and his thoughts were all
Fixed on his sins, his sufferings, and his fall:
His ruffled mind was pictured in his face,
Once the fair seat of dignity and grace:
Great was the danger of a man so prone
To think of madness, and to think alone;
400   Yet pride still lived, and struggled to sustain
The drooping spirit, and the roving brain;
But this too failed: a Friend his freedom gave,
And sent him help the threatening world to brave;
Gave solid counsel what to seek or flee,
But still would stranger to his person be:
In vain! the truth determined to explore,
He traced the Friend whom he had wronged before.

   This was too much; both aided and advised
By one who shunned him, pitied, and despised:
410   He bore it not: 'twas a deciding stroke,
And on his reason like a torrent broke;
In dreadful stillness he appeared awhile,
With vacant horror, and a ghastly smile;
Then rose at once into the frantic rage,
That force controlled not, nor could love assuage.

   Friends now appeared, but in the Man was seen
The angry Maniac, with vindictive mien;
Too late their pity gave to care and skill
The hurried mind and ever-wandering will;
420   Unnoticed passed all time, and not a ray
Of reason broke on his benighted way;
But now he spurned the straw in pure disdain,
And now laughed loudly at the clinking chain.

   Then as its wrath subsided, by degrees
The mind sank slowly to infantine ease;

To playful folly, and to causeless joy,
Speech without aim, and without end, employ;
He drew fantastic figures on the wall,
And gave some wild relation of them all;
With brutal shape he joined the human face,   430
And idiot smiles approved the motley race.

  Harmless at length the unhappy man was found,
The spirit settled, but the reason drowned;
And all the dreadful tempest died away
To the dull stillness of the misty day.

  And now his freedom he attained, – if free
The lost to reason, truth, and hope, can be;
His friends, or wearied with the charge, or sure
The harmless wretch was now beyond a cure,
Gave him to wander where he pleased, and find   440
His own resources for the eager mind:
The playful children of the place he meets,
Playful with them he rambles through the streets;
In all they need, his stronger arm he lends,
And his lost mind to these approving friends.

  That gentle Maid, whom once the Youth had loved,
Is now with mild religious pity moved;
Kindly she chides his boyish flights, while he
Will for a moment fixed and pensive be;
And as she trembling speaks, his lively eyes   450
Explore her looks, he listens to her sighs;
Charmed by her voice, the harmonious sounds invade
His clouded mind, and for a time persuade:
Like a pleased Infant, who has newly caught
From the maternal glance a gleam of thought;
He stands enrapt, the half-known voice to hear,
And starts, half-conscious, at the falling tear.

  Rarely from town, nor then unwatched, he goes,
In darker mood, as if to hide his woes;
Returning soon, he with impatience seeks   460

His youthful friends, and shouts, and sings, and speaks;
Speaks a wild speech with action all as wild –
The children's leader, and himself a child;
He spins their top, or, at their bidding, bends
His back, while o'er it leap his laughing friends;
Simple and weak, he acts the boy once more,
And heedless children call him *Silly Shore*.

'SQUIRE THOMAS;

OR,

THE PRECIPITATE CHOICE

Such smiling rogues as these,
Like rats oft bite the holy cords in twain,
Too intrinsicate t' unloose. –
                                    Lear, Act II. Scene 2.

My other self, my Counsel's Consistory,
My Oracle, my Prophet, –
I as a Child will go by thy direction.
                                    Richard III, Act II. Scene 2.

If I do not have pity upon her, I'm a villain;
If I do not love her, I am a Jew.
                    Much Ado about Nothing, Act II. Scene 2.

Women are soft, mild, pitiable, flexible,
But thou art obdurate, flinty, rough, remorseless.
                                    3 Henry VI, Act I. Scene 4.

He must be told of it, and he shall, the office
Becomes a Woman best; I'll take it upon me:
If I prove honey-mouth'd, let my tongue blister.
                            Winter's Tale, Act II. Scene 2.

Disguise – I see thou art a wickedness.
                            Twelfth Night, Act II. Scene 2.

'Squire *Thomas* flattered long a wealthy Aunt,
Who left him all that she could give or grant;
Ten years he tried, with all his craft and skill,

To fix the sovereign Lady's varying will;
Ten years enduring at her board to sit,
He meekly listened to her tales and wit;
He took the meanest office man can take,
And his Aunt's vices for her money's sake:
By many a threatening hint she waked his fear,
And he was pained to see a rival near;
Yet all the taunts of her contemptuous pride
He bore, nor found his grovelling spirit tried;
Nay, when she wished his parents to traduce,
Fawning he smiled, and justice called the abuse;
'They taught you nothing, are you not at best,'
Said the proud Dame, 'a trifler, and a jest?
Confess you are a Fool!' – he bowed and he confessed.

This vexed him much, but could not always last;
The Dame is buried, and the trial past.

There was a Female, who had courted long
Her Cousin's gifts, and deeply felt the wrong;
By a vain Boy forbidden to attend
The private councils of her wealthy friend,
She vowed revenge, nor should that crafty boy
In triumph undisturbed his spoils enjoy:
He heard, he smiled, and when the Will was read,
Kindly dismissed the Kindred of the dead;
'The dear deceased,' he called her, and the crowd
Moved off with curses deep and threatenings loud.

The Youth retired, and, with a mind at ease,
Found he was rich, and fancied he must please:
He might have pleased, and to his comfort found
The Wife he wished, if he had sought around;
For there were Lasses of his own degree,
With no more hatred to the state than he:
But he had courted spleen and age so long,
His heart refused to woo the fair and young;
So long attended on caprice and whim,

He thought attention now was due to him;
And as his flattery pleased the wealthy Dame,   40
Heir to the wealth, he might the flattery claim;
But this the Fair, with one accord, denied,
Nor waived for Man's caprice the Sex's pride;
There is a season when to them is due
Worship and awe, and they will claim it too;
'Fathers,' they cry, 'long hold us in their chain,
Nay, tyrant Brothers claim a right to reign;
Uncles and Guardians we in turn obey,
And Husbands rule with ever-during sway;
Short is the time when Lovers at the feet   50
Of Beauty kneel, and own the slavery sweet;
And shall we this our triumph, this the aim
And boast of female power, forbear to claim?
No! we demand that homage, that respect,
Or the proud rebel punish and reject.'

Our Hero, still too indolent, too nice
To pay for Beauty the accustomed price,
No less forbore to address the humbler Maid,
Who might have yielded with the price unpaid;
But lived, himself to humour and to please,   60
To count his money, and enjoy his ease.

It pleased a neighbouring 'Squire to recommend
A faithful Youth, as servant to his friend;
Nay, more than servant, whom he praised for parts
Ductile yet strong, and for the best of hearts;
One who might ease him in his small affairs,
With tenants, tradesmen, taxes, and repairs;
Answer his letters, look to all his dues,
And entertain him with discourse and news.

The 'Squire believed, and found the trusted Youth   70
A very pattern for his care and truth;
Not for his virtues to be praised alone,
But for a modest mien and humble tone;

Assenting always, but as if he meant
Only to strength of reasons to assent;
For he was stubborn, and retained his doubt,
Till the more subtle 'Squire had forced it out;
'Nay, still was right, but he perceived that strong
And powerful minds could make the right the wrong.'

80   When the 'Squire's thoughts on some fair damsel dwelt,
The faithful Friend his apprehensions felt;
It would rejoice his faithful heart to find
A Lady suited to his Master's mind;
But who deserved that Master? who would prove
That hers was pure, uninterested love?
Although a Servant, he would scorn to take
A Countess, till she suffered for his sake;
Some tender spirit, humble, faithful, true,
Such, my dear Master! must be sought for you!

90   Six months had passed, and not a Lady seen,
With just this love, 'twixt fifty and fifteen;
All seemed his doctrine or his pride to shun,
All would be wooed, before they would be won;
When the chance naming of a race and fair,
Our 'Squire disposed to take his pleasure there:
The Friend professed, 'although he first began
To hint the thing, it seemed a thoughtless plan;
The roads, he feared, were foul, the days were short,
The village far, and yet there might be sport.'

100   'What! you of roads and starless nights afraid?
You think to govern! you to be obey'd!'
Smiling he spoke, the humble Friend declared
His soul's obedience, and to go prepared.

The place was distant, but with great delight
They saw a race, and hailed the glorious sight;
The 'Squire exulted, and declared the ride
Had amply paid, and he was satisfied.
They gazed, they feasted, and, in happy mood,

Homeward returned, and hastening as they rode;
For short the day, and sudden was the change   110
From light to darkness, and the way was strange;
Our Hero soon grew peevish, then distressed,
He dreaded darkness, and he sighed for rest:
Going, they passed a village; but, alas!
Returning saw no village to repass;
The 'Squire remembered too a noble hall,
Large as a church, and whiter than its wall;
This he had noticed as they rode along,
And justly reasoned that their road was wrong:
George, full of awe, was modest in reply, –   120
'The fault was his, 'twas folly to deny;
And of his Master's safety were he sure,
There was no grievance he would not endure.'
This made his peace with the relenting 'Squire,
Whose thoughts yet dwelt on supper and a fire;
When, as they reached a long and pleasant green,
Dwellings of men, and next a man, were seen.

  'My friend,' said *George*, 'to travellers astray
Point out an inn, and guide us on the way;'

The man looked up; 'Surprising! can it be   130
My Master's Son? as I'm alive, 'tis he.'

  'How! *Robin*,' *George* replied, 'and are we near
My Father's house? how strangely things appear! –
Dear Sir, though wanderers, we at last are right,
Let us proceed, and glad my Father's sight;
We shall at least be fairly lodged and fed,
I can insure a supper and a bed;
Let us this night, as one of pleasure date,
And of surprise: it is an act of Fate.'
'Go on,' the 'Squire in happy temper cried,   140
'I like such blunder! I approve such guide.'

  They ride, they halt, the Farmer comes in haste,
Then tells his Wife how much their house is graced;

They bless the chance, they praise the lucky Son,
That caused the error – Nay! it was not one;
But their good fortune – Cheerful grew the 'Squire,
Who found dependants, flattery, wine, and fire;
He heard the jack turn round; the busy Dame
Produced her damask, and with supper came,
150   The Daughter dressed with care, and full of maiden shame.

Surprised, our Hero saw the air and dress,
And strove his admiration to express;
Nay! felt it too – for *Harriot* was, in truth,
A tall fair beauty in the bloom of youth;
And from the pleasure and surprise, a grace
Adorned the blooming damsel's form and face;
Then too, such high respect and duty paid
By all – such silent reverence in the Maid;
Venturing with caution, yet with haste, a glance;
160   Loth to retire, yet trembling to advance,
Appeared the Nymph, and, in her gentle Guest,
Stirred soft emotions till the hour of rest:
Sweet was his sleep, and in the morn again
He felt a mixture of delight and pain:
'How fair, how gentle,' said the 'Squire, 'how meek,
And yet how sprightly, when disposed to speak!
Nature has blessed her form, and Heaven her mind,
But in her favours Fortune is unkind;
Poor is the Maid – nay, poor she cannot prove
170   Who is enriched with beauty, worth, and love.'

The 'Squire arose, with no precise intent
To go or stay – uncertain what he meant:
He moved to part – they begged him first to dine;
And who could then escape from Love and Wine?
As came the night, more charming grew the Fair,
And seemed to watch him with a two-fold care:
On the third morn resolving not to stay,
Though urged by Love, he bravely rode away.

Arrived at home, three pensive days he gave
To feelings fond and meditations grave;   180
Lovely she was, and, if he did not err,
As fond of him as his fond heart of her;
Still he delayed, unable to decide,
Which was the master-passion, Love or Pride:
He sometimes wondered how his friend could make,
And then exulted in, the night's mistake;
Had she but fortune, 'doubtless then,' he cried,
'Some happier man had won the wealthy bride.'

While thus he hung in balance, now inclined
To change his State, and then to change his Mind, –   190
That careless *George* dropped idly on the ground
A Letter, which his crafty Master found;
The stupid Youth confessed his fault, and prayed
The generous 'Squire to spare a gentle Maid;
Of whom her tender Mother, full of fears,
Had written much – 'She caught her oft in tears,
For ever thinking on a Youth above
Her humble fortune – still she owned not love;
Nor can define, dear Girl! the cherished pain,
But would rejoice to see the cause again: 200
That neighbouring youth, whom she endured before,
She now rejects, and will behold no more;
Raised by her passion, she no longer stoops,
To her own equals, but she pines and droops
Like to a lily, on whose sweets the Sun
Has withering gazed – she saw and was undone:
His wealth allured her not – nor was she moved
By his superior state, himself she loved;
So mild, so good, so gracious, so genteel, –
But spare your Sister, and her love conceal;   210
We must the fault forgive, since she the pain must feel.'

'Fault!' said the 'Squire, 'there's coarseness in the mind
That thus conceives of feelings so refined;
Here end my doubts, nor blame yourself, my friend,

Fate made you careless – here my doubts have end.'

    The way is plain before us – there is now
The Lover's visit first, and then the vow
Mutual and fond, the marriage-rite, the Bride
Brought to her home with all a husband's pride;
The 'Squire receives the prize his merits won,
And the glad Parents leave the Patron-Son.

    But in short time he saw with much surprise,
First gloom, then grief, and then resentment rise,
From proud commanding frowns and anger-darting eyes:
'Is there in *Harriot*'s humble mind this fire,
This fierce impatience?' asked the puzzled 'Squire:
'Has marriage changed her? or the mask she wore
Has she thrown by, and is herself once more?'

    Hour after hour, when clouds on clouds appear,
Dark and more dark, we know the tempest near;
And thus the frowning brow, the restless form,
And threatening glance, forerun domestic storm:
So read the Husband, and, with troubled mind,
Revealed his fears – 'My Love, I hope you find
All here is pleasant – but I must confess
You seem offended, or in some distress;
Explain the grief you feel, and leave me to redress.'

    'Leave it to you?' replied the Nymph – 'indeed!
What – to the cause from whence the ills proceed?
Good Heaven! to take me from a place, where I
Had every comfort underneath the sky;
And then immure me in a gloomy place,
With the grim Monsters of your ugly race,
That from their canvass staring, make me dread,
Through the dark chambers where they hang, to tread!
No friend nor neighbour comes to give that joy,
Which all things here must banish or destroy:
Where is the promised coach, the pleasant ride?
Oh! what a fortune has a Farmer's bride!

220

230

240

Your sordid pride has placed me just above 250
Your hired domestics – and what pays me? Love! –
A selfish fondness I endure each hour,
And share unwitnessed pomp, unenvied power;
I hear your folly, smile at your parade,
And see your favourite dishes duly made;
Then am I richly dressed for you to admire,
Such is my duty and my Lord's desire:
Is this a life for youth, for health, for joy?
Are these my duties – this my base employ?
No! to my Father's house will I repair, 260
And make your idle wealth support me there;
Was it your wish to have an humble Bride
For bondage thankful? Curse upon your pride!
Was it a slave you wanted? You shall see,
That, if not happy, I at least am free;
Well, Sir, your answer:' – silent stood the 'Squire,
As looks a Miser at his house on fire;
Where all, he deems, is vanished in that flame,
Swept from the earth his substance and his name;
So, lost to every promised joy of life, 270
Our 'Squire stood gaping at his angry Wife; –
His fate, his ruin, where he saw it vain,
To hope for peace, pray, threaten, or complain;
And thus, betwixt his wonder at the ill
And his despair – there stood he gaping still.

'Your answer, Sir, – shall I depart a spot
I thus detest?' – 'Oh miserable lot!'
Exclaimed the Man, 'Go, serpent! nor remain
To sharpen woe by insult and disdain:
A nest of harpies was I doomed to meet; 280
What plots, what combinations of deceit!
I see it now – all planned, designed, contrived;
Served by that Villain – by this Fury wived –
What fate is mine! What wisdom, virtue, truth,
Can stand, if Demons set their traps for Youth?

He lose his way! vile dog! he cannot lose
The way a villain through his life pursues;
And thou, Deceiver! thou afraid to move,
And hiding close the Serpent in the Dove!
290   I saw – but, fated to endure disgrace, –
Unheeding saw, the fury in thy face;
And called it spirit – Oh! I might have found
Fraud and imposture – all the kindred round!
A nest of Vipers' ———

———————————'Sir, I'll not admit
These wild effusions of your angry wit:
Have you that value, that we all should use
Such mighty arts for such important views?
Are you such prize – and is my state so fair,
That they should sell their souls to get me there?
300   Think you that we alone our thoughts disguise?
When in pursuit of some contended prize,
Mask we alone the heart, and soothe whom we despise?
Speak you of craft and subtle schemes, who know
That all your wealth you to deception owe;
Who played for ten dull years a scoundrel-part,
To worm yourself into a Widow's heart?
Now, when you guarded, with superior skill,
That Lady's closet, and preserved her Will,
Blind in your craft, you saw not one of those
310   Opposed by you might you in turn oppose;
Or watch your motions, and by art obtain
Share of that wealth you gave your peace to gain.
Did conscience never' ———

——— 'Cease, Tormentor, cease –
Or reach me poison – let me rest in peace!'

'Agreed – but hear me – let the truth appear;'
'Then state your purpose – I'll be calm, and hear.' –
'Know then, this wealth, sole object of your care,
I had some right, without your hand, to share;

My Mother's claim was just – but soon she saw
Your power, compelled, insulted, to withdraw; 320
'Twas then my Father, in his anger, swore
You should divide the fortune, or restore;
Long we debated – and you find me now
Heroic victim to a Father's vow;
Like *Jephtha*'s Daughter, but in different state,
And both decreed to mourn our early fate;
Hence was my Brother servant to your pride,
Vengeance made him your Slave – and me your Bride:
Now all is known – a dreadful price I pay
For our revenge – but still we have our day; 330
All that you love, you must with others share,
Or all you dread from their resentment dare!
Yet terms I offer – let contention cease;
Divide the spoil, and let us part in peace.'

   Our Hero trembling heard – he sat – he rose –
Nor could his motions nor his mind compose;
He paced the room – and, stalking to her side,
Gazed on the face of his undaunted Bride;
And nothing there but scorn and calm aversion spied:
He would have vengeance, yet he feared the law; 340
Her friends would threaten, and their power he saw;
'Then let her go:' – but oh! a mighty sum
Would that demand, since he had let her come;
Nor from his sorrows could he find redress,
Save that which led him to a like distress;
And all his ease was in his Wife to see
A wretch as anxious and distressed as he:
Her strongest wish, the fortune to divide
And part in peace, his avarice denied;
And thus it happened, as in all deceit, 350
The cheater found the evil of the cheat:
The Husband grieved – nor was the Wife at rest;
Him she could vex, and he could her molest;
She could his passion into frenzy raise,

But when the fire was kindled, feared the blaze:
As much they studied, so in time they found
The easiest way to give the deepest wound;
But then, like Fencers, they were equal still,
Both lost in danger what they gained in skill;
Each heart a keener kind of rancour gained,
And paining more, was more severely pained;
And thus by both were equal vengeance dealt,
And both the anguish they inflicted felt.

360

TALE XIII
JESSE AND COLIN

Then she plots, then she ruminates, then she devises, and what they think
in their hearts they may effect, they will break their hearts but they will
effect.

Merry Wives of Windsor, Act II. Scene 2.

She hath spoken that she should not, I am sure of that;
Heaven knows what she hath known.

Macbeth, Act V. Scene 1.

Our house is hell, and thou a merry devil.
Merchant of Venice, Act II. Scene 3.

And yet, for aught I see, they are as sick that surfeit of too much, as they
that starve with nothing; it is no mean happiness, therefore, to be seated in
the mean.

Merchant of Venice, Act I. Scene 2.

A Vicar died, and left his Daughter poor –
It hurt her not, she was not rich before:
Her humble share of worldly goods she sold,
Paid every debt, and then her fortune told;
And found, with youth and beauty, hope and health,
Two hundred guineas was her worldly wealth;
It then remained to choose her path in life,
And first, said *Jesse*, 'Shall I be a wife? –
Colin is mild and civil, kind and just,
I know his love, his temper I can trust;
But small his farm, it asks perpetual care,
And we must toil as well as trouble share:

10

True, he was taught in all the gentle arts
That raise the soul, and soften human hearts;
And boasts a Parent, that deserves to shine
In higher class, and I could wish her mine;
Nor wants he will his station to improve,
A just ambition waked by faithful love; —
Still is he poor — and here my Father's Friend
20   Deigns for his Daughter, as her own, to send;
A worthy lady, who it seems has known
A world of griefs and troubles of her own:
I was an infant, when she came, a guest
Beneath my Father's humble roof to rest;
Her kindred all unfeeling, vast her woes,
Such her complaint, and there she found repose;
Enriched by fortune, now she nobly lives,
And nobly, from the blessed abundance, gives;
The grief, the want of human life she knows,
30   And comfort there and here relief bestows;
But, are they not dependants? — Foolish pride!
Am I not honoured by such friend and guide?
Have I a home,' (here *Jesse* dropped a tear,)
'Or friend beside?' — A faithful friend was near.

Now *Colin* came, at length resolved to lay
His heart before her, and to urge her stay;
True, his own plough the gentle *Colin* drove,
An humble farmer with aspiring love;
Who, urged by passion, never dared till now,
40   Thus urged by fears, his trembling hopes avow;
Her father's glebe he managed; every year
The grateful Vicar held the Youth more dear;
He saw indeed the prize in *Colin*'s view,
And wished his *Jesse* with a man so true;
Timid as true, he urged with anxious air
His tender hope, and made the trembling prayer;
When *Jesse* saw, nor could with coldness see,
Such fond respect, such tried sincerity:

Grateful for favours to her Father dealt,
She more than grateful for his passion felt;   50
Nor could she frown on one so good and kind,
Yet feared to smile, and was unfixed in mind;
But prudence placed the Female Friend in view –
What might not one so rich and grateful do?
So lately, too, the good old Vicar died,
His faithful daughter must not cast aside
The signs of filial grief, and be a ready bride:
Thus, led by prudence, to the Lady's seat,
The Village-Beauty purposed to retreat;
But, as in hard-fought fields the victor knows   60
What to the vanquished he, in honour, owes,
So in this conquest over powerful love,
Prudence resolved a generous foe to prove;
And *Jesse* felt a mingled fear and pain
In her dismission of her faithful swain,
Gave her kind thanks, and when she saw his woe,
Kindly betrayed that she was loth to go;
'But would she promise, if abroad she met
A frowning world, she would remember yet
Where dwelt a friend?' – 'That could she not forget.'   70
And thus they parted; but each faithful heart
Felt the compulsion, and refused to part.

  Now by the morning mail the timid Maid
Was to that kind and wealthy Dame conveyed;
Whose invitation, when her Father died,
Jesse as comfort to her heart applied;
She knew the days her generous Friend had seen –
As wife and widow, evil days had been;
She married early, and for half her life
Was an insulted and forsaken wife;   80
Widowed and poor, her angry father gave,
Mixed with reproach, the pittance of a slave;
Forgetful brothers passed her, but she knew
Her humbler friends, and to their home withdrew;

The good old Vicar to her sire applied
For help, and helped her when her sire denied;
When in few years Death stalked through bower and hall,
Sires, sons, and sons of sons were buried all:
She then abounded, and had wealth to spare;
90   For softening grief she once was doomed to share;
Thus trained in Misery's school, and taught to feel,
She would rejoice an orphan's woes to heal: —
So *Jesse* thought, who looked within her breast,
And thence conceived how bounteous minds are blessed.

From her vast mansion looked the Lady down
On humbler buildings of a busy town;
Thence came her friends of either sex, and all
With whom she lived on terms reciprocal:
They passed the hours with their accustomed ease,
100   As guests inclined, but not compelled to please;
But there were others in the mansion found,
For office chosen, and by duties bound;
Three female rivals, each of power possessed,
The attendant-Maid, poor Friend, and kindred-Guest.

To these came *Jesse*, as a seaman thrown
By the rude storm upon a coast unknown:
The view was flattering, civil seemed the race,
But all unknown the dangers of the place.

Few hours had passed, when, from attendants freed,
110   The Lady uttered — 'This is kind indeed;
Believe me, love! that I for one like you
Have daily prayed, a friend discreet and true,
Oh! wonder not that I on you depend,
You are mine own hereditary friend;
Hearken, my *Jesse*, never can I trust
Beings ungrateful, selfish, and unjust;
But you are present, and my load of care
Your love will serve to lighten and to share:
Come near me, *Jesse* — let not those below,

Of my reliance on your friendship know;   120
Look as they look, be in their freedoms free –
But all they say, do you convey to me.'

Here *Jesse*'s thoughts to *Colin*'s cottage flew,
And with such speed she scarce their absence knew.

'*Jane* loves her mistress, and should she depart,
I lose her service, and she breaks her heart;
My ways and wishes, looks and thoughts she knows,
And duteous care by close attention shows:
But is she faithful? in temptation strong?
Will she not wrong me? ah! I fear the wrong: 130
Your Father loved me; now, in time of need,
Watch for my good, and to his place succeed.

'Blood doesn't bind – that Girl, who every day
Eats of my bread, would wish my life away;
I am her *dear relation*, and she thinks
To make her fortune, an ambitious minx!
She only courts me for the prospect's sake,
Because she knows I have a will to make;
Yes, love! my will delayed, I know not how –
But you are here, and I will make it now.   140

'That idle Creature, keep her in your view,
See what she does, what she desires to do;
On her young mind may artful villains prey,
And to my plate and jewels find a way;
A pleasant humour has the girl; her smile
And cheerful manner, tedious hours beguile:
But well observe her, ever near her be,
Close in your thoughts, in your professions free.

'Again, my *Jesse*, hear what I advise,
And watch a woman ever in disguise;   150
Issop, that widow, serious, subtle, sly –
But what of this? – I must have company:
She markets for me, and although she makes

Profit, no doubt, of all she undertakes,
Yet she is one I can to all produce,
And all her talents are in daily use;
Deprived of her, I may another find
As sly and selfish, with a weaker mind:
But never trust her, she is full of art,
And worms herself into the closest heart;
Seem then, I pray you, careless in her sight,
Nor let her know, my love, how we unite.

'Do, my good *Jesse*, cast a view around,
And let no wrong within my house by found;
That Girl associates with – I know not who
Are her companions, nor what ill they do;
'Tis then the Widow plans, 'tis then she tries
Her various arts and schemes for fresh supplies;
'Tis then, if ever, *Jane* her duty quits,
And, whom I know not, favours and admits:
Oh! watch their movements all; for me 'tis hard,
Indeed is vain, but you may keep a guard;
And I, when none your watchful glance deceive,
May make my will, and think what I shall leave.'

Jesse, with fear, disgust, alarm, surprise,
Heard of these duties for her ears and eyes;
Heard by what service she must gain her bread,
And went with scorn and sorrow to her bed.

Jane was a servant fitted for her place,
Experienced, cunning, fraudful, selfish, base;
Skilled in those mean humiliating arts
That make their way to proud and selfish hearts;
By instinct taught, she felt an awe, a fear,
For *Jesse*'s upright, simple character;
Whom with gross flattery she awhile assailed,
And then beheld with hatred when it failed;
Yet trying still upon her mind for hold,
She all the secrets of the mansion told;

And to invite an equal trust, she drew
Of every mind a bold and rapid view;   190
But on the widowed Friend with deep disdain,
And rancorous envy, dwelt the treacherous *Jane*: –
In vain such arts; without deceit or pride,
With a just taste and feeling for her guide,
From all contagion *Jesse* kept apart,
Free in her manners, guarded in her heart.

Jesse one morn was thoughtful, and her sigh
The Widow heard as she was passing by:
And – 'Well!' she said, 'is that some distant swain,
Or aught with us, that gives your bosom pain?   200
Come, we are fellow-sufferers, slaves in thrall,
And tasks and griefs are common to us all;
Think not my frankness strange; they love to paint
Their state with freedom, who endure restraint;
And there is something in that speaking eye
And sober mien, that prove I may rely: –
You came a stranger; to my words attend,
Accept my offer, and you find a friend;
It is a labyrinth in which you stray,
Come, hold my clue, and I will lead the way.   210

'Good Heaven! that one so jealous, envious, base,
Should be the mistress of so sweet a place;
She, who so long herself was low and poor,
Now broods suspicious on her useless store,
She loves to see us abject, loves to deal
Her insult round, and then pretends to feel;
Prepare to cast all dignity aside,
For know your talents will be quickly tried;
Nor think, from favours past, a friend to gain,
'Tis but by duties we our posts maintain: 220
I read her novels, gossip through the town,
And daily go for idle stories, down;
I cheapen all she buys, and bear the curse
Of honest tradesmen for my niggard-purse;

And, when for her this meanness I display,
She cries, "I heed not what I throw away;"
Of secret bargains I endure the shame,
And stake my credit for our fish and game;
Oft has she smiled to hear "her generous soul
Would gladly give, but stoops to my control:"
Nay! I have heard her, when she chanced to come
Where I contended for a petty sum,
Affirm 'twas painful to behold such care,
"But *Issop*'s nature is to pinch and spare:"
Thus all the meanness of the house is mine,
And my reward, — to scorn her, and to dine.

'See next that giddy thing, with neither pride
To keep her safe, nor principle to guide;
Poor, idle, simple flirt! as sure as fate
Her maiden-fame will have an early date:
Of her beware; for all who live below
Have faults they wish not all the world to know;
And she is fond of listening, full of doubt,
And stoops to guilt to find an error out.

'And now once more observe the artful Maid,
A lying, prying, jilting, thievish jade;
I think, my love, you would not condescend
To call a low, illiterate girl, your friend:
But in our troubles we are apt, you know,
To lean on all who some compassion show;
And she has flexile features, acting eyes,
And seems with every look to sympathise;
No mirror can a mortal's grief express
With more precision, or can feel it less;
That proud, mean spirit, she by fawning courts,
By vulgar flattery, and by vile reports;
And, by that proof she every instant gives
To one so mean, that yet a meaner lives. —

'Come, I have drawn the curtain, and you see

Your fellow-actors, all our company;   260
Should you incline to throw reserve aside,
And in my judgement and my love confide;
I could some prospects open to your view,
That ask attention – and, till then, adieu.'

   'Farewell,' said *Jesse*, hastening to her room,
Where all she saw within, without, was gloom:
Confused, perplexed, she passed a dreary hour,
Before her reason could exert its power;
To her all seemed mysterious, all allied
To avarice, meanness, folly, craft, and pride;   270
Wearied with thought, she breathed the garden's air,
When came the laughing Lass, and joined her there.

   'My sweetest friend has dwelt with us a week,
And does she love us? be sincere and speak;
My Aunt you cannot – Lord! how I should hate
To be like her, all misery and state;
Proud, and yet envious, she disgusted sees
All who are happy, and who look at ease.
Let friendship bind us, I will quickly show
Some favourites near us, you'll be blessed to know;   280
My Aunt forbids it – but, can she expect,
To soothe her spleen, we shall ourselves neglect?
Jane and the Widow were to watch and stay
My free-born feet; I watched as well as they;
Lo! what is this? this simple key explores
The dark recess that holds the *Spinster*'s stores;
And, led by her ill star, I chanced to see
Where *Issop* keeps her stock of ratafie;
Used in the hours of anger and alarm,
It makes her civil, and it keeps her warm;   290
Thus blessed with secrets, both would choose to hide,
Their fears now grant me, what their scorn denied.

   'My freedom thus by their assent secured,
Bad as it is, the place may be endured;

And bad it is, but her estates, you know,
And her beloved hoards, she must bestow;
So we can slyly our amusements take,
And friends of demons, if they help us, make.'

'Strange creatures these,' thought *Jesse*, half inclined
To smile at one malicious and yet kind;
Frank and yet cunning, with a heart to love
And malice prompt – the serpent and the dove;
Here could she dwell? or could she yet depart?
Could she be artful? could she bear with art? –
This splendid Mansion gave the Cottage grace,
She thought a dungeon was a happier place;
And *Colin* pleading, when he pleaded best,
Wrought not such sudden change in *Jesse*'s breast.

The wondering Maiden, who had only read
Of such vile beings, saw them now with dread;
Safe in themselves – for Nature has designed
The creature's poison harmless to the kind;
But all beside who in the haunts are found,
Must dread the poison, and must feel the wound.

Days full of care, slow weary weeks passed on,
Eager to go, still *Jesse* was not gone;
Her time in trifling, or in tears she spent,
She never gave, she never felt content:
The Lady wondered that her humble guest
Strove not to please, would neither lie nor jest;
She sought no news, no scandal would convey,
But walked for health, and was at church to pray;
All this displeased, and soon the Widow cried:
'Let me be frank – I am not satisfied;
You know my wishes, I your judgement trust;
You can be useful, *Jesse*, and you must;
Let me be plainer, child, – I want an ear,
When I am deaf, instead of mine, to hear;
When mine is sleeping, let your eye awake;

300

310

320

When I observe not, observation take;   330
Alas! I rest not on my pillow laid,
Then threatening whispers make my soul afraid;
The tread of strangers to my ear ascends,
Fed at my cost, the minions of my friends;
While you, without a care, a wish to please,
Eat the vile bread of idleness and ease.'
The indignant Girl, astonished, answered – 'Nay!
This instant, Madam, let me haste away,
Thus speaks my father's, thus an orphan's friend?
This instant, Lady, let your bounty end.'   340

    The Lady frowned, indignant, – 'What!' she cried,
'A Vicar's Daughter with a Princess' pride!
And Pauper's lot! but pitying I forgive;
How, simple *Jesse*, do you think to live?
Have I not power to help you, foolish Maid?
To my concerns be your attention paid;
With cheerful mind the allotted duties take,
And recollect I have a will to make.'

    Jesse, who felt as liberal natures feel,
When thus the baser their designs reveal,   350
Replied – 'Those duties were to her unfit,
Nor would her spirit to her tasks submit.'

    In silent scorn the Lady sate awhile,
And then replied with stern contemptuous smile –

    'Think you, fair Madam, that you came to share
Fortunes like mine without a thought or care?
A guest indeed! from every trouble free,
Dressed by my help, with not a care for me;
When I a visit to your Father made,
I for the poor assistance largely paid;   360
To his domestics I their tasks assigned,
I fixed the portion for his hungry hind;
And had your Father (simple man!) obeyed

My good advice, and watched as well as prayed,
He might have left you something with his prayers,
And lent some colour for these lofty airs. –

'In tears! my love! Oh, then my softened heart
Cannot resist – we never more will part;
I need your friendship – I will be your friend,
370   And thus determined, to my will attend.'

Jesse went forth, but with determined soul
To fly such love, to break from such control;
'I hear enough,' the trembling Damsel cried,
'Flight be my care, and Providence my guide;
Ere yet a prisoner, I escape will make,
Will, thus displayed, the insidious arts forsake,
And, as the rattle sounds, will fly the fatal snake.'

Jesse her thanks upon the morrow paid,
Prepared to go, determined though afraid.

'Ungrateful creature,' said the Lady, 'this
380   Could I imagine? – are you frantic, Miss?
What! leave your friend, your prospects, – is it true?'
This *Jesse* answered by a mild 'Adieu!'

The Dame replied, 'Then houseless may you rove,
The starving victim to a guilty love;
Branded with shame, in sickness doomed to nurse
An ill-formed cub, your scandal and your curse;
Spurned by its scoundrel father, and ill fed
By surly rustics with the parish-bread! –
390   Relent you not? – speak – yet I can forgive;
Still live with me' – 'With you,' said *Jesse*, 'live?
No! I would first endure what you describe,
Rather than breathe with your detested tribe;
Who long have feigned, till now their very hearts
Are firmly fixed in their accursed parts;
Who all profess esteem, and feel disdain,
And all with justice of deceit complain;

Whom I could pity, but that, while I stay,
My terror drives all kinder thoughts away;
Grateful for this, that when I think of you, 400
I little fear what poverty can do.'

The angry Matron her attendant *Jane*
Summoned in haste, to soothe the fierce disdain:

'A vile detested wretch!' the Lady cried,
'Yet shall she be, by many an effort, tried,
And, clogged with debt and fear, against her will abide;
And, once secured, she never shall depart
Till I have proved the firmness of her heart;
Then when she dares not, would not, cannot go,
I'll make her feel, what 'tis to use me so.' 410

The pensive *Colin* in his garden strayed,
But felt not then the beauties it displayed;
There many a pleasant object met his view,
A rising wood of oaks behind it grew;
A stream ran by it, and the village-green
And public road were from the garden seen;
Save where the pine and larch the boundary made,
And on the rose-beds threw a softening shade.

The Mother sat beside the garden door,
Dressed as in times ere she and hers were poor; 420
The broad-laced cap was known in ancient days,
When Madam's dress compelled the village praise;
And still she looked as in the times of old,
Ere his last farm the erring husband sold;
While yet the Mansion stood in decent state,
And paupers waited at the well-known gate.

'Alas! my Son!' the Mother cried, 'and why
That silent grief and oft-repeated sigh?
True we are poor, but thou hast never felt
Pangs to thy father for his error dealt; 430
Pangs from strong hopes of visionary gain,

For ever raised, and ever found in vain.
He rose unhappy! from his fruitless schemes,
As guilty wretches from their blissful dreams;
But thou wert then, my Son, a playful child,
Wondering at grief, gay, innocent, and wild;
Listening at times to thy poor mother's sighs,
With curious looks and innocent surprise;
Thy father dying, thou, my virtuous boy,
My comfort always, waked my soul to joy;
With the poor remnant of our fortune left,
Thou hast our station of its gloom bereft;
Thy lively temper, and thy cheerful air,
Have cast a smile on sadness and despair;
Thy active hand has dealt to this poor space,
The bliss of plenty and the charm of grace;
And all around us wonder when they find
Such taste and strength, such skill and power combined;
There is no mother, *Colin*, no not one,
But envies me so kind, so good a son;
By thee supported on this failing side,
Weakness itself awakes a parent's pride:
I bless the stroke that was my grief before,
And feel such joy that 'tis disease no more;
Shielded by thee, my want becomes my wealth, –
And soothed by *Colin*, sickness smiles at health;
The old men love thee, they repeat thy praise,
And say, like thee were youth in earlier days;
While every village-maiden cries, "How gay,
How smart, how brave, how good is *Colin Grey!*"

'Yet art thou sad; alas! my Son, I know
Thy heart is wounded, and the cure is slow;
Fain would I think that *Jesse* still may come
To share the comforts of our rustic home:
She surely loved thee; I have seen the maid,
When thou hast kindly brought the Vicar aid, –
When thou hast eased his bosom of its pain,

Oh! I have seen her – she will come again.'

The Matron ceased; and *Colin* stood the while
Silent, but striving for a grateful smile;   470
He then replied – 'Ah! sure, had *Jesse* stayed,
And shared the comforts of our sylvan shade;
The tenderest duty and the fondest love
Would not have failed that generous heart to move;
A grateful pity would have ruled her breast,
And my distresses would have made me blessed.

'But she is gone, and ever has in view
Grandeur and taste, – and what will then ensue?
Surprise and then delight in scenes so fair and new;
For many a day, perhaps for many a week,   480
Home will have charms, and to her bosom speak;
But thoughtless ease, and affluence, and pride,
Seen day by day, will draw the heart aside;
And she at length, though gentle and sincere,
Will think no more of our enjoyments here.'

Sighing he spake – but hark! he hears the approach
Of rattling wheels! and lo! the evening-coach;
Once more the movement of the horses' feet
Makes the fond heart with strong emotion beat:
Faint were his hopes, but ever had the sight   490
Drawn him to gaze beside his gate at night;
And when with rapid wheels it hurried by,
He grieved his Parent with a hopeless sigh;
And could the blessing have been bought – what sum
Had he not offered, to have *Jesse* come?
She came – he saw her bending from the door,
Her face, her smile, and he beheld no more;
Lost in his joy – the mother lent her aid
To assist and to detain the willing Maid;
Who thought her late, her present home to make,   500
Sure of a welcome for the Vicar's sake;
But the good Parent was so pleased, so kind,
So pressing *Colin*, she so much inclined,

That night advanced; and then so long detained,
No wishes to depart she felt, or feigned;
Yet long in doubt she stood, and then perforce remained.

Here was a lover fond, a friend sincere;
Here was content and joy, for she was here:
In the mild evening, in the scene around,
The Maid, now free, peculiar beauties found;
Blended with village-tones, the evening-gale
Gave the sweet night-bird's warblings to the vale;
The Youth emboldened, yet abashed, now told
His fondest wish, nor found the Maiden cold;
The Mother smiling whispered – 'Let him go
And seek the licence!' *Jesse* answered 'No:'
But *Colin* went. – I know not if they live
With all the comforts wealth and plenty give;
But with pure joy to envious souls denied,
To suppliant meanness and suspicious pride;
And village-maids of happy couples say,
'They live like *Jesse Bourn* and *Colin Grey*.'

THE STRUGGLES OF CONSCIENCE

I am a villain; yet I lie, I am not;
Fool! of thyself speak well: – Fool! do not flatter.
  My Conscience hath a thousand several tongues,
And every tongue brings in a several tale.
                    Richard III, Act V. Scene 3.

  My Conscience is but a kind of hard Conscience,
The fiend gives the more friendly counsel.
                    Merchant of Venice, Act II. Scene 2.

  Thou hast it now – and I fear
Thou play'dst most foully for it.
                    Macbeth, Act III. Scene 1.

Canst thou not minister to a mind diseas'd,
Pluck from the memory a rooted sinew,
Rase out the written troubles of the brain,
And with some sweet oblivious antidote
Cleanse the foul bosom of that perilous stuff
Which weighs upon the heart?
                    Macbeth, Act V. Scene 3.

  Soft! I did but dream –
Oh! coward Conscience, how dost thou afflict me!
                    Richard III, Act V. Scene 3.

A serious Toyman in the City dwelt,
Who much concern for his religion felt;
Reading, he changed his tenets, read again,

And various questions could with skill maintain;
Papist and Quaker if we set aside,
He had the road of every traveller tried;
There walked awhile, and on a sudden turned
Into some bye-way he had just discerned:
He had a nephew, *Fulham — Fulham* went
His Uncle's way, with every turn content;
He saw his pious kinsman's watchful care,
And thought such anxious pains his own might spare,
And he, the truth obtained, without the toil, might share.
In fact young *Fulham*, though he little read,
Perceived his Uncle was by fancy led;
And smiled to see the constant care he took,
Collating creed with creed, and book with book.

    At length the senior fixed; I pass the sect
He called a Church, 'twas precious and elect;
Yet the seed fell not in the richest soil,
For few disciples paid the Preacher's toil;
All in an attic-room were wont to meet,
These few disciples at their Pastor's feet;
With these went *Fulham*, who, discreet and grave,
Followed the light his worthy Uncle gave;
Till a warm Preacher found a way to impart
Awakening feelings to his torpid heart:
Some weighty truths, and of unpleasant kind,
Sank, though resisted, in his struggling mind;
He wished to fly them, but compelled to stay,
Truth to the waking Conscience found her way;
For though the Youth was called a prudent lad,
And prudent was, yet serious faults he had;
Who now reflected — 'Much am I surprised,
I find these notions cannot be despised;
No! there is something I perceive at last,
Although my Uncle cannot hold it fast;
Though I the strictness of these men reject,
Yet I determine to be circumspect;

This man alarms me, and I must begin 40
To look more closely to the things within;
These sons of zeal have I derided long,
But now begin to think the laughers wrong;
Nay! my good Uncle, by all teachers moved,
Will be preferred to him who none approved,
Better to love amiss than nothing to have loved.'
Such were his thoughts, when Conscience first began
To hold close converse with the awakened man:
He from that time reserved and cautious grew,
And for his duties felt obedience due; 50
Pious he was not, but he feared the pain
Of sins committed, nor would sin again.
Whene'er he strayed, he found his Conscience rose,
Like one determined what was ill to oppose
What wrong to accuse, what secret to disclose;
To drag forth every latent act to light,
And fix them fully in the actor's sight:
This gave him trouble, but he still confessed
The labour useful, for it brought him rest.

The Uncle died, and when the Nephew read 60
The will, and saw the substance of the dead –
Five hundred guineas, with a stock in trade, –
He much rejoiced, and thought his fortune made;
Yet felt aspiring pleasure at the sight,
And for increase, increasing appetite:
Desire of profit, idle habits checked,
(For *Fulham*'s virtue was, to be correct);
He and his Conscience had their compact made –
'Urge me with truth, and you will soon persuade;
But not,' he cried, 'for mere ideal things 70
Give me to feel those terror-breeding stings.'

'Let not such thoughts,' she said, 'your mind confound,
Trifles may wake me, but they never wound;
In them indeed there is a wrong and right,

But you will find me pliant and polite;
Not like a Conscience of the dotard kind,
Awake to dreams, to dire offences blind;
Let all within be pure, in all beside
Be your own master, governor, and guide;
Alive to danger, in temptation strong,
And I shall sleep our whole existence long.'

'Sweet be thy sleep' said *Fulham*, 'strong must be
The tempting ill that gains access to me;
Never will I to evil deed consent,
Or, if surprised, oh! how will I repent!
Should gain be doubtful, soon would I restore
The dangerous good, or give it to the poor:
Repose for them my growing wealth shall buy –
Or build – who knows? – an hospital like Guy? –
Yet why such means to soothe the smart within,
While firmly purposed to renounce the sin?'

Thus our young Trader and his *Conscience* dwelt
In mutual love, and great the joy they felt;
But yet in small concerns, in trivial things,
'She was,' he said, 'too ready with the stings,'
And he too apt, in search of growing gains,
To lose the fear of penalties and pains:
Yet these were trifling bickerings, petty jars,
Domestic strifes, preliminary wars;
He ventured little, little she expressed
Of indignation, and they both had rest.

Thus was he fixed to walk the worthy way,
When profit urged him to a bold essay: –
A time was that when all at pleasure gamed
In lottery-chances, yet of law unblamed;
This *Fulham* tried: who would to him advance
A pound or crown, he gave in turn a chance
For weighty prize, – and should they nothing share,

They had their crown or pound in *Fulham*'s ware;
Thus the old stores within the shop were sold   110
For that which none refuses, new or old.

Was this unjust? yet *Conscience* could not rest,
But made a mighty struggle in the breast;
And gave the aspiring man an early proof,
That should they war he would have work enough;
'Suppose,' she said, 'your vended numbers rise
The same with those which gain each real prize,
Such your proposal, can you ruin shun?'
'A hundred thousand,' he replied, 'to one;'
'Still it may happen,' 'I the sum must pay,'   120
'You know you cannot,' 'I can run away;'
'That is dishonest,' – 'Nay, but you must wink
At a chance-hit; it cannot be, I think:
Upon my conduct as a whole decide,
Such trifling errors let my virtues hide;
Fail I at Meeting? am I sleepy there?
My purse refuse I with the Priest to share?
Do I deny the poor a helping hand?
Or stop the wicked women in the Strand?
Or drink at club beyond a certain pitch?   130
Which are your charges? Conscience, tell me which?'

' 'Tis well,' said she, 'but –' 'Nay, I pray, have done –
Trust me, I will not into danger run.'

The lottery drawn, not one demand was made,
Fulham gained profit and increase of trade;
'See now,' said he – for Conscience yet arose, –
'How foolish 'tis such measures to oppose;
Have I not blameless thus my state advanced?'
'Still,' muttered Conscience, 'still it might have chanced;'
'Might!' said our Hero, 'who is so exact   140
As to inquire what might have been a fact?'

Now *Fulham*'s shop contained a curious view
Of costly trifles elegant and new;

The Papers told where kind mammas might buy
The gayest toys to charm an infant's eye;
Where generous beaux might gentle damsels please,
And travellers call who cross the land or seas,
And find the curious art, the neat device
Of precious value and of trifling price.

150   Here *Conscience* rested, she was pleased to find
No less an active than an honest mind;
But when he named his price, and when he swore,
His *Conscience* checked him, that he asked no more,
When half he sought had been a large increase
On fair demand, she could not rest in peace:
(Beside the affront to call the adviser in,
Who would prevent, to justify the sin?)
She therefore told him, that 'he vainly tried
To soothe her anger, conscious that he lied;
160   If thus he grasped at such usurious gains,
He must deserve, and should expect her pains.'

The charge was strong; he would in part confess
Offence there was – But, who offended less?
'What! is a mere assertion called a lie?
And if it be, are men compelled to buy?
'Twas strange that *Conscience* on such points should dwell,
While he was acting (he would call it) well;
He bought as others buy, he sold as others sell:
There was no fraud, and he demanded cause
170   Why he was troubled, when he kept the laws?'

'My laws?' said *Conscience*, 'What,' said he, 'are thine?
Oral or written, human or divine?
Show me the chapter, let me see the text;
By laws uncertain subjects are perplexed;
Let me my finger on the statute lay,
And I shall feel it duty to obey.'

'Reflect,' said *Conscience*, ''twas your own desire

That I should warn you, – does the compact tire?
Repent you this? then bid me not advise,
And rather hear your passions as they rise;   180
So you may counsel and remonstrance shun,
But then remember it is war begun:
And you may judge from some attacks, my friend,
What serious conflicts will on war attend.'

   'Nay, but,' at length the thoughtful man replied,
'I say not that; I wish you for my guide;
Wish for your checks, and your reproofs – but then
Be like a *Conscience* of my fellow-men;
Worthy I mean, and men of good report,
And not the wretches who with conscience sport: 190
There's *Bice* my friend, who passes off his grease
Of pigs for bears', in pots a crown a-piece;
His *Conscience* never checks him when he swears
The fat he sells is honest fat of bears;
And so it is, for he contrives to give
A drachm to each – 'tis thus that tradesmen live:
Now why should you and I be over-nice?
What man is held in more repute than *Bice*?'

   Here ended the dispute; but yet 'twas plain
The parties both expected strife again: 200
Their friendship cooled, he looked about and saw
Numbers who seemed unshackled by his awe;
While like a school-boy he was threatened still,
Now for the deed, now only for the will;
Here Conscience answered, 'To thy neighbour's guide
Thy neighbour leave, and in thine own confide.'

   Such were each day the charges and replies,
When a new object caught the Trader's eyes: –
A Vestry-Patriot, could he gain the name,
Would famous make him, and would pay the fame;   210
He knew full well the sums bequeathed in charge
For schools, for alms-men, for the poor, were large;

Report had told, and he could feel it true
That most unfairly dealt the trusted few;
No partners would they in their office take,
Nor clear accounts at annual meetings make;
Aloud our Hero in the vestry spoke
Of hidden deeds, and vowed to draw the cloak;
It was the poor man's cause, and he for one
220   Was quite determined to see justice done;
His foes affected laughter, then disdain,
They too were loud and threatening, but in vain;
The pauper's friend, their foe, arose and spoke again:
Fiercely he cried, 'Your garbled statements show
That you determine we shall nothing know;
But we shall bring your hidden crimes to light,
Give you to shame, and to the poor their right.'

Virtue like this might some approval ask —
But Conscience sternly said, 'You wear a mask;'
230   'At least,' said *Fulham*, 'If I have a view
To serve myself, I serve the public too.'

Fulham, though checked, retained his former zeal,
And this the cautious rogues began to feel:
'Thus will he ever bark,' in peevish tone,
An Elder cried — 'the cur must have a bone:'
They then began to hint, and to begin
Was all they needed — it was felt within;
In terms less veiled an offer then was made,
Though distant still, it failed not to persuade:
240   More plainly then was every point proposed,
Approved, accepted, and the bargain closed.
The exulting Paupers hailed their Friend's success,
And bade adieu tó murmurs and distress.

Alas! their Friend had now superior light,
And, viewed by that, he found that all was right;
'There were no errors, the disbursements small,
This was the truth, and truth was due to all.'

And rested Conscience? No! she would not rest,
Yet was content with making a protest:
Some acts she now with less reluctance bore,   250
Nor took alarm so quickly as before;
Like those in towns besieged, who every ball
At first with terror view, and dread them all,
But, grown familiar with the scenes, they fear
The danger less, as it approaches near;
So Conscience, more familiar with the view
Of growing evils, less attentive grew:
Yet he who felt some pain, and dreaded more,
Gave a peace-offering to the angry poor.

Thus had he quiet, – but the time was brief,   260
From his new triumph sprang a cause of grief;
In office joined, and acting with the rest,
He must admit the sacramental test:
Now, as a Sectary, who had all his life,
As he supposed, been with the Church at strife,
(No rules of hers, no laws had he perused
Nor knew the tenets he by rote abused;)
Yet Conscience here arose more fierce and strong,
Than when she told of robbery and wrong;
'Change his religion! No! he must be sure   270
That was a blow no conscience could endure.'

Though friend to virtue, yet she oft abides
In early notions, fixed by erring guides;
And is more startled by a call from those,
Than when the foulest crimes her rest oppose;
By error taught, by prejudice misled,
She yields her rights, and fancy rules instead;
When Conscience all her stings and terror deals,
Not as truth dictates, but as fancy feels:
And thus within our Hero's troubled breast,   280
Crime was less torture than the odious test.
New forms, new measures, he must now embrace,
With sad conviction that they warred with grace;

To his new church no former friend would come,
They scarce preferred her to the Church of *Rome:*
But thinking much, and weighing guilt and gain,
Conscience and he commuted for the pain;
Then promised *Fulham* to retain his creed,
And their peculiar paupers still to feed;
290   Their attic room (in secret) to attend,
And not forget he was the Preacher's friend;
Thus he proposed, and Conscience, troubled, tried
And wanting peace, reluctantly complied.

Now care subdued, and apprehensions gone,
In peace our Hero went aspiring on;
But short the period – soon a quarrel rose,
Fierce in the birth, and fatal in the close;
With times of truce between, which rather proved
That both were weary, than that either loved.

300   *Fulham* even now disliked the heavy thrall,
And for her death would in his anguish call,
As *Rome*'s mistaken friend exclaimed, *Let Carthage fall!*
So felt our Hero, so his wish expressed,
Against his powerful Sprite – *delenda est:*
Rome in her conquest saw not danger near,
Freed from her rival, and without a fear;
So, Conscience conquered, men perceive how free,
But not how fatal such a state must be.
Fatal not free our Hero's; foe or friend,
310   Conscience on him was destined to attend:
She dozed indeed, grew dull, nor seemed to spy
Crime following crime, and each of deeper dye;
But all were noticed, and the reckoning time
With her account came on – crime following crime.

This, once a foe, now Brother in the Trust,
Whom *Fulham* late described as fair and just,
Was the sole Guardian of a wealthy Maid,

Placed in his power, and of his frown afraid:
Not quite an idiot, for her busy brain
Sought, by poor cunning, trifling points to gain;　　　　320
Success in childish projects her delight,
She took no heed of each important right.

　　The friendly parties met – the Guardian cried,
'I am too old; my Sons have each a Bride:
Martha, my Ward, would make an easy Wife,
On easy terms I'll make her yours for life;
And then the creature is so weak and mild,
She may be soothed and threatened as a child;' –
'Yet not obey,' said *Fulham*, 'for your fools,
Female and male, are obstinate as mules.'　　　　330

　　Some points adjusted, these new friends agreed,
Proposed the day, and hurried on the deed.

　　' 'Tis a vile act,' said *Conscience*, – 'it will prove,'
Replied the bolder Man, 'an act of love;
Her wicked Guardian might the Girl have sold
To endless misery, for a Tyrant's gold;
Now may her life be happy – for I mean
To keep my temper even and serene:'
'I cannot thus compound,' the Spirit cried,
'Nor have my laws thus broken and defied:　　　　340
This is a fraud, a bargain for a Wife;
Expect my vengeance, or amend your life.'

　　The Wife was pretty, trifling, childish, weak;
She could not think, but would not cease to speak:
This he forbad – she took the caution ill,
And boldly rose against his sovereign will;
With idiot-cunning she would watch the hour,
When friends were present, to dispute his power:
With tyrant-craft, he then was still and calm,
But raised in private terror and alarm:　　　　350
By many trials, she perceived how far
To vex and tease, without an open war;

And he discovered that so weak a mind
No art could lead, and no compulsion bind;
The rudest force would fail such mind to tame,
And she was callous to rebuke and shame;
Proud of her wealth, the power of law she knew,
And would assist him in the spending too:
His threatening words with insult she defied,
To all his reasoning with a stare replied;
And when he begged her to attend, would say,
'Attend I will – but, let me have my way.'

Nor rest had Conscience: 'While you merit pain
From me,' she cried, 'you seek redress in vain.'
His thoughts were grievous: 'All that I possess
From this vile bargain, adds to my distress;
To pass a life with one who will not mend,
Who cannot love, nor save, nor wisely spend,
Is a vile prospect, and I see no end:
For if we part, I must of course restore
Much of her money, and must wed no more.'

'Is there no way?' – here *Conscience* rose in power,
'Oh! fly the danger of this fatal hour;
I am thy Conscience, faithful, fond, and true,
Ah! fly this thought, or evil must ensue;
Fall on thy knees, and pray with all thy soul,
Thy purpose banish, thy design control:
Let every hope of such advantage cease,
Or never more expect a moment's peace.'

The affrighted Man a due attention paid,
Felt the rebuke, and the command obeyed.

Again the Wife rebelled, again expressed
A love for pleasure – a contempt of rest:
'She, whom she pleased, would visit, would receive
Those who pleased her, nor deign to ask for leave.'

'One way there is,' said he; 'I might contrive
Into a trap this foolish thing to drive:
Who pleased her, said she? – I'll be certain who – '
'Take heed,' said Conscience, 'what thou mean'st to do;
Ensnare thy wife?' – 'Why yes,' he must confess,   390
'It might be wrong – but there was no redress:
Beside, to think,' said he, 'is not to sin.'
'Mistaken Man!' replied the Power within.
No guest unnoticed to the Lady came,
He judged the event with mingled joy and shame:
Oft he withdrew, and seemed to leave her free,
But still as watchful as a lynx was he;
Meanwhile the Wife was thoughtless, cool, and gay,
And, without virtue, had no wish to stray.

Though thus opposed, his plans were not resigned: 400
'Revenge,' said he, 'will prompt that daring mind;
Refused supplies, insulted and distressed,
Enraged with me, and near a favourite guest –
Then will her vengeance prompt the daring deed,
And I shall watch, detect her, and be freed.'

There was a Youth – but let me hide the name,
With all the progress of this deed of shame: –
He had his views – on him the Husband cast
His net, and saw him in his trammels fast.

'Pause but a moment – think what you intend,'   410
Said the roused Sleeper: 'I am yet a friend;
Must all our days in enmity be spent?'
'No!' and he paused – 'I surely shall repent:'
Then hurried on – the evil plan was laid,
The Wife was guilty, and her Friend betrayed,
And *Fulham* gained his wish, and for his will was paid.

Had crimes less weighty on the spirit pressed,
This troubled Conscience might have sunk to rest;
And, like a foolish guard, been bribed to peace,
By a false promise, that offence should cease;   420

Past faults had seemed familiar to the view,
Confused if many, and obscure though true;
And Conscience, troubled with the dull account,
Had dropped her tale, and slumbered o'er the amount:
But, struck by daring guilt, alert she rose,
Disturbed, alarmed, and could no more repose;
All hopes of friendship, and of peace, were past,
And every view with gloom was overcast.
Hence from that day, that day of shame and sin,
430   Arose the restless enmity within;
On no resource could *Fulham* now rely,
Doomed all expedients, and in vain, to try;
For *Conscience*, roused, sat boldly on her throne,
Watched every thought, attacked the foe alone,
And with envenomed sting drew forth the inward groan:
Expedients failed that brought relief before,
In vain his alms gave comfort to the poor;
Give what he would, to him the comfort came no more:
Not prayer availed, and when (his crimes confessed)
440   He felt some ease – she said – 'are they redressed?
You still retain the profit, and be sure,
Long as it lasts, this anguish shall endure.'

    Fulham still tried to soothe her, cheat, mislead;
But *Conscience* laid her finger on the Deed,
And read the crime with power, and all that must succeed:
He tried to expel her, but was sure to find
Her strength increased by all that he designed;
Nor ever was his groan more loud and deep,
Than when refreshed she rose from momentary sleep.

450   Now desperate grown, weak, harassed, and afraid,
From new allies he sought for doubtful aid;
To thought itself he strove to bid adieu,
And from devotions to diversions flew;
He took a poor domestic for a slave,
(Though Avarice grieved to see the price he gave);
Upon his board, once frugal, pressed a load

Of viands rich, the appetite to goad;
The long-protracted meal, the sparkling cup,
Fought with his gloom, and kept his courage up:
Soon as the morning came, there met his eyes   460
Accounts of wealth, that he might reading rise;
To profit then he gave some active hours,
Till food and wine again should renovate his powers:
Yet, spite of all defence, of every aid,
The watchful Foe her close attention paid;
In every thoughtful moment, on she pressed,
And gave at once her dagger to his breast:
He waked at midnight, and the fears of sin,
As waters, through a bursten dam, broke in;
Nay, in the banquet, with his friends around,   470
When all their cares and half their crimes were drowned,
Would some chance act awake the slumbering fear,
And care and crime in all their strength appear:
The news is read, a guilty Victim swings,
And troubled looks proclaim the bosom-stings;
Some Pair are wed; this brings the Wife in view,
And some divorced; this shows the parting too:
Nor can he hear of evil word or deed,
But they to thought, and thought to sufferings lead.

    Such was his life – no other changes came,   480
The hurrying day, the conscious night the same;
The night of horror – when he, starting, cried,
To the poor startled Sinner at his side:
'Is it in law? am I condemned to die?
Let me escape! – I'll give – oh! let me fly –
How! but a Dream – no Judges! Dungeon! Chain!
Or these grim Men! – I will not sleep again. –
Wilt thou, dread Being! thus thy promise keep?
Day is thy time – and wilt thou murder sleep?
Sorrow and Want repose, and wilt thou come,   490
Nor give one hour of pure untroubled gloom?

    Oh! Conscience! Conscience! Man's most faithful friend,

Him canst thou comfort, ease, relieve, defend:
But if he will thy friendly checks forgo,
Thou art, oh! woe for me, his deadliest foe!'

ADVICE;

OR,

THE 'SQUIRE AND THE PRIEST

━━━━━━━━

His hours fill'd up with riots, banquets, sports, –
And never noted in him any study,
Any retirement, any sequestration.
Henry V, Act I. Scene 1.

I will converse with iron-witted fools,
With unrespective boys; none are for me,
Who look into me with considerate eyes.
Richard III, Act IV. Scene 2.

You cram these words into mine ears, against
The stomach of my sense.
Tempest, Act II. Scene 1.

A wealthy Lord of far-extended land
Had all that pleased him placed at his command;
Widowed of late, but finding much relief
In the world's comforts, he dismissed his grief.
He was by marriage of his daughters eased,
And knew his sons could marry if they pleased;
Meantime in travel he indulged the boys,
And kept no spy nor partner of his joys.

These joys, indeed, were of the grosser kind,
That fed the cravings of an earthy mind;
A mind that, conscious of its own excess,

10

Felt the reproach his neighbours would express.
Long at the indulgent board he loved to sit,
Where joy was laughter, and profaneness wit;
And such the Guest and manners of the Hall,
No wedded Lady on the 'Squire would call;
Here reigned a Favourite, and her triumph gained
O'er other favourites who before had reigned;
Reserved and modest seemed the Nymph to be,
20 Knowing her Lord was charmed with modesty;
For he, a sportsman keen, the more enjoyed,
The greater value had the thing destroyed.

Our 'Squire declared that, from a Wife released,
He would no more give trouble to a Priest;
Seemed it not, then, ungrateful and unkind,
That he should trouble from the Priesthood find?
The church he honoured, and he gave the due
And full respect to every Son he knew;
But envied those who had the luck to meet
30 A gentle Pastor, civil, and discreet;
Who never bold and hostile sermon penned,
To wound a sinner, or to shame a friend;
One whom no being either shunned or feared,
Such must be loved wherever they appeared.

Not such the stern old Rector of the time,
Who soothed no culprit, and who spared no crime;
Who would his fears and his contempt express,
For irreligion and licentiousness;
Of him our Village Lord, his guests among,
40 By speech vindictive proved his feelings stung.

'Were he a bigot,' said the 'Squire, 'whose zeal
Condemned us all, I should disdain to feel:
But when a man of parts, in College trained,
Prates of our conduct, – who would not be pained?
While he declaims (where no one dares reply)
On men abandoned, grovelling in the stye
(Like beasts in human shape) of shameless luxury.

Yet with a patriot's zeal I stand the shock
Of vile rebuke, example to his flock:
But let this Rector, thus severe and proud,   50
Change his wide surplice for a narrow shroud;
And I will place within his seat a Youth,
Trained by the Graces, to explain the Truth;
Then shall the flock with gentle hand be led,
By Wisdom won, and by Compassion fed.'

   This purposed Teacher was a Sister's Son,
Who of her children gave the Priesthood one;
And she had early trained for this employ
The pliant talents of her College-Boy:
At various times her letters painted all   60
Her Brothers' views – the manners of the Hall;
The Rector's harshness, and the mischief made
By chiding those whom Preachers should persuade:
This led the Youth to views of easy life,
A friendly Patron, an obliging Wife;
His tithe, his glebe, the garden, and the steed,
With books as many as he wished to read.

   All this accorded with the Uncle's will;
He loved a Priest compliant, easy, still;
Sums he had often to his favourite sent,   70
'To be,' he wrote, 'in manly freedom spent;
For well it pleased his spirit to assist
An honest Lad, who scorned a Methodist:'
His Mother too, in her maternal care,
Bade him of canting hypocrites beware;
Who from his duties would his heart seduce,
And make his talents of no earthly use.

   Soon must a trial of his worth be made –
The ancient Priest is to the tomb conveyed;
And the Youth summoned from a serious friend;   80
His guide and host, new duties to attend.

   Three months before, the Nephew and the 'Squire
Saw mutual worth to praise and to admire;

And though the one too early left his wine,
The other still exclaimed – 'My Boy will shine:
Yes, I perceive that he will soon improve,
And I shall form the very guide I love;
Decent abroad, he will my name defend,
And, when at home, be social and unbend.'

90   The plan was specious, for the mind of *James*
Accorded duly with his Uncle's schemes:
He then aspired not to a higher name,
Than sober Clerks of moderate talents claim;
Gravely to pray, and reverendly to preach,
Was all he saw, good Youth! within his reach:
Thus may a mass of sulphur long abide
Cold and inert, but, to the flame applied,
Kindling it blazes, and consuming turns
To smoke and poison, as it boils and burns.

100   *James*, leaving College, to a Preacher strayed;
What called, he knew not – but the call obeyed:
Mild, idle, pensive, ever led by those
Who could some specious novelty propose;
Humbly he listened, while the Preacher dwelt
On touching themes, and strong emotions felt;
And in this night was fixed that pliant will,
To one sole point, and he retains it still.

At first his care was to himself confined;
Himself assured, he gave it to mankind:
110   His zeal grew active – honest, earnest zeal,
And comfort dealt to him, he longed to deal;
He to his favourite Preacher now withdrew,
Was taught to teach, instructed to subdue;
And trained for ghostly warfare, when the call
Of his new duties reached him from the Hall.

Now to the 'Squire, although alert and stout,
Came unexpected an attack of gout;
And the grieved Patron felt such serious pain,

He never thought to see a church again:
Thrice had the youthful Rector taught the crowd,   120
Whose growing numbers spoke his powers aloud,
Before the Patron could himself rejoice
(His pain still lingering) in the general voice;
For he imputed all this early fame
To graceful manner, and the well-known name;
And to himself assumed a share of praise,
For worth and talents he was pleased to raise.

A month had flown, and with it fled disease;
What pleased before began again to please:
Emerging daily from his chamber's gloom,   130
He found his old sensations hurrying home;
Then called his Nephew, and exclaimed, 'My Boy,
Let us again the balm of life enjoy;
The foe has left me, and I deem it right,
Should he return, to arm me for the fight.'

Thus spoke the 'Squire, the favourite Nymph stood by,
And viewed the Priest with insult in her eye;
She thrice had heard him when he boldly spoke
On dangerous points, and feared he would revoke:
For *James* she loved not – and her manner told,   140
'This warm affection will be quickly cold:'
And still she feared impression might be made
Upon a subject, nervous and decayed;
She knew her danger, and had no desire
Of reformation in the gallant 'Squire;
And felt an envious pleasure in her breast
To see the Rector daunted and distressed.

Again the Uncle to the Youth applied –
'Cast, my dear Lad, that cursèd gloom aside:
There are for all things time and place; appear   150
Grave in your pulpit, and be merry here:
Now take your wine – for woes a sure resource,
And the best prelude to a long discourse.'

James half obeyed, but cast an angry eye
On the fair Lass, who still stood watchful by:
Resolving thus, 'I have my fears – but still
I must perform my duties, and I will;
No love, no interest, shall my mind control;
Better to lose my comforts than my soul;
160   Better my Uncle's favour to abjure,
Than the upbraidings of my heart endure.'

He took his glass, and then addressed the 'Squire:
'I feel not well, permit me to retire.'
The 'Squire conceived that the ensuing day
Gave him these terrors for the grand essay,
When he himself should this young Preacher try,
And stand before him with observant eye;
This raised compassion in his manly breast,
And he would send the Rector to his rest:
170   Yet first, in soothing voice – 'A moment stay,
And these suggestions of a friend obey;
Treasure these hints, if fame or peace you prize, –
The bottle emptied, I shall close my eyes.

'On every Priest a two-fold care attends,
To prove his talents, and insure his friends:
First, of the first – your stores at once produce,
And bring your reading to its proper use:
On doctrines dwell, and every point enforce
By quoting much, the Scholar's sure resource;
180   For he alone can show us on each head
What ancient Schoolmen and sage Fathers said:
No worth has knowledge, if you fail to show
How well you studied, and how much you know:
Is Faith your subject, and you judge it right
On theme so dark to cast a ray of light;
Be it that faith the Orthodox maintain,
Found in the Rubrick, what the Creeds explain;
Fail not to show us on this ancient faith,
(And quote the passage) what some Martyr saith:

Dwell not one moment on a faith that shocks 190
The minds of men sincere and orthodox;
That gloomy faith, that robs the wounded mind
Of all the comfort it was wont to find
From virtuous acts, and to the soul denies
Its proper due for alms and charities;
That partial faith, that, weighing sins alone,
Lets not a virtue for a fault atone;
That starving faith, that would our tables clear,
And make one dreadful Lent of all the year;
And cruel too, for this is faith that rends 200
Confiding beauties from protecting friends;
A faith that all embracing, what a gloom
Deep and terrific o'er the land would come!
What scenes of horror would that time disclose!
No sight but misery, and no sound but woes:
Your nobler faith, in loftier style conveyed,
Shall be with praise and admiration paid:
On points like these your hearers all admire
A preacher's depth, and nothing more require;
Shall we a studious youth to *College* send 210
That every clown his words may comprehend?
'Tis for your glory, when your hearers own
Your learning matchless, but the sense unknown.

'Thus honour gained, learn now to gain a friend,
And the sure way is – never to offend;
For, *James*, consider – what your neighbours do
Is their own business, and concerns not you:
Shun all resemblance to that forward race
Who preach of sins before a sinner's face;
And seem as if they overlooked a pew, 220
Only to drag a failing man in view:
Much should I feel, when groaning in disease,
If a rough hand upon my limb should seize;
But great my anger, if this hand were found
The very Doctor's, who should make it sound:

So feel our minds, young Priest, so doubly feel,
When hurt by those whose office is to heal.

    'Yet of our duties you must something tell,
And must at times on sin and frailty dwell;
Here you may preach in easy, flowing style,
How errors cloud us, and how sins defile:
Here bring persuasive tropes and figures forth,
To show the poor that wealth is nothing worth;
That they, in fact, possess an ample share
Of the world's good and feel not half its care;
Give them this comfort, and, indeed, my gout
In its full vigour causes me some doubt;
And let it always, for your zeal, suffice,
That Vice you combat, in the abstract —— Vice:
The very captious will be quiet then,
We all confess we are offending men:
In lashing sin, of every stroke beware,
For sinners feel, and sinners you must spare:
In general satire, every man perceives
A slight attack, yet neither fears nor grieves;
But name the offence, and you absolve the rest,
And point the danger at a single breast,

    'Yet are these sinners of a class so low,
That you with safety may the lash bestow;
Poachers, and drunkards, idle rogues, who feed
At others' cost, a marked correction need:
And all the better sort, who see your zeal,
Will love and reverence for their Pastor feel;
Reverence for One who can inflict the smart,
And love, because he deals them not a part.

    'Remember well what love and age advise,
A quiet Rector is a parish prize;
Who in his learning has a decent pride,
Who to his people is a gentle guide;
Who only hints at failings that he sees;

Who loves his glebe, his patron, and his ease,
And finds the way to fame and profit is to please.'

    The Nephew answered not, except a sigh
And look of sorrow might be termed reply:
He saw the fearful hazard of his state,
And held with truth and safety strong debate;
Nor long he reasoned, for the zealous Youth
Resolved, though timid, to profess the truth;
And though his Friend should like a lion roar,
Truth would he preach, and neither less nor more.   270

    The bells had tolled – arrived the time of prayer,
The flock assembled, and the 'Squire was there:
And now can Poet sing, or Proseman say,
The disappointment of that trying day?

    As he who long had trained a favourite steed,
(Whose blood and bone gave promise of his speed,)
Sanguine with hope, he runs with partial eye
O'er every feature, and his bets are high;
Of triumph sure, he sees the Rivals start,
And waits their coming with exulting heart;   280
Forestalling glory, with impatient glance,
And sure to see his conquering steed advance;
The conquering steed advances – luckless day!
A rival's *Herod* bears the prize away;
Nor second his, nor third, but lagging last,
With hanging head he comes, by all surpassed;
Surprise and wrath the owner's mind inflame,
Love turns to scorn, and glory ends in shame; –
Thus waited, high in hope, the partial 'Squire,
Eager to hear, impatient to admire: 290
When the young Preacher, in the tones that find
A certain passage to the kindling mind,
With air and accent strange, impressive, sad,
Alarmed the Judge – he trembled for the Lad:
But when the text announced the power of grace,

Amazement scowled upon his clouded face,
At this degenerate Son of his illustrious race;
Staring he stood, till hope again arose,
That *James* might well define the words he chose;
For this he listened – but, alas! he found
The Preacher always on forbidden ground.

And now the Uncle left the hated pew,
With *James*, and *James*'s conduct in his view:
A long farewell to all his favourite schemes!
For now no crazed Fanatic's frantic dreams
Seemed vile as *James*'s conduct, or as *James*:
All he had long derided, hated, feared
This, from the chosen Youth, the Uncle heard; –
The needless pause, the fierce disordered air,
The groan for sin, the vehemence of prayer,
Gave birth to wrath, that, in a long discourse
Of grace, triumphant rose to four-fold force:
He found his thoughts despised, his rules transgressed
And while the anger kindled in his breast,
The pain must be endured that could not be expressed:
Each new idea more inflamed his ire,
As fuel thrown upon a rising fire:
A hearer yet, he sought by threatening sign
To ease his heart, and awe the young Divine;
But *James* refused those angry looks to meet,
Till he dismissed his flock, and left his seat:
Exhausted then he felt his trembling frame,
But fixed his soul, – his sentiments the same;
And therefore wise it seemed to fly from rage,
And seek for shelter in his Parsonage:
There, if forsaken, yet consoled to find
Some comforts left, though not a few resigned;
There if he lost an erring parent's love,
An honest Conscience must the cause approve;
If the nice palate were no longer fed,
The mind enjoyed delicious thoughts instead;

300

310

320

330

And if some part of earthly good was flown,
Still was the tithe of ten good farms his own.

Fear now, and discord, in the village reign,
The cool remonstrate, and the meek complain;
But there is war within, and wisdom pleads in vain:
Now dreads the Uncle, and proclaims his dread,
Lest the Boy-Priest should turn each rustic head;
The certain converts cost him certain woe,
The doubtful fear lest they should join the foe: 340
Matrons of old, with whom he used to joke,
Now pass his Honour with a pious look;
Lasses, who met him once with lively airs,
Now cross his way, and gravely walk to prayers:
An old Companion, whom he long has loved,
By coward fears confessed his conscience moved;
As the third bottle gave its spirit forth,
And they bore witness to departed worth,
The Friend arose, and he too would depart; –
'Man,' said the 'Squire, 'thou wert not wont to start;   350
Hast thou attended to that foolish Boy,
Who would abridge all comforts, or destroy?'

Yes, he had listened, who had slumbered long,
And was convinced that something must be wrong:
But, though affected, still his yielding heart,
And craving palate, took the Uncle's part;
Wine now oppressed him, who, when free from wine,
Could seldom clearly utter his design;
But though by nature and indulgence weak,
Yet, half converted, he resolved to speak;   360
And, speaking, owned, 'that in his mind the Youth
Had gifts and learning, and that truth was truth;
The 'Squire he honoured, and, for his poor part,
He hated nothing like a hollow heart:
But 'twas a maxim he had often tried,
That right was right, and there he would abide;
He honoured learning, and he would confess,

The Preacher had his talents, – more or less: –
Why not agree? he thought the young Divine
370   Had no such strictness – they might drink and dine;
For them sufficient, – but he said before, –
That truth was truth, and he would drink no more.'

   This heard the 'Squire with mixed contempt and pain,
He feared the Priest this recreant Sot would gain.
The favourite Nymph, though not a convert made,
Conceived the Man she scorned her cause would aid;
And when the spirits of her Lord were low,
The Lass presumed the wicked cause to show:
'It was the wretched life his Honour led,
380   And would draw vengeance on his guilty head;
Their loves (Heaven knew how dreadfully distressed
The thought had made her) were as yet unblessed:
And till the Church had sanctioned' – Here she saw
The wrath that forced her, trembling, to withdraw.

Add to these outward ills, some inward light,
That showed him all was not correct and right:
Though now he less indulged – and to the poor,
From day to day, sent alms from door to door;
Though he some ease from easy virtues found,
390   Yet Conscience told him he could not compound;
But must himself the darling sin deny,
Change the whole heart, —— but here a heavy sigh
Proclaimed 'How vast the toil! and ah! how weak am I!'

James too has trouble, – he divided sees
A parish, once harmonious and at ease:
With him united are the simply meek,
The warm, the sad, the nervous and the weak;
The rest his Uncle's, save the few beside,
Who own no doctrine, and obey no guide;
400   With stragglers of each adverse camp, who lend
Their aid to both, but each in turn offend.

Though zealous still, yet he begins to feel

The heat too fierce, that glows in vulgar zeal;
With pain he hears his simple friends relate
Their week's experience, and their woeful state:
With small temptations struggling every hour,
And bravely battling with the tempting power;
His native sense is hurt by strange complaints,
Of inward motions in these warring saints;
Who never cast on sinful bait a look,   410
But they perceive the Devil at the hook:
Grieved, yet compelled to smile, he finds it hard
Against the blunders of conceit to guard;
He sighs to hear the jests his converts cause,
He cannot give their erring zeal applause;
But finds it inconsistent to condemn
The flights and follies he has nursed in them:
These, in opposing minds, contempt produce,
Or mirth occasion, or provoke abuse;
On each momentous theme disgrace they bring,
And give to Scorn her poison and her sting.

THE CONFIDANT

Think'st thou I'd make a life of jealousy
To follow still the changes of the Moon,
With fresh suspicion?
      Othello, Act III. Scene 3.

Why has thou lost the fresh blood in thy cheeks,
And given my treasure and my rights in thee
To thick-ey'd musing and curs'd melancholy?
     1 Henry IV, Act II. Scene 3.

       It is excellent
To have a Giant's strength, but tyrannous
To use it as a Giant.
    Measure for Measure, Act II. Scene 2.

Anna was young and lovely – in her eye
The glance of beauty, in her cheek the dye;
Her shape was slender, and her features small,
But graceful, easy, unaffected all:
The liveliest tints her youthful face disclosed,
There beauty sparkled and there health reposed;
For the pure blood that flushed that rosy cheek,
Spoke what the heart forbad the tongue to speak;
And told the feelings of that heart as well,
Nay, with more candour than the tongue could tell:
Though this fair Lass had with the wealthy dwelt,
Yet, like the damsel of the cot she felt;
And, at the distant hint or dark surmise,
The blood into the mantling cheek would rise.

10

Now *Anna*'s station frequent terrors wrought,
In one whose looks were with such meaning fraught;
For on a Lady, as an humble friend,
It was her painful office to attend.

Her duties here were of the usual kind, –
And some the body harassed, some the mind: 20
Billets she wrote, and tender stories read,
To make the Lady sleepy in her bed;
She played at whist, but with inferior skill,
And heard the summons as a call to drill;
Music was ever pleasant till she played
At a request that no request conveyed;
The Lady's tales with anxious looks she heard,
For she must witness what her Friend averred;
The Lady's taste she must in all approve,
Hate whom she hated, whom she loved must love: 30
These, with the various duties of her place,
With care she studied, and performed with grace;
She veiled her troubles in a mask of ease,
And showed her pleasure was a power to please.

Such were the Damsel's duties; she was poor, –
Above a servant, but with service more;
Men on her face with careless freedom gazed,
Nor thought how painful was the glow they raised;
A wealthy few to gain her favour tried,
But not the favour of a grateful bride;   40
They spoke their purpose with an easy air,
That shamed and frightened the dependent fair;
Past time she viewed, the passing time to cheat,
But nothing found to make the present sweet;
With pensive soul she read life's future page,
And saw dependent, poor, repining age.

But who shall dare to assert what *years* may bring,
When wonders from the passing *hour* may spring? –
There dwelt a Yeoman in the place, whose mind

50   Was gentle, generous, cultivated, kind;
      For thirty years he laboured; Fortune then
      Placed the mild rustic with superior men:
      A richer *Stafford*, who had lived to save,
      What he had treasured to the poorer gave;
      Who with a sober mind that treasure viewed,
      And the slight studies of his youth renewed:
      He not profoundly, but discreetly read,
      And a fair mind with useful culture fed;
      Then thought of marriage, 'But the great,' said he,
60   'I shall not suit, nor will the meaner me:'
      Anna he saw, admired her modest air;
      He thought her virtuous, and he knew her fair;
      Love raised his pity for her humble state,
      And prompted wishes for her happier fate;
      No pride in money would his feelings wound,
      No vulgar manners hurt him and confound:
      He then the Lady at the Hall addressed,
      Sought her consent, and his regard expressed;
      Yet if some cause his earnest wish denied,
70   He begged to know it, and he bowed and sighed.

      The Lady owned that she was loth to part,
      But praised the Damsel for her gentle heart,
      Her pleasing person, and her blooming health;
      But ended thus, 'Her virtue is her wealth.'

      'Then is she rich!' he cried, with lively air;
      'But whence, so please you, came a lass so fair?'

      'A placeman's child was *Anna*, one who died
      And left a widow by afflictions tried;
      She to support her infant-daughter strove,
80   But early left the object of her love:
      Her youth, her beauty, and her orphan-state
      Gave a kind Countess interest in her fate;
      With her she dwelt and still might dwelling be,
      When the *Earl*'s folly caused the Lass to flee;

A second Friend was she compelled to shun,
By the rude offers of an unchecked son;
I found her then, and with a mother's love
Regard the gentle Girl whom you approve;
Yet, e'en with me protection is not peace,
Nor man's designs, nor beauty's trials cease;   90
Like sordid boys by costly fruit they feel,
They will not purchase, but they try to steal.'

   Now this good Lady, like a witness true,
Told but the truth, and all the truth she knew;
And 'tis our duty and our pain to show
Truth this good Lady had not means to know.
Yes, there was locked within the Damsel's breast,
A fact important to be now confessed;
Gently, my Muse, the afflicting tale relate,
And have some feeling for a sister's fate.   100

   Where *Anna* dwelt, a conquering Hero came, –
An Irish Captain, *Sedley* was his name;
And he too had that same prevailing art,
That gave soft wishes to the Virgin's heart;
In years they differed; he had thirty seen
When this young Beauty counted just fifteen;
But still they were a lovely lively pair,
And trod on earth as if they trod on air.

   On Love, delightful theme! the Captain dwelt
With force still growing with the hopes he felt;   110
But with some caution and reluctance told,
He had a father crafty, harsh, and old;
Who, as possessing much, would much expect,
Or both, for ever, from his love reject:
Why then offence to one so powerful give,
Who (for their comfort) had not long to live?

   With this poor prospect the deluded Maid,
In words confiding, was indeed betrayed;
And, soon as terrors in her bosom rose,

120 The Hero fled; they hindered his repose;
Deprived of him, she to a parent's breast
Her secret trusted, and her pains impressed:
Let her to Town (so Prudence urged) repair,
To shun disgrace, at least to hide it there;
But ere she went, the luckless Damsel prayed
A chosen Friend might lend her timely aid;
'Yes! my soul's sister, my *Eliza*, come,
Hear her last sigh, and ease thy *Anna*'s doom:'
'"Tis a fool's wish,' the angry father cried,
130 But, lost in troubles of his own, complied;
And dear *Eliza* to her friend was sent,
To indulge that wish, and be her punishment:
The time arrived, and brought a tenfold dread;
The time was passed, and all the terror fled;
The infant died; the face resumed each charm,
And reason now brought trouble and alarm;
'Should her *Eliza* – no! she was too just,
Too good and kind – but ah! too young to trust:'
Anna returned, her former place resumed,
140 And faded beauty with new grace re-bloomed;
And if some whispers of the past were heard,
They died innoxious, as no cause appeared;
But other cares on *Anna*'s bosom pressed,
She saw her father gloomy and distressed;
He died o'erwhelmed with debt, and soon was shed
The filial sorrow o'er a mother dead;
She sought *Eliza*'s arms, that faithful friend was wed:
Then was compassion by the Countess shown,
And all the adventures of her life are known.

150 And now beyond her hopes – no longer tried
By slavish awe – she lived a Yeoman's bride;
Then blessed her lot, and with a grateful mind
Was careful, cheerful, vigilant, and kind:
The gentle Husband felt supreme delight,
Blessed by her joy, and happy in her sight:

He saw with pride in every friend and guest
High admiration and regard expressed;
With greater pride, and with superior joy,
He looked exulting on his first-born boy;
To her fond breast the Wife her infant strained.   160
Some feelings uttered, some were not explained;
And she enraptured with her treasure grew,
The sight familiar, but the pleasure new.

Yet there appeared within that tranquil state,
Some threatening prospect of uncertain fate:
Between the married when a secret lies,
It wakes suspicion from enforced disguise;
Still thought the Wife upon her absent Friend,
With all that must upon her truth depend;
'There is no being in the world beside,   170
Who can discover what that Friend will hide;
Who knew the fact, knew not my name or state,
Who these can tell, cannot the fact relate;
But thou, *Eliza*, canst the whole impart,
And all my safety is thy generous heart.'

Mixed with these fears – but light and transient these –
Fled years of peace, prosperity, and ease;
So tranquil all, that scarce a gloomy day
For days of gloom unmixed prepared the way:
One eve, the Wife, still happy in her state,   180
Sang gaily thoughtless of approaching fate;
Then came a letter, that (received in dread
Not unobserved) she in confusion read;
The substance this – 'Her friend rejoiced to find
That she had riches with a grateful mind;
While poor *Eliza* had from place to place
Been lured by hope to labour for disgrace;
That every scheme her wandering husband tried,
Pained while he lived and perished when he died.'
She then of want in angry style complained,   190

Her child a burden to her life remained,
Her kindred shunned her prayers, no friend her soul sustained:

'Yet why neglected? Dearest *Anna* knew
Her worth once tried, her friendship ever true;
She hoped, she trusted, though by wants oppressed,
To lock the treasured secret in her breast;
Yet, vexed by trouble, must apply to one
For kindness due to her for kindness done.'

In *Anna*'s mind was tumult, in her face
200   Flushings of dread had momentary place;
'I must,' she judged, 'these cruel lines expose,
Or fears, or worse than fears, my crime disclose.'

The letter shown, he said, with sober smile: –
'*Anna*, your Friend has not a friendly style;
Say, where could you with this fair lady dwell,
Who boasts of secrets that she scorns to tell?'
'At school,' she answered, he 'at school?' replied,
'Nay, then I know the secrets you would hide;
Some early longings these, without dispute,
210   Some youthful gaspings for forbidden fruit:
Why so disordered, love? are such the crimes
That give us sorrow in our graver times?
Come, take a present for your Friend, and rest
In perfect peace – you find you are confessed.'

This cloud, though passed, alarmed the conscious Wife,
Presaging gloom and sorrow for her life;
Who to her answer joined a fervent prayer,
That her *Eliza* would a sister spare;
If she again – but was there cause? – should send,
220   Let her direct – and then she named a friend:
A sad expedient untried friends to trust,
And still to fear the tried may be unjust;
Such is his pain, who, by his debt oppressed,
Seeks by new bonds, a temporary rest.

Few were her peaceful days, till *Anna* read
The words she dreaded, and had cause to dread: –

'Did she believe, did she, unkind, suppose
That thus *Eliza*'s friendship was to close?
No! though she tried (and her desire was plain)
To break the friendly bond, she strove in vain;   230
Asked she for silence? why so loud the call,
And yet the token of her love so small?
By means like these will you attempt to bind
And check the movements of an injured mind?
Poor as I am, I should be proud to show
What dangerous secrets I may safely know;
Secrets to men of jealous minds conveyed,
Have many a noble house in ruins laid;
Anna, I trust, although with wrongs beset,
And urged by want, I shall be faithful yet;   240
But what temptation may from these arise,
To take a slighted woman by surprise,
Becomes a subject of your serious care –
For who offends, must for offence prepare.'

Perplexed, dismayed, the Wife foresaw her doom;
A day deferred was yet a day to come;
But still, though painful her suspended state,
She dreaded more the crisis of her fate;
Better to die than *Stafford*'s scorn to meet,
And her strange Friend perhaps would be discreet: 250
Presents she sent, and made a strong appeal
To woman's feelings, begging her to feel;
With too much force she wrote of jealous men,
And her tears falling spoke beyond the pen;
Eliza's silence she again implored,
And promised all that prudence could afford.

For looks composed and careless, *Anna* tried;
She seemed in trouble, and unconscious sighed;
The faithful Husband, who devoutly loved

260   His silent partner, with concern reproved:
       'What secret sorrows on my *Anna* press,
       That love may not partake, nor care redress?'
       'None, none,' she answered, with a look so kind,
       That the fond man determined to be blind.

       A few succeeding weeks of brief repose
       In *Anna*'s cheek revived the faded rose;
       A hue like this the western sky displays,
       That glows awhile, and withers as we gaze.

       Again the Friend's tormenting letter came —
270   'The wants she suffered were affection's shame:
       She with her child a life of terrors led,
       Unhappy fruit! but of a lawful bed;
       Her friend was tasting every bliss in life,
       The joyful mother, and the wealthy wife;
       While she was placed in doubt, in fear, in want,
       To starve on trifles that the happy grant;
       Poorly for all her faithful silence paid,
       And tantalized by ineffectual aid;
       She could not thus a beggar's lot endure,
280   She wanted something permanent and sure;
       If they were friends, then equal be their lot,
       And she was free to speak if they were not.'

       Despair and terror seized the Wife, to find
       The artful workings of a vulgar mind:
       Money she had not, but the hint of dress
       Taught her new bribes, new terrors to redress:
       She with such feeling then described her woes,
       That envy's self might on the view repose;
       Then to a mother's pains she made appeal,
290   And painted grief like one compelled to feel.

       Yes! so she felt, that in her air, her face,
       In every purpose, and in every place;
       In her slow motion, in her languid mien,
       The grief, the sickness of her soul, were seen.

Of some mysterious ill, the Husband sure,
Desired to trace it, for he hoped to cure;
Something he knew obscurely, and had seen
His Wife attend a cottage on the Green;
Love, loth to wound, endured conjecture long,
Till fear would speak, and spoke in language strong.   300

'All I must know, my *Anna*, – truly know
Whence these emotions, terrors, troubles flow:
Give me thy grief, and I will fairly prove
Mine is no selfish, no ungenerous love.'

Now *Anna*'s soul the seat of strife became,
Fear with respect contended, love with shame;
But fear prevailing was the ruling guide,
Prescribing what to show and what to hide.

'It is my friend' she said, – 'but why disclose
A woman's weakness struggling with her woes?   310
Yes, she has grieved me by her fond complaints,
The wrongs she suffers, the distress she paints;
Something we do, – but she afflicts me still,
And says, with power to help, I want the will;
This plaintive style I pity and excuse,
Help when I can, and grieve when I refuse;
But here my useless sorrows I resign,
And will be happy in a love like thine.'

The Husband doubted, he was kind but cool: –
''Tis a strong friendship to arise at school;   320
Once more then, Love, once more the sufferer aid, –
I too can pity, but I must upbraid;
Of these vain feelings then thy bosom free,
Nor be o'erwhelmed by useless sympathy.'

The wife again dispatched the useless bribe,
Again essayed her terrors to describe;
Again with kindest words entreated peace,
And begged her offerings for a time might cease.

A calm succeeded, but too like the one
330   That causes terror ere the storm comes on:
A secret sorrow lived in *Anna*'s heart,
In *Stafford*'s mind a secret fear of art;
Not long they lasted, – this determined Foe
Knew all her claims, and nothing would forgo;
Again her letter came, where *Anna* read –
'My child, one cause of my distress, is dead;
Heaven has my infant;' 'Heartless wretch!' she cried,
'Is this thy joy?' – 'I am no longer tied;
Now will I, hastening to my Friend, partake
340   Her cares and comforts, and no more forsake;
Now shall we both in equal station move,
Save that my Friend enjoys a husband's love.'

Complaint and threats so strong, the Wife amazed,
Who wildly on her cottage-neighbour gazed;
Her tones, her trembling, first betrayed her grief,
When floods of tears gave anguish its relief.

She feared that *Stafford* would refuse assent,
And knew her selfish Friend would not relent;
She must petition, yet delayed the task,
350   Ashamed, afraid, and yet compelled to ask;
Unknown to him some object filled her mind,
And, once suspicious, he became unkind;
They sat one evening, each absorbed in gloom,
When, hark! a noise and rushing to the room,
The Friend tripped lightly in, and laughing said, 'I come.'

Anna received her with an anxious mind;
And meeting whispered, 'Is *Eliza* kind?'
Reserved and cool, the Husband sought to prove
The depth and force of this mysterious love.
360   To nought that passed between the Stranger-Friend
And his meek Partner seemed he to attend;
But, anxious, listened to the lightest word
That might some knowledge of his guest afford;

And learn the reason one to him so dear
Should feel such fondness, yet betray such fear.

   Soon he perceived this uninvited Guest,
Unwelcome too, a sovereign power possessed;
Lofty she was and careless, while the meek
And humbled *Anna* was afraid to speak:
As mute she listened with a painful smile,   370
Her Friend sate laughing and at ease the while,
Telling her idle tales with all the glee
Of careless and unfeeling levity.
With calm good sense he knew his Wife endued,
And now with wounded pride her conduct viewed;
Her speech was low, her every look conveyed
'I am a slave, subservient and afraid.'
All trace of comfort vanished; if she spoke,
The noisy Friend upon her purpose broke;
To her remarks with insolence replied,   380
And her assertions doubted or denied;
While the meek *Anna* like an infant shook,
Woe-struck and trembling at the serpent's look.

   'There is,' said *Stafford*, 'yes, there is a cause –
This creature fights her, overpowers and awes:'
Six weeks had passed – 'In truth, my Love, this Friend
Has liberal notions; what does she intend?
Without a hint she came, and will she stay
Till she receives the hint to go away?'

   Confused the Wife replied, in spite of truth,   390
'I love the dear companion of my youth:'
''Tis well,' said *Stafford*; 'then your loves renew,
Trust me, your rivals, *Anna*, will be few.'

   Though playful this, she felt too much distressed
To admit the consolation of a jest;
Ill she reposed, and in her dreams would sigh,
And, murmuring forth her anguish, beg to die;

With sunken eye, slow pace and pallid cheek,
She looked confusion and she feared to speak.

400   All this the Friend beheld, for, quick of sight,
She knew the Husband eager for her flight;
And that by force alone she could retain
The lasting comforts she had hope to gain:
She now perceived, to win her post for life,
She must infuse fresh terrors in the Wife;
Must bid to friendship's feebler ties adieu,
And boldly claim the object in her view;
She saw the Husband's love, and knew the power
Her Friend might use in some propitious hour.

410   Meantime the anxious Wife, from pure distress
Assuming courage, said, 'I will confess;'
But with her children felt a parent's pride,
And sought once more the hated truth to hide.

Offended, grieved, impatient, *Stafford* bore
The odious change, till he could bear no more;
A friend to truth, in speech and action plain,
He held all fraud and cunning in disdain;
But fraud to find, and falsehood to detect,
For once he fled to measures indirect.

420   One day the Friends were seated in that Room
The Guest with care adorned, and named her Home:
To please the eye, there curious prints were placed,
And some light volumes to amuse the taste;
Letters and music, on a table laid,
The favourite studies of the Fair betrayed;
Beneath the window was the toilet spread,
And the fire gleamed upon a crimson bed.

In *Anna*'s looks and falling tears were seen,
How interesting had their subjects been;
430   'Oh! then,' resumed the Friend, 'I plainly find

That you and *Stafford* know each other's mind;
I must depart, must on the world be thrown,
Like one discarded, worthless and unknown;
But, shall I carry, and to please a foe,
A painful secret in my bosom? No!
Think not your Friend a reptile you may tread
Beneath your feet, and say, the worm is dead;
I have some feeling, and will not be made
The scorn of her whom love cannot persuade:
Would not your word, your slightest wish, effect   440
All that I hope, petition, or expect?
The power you have, but you the use decline, –
Proof that you feel not, or you fear not mine.
There was a time, when I, a tender maid,
Flew at a call, and your desires obeyed;
A very mother to the child became,
Consoled your sorrow, and concealed your shame;
But now, grown rich and happy, from the door
You thrust a bosom-friend, despised and poor;
That child alive, its mother might have known   450
The hard, ungrateful spirit she has shown.'

Here paused the Guest, and *Anna* cried at length –
'You try me, cruel friend! beyond my strength;
Would I had been beside my infant laid,
Where none would vex me, threaten or upbraid.'

In *Anna*'s looks the Friend beheld despair;
Her speech she softened, and composed her air;
Yet, while professing love, she answered still –
'You can befriend me, but you want the will.'
They parted thus, and *Anna* went her way,   460
To shed her secret sorrows, and to pray.

Stafford, amused with books, and fond of home,
By reading oft dispelled the evening gloom;
History or tale – all heard him with delight,
And thus was passed this memorable night.

The listening Friend bestowed a flattering smile,
A sleeping boy the Mother held the while;
And ere she fondly bore him to his bed,
On his fair face the tear of anguish shed.

470   And now his task resumed, 'My tale,' said he,
'Is short and sad, short may our sadness be! –

'The Caliph *Harun*,* as historians tell,
Ruled, for a tyrant, admirably well;
Where his own pleasures were not touched, to men
He was humane, and sometimes even then:
Harun was fond of fruits, and gardens fair,
And woe to all whom he found poaching there:
Among his pages was a lively Boy,
Eager in search of every trifling joy;
480   His feelings vivid, and his fancy strong,
He sighed for pleasure while he shrank from wrong;
When by the Caliph in the garden placed
He saw the treasures which he longed to taste;
And oft alone he ventured to behold
Rich hanging fruits with rind of glowing gold;
Too long he stayed forbidden bliss to view,
His virtue failing, as his longings grew;
Athirst and wearied with the noon-tide heat,
Fate to the garden led his luckless feet;
490   With eager eyes and open mouth he stood,
Smelt the sweet breath, and touched the fragrant food,
The tempting beauty sparkling in the sun
Charmed his young sense – he ate, and was undone:
When the fond glutton paused, his eyes around
He turned, and eyes upon him turning, found;
Pleased he beheld the spy, a brother-Page,
A friend allied in office and in age;

---

* The Sovereign here meant is *Haroun Alraschid*, or *Harun al Rashid*, who died early
  in the ninth century; he is often the hearer, and sometimes the hero, of a Tale in the
  Arabian Nights Entertainments.

Who promised much that secret he would be,
But high the price he fixed on secrecy.

'"Were you suspected, my unhappy friend,"   500
Began the Boy, "where would your sorrows end?
In all the palace there is not a page
The Caliph would not torture in his rage;
I think I see thee now impaled alive,
Writhing in pangs – but come, my friend! revive!
Had some beheld you, all your purse contains
Could not have saved you from terrific pains;
I scorn such meanness, and, if not in debt,
Would not an asper on your folly set."

'The hint was strong; young *Osmyn* searched his store   510
For bribes, and found he soon could bribe no more;
That time arrived, for *Osmyn*'s stock was small,
And the young Tyrant now possessed it all;
The cruel Youth, with his companions near,
Gave the broad hint that raised the sudden fear;
The ungenerous insult now was daily shown,
And *Osmyn*'s peace and honest pride were flown;
Then came augmenting woes, and fancy strong
Drew forms of suffering, a tormenting throng;
He felt degraded, and the struggling mind   520
Dared not be free, and could not be resigned;
And, all his pains and fervent prayers obtained,
Was truce from insult, while the fears remained.

'One day it chanced that this degraded Boy
And tyrant-Friend were fixed at their employ
Who now had thrown restraint and form aside,
And for his bribe in plainer speech applied;
"Long have I waited, and the last supply
Was but a pittance, yet how patient I!
But give me now what thy first terrors gave,   530
My speech shall praise thee, and my silence save."

'*Osmyn* had found, in many a dreadful day,
The Tyrant fiercer when he seemed in play;
He begged forbearance; "I have not to give,
Spare me awhile, although 'tis pain to live;
Oh! had that stolen fruit the power possessed
To war with life, I now had been at rest."

'"So fond of death," replied the Boy, "'tis plain
Thou hast no certain notion of the pain;
But to the Caliph were a secret shown,
Death has no pains that would be then unknown."

'Now, says the story, in a closet near,
The Monarch seated, chanced the Boys to hear;
There oft he came, when wearied on his throne,
To read, sleep, listen, pray, or be alone.

'The tale proceeds, when first the Caliph found
That he was robbed, although alone, he frowned;
And swore in wrath, that he would send the Boy
Far from his notice, favour or employ;
But gentler movements soothed his ruffled mind,
And his own failings taught him to be kind.

'Relenting thoughts then painted *Osmyn* young,
His passion urgent, and temptation strong;
And that he suffered from that villain-Spy
Pains worse than death, till he desired to die;
Then if his morals had received a stain,
His bitter sorrows made him pure again:
To Reason, Pity lent her powerful aid,
For one so tempted, troubled, and betrayed;
And a free pardon the glad Boy restored
To the kind presence of a gentle Lord;
Who from his office and his country drove
That traitor-Friend, whom pains nor prayers could move;
Who raised the fears no mortal could endure,
And then with cruel avarice sold the cure.

'My tale is ended; but, to be applied,
I must describe the place where Caliphs hide:'

Here both the Females looked alarmed, distressed,
With hurried passions hard to be expressed.

'It was a closet by a chamber placed,   570
Where slept a Lady of no vulgar taste;
Her Friend attended in that chosen Room
That she had honoured and proclaimed her Home;
To please the eye were chosen pictures placed,
And some light volumes to amuse the taste;
Letters and music on a table laid,
For much the Lady wrote, and often played;
Beneath the window was a toilet spread,
And a fire gleamed upon a crimson bed.'

He paused, he rose; with troubled joy the Wife   580
Felt the new era of her changeful life;
Frankness and love appeared in *Stafford*'s face,
And all her trouble to delight gave place.

Twice made the Guest an effort to sustain
Her feelings, twice resumed her seat in vain,
Nor could suppress her shame, nor could support her pain:
Quick she retired, and all the dismal night
Thought of her guilt, her folly, and her flight;
Then sought unseen her miserable home,
To think of comforts lost, and brood on wants to come.   590

RESENTMENT

_____

> She hath a tear for pity, and a hand
> Open as day for melting charity;
> Yet, notwithstanding, being incens'd, is flint –
> Her temper, therefore, must be well observ'd.
> 2 Henry IV, Act IV. Scene 4.

> Three or four wenches, where I stood, cried – 'Alas good soul!' and forgave him with all their hearts; but there is no heed to be taken of them; if Caesar had stabbed their Mothers, they would have done no less.
> Julius Caesar, Act I. Scene 2.

> How dost? Art cold?
> I'm cold myself – Where is the straw, my fellow?
> The act of our necessities is strange,
> That can make vile things precious.
> King Lear, Act III. Scene 2.

Females there are of unsuspicious mind,
Easy and soft, and credulous and kind;
Who, when offended for the twentieth time,
Will hear the offender and forgive the crime;
And there are others whom like these to cheat,
Asks but the humblest effort of deceit;
But they, once injured, feel a strong disdain,
And, seldom pardoning, never trust again:
Urged by religion, they forgive – but yet
Guard the warm heart, and never more forget: –
Those are like wax – apply them to the fire,
Melting, they take the impressions you desire;

Easy to mould, and fashion as you please,
And again moulded with an equal ease;
Like smelted iron these the forms retain,
But once impressed will never melt again.

A busy port, a serious Merchant made
His chosen place to re-commence his trade:
And brought his Lady, who, their children dead,
Their native seat of recent sorrow fled;   20
The Husband duly on the quay was seen,
The Wife at home became at length serene
There in short time the social couple grew
With all acquainted, friendly with a few;
When the good Lady, by disease assailed,
In vain resisted – hope and science failed:
Then spake the female friends, by pity led,
'Poor Merchant *Paul!* what think ye? will he wed?
A quiet, easy, kind, religious Man,
Thus can he rest? – I wonder if he can.'   30

He too, as grief subsided in his mind,
Gave place to notions of congenial kind:
Grave was the Man, as we have told before;
His years were forty – he might pass for more;
Composed his features were, his stature low,
His air important, and his motions slow;
His dress became him, it was neat and plain,
The colour purple, and without a stain;
His words were few, and special was his care,
In simplest terms his purpose to declare;   40
A man more civil, sober, and discreet,
More grave and courteous, you could seldom meet:
Though frugal he, yet sumptuous was his board,
As if to prove how much he could afford;
For though reserved himself, he loved to see
His table plenteous, and his neighbours free:
Among these friends he sat in solemn style,
And rarely softened to a sober smile;
For this, observant friends their reasons gave –

50   'Concerns so vast would make the idlest grave;
     And for such man to be of language free,
     Would seem incongruous as a singing tree:
     Trees have their music, but the birds they shield,
     The pleasing tribute for protection yield;
     Each ample tree the tuneful choir defends,
     As this rich Merchant cheers his happy friends!'

        In the same town it was his chance to meet
     A gentle Lady, with a mind discreet;
     Neither in life's decline, nor bloom of youth,
60   One famed for maiden modesty and truth:
     By nature cool, in pious habits bred,
     She looked on lovers with a Virgin's dread;
     Deceivers, rakes, and libertines were they,
     And harmless beauty their pursuit and prey;
     As bad as giants in the ancient times,
     Were modern lovers, and the same their crimes:
     Soon as she heard of her all-conquering charms,
     At once she fled to her defensive arms;
     Conned o'er the tales her maiden Aunt had told,
70   And, statue-like, was motionless and cold;
     From prayer of love, like that *Pygmalion* prayed,
     Ere the hard stone became the yielding Maid, –
     A different change in this chaste Nymph ensued,
     And turned to stone the breathing flesh and blood:
     Whatever youth described his wounded heart,
     'He came to rob her, and she scorned his art;
     And who of raptures once presumed to speak,
     Told listening maids he thought them fond and weak:
     But should a worthy Man his hopes display
80   In few plain words, and beg a *yes* or *nay*;
     He would deserve an answer just and plain,
     Since adulation only moved disdain, –
     Sir, if my friends object not, come again.'

        Hence, our grave Lover, though he liked the face,
     Praised not a feature – dwelt not on a grace:

But in the simplest terms declared his state,
'A widowed Man, who wished a virtuous Mate;
Who feared neglect, and was compelled to trust
Dependants wasteful, idle, or unjust;
Or should they not the trusted stores destroy,   90
At best, they could not help him to enjoy;
But with her person, and her prudence blessed,
His acts would prosper, and his soul have rest:
Would she be his?' – 'Why, that was much to say;
She would consider: he awhile might stay;
She liked his manners, and believed his word;
He did not flatter, flattery she abhorred:
It was her happy lot in peace to dwell –
Would change make better what was now so well?
But she would ponder:' – 'This,' he said, 'was kind,'   100
And begged to know 'when she had fixed her mind.'

Romantic Maidens would have scorned the air,
And the cool prudence of a mind so fair;
But well it pleased this wiser Maid to find
Her own mild virtues in her Lover's mind.

His worldly wealth she sought, and quickly grew
Pleased with her search, and happy in the view
Of vessels freighted with abundant stores,
Of rooms whose treasures pressed the groaning floors;
And he of clerks and servants could display   110
A little army, on a public day;
Was this a Man like needy Bard to speak
Of balmy lip, bright eye, or rosy cheek?

The sum appointed for her widowed state,
Fixed by her Friend, excited no debate;
Then the kind Lady gave her hand and heart,
And, never finding, never dealt with art:
In his engagements she had no concern;
He taught her not, nor had she wish to learn:

120   On him in all occasions she relied –
      His word her surety, and his worth her pride.

          When ship was launched, and Merchant *Paul* had share,
      A bounteous feast became the Lady's care;
      Who then her entry to the dinner made,
      In costly raiment, and with kind parade.

          Called by this duty on a certain day,
      And robed to grace it in a rich array;
      Forth from her room, with measured step she came,
      Proud of the event, and stately looked the Dame:
130   The Husband met her at his study-door –
      'This way, my Love – one moment and no more:
      A trifling business – you will understand
      The law requires that you affix your hand;
      But first attend, and you shall learn the cause
      Why forms like these have been prescribed by laws;'
      Then from his chair a Man in black arose,
      And with much quickness hurried off his prose:
      That '*Ellen Paul* the Wife and so forth, freed
      From all control, her own the act and deed,
140   And forasmuch' – said she, 'I've no distrust,
      For he that asks it is discreet and just;
      Our friends are waiting – where am I to sign? –
      There! – Now be ready when we meet to dine.'

          This said, she hurried off in great delight,
      The ship was launched, and joyful was the night.

          Now, says the Reader, and in much disdain,
      This serious Merchant was a rogue in grain;
      A treacherous wretch, an artful, sober knave,
      And ten times worse for manners cool and grave;
150   And she devoid of sense, to set her hand
      To scoundrel deeds, she could not understand.

          Alas! 'tis true, and I in vain had tried
      To soften crime, that cannot be denied;

And might have laboured many a tedious verse
The latent cause of mischief to rehearse: –
Be it confessed, that long, with troubled look,
This Trader viewed a huge accompting-book;
(His former marriage for a time delayed
The dreaded hour, the present lent its aid);
But he too clearly saw the evil day,   160
And put the terror, by deceit, away;
Thus by connecting with his sorrows, crime,
He gained a portion of uneasy time. –
All this too late the injured Lady saw,
What law had given, again she gave to law;
His guilt, her folly – these at once impressed
Their lasting feelings on her guileless breast.

'Shame I can bear,' she cried, 'and want sustain,
But will not see this guilty wretch again,'
For all was lost, and he, with many a tear,   170
Confessed the fault – she turning scorned to hear.
To legal claims he yielded all his worth,
But small the portion, and the wronged were wroth;
Nor to their debtor would a part allow;
And where to live he knew not – knew not how.

The Wife a cottage found, and thither went
The suppliant Man, but she would not relent:
Thenceforth she uttered with indignant tone,
'I feel the misery, and will feel alone;' –
He would turn servant for her sake, would keep   180
The poorest school; the very streets would sweep,
To show his love – 'It was already shown:
And her afflictions should be all her own.
His wants and weakness might have touched her heart,
But from his meanness she resolved to part.'

In a small alley was she lodged, beside
Its humblest poor, and at the view she cried: –
'Welcome – yes! let me welcome, if I can,

The fortune dealt me by this cruel Man;
Welcome this low-thatched roof, this shattered door,
These walls of clay, this miserable floor;
Welcome my envied neighbours; this, to you,
Is all familiar – all to me is new:
You have no hatred to the loathsome meal;
Your firmer nerves no trembling terrors feel,
Nor, what you must expose, desire you to conceal;
What your coarse feelings bear without offence,
Disgusts my taste, and poisons every sense:
Daily shall I your sad relations hear,
Of wanton women, and of men severe;
There will dire curses, dreadful oaths abound,
And vile expressions shock me and confound;
Noise of dull wheels, and songs with horrid words,
Will be the music that this lane affords;
Mirth that disgusts, and quarrels that degrade
The human mind, must my retreat invade:
Hard is my fate! yet easier to sustain,
Than to abide with guilt and fraud again;
A grave impostor! who expects to meet,
In such grey locks and gravity, deceit?
Where the sea rages, and the billows roar,
Men know the danger, and they quit the shore;
But, be there nothing in the way descried,
When o'er the rocks smooth runs the wicked tide, –
Sinking unwarned, they execrate the shock,
And the dread peril of the sunken rock.'

A frowning World had now the Man to dread,
Taught in no arts, to no profession bred:
Pining in grief, beset with constant care,
Wandering he went, to rest he knew not where.

Meantime the Wife – but she abjured the name,
Endured her lot, and struggled with the shame;
When lo! an Uncle on the mother's side,
In nature something, as in blood allied,

Admired her firmness, his protection gave,
And showed a kindness she disdained to crave.

Frugal and rich the Man, and frugal grew
The sister-mind, without a selfish view;
And further still – the temperate pair agreed
With what they saved the patient poor to feed: 230
His whole estate, when to the grave consigned,
Left the good Kinsman to the kindred mind:
Assured that law, with spell secure and tight,
Had fixed it as her own peculiar right.

Now to her ancient residence removed,
She lived as Widow, well endowed and loved;
Decent her table was, and to her door
Came daily welcomed the neglected poor:
The absent sick were soothed by her relief,
As her free bounty sought the haunts of grief;   240
A plain and homely charity had she,
And loved the object of her alms to see;
With her own hands she dressed the savoury meat,
With her own fingers wrote the choice receipt:
She heard all tales that injured Wives relate,
And took a double interest in their fate;
But of all Husbands not a wretch was known,
So vile, so mean, so cruel, as her own.

This bounteous Lady kept an active spy,
To search the abodes of want, and to supply;   250
The gentle *Susan* served the liberal Dame, –
Unlike their notions, yet their deeds the same:
No practiced villain could a victim find,
Than this stern Lady more completely blind;
Nor (if detected in his fraud) could meet
One less disposed to pardon a deceit;
The wrong she treasured, and on no pretence
Received the offender, or forgot the offence:
But the kind Servant, to the thrice-proved knave,
A fourth time listened, and the past forgave.   260

First in her youth, when she was blithe and gay,
Came a smooth Rogue, and stole her love away;
Then to another and another flew,
To boast the wanton mischief he could do:
Yet she forgave him, though so great her pain,
That she was never blithe or gay again.

Then came a Spoiler, who, with villain-art,
Implored her hand, and agonized her heart;
He seized her purse, in idle waste to spend
270   With a vile wanton, whom she called her friend:
Five years she suffered — he had revelled five —
Then came to show her he was just alive;
Alone he came, his vile Companion dead,
And he, a wandering Pauper, wanting bread;
His body wasted, withered life and limb,
When this kind soul became a slave to him:
Nay! she was sure that, should he now survive,
No better Husband would be left alive;
For him she mourned, and then, alone and poor,
280   Sought and found comfort at her Lady's door:
Ten years she served, and, mercy her employ,
Her tasks were pleasure, and her duty, joy.

Thus lived the Mistress and the Maid, designed
Each other's aid, — one cautious, and both kind:
Oft at their window, working, they would sigh
To see the agèd and the sick go by;
Like wounded bees, that at their home arrive,
Slowly and weak, but labouring for the hive.

The busy people of a Mason's yard
290   The curious Lady viewed with much regard;
With steady motion she perceived them draw
Through blocks of stone the slowly-working saw;
It gave her pleasure and surprise to see
Among these men the signs of revelry:
Cold was the season, and confined their view,

Tedious their tasks, but merry were the crew:
There she beheld an aged Pauper wait,
Patient and still, to take an humble freight;
Within the paniers on an ass he laid
The ponderous grit, and for the portion paid;   300
This he re-sold, and, with each trifling gift,
Made shift to live, and wretched was the shift.

Now will it be by every Reader told
Who was this humble Trader, poor and old. –
In vain an Author would a Name suppress,
From the least hint a Reader learns to guess;
Of Children lost, our Novels sometimes treat,
We never care – assured again to meet:
In vain the Writer for concealment tries,
We trace his purpose under all disguise;   310
Nay, though he tells us they are dead and gone,
Of whom we wot – they will appear anon;
Our favourites fight, are wounded, hopeless lie,
Survive they cannot – nay! they cannot die:
Now, as these tricks and stratagems are known,
'Tis best, at once, the simple truth to own.

This was the Husband – in an humble shed
He nightly slept, and daily sought his bread:
Once for relief the weary Man applied;
'Your Wife is rich,' the angry Vestry cried;   320
Alas! he dared not to his Wife complain,
Feeling her wrongs, and fearing her disdain:
By various methods he had tried to live,
But not one effort would subsistence give:
He was an Usher in a School, till noise
Made him less able than the weaker boys;
On messages he went, till he in vain
Strove names, or words, or meaning to retain;
Each small employment in each neighbouring town,
By turn he took to lay as quickly down: 330
For such his fate, he failed in all he planned,
And nothing prospered in his luckless hand.

At his old home, his motive half suppressed,
He sought no more for riches, but for rest:
There lived the bounteous Wife, and at her gate
He saw in cheerful groups the needy wait;
'Had he a right with bolder hope to apply?'
He asked, – was answered, and went groaning by:
For some remains of spirit, temper, pride,
340   Forbade a prayer he knew would be denied.

Thus was the grieving Man, with burdened ass,
Seen day by day along the street to pass:
'Who is he, *Susan?* who the poor old Man?
He never calls – do make him, if you can.' –
The conscious Damsel still delayed to speak,
She stopped confused, and had her words to seek;
From *Susan*'s fears the fact her Mistress knew,
And cried – 'The Wretch! what scheme has he in view?
Is this his lot? – but let him, let him feel, –
350   Who wants the courage, not the will, to steal.'

A dreadful winter came, each day severe,
Misty when mild, and icy-cold when clear;
And still the humble dealer took his load,
Returning slow, and shivering on the road:
The Lady, still relentless, saw him come,
And said, – 'I wonder, has the Wretch a home!'
'A hut! a hovel!' – 'Then his fate appears
To suit his crime;' – 'Yes, Lady, not his years; –
No! nor his sufferings – nor that form decayed:' –
360   'Well! let the Parish give its Paupers aid:
You must the vileness of his acts allow;'
'And you, dear Lady, that he feels it now:'
'When such dissemblers on their deeds reflect,
Can they the pity they refused expect?
He that doth evil, evil shall he dread.' –
'The snow,' quoth *Susan*, 'falls upon his bed, –
It blows beside the thatch, – it melts upon his head.' –

''Tis weakness, child, for grieving guilt to feel:'
'Yes, but he never sees a wholesome meal;
Through his bare dress appears his shrivelled skin,   370
And ill he fares without, and worse within:
With that weak body, lame, diseased, and slow,
What cold, pain, peril, must the sufferer know!'
'Think on his crime.' – 'Yes, sure 'twas very wrong;
But look (God bless him!) how he gropes along.' –
'Brought me to shame.' – 'Oh! yes, I know it all –
What cutting blast! and he can scarcely crawl;
He freezes as he moves, – he dies! if he should fall:
With cruel fierceness drives this icy sleet, –
And must a Christian perish in the street,   380
In sight of Christians? – There! at last, he lies; –
Nor unsupported can he ever rise:
He cannot live.' – 'But is he fit to die?' –
Here *Susan* softly muttered a reply,
Looked round the room – said something of its state,
Dives the rich, and *Lazarus* at his gate;
And then aloud – 'In pity do behold
The Man affrightened, weeping, trembling, cold:
Oh! how those flakes of snow their entrance win
Through the poor rags, and keep the frost within;   390
His very heart seems frozen as he goes,
Leading that starved companion of his woes:
He tried to pray – his lips I saw them move,
And he so turned his piteous looks above;
But the fierce wind the willing heart opposed,
And, ere he spoke, the lip in misery closed:
Poor suffering object! yes, for ease you prayed,
And God will hear – he only, I'm afraid.'

'Peace, *Susan*, peace: Pain ever follows Sin,' –
Ah! then, thought *Susan*, when will ours begin?   400
'When reached his home, to what a cheerless fire
And chilling bed will those cold limbs retire!
Yet ragged, wretched as it is, that bed

Takes half the space of his contracted shed;
I saw the thorns beside the narrow grate,
With straw collected in a putrid state:
There will he, kneeling, strive the fire to raise,
And that will warm him, rather than the blaze;
The sullen, smoky blaze, that cannot last
410   One moment after his attempt is past:
And I so warmly and so purely laid,
To sink to rest – indeed, I am afraid.' –
'Know you his conduct?' – 'Yes, indeed, I know, –
And how he wanders in the wind and snow;
Safe in our rooms the threatening storm we hear,
But he feels strongly what we faintly fear.'
'*Wilful* was rich, and he the storm defied;
Wilful is poor, and must the storm abide;'
Said the stern Lady. – ''Tis in vain to feel;
420   Go and prepare the chicken for our meal.'

Susan her task reluctantly began,
And uttered, as she went, – 'The poor old Man!' –
But while her soft and ever-yielding heart
Made strong protest against her Lady's part,
The Lady's self began to think it wrong
To feel so wrathful and resent so long.

'No more the Wretch would she receive again,
No more behold him – but she would sustain;
Great his offence, and evil was his mind, –
430   But he had suffered, and she would be kind:
She spurned such baseness, and she found within
A fair acquittal from so foul a sin;
Yet she too erred, and must of Heaven expect
To be rejected, him should she reject.'

Susan was summoned – 'I'm about to do
A foolish act, in part seduced by you;
Go to the Creature – say that I intend,
Foe to his sins, to be his sorrow's friend;

Take, for his present comforts, food and wine,
And mark his feelings at this act of mine: 440
Observe if shame be o'er his features spread,
By his own Victim to be soothed and fed;
But, this inform him, that it is not love
That prompts my heart, that duties only move:
Say, that no merits in his favour plead,
But miseries only, and his abject need;
Nor bring me grovelling thanks, nor high-flown praise;
I would his spirits, not his fancy raise:
Give him no hope that I shall ever more
A man so vile to my esteem restore;   450
But warn him rather, that, in time of rest,
His crimes be all remembered and confessed:
I know not all that form the sinner's debt,
But there is one that he must not forget.'

   The mind of *Susan* prompted her with speed
To act her part in every courteous deed:
All that was kind she was prepared to say,
And keep the lecture for a future day;
When he had all life's comforts by his side,
Pity might sleep, and good advice be tried.   460

   This done, the Mistress felt disposed to look,
As self-approving, on a pious book:
Yet, to her native bias still inclined,
She felt her act too merciful and kind;
But, when long musing on the chilling scene
So lately past – the frost and sleet so keen –
The Man's whole misery in a single view, –
Yes! she could think some pity was his due.

   Thus fixed, she heard not her Attendant glide
With soft slow step – till, standing by her side,   470
The trembling Servant gasped for breath, and shed
Relieving tears, then uttered – 'He is dead!'

   'Dead!' said the startled Lady, 'Yes, he fell

Close at the door where he was wont to dwell;
There his sole friend, the Ass, was standing by,
Half dead himself, to see his Master die.'

'Expired he then, good Heaven! for want of food?'
'No! crusts and water in a corner stood; –
To have this plenty, and to wait so long,
480   And to be right too late, is doubly wrong:
Then, every day to see him totter by,
And to forbear – Oh! what a heart had I!'

'Blame me not, child – I tremble at the news:'
''Tis my own heart,' said *Susan*, 'I accuse:
To have this money in my purse – to know
What grief was his, and what to grief we owe;
To see him often, always to conceive
How he must pine and languish, groan and grieve;
And every day in ease and peace to dine,
490   And rest in comfort! – what a heart is mine!' –

TALE XVIII

THE WAGER

'Tis thought your deer doth hold you at a bay.
Taming the Shrew, Act V. Scene 2.

I choose her for myself,
If she and I are pleas'd, what's that to you?
—, Act V, Scene 2.

Let's send each one to his wife,
And he whose wife is most obedient
Shall win the wager.
—, Act V. Scene 2.

Now by the world it is a lusty wench,
I love her ten times more than e'er I did.
—, Act II. Scene 1.

Counter and *Clubb* were men in trade, whose pains,
Credit, and prudence, brought them constant gains;
Partners and punctual, every friend agreed
Counter and *Clubb* were men who must succeed.
When they had fixed some little time in life,
Each thought of taking to himself a wife:
As men in trade alike, as men in love
They seemed with no according views to move;
As certain ores in outward view the same,
They showed their difference when the magnet came.   10
Counter was vain; with spirit strong and high,
'Twas not in him like suppliant swain to sigh:
'His wife might o'er his men and maids preside,

And in her province be a judge and guide;
But what he thought, or did, or wished to do,
She must not know, or censure if she knew;
At home, abroad, by day, by night, if he
On aught determined, so it was to be:
20 'How is a man,' he asked, 'for business fit,
Who to a female can his will submit?
Absent awhile, let no inquiring eye
Or plainer speech presume to question why;
But all be silent; and, when seen again,
Let all be cheerful – shall a wife complain?
Friends I invite, and who shall dare to object,
Or look on them with coolness or neglect?
No! I must ever of my house be head,
And, thus obeyed, I condescend to wed.'

Clubb heard the speech – 'My Friend is nice,' said he;
30 'A wife with less respect will do for me:
How is he certain such a prize to gain?
What he approves, a lass may learn to feign,
And so affect to obey till she begins to reign;
Awhile complying, she may vary then,
And be as wives of more unwary men:
Beside, to him who plays such lordly part,
How shall a tender creature yield her heart?
Should he the promised confidence refuse,
She may another more confiding choose;
40 May show her anger, yet her purpose hide,
And wake his jealousy, and wound his pride.
In one so humbled, who can trace the friend?
I, on an equal, not a slave, depend;
If true, my confidence is wisely placed,
And being false, she only is disgraced.'

Clubb, with these notions, cast his eye around,
And one so easy soon a partner found.
The Lady chosen was of good repute;
Meekness she had not, and was seldom mute;

Though quick to anger, still she loved to smile,   50
And would be calm if men would wait awhile:
She knew her duty, and she loved her way,
More pleased in truth to govern than obey;
She heard her Priest with reverence, and her Spouse
As one who felt the pressure of her vows;
Useful and civil, all her friends confessed –
Give her her way, and she would choose the best;
Though some indeed a sly remark would make, –
Give it her not, and she would choose to take.

All this, when *Clubb* some cheerful months had spent,   60
He saw, confessed, and said he was content.

Counter meantime selected, doubted, weighed,
And then brought home a young complying Maid; –
A tender creature, full of fears as charms,
A beauteous nursling from its mother's arms;
A soft, sweet blossom, such as men must love,
But to preserve must keep it in the stove:
She had a mild, subdued, expiring look –
Raise but the voice, and this fair creature shook;
Leave her alone, she felt a thousand fears –   70
Chide, and she melted into floods of tears;
Fondly she pleaded and would gently sigh,
For very pity, or she knew not why;
One whom to govern none could be afraid –
Hold up the finger, this meek thing obeyed;
Her happy Husband had the easiest task –
Say but his will, no question would she ask;
She sought no reasons, no affairs she knew,
Of business spoke not, and had nought to do.

Oft he exclaimd, 'How meek! how mild! how kind!   80
With her 'twere cruel but to seem unkind;
Though ever silent when I take my leave,
It pains my heart to think how hers will grieve;
'Tis Heaven on earth with such a wife to dwell,

I am in raptures to have sped so well;
But let me not, my friend, your envy raise,
No! on my life, your patience has my praise.'

    His Friend, though silent, felt the scorn implied –
'What need of patience?' to himself he cried:
90   'Better a woman o'er her house to rule,
Than a poor child just hurried from her school;
Who has no care, yet never lives at ease;
Unfit to rule, and indisposed to please;
What if he govern, there his boast should end,
No husband's power can make a slave his friend.'

    It was the custom of these Friends to meet
With a few neighbours in a neighbouring street;
Where *Counter* oft-times would occasion seize,
100   To move his silent Friend by words like these:
'A man,' said he, 'if governed by his wife,
Gives up his rank and dignity in life;
Now, better fate befalls my Friend and me' –
He spoke, and looked the approving smile to see.

    The quiet Partner, when he chose to speak,
Desired his Friend 'another theme to seek;
When thus they met, he judged that state-affairs
And such important subjects should be theirs:'
But still the Partner, in his lighter vein,
Would cause in *Clubb* affliction or disdain;
110   It made him anxious to detect the cause
Of all that boasting – 'Wants my friend applause?
This plainly proves him not at perfect ease,
For, felt he pleasure, he would wish to please. –
These triumphs here for some regrets atone, –
Men who are blessed, let other men alone.'
Thus made suspicious, he observed and saw
His Friend each night at early hour withdraw;
He sometimes mentioned *Juliet*'s tender nerves,
And what attention such a wife deserves:

'In this,' thought *Clubb*, 'full sure some mystery lies –   120
He laughs at me, yet he with much complies,
And all his vaunts of bliss are proud apologies.'

   With such ideas treasured in his breast,
He grew composed, and let his anger rest;
Till *Counter* once (when wine so long went round
That Friendship and Discretion both were drowned)
Began in teasing and triumphant mood
His evening banter – 'Of all earthly good,
The best,' he said, 'was an obedient spouse,   130
Such as my Friend's – that every one allows;
What if she wishes his designs to know?
It is because she would her praise bestow;
What if she will that he remains at home?
She knows that mischief may from travel come.
I, who am free to venture where I please,
Have no such kind preventing checks as these;
But mine is double duty, first to guide
Myself aright, then rule a house beside;
While this our Friend, more happy than the free,
Resigns all power, and laughs at liberty.'   140

   'By Heaven!' said *Clubb*, 'excuse me if I swear –
I'll bet a hundred guineas, if he dare,
That uncontrolled I will such freedoms take,
That he will fear to equal – there's my stake.'

   'A match!' said *Counter*, much by wine inflamed;
'But we are friends – let smaller stake be named;
Wine for our future meeting, that will I
Take and no more – what peril shall we try?'
'Let's to *Newmarket*,' *Clubb* replied; 'or choose
Yourself the place, and what you like to lose;   150
And he who first returns, or fears to go,
Forfeits his cash –' Said *Counter*, 'Be it so.'

   The friends around them saw with much delight
The social war, and hailed the pleasant night;

Nor would they further hear the cause discussed,
Afraid the recreant heart of *Clubb* to trust.

   Now sober thoughts returned as each withdrew,
And of the subject took a serious view:
''Twas wrong,' thought *Counter*, 'and will grieve my love;'
160   ''Twas wrong,' thought *Clubb*, 'my wife will not approve;
But friends were present; I must try the thing,
Or with my folly half the town will ring.'

   He sought his Lady – 'Madam, I'm to blame,
But was reproached, and could not bear the shame;
Here in my folly – for 'tis best to say
The very truth – I've sworn to have my way;
To that *Newmarket* – (though I hate the place,
And have no taste or talents for a race,
Yet so it is – well, now prepare to chide –)
170   I laid a wager that I dared to ride;
And I must go; by Heaven, if you resist
I shall be scorned, and ridiculed, and hissed;
Let me with grace before my friends appear,
You know the truth, and must not be severe;
He too must go, but that he will of course;
Do you consent? – I never think of force.'

   'You never need,' the worthy Dame replied;
'The husband's honour is the woman's pride;
If I in trifles be the wilful wife,
180   Still for your credit I would lose my life;
Go! and when fixed the day of your return,
Stay longer yet, and let the blockheads learn
That though a wife may sometimes wish to rule,
She would not make the indulgent man a fool;
I would at times advise – but idle they
Who think the assenting husband *must* obey.'

   The happy Man, who thought his Lady right
In other cases, was assured tonight;

Then for the day with proud delight prepared,
To show his doubting friends how much he dared.   190

   Counter, – who grieving sought his bed, his rest,
Broken by pictures of his Love distressed, –
With soft and winning speech the Fair prepared;
'She all his councils, comforts, pleasures shared;
She was assured he loved her from his soul,
She never knew, and need not fear control;
But so it happened – he was grieved at heart,
It happened so, that they awhile must part
A little time – the distance was but short,
And business called him – he despised the sport;   200
But to *Newmarket* he engaged to ride
With his friend *Clubb*,' and there he stopped and sighed.

   Awhile the tender creature looked dismayed,
Then floods of tears the call of grief obeyed: –

   'She an objection! No!' she sobbed, 'not one;
Her work was finished, and her race was run;
For die she must, indeed she would not live
A week alone, for all the world could give;
He too must die in that same wicked place;
It always happened – was a common case;   210
Among those horrid horses, jockeys, crowds,
'Twas certain death – they might bespeak their shrouds;
He would attempt a race, be sure to fall –
And she expire with terror – that was all;
With love like hers, she was indeed unfit
To bear such horrors, but she must submit.'

   'But for three days, my Love! three days at most –'
'Enough for me; I then shall be a ghost –'
'My honour's pledged;' – 'Oh yes, my dearest life,
I know your honour must outweigh your wife;   220
But, ere this absence, have you sought a friend?
I shall be dead – on whom you can depend? –

Let me one favour of your kindness crave,
Grant me the stone I mentioned for my grave. –'

'Nay, Love, attend – why, bless my soul –I say
I will return – there – weep no longer –nay! –'
'Well! I obey, and to the last am true,
But spirits fail me; I must die, adieu!'

'What, Madam! must? – 'tis wrong – I'm angry –zounds!
230   Can I remain and lose a thousand pounds?'

'Go, then, my love! it is a monstrous sum,
Worth twenty wives – go, love! and I am dumb –
Nor be displeased – had I the power to live,
You might be angry, now you must forgive;
Alas! I faint – ah! cruel – there's no need
Of wounds or fevers – this has done the deed.'

The Lady fainted, and the Husband sent
For every aid, for every comfort went;
Strong terror seized him; 'Oh! she loved so well,
240   And who the effect of tenderness could tell?'

She now recovered, and again began
With accent querulous, – 'Ah! cruel man –'
Till the sad Husband, conscience-struck, confessed
'Twas very wicked with his Friend to jest;
For now he saw that those who were obeyed,
Could like the most subservient feel afraid;
And though a wife might not dispute the will
Of her liege Lord, she could prevent it still.

The morning came, and *Clubb* prepared to ride
250   With a smart boy, his servant and his guide;
When, ere he mounted on the ready steed,
Arrived a letter, and he stopped to read.

'My friend,' he read – 'our journey I decline,
A heart too tender for such strife is mine;
Yours is the triumph, be you so inclined;

But you are too considerate and kind:
In tender pity to my *Juliet*'s fears
I thus relent, o'ercome by love and tears;
She knows your kindness; I have heard her say,
A man like you 'tis pleasure to obey: 260
Each faithful wife, like ours, must disapprove
Such dangerous trifling with connubial love;
What has the idle world, my friend, to do
With our affairs? they envy me and you:
What if I could my gentle spouse command, –
Is that a cause I should her tears withstand?
And what if you, a friend of peace, submit
To one you love, – is that a theme for wit?
'Twas wrong, and I shall henceforth judge it weak
Both of submission and control to speak: 270
Be it agreed that all contention cease,
And no such follies vex our future peace;
Let each keep guard against domestic strife,
And find nor slave nor tyrant in his wife.' –

'Agreed,' said *Clubb*, 'with all my soul agreed –'
And to the boy, delighted, gave his steed;
'I think my friend has well his mind expressed,
And I assent; such things are not a jest.'

'True,' said the Wife, 'no longer he can hide
The truth that pains him by his wounded pride;   280
Your Friend has found it not an easy thing,
Beneath his yoke, this yielding soul to bring;
These weeping willows, though they seem inclined
By every breeze, yet not the strongest wind
Can from their bent divert this weak but stubborn kind;
Drooping they seek your pity to excite,
But 'tis at once their nature and delight;
Such women feel not; while they sigh and weep,
'Tis but their habit – their affections sleep;
They are like ice that in the hand we hold,   290
So very melting, yet so very cold;

On such affection let not man rely,
The husbands suffer, and the ladies sigh:
But your friend's offer let us kindly take,
And spare his pride for his vexation's sake;
For he has found, and through his life will find,
'Tis easiest dealing with the firmest mind –
More just when it resists, and, when it yields, more kind.'

THE CONVERT

A Tapster is a good trade,
And an old cloak makes a new jerkin,
A wither'd serving-man, a fresh tapster.
Merry Wives of Windsor, Act I. Scene 3.

A fellow, sir, that I have known go about with my troll-my-dames.
Winter's Tale, Act IV. Scene 2.

I myself, sometimes leaving the fear of Heaven
on my left hand, and hiding mine honour in my necessity, am forced to
shuffle, to hedge, and to lurch.
Merry Wives of Windsor, Act II. Scene 2.

Yea, and at that very moment,
Consideration like an Angel came,
And whipp'd th' offending Adam out of him.
Henry V, Act I. Scene 1.

I have liv'd long enough; my May of life
Is fall'n into the sear, the yellow leaf;
And that which should accompany old age,
As honour, love, obedience, troops of friends,
I must not look to have.
Macbeth, Act V. Scene 3.

Some to our Hero have a hero's name
Denied, because no father's he could claim;
Nor could his mother with precision state
A full fair claim to her certificate;
On her own word the marriage must depend, –
A point she was not eager to defend:

But who, without a father's name, can raise
His own so high, deserves the greater praise;
The less advantage to the strife he brought,
10   The greater wonders has his prowess wrought;
He who depends upon his wind and limbs,
Needs neither cork nor bladder when he swims;
Nor will by empty breath be puffed along,
As not himself – but in his helpers – strong.

Suffice it then, our Hero's name was clear,
For, call *John Dighton*, and he answered 'Here!'
But who that name in early life assigned,
He never found, he never tried to find:
Whether his kindred were to *John* disgrace,
20   Or *John* to them, is a disputed case;
His infant-state owed nothing to their care –
His mind neglected, and his body bare;
All his success must on himself depend,
He had no money, counsel, guide, or friend;
But in a market-town an active boy
Appeared, and sought in various ways employ;
Who soon, thus cast upon the world, began
To show the talents of a thriving man.

With spirit high, *John* learned the world to brave,
30   And in both senses was a ready knave;
Knave as of old, obedient, keen, and quick,
Knave as at present, skilled to shift and trick;
Some humble part of many trades he caught,
He for the builder and the painter wrought;
For serving-maids on secret errands ran,
The waiter's helper, and the hostler's man;
And when he chanced (oft chanced he) place to lose,
His varying genius shone in blacking shoes:
A midnight fisher by the pond he stood,
40   Assistant poacher he o'erlook'd the wood;
At an election, *John*'s impartial mind
Was to no cause nor candidate confined;
To all in turn he full allegiance swore,

And in his hat the various badges bore:
His liberal soul with every sect agreed,
Unheard their reasons, he received their creed;
At Church he deigned the organ-pipes to fill,
And at the meeting sang both loud and shrill:
But the full purse these different merits gained,
By strong demands his lively passions drained;   50
Liquors he loved of each inflaming kind,
To midnight revels flew with ardent mind;
Too warm at cards, a losing game he played,
To fleecing beauty his attention paid;
His boiling passions were by oaths expressed,
And lies he made his profit and his jest.

Such was the boy, and such the man had been,
But fate or happier fortune changed the scene;
A fever seized him, 'He should surely die –'
He feared, and lo! a friend was praying by;   60
With terror moved, this Teacher he addressed,
And all the errors of his youth confessed:
The good man kindly cleared the Sinner's way
To lively hope, and counselled him to pray;
Who then resolved, should he from sickness rise,
To quit cards, liquors, poaching, oaths, and lies:
His health restored, he yet resolved, and grew
True to his masters, to their Meeting true;
His old companions at his sober face
Laughed loud, while he, attesting it was grace,   70
With tears besought them all his calling to embrace:
To his new friends such convert gave applause,
Life to their zeal, and glory to their cause:
Though terror wrought the mighty change, yet strong
Was the impression, and it lasted long;
John at the lectures due attendance paid,
A convert meek, obedient, and afraid.
His manners strict, though formed on fear alone,
Pleased the grave friends, nor less his solemn tone,
The lengthened face of care, the low and inward groan: 80

The stern good men exulted, when they saw
Those timid looks of penitence and awe;
Nor thought that one so passive, humble, meek,
Had yet a creed and principles to seek.

The faith that Reason finds, confirms, avows,
The hopes, the views, the comforts she allows, –
These were not his, who by his feelings found,
And by them only, that his faith was sound;
Feelings of terror these, for evil past,
90   Feelings of hope, to be received at last;
Now weak, now lively, changing with the day,
These were his feelings, and he felt his way.

Sprung from such sources, will this faith remain
While these supporters can their strength retain:
As heaviest weights the deepest rivers pass,
While icy chains fast bind the solid mass;
So, born of feelings, faith remains secure,
Long as their firmness and their strength endure:
But when the waters in their channel glide,
100   A bridge must bear us o'er the threatening tide;
Such bridge is Reason, and there Faith relies,
Whether the varying spirits fall or rise.

His Patrons, still disposed their aid to lend,
Behind a counter placed their humble friend;
Where pens and paper were on shelves displayed,
And pious pamphlets on the windows laid:
By nature active, and from vice restrained,
Increasing trade his bolder views sustained;
His friends and teachers, finding so much zeal
110   In that young convert whom they taught to feel,
His trade encouraged, and were pleased to find
A hand so ready, with such humble mind.

And now, his health restored, his spirits eased,
He wished to marry, if the Teachers pleased.
They, not unwilling, from the virgin-class

Took him a comely and a courteous lass;
Simple and civil, loving and beloved,
She long a fond and faithful partner proved;
In every year the Elders and the Priest
Were duly summoned to a christening feast;   120
Nor came a babe, but by his growing trade,
John had provison for the coming made;
For friends and strangers all were pleased to deal
With one whose care was equal to his zeal.

In human friendships, it compels a sigh,
To think what trifles will dissolve the tie.
John, now become a master of his trade,
Perceived how much improvement might be made;
And as this prospect opened to his view,
A certain portion of his zeal withdrew;   130
His fear abated, – 'What had he to fear, –
His profits certain, and his conscience clear?'
Above his door a board was placed by *John*,
And '*Dighton, Stationer*,' was gilt thereon;
His window next, enlarged to twice the size,
Shone with such trinkets as the simple prize;
While in the shop with pious works were seen
The last new play, review, or magazine:
In orders punctual, he observed – 'the books
He never read, and could he judge their looks?   140
Readers and critics should their merits try,
He had no office but to sell and buy;
Like other traders, profit was his care;
Of what they print, the authors must beware;'
He held his Patrons and his Teachers dear,
But with his trade – they must not interfere.

'Twas certain now that *John* had lost the dread
And pious thoughts that once such terrors bred;
His habits varied, and he more inclined
To the vain world, which he had half resigned: 150
He had moreover in his brethren seen,

Or he imagined, craft, conceit, and spleen;
'They are but men,' said *John*, 'and shall I then
Fear man's control, or stand in awe of men?
'Tis their advice, (their Convert's rule and law,)
And good it is – I will not stand in awe.'

Moreover *Dighton*, though he thought of books
As one who chiefly on the title looks,
Yet sometimes pondered o'er a page to find,
When vexed with cares, amusement for his mind;
And by degrees that mind had treasured much
From works his teachers were afraid to touch:
Satiric novels, poets bold and free,
And what their writers term philosophy;
All these were read, and he began to feel
Some self-approval on his bosom steal.
Wisdom creates humility, but he
Who thus collects it, will not humble be:
No longer *John* was filled with pure delight,
And humble reverence in a Pastor's sight;
Who, like a grateful zealot, listening stood,
To hear a man so friendly and so good;
But felt the dignity of one who made
Himself important by a thriving trade;
And growing pride in *Dighton*'s mind was bred
By the strange food on which it coarsely fed.

Their Brother's fall the grieving Brethren heard,
The pride indeed to all around appeared;
The world his friends agreed had won the soul
From its best hopes, the man from their control:
To make him humble, and confine his views
Within their bounds, and books which they peruse;
A deputation from these friends select,
Might reason with him to some good effect;
Armed with authority, and led by love,
They might those follies from his mind remove;

Deciding thus, and with this kind intent,
A chosen body with its speaker went.

'*John*,' said the Teacher, '*John*, with great concern
We see thy frailty, and thy fate discern, –   190
Satan with toils thy simple soul beset,
And thou art careless, slumbering in the net;
Unmindful art thou of thy early vow;
Who at the morning-meeting sees thee now?
Who at the evening? "Where is brother *John*?"
We ask – are answered, "To the tavern gone;"
Thee on the Sabbath seldom we behold,
Thou canst not sing, thou art nursing for a cold:
This from the Churchmen thou hast learned, for they
Have colds and fevers on the Sabbath-day;   200
When in some snug warm room they sit, and pen
Bills from their ledgers, (world-entangled men!)

'See with what pride thou hast enlarged thy shop;
To view thy tempting stores, the heedless stop;
By what strange names dost thou these baubles know,
Which wantons wear, to make a sinful show?
Hast thou in view these idle volumes placed
To be the pander of a vicious taste?
What's here? a book of dances! – you advance
In goodly knowledge – *John*, wilt learn to dance?   210
How! "Go –" it says, and "*to the devil go!*
And shake thyself!" I tremble – but 'tis so –
Wretch as thou art, what answer canst thou make?
Oh! without question thou wilt go and shake.
What's here? the *School for Scandal!* – pretty schools!
Well, and art thou proficient in the rules?
Art thou a pupil, is it thy design
To make our names contemptible as thine?
Old Nick, a Novel! oh! 'tis mighty well –
A fool has courage when he laughs at hell;   220
Frolic and Fun, the Humours of *Tim Grin*;

Why, *John*, thou grow'st facetious in thy sin;
And what? *the Archdeacon's Charge* – 'tis mighty well –
If Satan published, thou wouldst doubtless sell;
Jests, novels, dances, and this precious stuff,
To crown thy folly – we have seen enough;
We find thee fitted for each evil work –
Do print the *Koran* and become a Turk.

    '*John*, thou art lost, success and worldly pride
230   O'er all thy thoughts and purposes preside,
Have bound thee fast, and drawn thee far aside;
Yet turn; these sin-traps from thy shop expel,
Repent and pray, and all may yet be well.

    'And here thy wife, thy *Dorothy* behold,
How fashion's wanton robes her form infold!
Can grace, can goodness with such trappings dwell?
John, thou hast made thy wife a *Jezebel*:
See! on her bosom rests the sign of sin,
The glaring proof of naughty thoughts within;
240   What! 'tis a cross; come hither – as a friend,
Thus from thy neck the shameful badge I rend.' –

    'Rend, if you dare,' said *Dighton*, 'you shall find
A man of spirit, though to peace inclined;
Call me ungrateful! have I not my pay
At all times ready for the expected day? –
To share my plenteous board you deign to come,
Myself your pupil, and my house your home?
And shall the persons who my meat enjoy,
Talk of my faults, and treat me as a boy?
250   Have you not told how *Rome*'s insulting priests
Led their meek Laymen like a herd of beasts;
And by their fleecing and their forgery made
Their holy calling an accursed trade?
Can you such acts and insolence condemn,
Who to your utmost power resemble them?

    'Concerns it you what books I set for sale?
The tale perchance may be a virtuous tale;

And for the rest, 'tis neither wise nor just,
In you, who read not, to condemn on trust;
Why should the Archdeacon's Charge your spleen excite?   260
He, or perchance the Archbishop, may be right.

'That from your meetings I refrain, is true;
I meet with nothing pleasant – nothing new;
But the same proofs, that not one text explain,
And the same lights, where all things dark remain;
I thought you Saints on earth, – but I have found
Some sins among you, and the best unsound;
You have your failings, like the crowds below,
And at your pleasure, hot and cold can blow:
When I at first your grave deportment saw,   270
(I own my folly,) I was filled with awe;
You spoke so warmly, and it seems so well,
I should have thought it treason to rebel;
Is it a wonder that a man like me
Should such perfection in such teachers see?
Nay, should conceive you sent from Heaven to brave
The host of sin, and sinful souls to save?
But as our reason wakes, our prospects clear,
And failings, flaws, and blemishes appear.

'When you were mounted in your rostrum high,   280
We shrank beneath your tone, your frown, your eye:
Then you beheld us abject, fallen, low,
And felt your glory from our baseness grow;
Touched by your words, I trembled like the rest,
And my own vileness, and your power confessed:
These, I exclaimed, are men divine, and gazed
On him who taught, delighted and amazed;
Glad when he finished, if by chance he cast
One look on such a sinner, as he passed.

'But when I viewed you in a clearer light,   290
And saw the frail and carnal appetite;
When, at his humble prayer, you deigned to eat,
Saints as you are, a civil Sinner's meat;

When as you sat contented and at ease,
Nibbling at leisure on the ducks and peas,
And, pleased some comforts in such place to find,
You could descend to be a little kind;
And gave us hope, in Heaven there might be room
For a few souls beside your own to come;
While this world's good engaged your carnal view,
And like a sinner you enjoyed it too;
All this perceiving, can you think it strange
That change in you should work an equal change?'

    'Wretch that thou art,' an Elder cried, 'and gone
For everlasting.' – 'Go thyself,' said *John*;
'Depart this instant, let me hear no more;
My house my castle is, and that my door.'

    The hint they took, and from the door withdrew,
And *John* to Meeting bade a long adieu;
Attached to business, he in time became
A wealthy man of no inferior name.
It seemed, alas! in *John*'s deluded sight,
That all was wrong because not all was right;
And when he found his Teachers had their stains,
Resentment and not reason broke his chains;
Thus on his feelings he again relied,
And never looked to Reason for his guide:
Could he have wisely viewed the frailty shown,
And rightly weighed their wanderings and his own;
He might have known that men may be sincere,
Though gay and feasting on the savoury cheer;
That doctrines sound and sober they may teach,
Who love to eat with all the glee they preach;
Nay! who believe the duck, the grape, the pine,
Were not intended for the dog and swine:
But *Dighton*'s hasty mind on every theme
Ran from the truth, and rested in the extreme;
Flaws in his friends he found, and then withdrew
(Vain of his knowledge) from their virtues too.

300

310

320

Best of his books he loved the liberal kind, 330
That, if they improve not, still enlarge the mind;
And found himself, with such advisers, free
From a fixed creed as mind enlarged could be.
His humble wife at these opinions sighed,
But her he never heeded till she died;
He then assented to a last request,
And by the Meeting-window let her rest;
And on her stone the sacred text was seen,
Which had her comfort in departing been.

Dighton with joy beheld his trade advance, 340
Yet seldom published, loth to trust to chance;
Then wed a Doctor's sister – poor indeed,
But skilled in works her husband could not read;
Who, if he wished new ways of wealth to seek,
Could make her half-crown pamphlet in a week;
This he rejected, though without disdain,
And chose the old and certain way to gain.

Thus he proceeded; trade increased the while,
And Fortune wooed him with perpetual smile:
On early scenes he sometimes cast a thought, 350
When on his heart the mighty change was wrought;
And all the ease and comfort Converts find,
Was magnified in his reflecting mind;
Then on the Teacher's priestly pride he dwelt,
That caused his freedom; but with this he felt
The danger of the free – for since that day
No guide had shown, no Brethren joined his way;
Forsaking one, he found no second creed,
But reading doubted, doubting what to read.

Still, though reproof had brought some present pain, 360
The gain he made was fair and honest gain;
He laid his wares indeed in public view,
But that all traders claim a right to do:
By means like these, he saw his wealth increase,
And felt his consequence, and dwelt in peace.

Our Hero's age was threescore years and five,
When he exclaimed, 'Why longer should I strive?
Why more amass, who never must behold
A young *John Dighton* to make glad the old?'
370   (The sons he had, to early graves were gone,
And girls were burdens to the mind of *John*.)
'Had I a boy, he would our name sustain,
That now to nothing must return again;
But what are all my profits, credit, trade,
And parish-honours? – folly and parade.'

Thus *Dighton* thought, and in his looks appeared
Sadness, increased by much he saw and heard:
The Brethren often at the shop would stay,
And make their comments ere they walked away;
380   They marked the window, filled in every pane,
With lawless prints of reputations slain;
Distorted forms of men with honours graced,
And our chief rulers in derision placed:
Amazed they stood, remembering well the days,
When to be humble was their brother's praise;
When at the dwelling of their friend they stopped
To drop a word, or to receive it dropped;
Where they beheld the prints of men renowned,
And far-famed Preachers pasted all round;
390   (Such mouths! eyes! hair! so prim! so fierce! so sleek!
They looked as speaking what is woe to speak):
On these the passing Brethren loved to dwell –
How long they spoke! how strongly! warmly! well!
What power had each to dive in mysteries deep,
To warm the cold, to make the hardened weep;
To lure, to fright, to soothe, to awe the soul,
And listening flocks to lead and to control!

But now discoursing, as they lingered near,
They tempted *John* (whom they accused) to hear
400   Their weighty charge, – 'And can the lost-one feel,

As in the time of duty, love, and zeal;
When all were summoned at the rising sun,
And he was ready with his friends to run;
When he, partaking with a chosen few,
Felt the great change, sensation rich and new?
No! all is lost, her favours Fortune showered
Upon the man, and he is overpowered;
The world has won him with its tempting store
Of needless wealth, and that has made him poor:
Success undoes him; he has risen to fall,   410
Has gained a fortune, and has lost his all;
Gone back from Sion, he will find his age
Loth to commence a second pilgrimage;
He has retreated from the chosen track,
And now must ever bear the burden on his back.'

Hurt by such censure, *John* began to find
Fresh revolutions working in his mind;
He sought for comfort in his books, but read
Without a plan or method in his head;
What once amused, now rather made him sad,   420
What should inform, increased the doubts he had;
Shame would not let him seek at Church a guide,
And from his Meeting he was held by pride;
His Wife derided fears she never felt,
And passing Brethren daily censures dealt;
Hope for a son was now for ever past,
He was the first *John Dighton*, and the last;
His stomach failed, his case the Doctor knew,
But said, 'he still might hold a year or two;'
'No more!' he said, 'but why should I complain?   430
A life of doubt must be a life of pain:
Could I be sure – but why should I despair?
I'm sure my conduct has been just and fair;
In youth indeed I had a wicked will,
But I repented, and have sorrow still:
I had my comforts, and a growing trade

Gave greater pleasure than a fortune made;
And as I more possessed and reasoned more,
I lost those comforts I enjoyed before,
When reverend guides I saw my table round,
And in my guardian guests my safety found:
Now sick and sad, no appetite, no ease,
Nor pleasure have I, nor a wish to please;
Nor views, nor hopes, nor plans, nor taste have I,
Yet sick of life, have no desire to die.'

He said and died; his trade, his name is gone,
And all that once gave consequence to *John*.

Unhappy *Dighton*! had he found a friend,
When conscience told him it was time to mend;
A friend discreet, considerate, kind, sincere,
Who would have shown the grounds of hope and fear;
And proved that spirits, whether high or low,
No certain tokens of man's safety show;
Had Reason ruled him in her proper place,
And Virtue led him while he leaned on Grace;
Had he while zealous been discreet and pure,
His knowledge humble, and his hope secure; —
These guides had placed him on the solid rock,
Where Faith had rested, nor received a shock;
But his, alas! was placed upon the sand,
Where long it stood not, and where none can stand.

THE BROTHERS

A Brother noble,
Whose nature is so far from doing harms,
That he suspects none; on whose foolish honesty
My practice may ride easy.
King Lear, Act I. Scene 2.

He lets me feed with hinds,
Bars me the place of Brother.
As You Like It, Act I. Scene 1.

'Twas I, but 'tis not I: I do not shame
To tell you what I was, being what I am.
As You Like It, Act IV. Scene 3.

Than old *George Fletcher*, on the British coast,
Dwelt not a seaman who had more to boast;
Kind, simple, and sincere, – he seldom spoke,
But sometimes sang and chorused – '*Hearts of Oak*;'
In dangers steady, with his lot content,
His days in labour and in love were spent.

He left a Son so like him, that the old
With joy exclaimed, ' 'Tis *Fletcher* we behold;'
But to his Brother when the kinsmen came,
And viewed his form, they grudged the father's name. 10

George was a bold, intrepid, careless lad,
With just the failings that his father had;
Isaac was weak, attentive, slow, exact,
With just the virtues that his father lacked.

George lived at sea; upon the land a guest,
He sought for recreation, not for rest, –
While, far unlike, his Brother's feebler form
Shrank from the cold, and shuddered at the storm;
Still with the Seaman's to connect his trade,
20   The boy was bound where blocks and ropes were made.

George, strong and sturdy, had a tender mind,
And was to Isaac pitiful and kind;
A very father, till his art was gained,
And then a friend unwearied he remained:
He saw his Brother was of spirit low,
His temper peevish, and his motions slow;
Not fit to bustle in a world, or make
Friends to his fortune for his merit's sake:
But the kind Sailor could not boast the art
30   Of looking deeply in the human heart;
Else had he seen that his weak Brother knew
What men to court – what objects to pursue;
That he to distant gain the way discerned,
And none so crooked but his genius learned.

Isaac was poor, and this the Brother felt;
He hired a house, and there the Landman dwelt;
Wrought at his trade, and had an easy home,
For there would George with cash and comforts come;
And when they parted, Isaac looked around,
40   Where other friends and helpers might be found.

He wished for some port-place, and one might fall,
He wisely thought, if he should try for all;
He had a vote, – and, were it well applied,
Might have its worth – and he had views beside;
Old Burgess Steel was able to promote
An humble man who served him with a vote;
For Isaac felt not what some tempers feel,
But bowed and bent the neck to Burgess Steel;
And great attention to a Lady gave,

His ancient friend, a maiden spare and grave: 50
One whom the visage long and look demure
Of *Isaac* pleased – he seemed sedate and pure;
And his soft heart conceived a gentle flame
For her who waited on this virtuous Dame:
Not an outrageous love, a scorching fire,
But friendly liking and chastised desire;
And thus he waited, patient in delay,
In present favour and in fortune's way.

  George then was coasting – war was yet delayed,
And what he gained was to his Brother paid;   60
Nor asked the Seaman what he saved or spent:
But took his grog, wrought hard, and was content;
Till war awaked the land, and *George* began
To think what part became a useful man:
'Pressed I must go – why, then, 'tis better far
At once to enter like a British tar,
Than a brave captain and the foe to shun,
As if I feared the music of a gun.'
'Go not!' said *Isaac* – 'You shall wear disguise:'
'What!' said the Seaman, 'clothe myself with lies?' –   70
'Oh! but there's danger.' – 'Danger in the fleet?
You cannot mean, good Brother, of defeat;
And other dangers I at land must share –
So now adieu! and trust a brother's care.'

  Isaac awhile demurred, – but, in his heart,
So might he share, he was disposed to part:
The better mind will sometimes feel the pain
Of benefactions – favour is a chain;
But they the feeling scorn, and what they wish, disdain; –
While beings formed in coarser mould will hate   80
The helping hand they ought to venerate;
No wonder *George* should in this cause prevail,
With one contending who was glad to fail: –
'*Isaac*, farewell! do wipe that doleful eye;

Crying we came, and groaning we may die;
Let us do something 'twixt the groan and cry;
And hear me, Brother, whether pay or prize,
One half to thee I give and I devise:
For thou hast oft occasion for the aid
90   Of learn'd physicians, and they will be paid:
Their wives and children, men support, at sea,
And thou, my Lad, art wife and child to me:
Farewell! – I go where hope and honour call,
Nor does it follow that who fights must fall.'

   Isaac here made a poor attempt to speak,
And a huge tear moved slowly down his cheek;
Like *Pluto*'s iron drop, hard sign of grace,
It slowly rolled upon the rueful face,
Forced by the striving will alone its way to trace.

100   Years fled – war lasted – *George* at sea remained,
While the slow Landman still his profits gained:
A humble place was vacant – he besought
His Patron's interest, and the office caught;
For still the Virgin was his faithful friend,
And one so sober could with truth commend,
Who of his own defects most humbly thought,
And their advice with zeal and reverence sought:
Whom thus the Mistress praised, the Maid approved,
And her he wedded whom he wisely loved.

110   No more he needs assistance – but, alas!
He fears the money will for liquor pass;
Or that the Seaman might to flatterers lend,
Or give support to some pretended friend:
Still he must write – he wrote, and he confessed
That, till absolved, he should be sore distressed;
But one so friendly would, he thought, forgive
The hasty deed – Heaven knew how he should live;
'But you,' he added, 'as a man of sense,
Have well considered danger and expense:

I ran, alas! into the fatal snare,   120
And now for trouble must my mind prepare;
And how, with children, I shall pick my way,
Through a hard world, is more than I can say:
Then change not, Brother, your more happy state,
Or on the hazard long deliberate.'

   George answered gravely, 'It is right and fit,
In all our crosses, humbly to submit:
Your apprehensions are unwise, unjust;
Forbear repining, and expel distrust.'
He added, 'Marriage was the joy of life,'   130
And gave his service to his Brother's Wife;
Then vowed to bear in all expense a part,
And thus concluded, 'Have a cheerful heart.'

   Had the glad *Isaac* been his Brother's guide,
In these same terms the Seaman had replied;
At such reproofs the crafty Landman smiled,
And softly said, – 'This creature is a child.'

   Twice had the gallant ship a capture made, –
And when in port the happy crew were paid,
Home went the Sailor, with his pocket stored,   140
Ease to enjoy, and pleasure to afford;
His time was short, joy shone in every face,
Isaac half fainted in the fond embrace:
The Wife resolved her honoured guest to please,
The Children clung upon their Uncle's knees;
The grog went round, the neighbours drank his health,
And *George* exclaimed, – 'Ah! what to this is wealth?
Better,' said he, 'to bear a loving heart,
Than roll in riches, – but we now must part!'

   All yet is still, – but hark! the winds o'ersweep   150
The rising waves, and howl upon the deep;
Ships late becalmed on mountain-billows ride, –
So life is threatened, and so man is tried.

Ill were the tidings that arrived from sea,
The worthy *George* must now a cripple be;
His leg was lopped; and though his heart was sound,
Though his brave Captain was with glory crowned, –
Yet much it vexed him to repose on shore,
An idle log, and be of use no more:
160   True, he was sure that *Isaac* would receive
All of his Brother that the foe might leave;
To whom the Seaman his design had sent,
Ere from the port the wounded hero went:
His wealth and expectations told, he 'knew
Wherein they failed, what *Isaac*'s love would do;
That he the grog and cabin would supply,
Where *George* at anchor during life would lie.'

The Landman read – and, reading, grew distressed: –
'Could he resolve to admit so poor a guest?
170   Better at Greenwich might the Sailor stay,
Unless his purse could for his comforts pay;
So *Isaac* judged, and to his Wife appealed,
But yet acknowledged it was best to yield:
Perhaps his pension, with what sums remain
Due or unsquandered, may the man maintain;
Refuse we must not.' – With a heavy sigh
The Lady heard, and made her kind reply: –
'Nor would I wish it, *Isaac*, were we sure
How long his crazy building will endure;
180   Like an old house, that every day appears
About to fall, – he may be propped for years;
For a few months, indeed, we might comply,
But these old battered fellows never die.'

The hand of *Isaac*, *George* on entering took,
With love and resignation in his look;
Declared his comfort in the fortune past,
And joy to find his anchor safely cast;
'Call then my nephews, let the grog be brought,
And I will tell them how the ship was fought.'

Alas! our simple Seaman should have known,   190
That all the care, the kindness, he had shown,
Were from his Brother's heart, if not his memory, flown:
All swept away to be perceived no more,
Like idle structures on the sandy shore;
The chance amusement of the playful boy,
That the rude billows in their rage destroy.

Poor *George* confessed, though loth the truth to find,
Slight was his knowledge of a Brother's mind:
The vulgar pipe was to the Wife offence,
The frequent grog to *Isaac* an expense;   200
Would friends like hers, she questioned, 'choose to come,
Where clouds of poisoned fume defile a room?
This, could their Lady-friend, and *Burgess Steel*,
(Teased with his Worship's asthma) bear to feel?
Could they associate or converse with him, –
A loud rough sailor with a timber limb?'

Cold as he grew, still *Isaac* strove to show,
By well-feigned care, that cold he could not grow;
And when he saw his Brother look distressed,
He strove some petty comforts to suggest;   210
On his Wife solely their neglect to lay,
And then to excuse it as a woman's way;
He too was chidden when her rules he broke,
And then she sickened at the scent of smoke.

George, though in doubt, was still consoled to find
His Brother wishing to be reckoned kind:
That *Isaac* seemed concerned by his distress,
Gave to his injured feelings some redress;
But none he found disposed to lend an ear
To stories, all were once intent to hear: 220
Except his Nephew, seated on his knee,
He found no creature cared about the sea;
But *George* indeed, – for *George* they called the boy,
When his good Uncle was their boast and joy, –

Would listen long, and would contend with sleep,
To hear the woes and wonders of the deep;
Till the fond Mother cried, – 'That man will teach
The foolish boy his loud and boisterous speech.'
So judged the Father – and the boy was taught
230 To shun the Uncle, whom his love had sought.

 The mask of kindness now but seldom worn,
George felt each evil harder to be borne;
And cried, (vexation growing day by day)
'Ah! brother *Isaac!* – What! I'm in the way!'
'No! on my credit, look ye, No! but I
Am fond of peace, and my repose would buy
On any terms – in short, we must comply:
My Spouse had money – she must have her will –
Ah! Brother, – marriage is a bitter pill.' –

240 *George* tried the Lady – 'Sister, I offend;'
'Me?' she replied – 'Oh no! – you may depend
On my regard – but watch your Brother's way,
Whom I, like you, must study and obey.'

 'Ah!' thought the Seaman, 'what a head was mine,
That easy birth at Greenwich to resign!
I'll to the parish' – but a little pride,
And some affection, put the thought aside.

 Now gross neglect and open scorn he bore
In silent sorrow – but he felt the more:
250 The odious pipe he to the kitchen took,
Or strove to profit by some pious book.

 When the mind stoops to this degraded state,
New griefs will darken the dependant's fate;
'Brother!' said *Isaac*, 'you will sure excuse
The little freedom I'm compelled to use:
My Wife's relations, – (curse the haughty crew,) –
Affect such niceness, and such dread of you:

You speak so loud – and they have natures soft, –
Brother – I wish – do go upon the loft!'

Poor *George* obeyed, and to the garret fled,   260
Where not a being saw the tears he shed:
But more was yet required, for guests were come,
Who could not dine if he disgraced the room.
It shocked his spirit to be esteemed unfit
With an own Brother and his Wife to sit;
He grew rebellious – at the Vestry spoke
For weekly aid – they heard it as a joke:
'So kind a Brother, and so wealthy – you
Apply to us? – No! this will never do:
Good neighbour *Fletcher*,' (said the Overseer,)   270
We are engaged – you can have nothing here!'

George muttered something in despairing tone,
Then sought his loft, to think and grieve alone:
Neglected, slighted, restless on his bed,
With heart half broken, and with scraps ill fed;
Yet was he pleased, that hours for play designed,
Were given to ease his ever-troubled mind;
The Child still listened with increasing joy,
And he was soothed by the attentive boy.

At length he sickened, and this duteous Child   280
Watched o'er his sickness, and his pains beguiled;
The Mother bade him from the loft refrain,
But, though with caution, yet he went again;
And now his tales the Sailor feebly told,
His heart was heavy and his limbs were cold:
The tender Boy came often to intreat
His good kind Friend would of his presents eat;
Purloined or purchased, for he saw, with shame,
The food untouched that to his Uncle came;
Who, sick in body and in mind, received   290
The Boy's indulgence, gratified and grieved.

'Uncle will die!' said *George*, – the piteous Wife
Exclaimed, 'she saw no value in his life;
But, sick or well, to my commands attend,
And go no more to your complaining Friend.'
The Boy was vexed, he felt his heart reprove
The stern decree. – What! punished for his love!
No! he would go, but softly, to the room,
Stealing in silence – for he knew his doom.

Once in a week the Father came to say,
'*George*, are you ill?' – and hurried him away;
Yet to his Wife would on their duties dwell,
And often cry, 'Do use my Brother well:'
And something kind, no question *Isaac* meant,
Who took vast credit for the vague intent.

But truly kind, the gentle Boy essayed
To cheer his Uncle, firm, although afraid;
But now the Father caught him at the door,
And, swearing – yes, the Man in Office swore,
And cried, 'Away! How! Brother, I'm surprised,
That one so old can be so ill advised:
Let him not dare to visit you again,
Your cursèd stories will disturb his brain;
Is it not vile to court a foolish boy,
Your own absurd narrations to enjoy?
What! sullen! – ha! *George Fletcher?* you shall see,
Proud as you are, your bread depends on me!'

He spoke, and, frowning, to his dinner went,
Then cooled and felt some qualms of discontent;
And thought on times when he compelled his Son
To hear these stories, nay, to beg for one:
But the Wife's wrath o'ercame the Brother's pain,
And shame was felt, and Conscience rose in vain.

George yet stole up, he saw his Uncle lie
Sick on the bed, and heard his heavy sigh:
So he resolved, before he went to rest,
To comfort one so dear and so distressed;

Then watched his time, but with a child-like art,
Betrayed a something treasured at his heart;
The observant Wife remarked, 'the Boy is grown   330
So like your Brother, that he seems his own;
So close and sullen! and I still suspect
They often meet – do watch them and detect!'

   George now remarked that all was still as night,
And hastened up with terror and delight;
'Uncle!' he cried, and softly tapped the door,
'Do let me in,' – but he could add no more;
The careful Father caught him in the fact,
And cried, – 'You serpent! is it thus you act?
Back to your Mother!' – and, with hasty blow,   340
He sent the indignant Boy to grieve below;
Then at the door an angry speech began –
'Is this your conduct? Is it thus you plan?
Seduce my child, and make my house a scene
Of vile dispute – What is it that you mean? –
George, are you dumb? do learn to know your friends,
And think awhile on whom your bread depends:
What! not a word? be thankful I am cool –
But, Sir, beware, nor longer play the fool;
Come, Brother, come! what is it that you seek   350
By this rebellion? – Speak, you villain, speak! –
Weeping! I warrant – sorrow makes you dumb:
I'll ope your mouth, impostor! if I come;
Let me approach – I'll shake you from the bed,
You stubborn dog – Oh God! my Brother's dead!' –

   Timid was *Isaac*, and in all the past
He felt a purpose to be kind at last;
Nor did he mean his Brother to depart,
Till he had shown the kindness of his heart:
But day by day he put the cause aside,   360
Induced by avarice, peevishness, or pride.

   But now awakened, from this fatal time
His conscience *Isaac* felt, and found his crime:

He raised to *George* a monumental stone,
And there retired to sigh and think alone;
An ague seized him, he grew pale, and shook, –
'So,' said his Son, 'would my poor Uncle look.'
'And so, my Child, shall I like him expire:'
'No! you have physic and a cheerful fire.'
'Unhappy sinner! yes, I'm well supplied
With every comfort my cold heart denied.' –
He viewed his Brother now, but not as one
Who vexed his Wife, by fondness for her Son;
Not as with wooden limb, and seaman's tale,
The odious pipe, vile grog, or humbler ale:
He now the worth and grief alone can view,
Of one so mild, so generous, and so true;
'The frank, kind Brother, with such open heart,
And I to break it – 'twas a Demon's part!'

So *Isaac* now, as led by conscience, feels,
Nor his unkindness palliates or conceals;
'This is your folly,' said his heartless Wife:
'Alas! my folly cost my Brother's life;
It suffered him to languish and decay,
My gentle Brother, whom I could not pay,
And therefore left to pine, and fret his life away.'

He takes his Son, and bids the boy unfold
All the good Uncle of his feelings told,
And he lamented – and the ready tear
Falls as he listens, soothed and grieved to hear.

'Did he not curse me, Child?' 'He never cursed,
But could not breathe, and said his heart would burst:'
'And so will mine:' – 'Then, Father, you must pray;
My Uncle said it took his pains away.'

Repeating thus his sorrows, *Isaac* shows
That he, repenting, feels the debt he owes,
And from this source alone his every comfort flows.

He takes no joy in office, honours, gain;
They make him humble, nay, they give him pain;
'These from my heart,' he cries, 'all feeling drove,   400
They made me cold to nature, dead to love;'
He takes no joy in home, but sighing sees
A Son in sorrow, and a Wife at ease;
He takes no joy in office – see him now,
And *Burgess Steel* has but a passing bow:
Of one sad train of gloomy thoughts possessed,
He takes no joy in friends, in food, in rest –
Dark are the evil days, and void of peace the best.
And thus he lives, if living be to sigh,
And from all comforts of the world to fly,   410
Without a hope in life – without a wish to die.

THE LEARNED BOY

Like one well studied in a sad ostent,
To please his grandam.
Merchant of Venice, Act II. Scene 2.

And then the whining school-boy, with his satchel
And shining morning face, creeping like snail
Unwillingly to school.
As You Like It, Act II. Scene 7.

He is a better scholar than I thought he was –
He has a good sprag memory.
Merry Wives of Windsor, Act IV. Scene 1.

One that feeds
On objects, arts, and imitations,
Which out of use, and stat'd by other men,
Begin his fashion.
Julius Caesar, Act IV. Scene 1.

Oh! torture me no more – I will confess.
2 Henry VI, Act III. Scene 3.

An honest man was Farmer *Jones*, and true,
He did by all as all by him should do;
Grave, cautious, careful, fond of gain was he,
Yet famed for rustic hospitality:
Left with his children in a widowed state,
The quiet man submitted to his fate;
Though prudent Matrons waited for his call,
With cool forbearance he avoided all;

Though each professed a pure maternal joy,
By kind attention to his feeble boy: 10
And though a friendly Widow knew no rest,
Whilst neighbour *Jones* was lonely and distressed;
Nay, though the maidens spoke in tender tone
Their hearts' concern to see him left alone –
Jones still persisted in that cheerless life,
As if 'twere sin to take a second wife.

Oh! 'tis a precious thing, when wives are dead,
To find such numbers who will serve instead:
And in whatever state a man be thrown,
'Tis that precisely they would wish their own;   20
Left the departed infants – then their joy
Is to sustain each lovely girl and boy;
Whatever calling his, whatever trade,
To that their chief attention has been paid;
His happy taste in all things they approve,
His friends they honour, and his food they love;
His wish for order, prudence in affairs,
And equal temper, (thank their stars!) are theirs:
In fact, it seemed to be a thing decreed,
And fixed as fate, that marriage must succeed;   30
Yet some, like *Jones*, with stubborn hearts and hard,
Can hear such claims, and show them no regard.

Soon as our Farmer, like a General, found
By what strong foes he was encompassed round, –
Engage he dared not, and he could not fly,
But saw his hope in gentle parley lie;
With looks of kindness then, and trembling heart,
He met the foe, and art opposed to art.

Now spoke that foe insidious – gentle tones,
And gentle looks, assumed for Farmer *Jones*;   40
'Three girls,' the Widow cried, 'a lively three
To govern well – indeed it cannot be.'
'Yes,' he replied, 'it calls for pains and care:

But I must bear it;' – 'Sir, you cannot bear;
Your son is weak, and asks a Mother's eye:'
'That, my kind friend, a Father's may supply;'
'Such growing griefs your very soul will tease;'
'To grieve another would not give me ease;
I have a Mother' – 'She, poor ancient soul!
Can she the spirits of the young control?
Can she thy peace promote, partake thy care,
Procure thy comforts, and thy sorrows share?
Age is itself impatient, uncontrolled:'
'But Wives like Mothers must at length be old.'
'Thou hast shrewd servants – they are evils sore;'
'Yet a shrewd Mistress might afflict me more.'
'Wilt thou not be a weary, wailing man?'
'Alas! and I must bear it as I can.'

Resisted thus, the Widow soon withdrew,
That in his pride the Hero might pursue;
And off his wonted guard, in some retreat,
Find from a foe prepared entire defeat:
But he was prudent, for he knew in flight
These Parthian warriors turn again and fight:
He but at freedom, not at glory aimed,
And only safety by his caution claimed.

Thus when a great and powerful State decrees,
Upon a small one, in its love, to seize, –
It vows in kindness to protect, defend,
And be the fond ally, the faithful friend;
It therefore wills that humbler State to place
Its hopes of safety in a fond embrace;
Then must that humbler State its wisdom prove,
By kind rejection of such pressing love;
Must dread such dangerous friendship to commence,
And stand collected in its own defence: –
Our Farmer thus the proffered kindness fled,
And shunned the love that into bondage led.

The Widow failing, fresh besiegers came,
To share the fate of this retiring Dame: 80
And each foresaw a thousand ills attend
The man, that fled from so discreet a friend;
And prayed, kind soul! that no event might make
The hardened heart of Farmer *Jones* to ache.

But he still governed with resistless hand,
And where he could not guide he would command:
With steady view in course direct he steered,
And his fair daughters loved him, though they feared;
Each had her school, and as his wealth was known,
Each had in time a household of her own. 90

The Boy indeed was at the Grandam's side,
Humoured and trained, her trouble and her pride:
Companions dear, with speech and spirits mild,
The childish widow and the vapourish child;
This nature prompts; minds uninformed and weak
In such alliance ease and comfort seek;
Pushed by the levity of youth aside,
The cares of man, his humour or his pride,
They feel, in their defenceless state, allied:
The child is pleased to meet regard from age, 100
The old are pleased even children to engage;
And all their wisdom, scorned by proud mankind,
They love to pour into the ductile mind;
By its own weakness into error led,
And by fond age with prejudices fed.

The Father, thankful for the good he had,
Yet saw with pain a whining, timid Lad;
Whom he instructing led through cultured fields,
To show that Man performs, what Nature yields:
But *Stephen*, listless, wandered from the view, 110
From beasts he fled, for butterflies he flew,
And idly gazed about, in search of something new.
The lambs indeed he loved, and wished to play

With things so mild, so harmless, and so gay;
Best pleased the weakest of the flock to see,
With whom he felt a sickly sympathy.

Meantime the Dame was anxious, day and night,
To guide the notions of her Babe aright,
And on the favourite mind to throw her glimmering light:
Her Bible-stories she impressed betimes,
And filled his head with hymns and holy rhymes;
On powers unseen, the good and ill, she dwelt,
And the poor Boy mysterious terrors felt;
From frightful dreams, he waking sobbed in dread,
Till the good Lady came to guard his bed.

The father wished such errors to correct,
But let them pass, in duty and respect;
But more it grieved his worthy mind to see
That *Stephen* never would a farmer be;
In vain he tried the shiftless Lad to guide,
And yet 'twas time that something should be tried:
He at the village-school perchance might gain
All that such mind could gather and retain;
Yet the good Dame affirmed her favourite child
Was apt and studious, though sedate and mild;
'That he on many a learnèd point could speak,
And that his body, not his mind, was weak.'

The Father doubted – but to school was sent
The timid *Stephen*, weeping as he went:
There the rude lads compelled the child to fight,
And sent him bleeding to his home at night;
At this the Grandam more indulgent grew,
And bade her Darling 'shun the beastly crew;
Whom *Satan* ruled, and who were sure to lie,
Howling in torments, when they came to die:'
This was such comfort, that in high disdain
He told their fate, and felt their blows again:
Yet if the Boy had not a hero's heart,

Within the school he played a better part;
He wrote a clean fine hand, and at his slate,   150
With more success than many a hero, sate;
He thought not much indeed – but what depends
On pains and care, was at his fingers' ends.

   This had his Father's praise, who now espied
A spark of merit, with a blaze of pride:
And though a farmer he would never make,
He might a pen with some advantage take;
And as a clerk that instrument employ,
So well adapted to a timid boy.

   A London Cousin soon a place obtained;   .160
Easy but humble – little could be gained:
The time arrived when youth and age must part,
Tears in each eye, and sorrow in each heart;
The careful Father bade his Son attend
To all his duties, and obey his Friend;
To keep his church and there behave aright,
As one existing in his Maker's sight,
Till acts to habits led, and duty to delight:
'Then try, my boy, as quickly as you can,
To assume the looks and spirit of a man;   170
I say, be honest, faithful, civil, true,
And this you may, and yet have courage too:
Heroic men, their country's boast and pride,
Have feared their God, and nothing feared beside;
While others daring, yet imbecile, fly
The power of man, and that of God defy:
Be manly then, though mild, for, sure as fate,
Thou art, my *Stephen*, too effeminate;
Here, take my purse, and make a worthy use
('Tis fairly stocked) of what it will produce: 180
And now my blessing, not as any charm
Or conjuration; but 'twill do no harm.'

   Stephen, whose thoughts were wandering up and down,

Now charmed with promised sights in *London-town*,
Now loth to leave his Grandam – lost the force,
The drift and tenor of this grave discourse;
But, in a general way, he understood
'Twas good advice, and meant, 'My Son, be good;'
And *Stephen* knew that all such precepts mean,
That lads should read their Bible, and be clean.

190

The good old Lady, though in some distress,
Begged her dear *Stephen* would his grief suppress;
'Nay, dry those eyes, my child – and first of all
Hold fast thy faith, whatever may befall:
Hear the best preacher, and preserve the text
For meditation, till you hear the next;
Within your Bible night and morning look –
There is your duty, read no other book;
Be not in crowds, in broils, in riots seen,
And keep your conscience and your linen clean:
Be you a *Joseph*, and the time may be,
When kings and rulers will be ruled by thee.'

200

'Nay,' said the Father – 'Hush, my Son,' replied
The Dame – 'The Scriptures must not be denied.'

The Lad, still weeping, heard the wheels approach,
And took his place within the evening coach,
With heart quite rent asunder: On one side
Was love, and grief, and fear, for scenes untried;
Wild-beasts and wax-work filled the happier part
Of *Stephen*'s varying and divided heart:
This he betrayed by sighs and questions strange,
Of famous shows, the Tower, and the Exchange.

210

Soon at his desk was placed the curious Boy,
Demure and silent at his new employ:
Yet as he could, he much attention paid
To all around him, cautious and afraid;
On older Clerks his eager eyes were fixed,

But *Stephen* never in their council mixed;
Much their contempt he feared, for if like them,
He felt assured he should himself condemn;   220
'Oh! they were all so eloquent, so free,
No! he was nothing – nothing could he be:
They dress so smartly, and so boldly look,
And talk as if they read it from a book;
But I,' said *Stephen*, 'will forbear to speak,
And they will think me prudent and not weak.
They talk, the instant they have dropped the pen,
Of singing-women and of acting-men;
Of plays and places where at night they walk
Beneath the lamps, and with the ladies talk;   230
While other ladies for their pleasure sing,
Oh! 'tis a glorious and a happy thing:
They would despise me, did they understand
I dare not look upon a scene so grand;
Or see the plays when critics rise and roar,
And hiss and groan and cry – Encore! encore! –
There's one among them looks a little kind;
If more encouraged, I would ope my mind.'

Alas! poor *Stephen*, happier had he kept
His purpose secret, while his envy slept;   240
Virtue perhaps had conquered, or his shame
At least preserved him simple as he came.
A year elapsed before this Clerk began
To treat the rustic something like a man;
He then in trifling points the youth advised,
Talked of his coat, and had it modernized:
Or with the lad a Sunday-walk would take,
And kindly strive his passions to awake;
Meanwhile explaining all they heard and saw,
Till *Stephen* stood in wonderment and awe: 250
To a neat garden near the town they strayed,
Where the Lad felt delighted and afraid;
There all he saw was smart, and fine, and fair, –

He could but marvel how he ventured there:
Soon he observed, with terror and alarm,
His friend enlocked within a lady's arm,
And freely talking – 'But it is,' said he,
'A near relation, and that makes him free;'
And much amazed was *Stephen*, when he knew
This was the first and only interview:
Nay, had that lovely arm by him been seized,
The lovely owner had been highly pleased;
'Alas!' he sighed, 'I never can contrive
At such bold, blessed freedoms to arrive;
Never shall I such happy courage boast,
I dare as soon encounter with a ghost.'

Now to a play the friendly couple went,
But the Boy murmured at the money spent;
'He loved,' he said, 'to buy, but not to spend –
They only talk awhile, and there's an end.'

'Come, you shall purchase books,' the Friend replied;
'You are bewildered, and you want a guide;
To me refer the choice, and you shall find
The light break in upon your stagnant mind!'
The cooler Clerks exclaimed, 'In vain your art,
To improve a cub without a head or heart;
Rustics though coarse, and savages though wild,
Our cares may render liberal and mild;
But what, my friend, can flow from all these pains?
There is no dealing with a lack of brains.' –

'True, I am hopeless to behold him man,
But let me make the booby what I can:
Though the rude stone no polish will display,
Yet you may strip the rugged coat away.'

Stephen beheld his books – 'I love to know
How money goes – now here is that to show:

260

270

280

And now,' he cried, 'I shall be pleased to get
Beyond the Bible – there I puzzle yet.'

He spoke abashed – 'Nay, nay!' the Friend replied,
'You need not lay the good old Book aside;   290
Antique and curious, I myself indeed
Read it at times, but as a man should read;
A fine old work it is, and I protest,
I hate to hear it treated as a jest;
The book has wisdom in it, if you look
Wisely upon it, as another book:
For superstition (as our Priests of Sin
Are pleased to tell us) makes us blind within:
Of this hereafter – we will now select
Some works to please you, others to direct;   300
Tales and Romances shall your fancy feed,
And reasoners form your morals and your creed.'

The books were viewed, the price was fairly paid,
And *Stephen* read undaunted, undismayed:
But not till first he papered all the row,
And placed in order, to enjoy the show;
Next lettered all their backs with care and speed,
Set them in ranks, and then began to read.

The love of order – I the thing receive
From reverend men, and I in part believe –   310
Shows a clear mind and clean, and whoso needs
This love, but seldom in the world succeeds;
And yet with this some other love must be,
Ere I can fully to the fact agree:
Valour and study may by order gain,
By order sovereigns hold more steady reign;
Through all the tribes of nature order runs,
And rules around in systems and in suns:
Still has the love of order found a place,
With all that's low, degrading, mean, and base,   320

With all that merits scorn, and all that meets disgrace:
In the cold Miser, of all change afraid,
In pompous men in public seats obeyed;
In humble Placemen, Heralds, solemn drones,
Fanciers of Flowers, and Lads like *Stephen Jones*;
Order to these is armour and defence,
And love of method serves in lack of sense.

For rustic youth could I a list produce
Of *Stephen*'s books, how great might be the use;
330   But evil fate was theirs – surveyed, enjoyed
Some happy months, and then by force destroyed:
So willed the Fates – but these, with patience read,
Had vast effect on *Stephen*'s heart and head.

This soon appeared – within a single week
He oped his lips, and made attempt to speak;
He failed indeed – but still his Friend confessed
The best have failed, and he had done his best:
The first of swimmers, when at first he swims,
Has little use or freedom in his limbs;
340   Nay, when at length he strikes with manly force,
The cramp may seize him, and impede his course.

Encouraged thus, our Clerk again essayed
The daring act, though daunted and afraid;
Succeeding now, though partial his success,
And pertness marked his manner and address,
Yet such improvement issued from his books,
That all discerned it in his speech and looks:
He ventured then on every theme to speak,
And felt no feverish tingling in his cheek;
350   His friend approving, hailed the happy change,
The Clerks exclaimed – ' 'Tis famous, and 'tis strange.'

Two years had passed; the Youth attended still,
(Though thus accomplished) with a ready quill;
He sat the allotted hours, though hard the case,
While timid prudence ruled in virtue's place;

By promise bound, the Son his letters penned
To his good parent, at the quarter's end.
At first he sent those lines, the state to tell
Of his own health, and hoped his friends were well;
He kept their virtuous precepts in his mind,   360
And needed nothing – then his name was signed:
But now he wrote of Sunday-walks and views,
Of actors' names, choice novels, and strange news;
How coats were cut, and of his urgent need
For fresh supply, which he desired with speed.
The Father doubted, when these letters came,
To what they tended, yet was loth to blame:
'*Stephen* was once *my duteous son*, and now
My most obedient – this can I allow?
Can I with pleasure or with patience see   370
A boy at once so heartless, and so free?'

But soon the kinsman heavy tidings told,
That love and prudence could no more withhold:
'*Stephen*, though steady at his desk, was grown
A rake and coxcomb – this he grieved to own;
His cousin left his church, and spent the day
Lounging about in quite a heathen way;
Sometimes he swore, but had indeed the grace
To show the shame imprinted on his face:
I searched his room, and in his absence read   380
Books that I knew would turn a stronger head;
The works of Atheists half the number made,
The rest were lives of harlots leaving trade;
Which neither man nor boy would deign to read,
If from the scandal and pollution freed:
I sometimes threatened, and would fairly state
My sense of things so vile and profligate;
But I'm a cit, such works are lost on me –
They're knowledge, and (good Lord!) philosophy!'

'Oh, send him down,' the Father soon replied;   390
'Let me behold him, and my skill be tried;

If care and kindness lose their wonted use,
Some rougher medicine will the end produce.'

Stephen with grief and anger heard his doom –
'Go to the farmer? to the rustic's home?
Curse the base threatening–' 'Nay, child, never curse;
Corrupted long, your case is growing worse;' –
'I!' quoth the Youth, 'I challenge all mankind
To find a fault; what fault have you to find?
Improve I not in manner, speech, and grace,
Inquire – my friends will tell it to your face;
Have I been taught to guard his kine and sheep?
A man like me has other things to keep;
This let him know,' – 'It would his wrath excite;
But come prepare, you must away tonight;'
'What! leave my studies, my improvements leave,
My faithful friends and intimates to grieve!' –
'Go to your father, *Stephen*, let him see
All these improvements – they are lost on me.'

The Youth, though loth, obeyed, and soon he saw
The Farmer-Father, with some signs of awe;
Who kind, yet silent, waited to behold
How one would act, so daring, yet so cold:
And soon he found, between the friendly pair
That secrets passed which he was not to share;
But he resolved those secrets to obtain,
And quash rebellion in his lawful reign.

Stephen, though vain, was with his Father mute,
He feared a crisis, and he shunned dispute;
And yet he longed with youthful pride to show,
He knew such things as farmers could not know;
These to the Grandam he with freedom spoke,
Saw her amazement, and enjoyed the joke:
But on the Father, when he cast his eye,
Something he found that made his valour shy;

And thus there seemed to be a hollow truce,
Still threatening something dismal to produce.

  Ere this the Father at his leisure read
The Son's choice volumes, and his wonder fled;
He saw how wrought the works of either kind,   430
On so presuming, yet so weak a mind;
These in a chosen hour he made his prey,
Condemned, and bore with vengeful thoughts away;
Then in a close recess the couple near,
He sate unseen to see, unheard to hear.

  There soon a trial for his patience came,
Beneath were placed the Youth and ancient Dame,
Each on a purpose fixed – but neither thought,
How near a foe, with power and vengeance fraught.

  And now the Matron told, as tidings sad,   440
What she had heard of her beloved Lad;
How he to graceless, wicked men gave heed,
And wicked books would night and morning read;
Some former lectures she again began,
And begged attention of her little man;
She brought, with many a pious boast, in view
His former studies, and condemned the new:
Once he the names of Saints and Patriarchs old,
Judges and Kings, and Chiefs and Prophets, told;
Then he, in winter-nights, the Bible took,   450
To count how often in the sacred book
The sacred name appeared, and could rehearse
Which were the middle chapter, word, and verse,
The very letter in the middle placed,
And so employed the hours that others waste.

'Such wert thou once; and now, my child, they say,
Thy faith, like water, runneth fast away;
The Prince of Devils hath, I fear, beguiled
The ready wit of my backsliding child.'

460   On this with lofty looks our Clerk began
      His grave rebuke, as he assumed the man —

      'There is no Devil,' said the hopeful Youth,
      'Nor Prince of Devils; that I know for truth:
      Have I not told you how my books describe
      The arts of Priests, and all the canting tribe?
      Your Bible mentions Egypt, where it seems
      Was *Joseph* found when *Pharaoh* dreamed his dreams;
      Now in that place, in some bewildered head,
      (The learned write) religious dreams were bred;
470   Whence through the earth, with various forms combined,
      They came to frighten and afflict mankind,
      Prone (so I read) to let a priest invade
      Their souls with awe, and by his craft be made
      Slave to his will, and profit to his trade:
      So say my books, and how the rogues agreed
      To blind the victims, to defraud and lead;
      When Joys above to ready Dupes were sold,
      And Hell was threatened to the shy and cold.

      'Why so amazed, and so prepared to pray?
480   As if a Being heard a word we say:
      This may surprise you; I myself began
      To feel disturbed, and to my Bible ran;
      I now am wiser — yet agree in this,
      The book has things that are not much amiss;
      It is a fine old work, and I protest
      I hate to hear it treated as a jest;
      The book has wisdom in it, if you look
      Wisely upon it as another book;' —

      'Oh! wicked! wicked! my unhappy child,
490   How hast thou been by evil men beguiled!'

      'How! wicked, say you? you can little guess
      The gain of that which you call wickedness:
      Why, sins you think it sinful but to name
      Have gained both wives and widows wealth and fame;

And this because such people never dread
Those threatened pains; hell comes not in their head;
Love is our nature, wealth we all desire,
And what we wish 'tis lawful to acquire;
So say my books — and what beside they show,
'Tis time to let this honest Farmer know;   500
Nay, look not grave, am I commanded down
To feed his cattle and become his clown?
Is such his purpose? then he shall be told
The vulgar insult —

               Hold, in mercy hold —
Father, oh! father! throw the whip away;
I was but jesting — on my knees I pray —
There, hold his arm — oh! leave us not alone:
In pity cease, and I will yet atone
For all my sin —' In vain; stroke after stroke,
On side and shoulder, quick as mill-wheels broke;   510
Quick as the patient's pulse, who trembling cried,
And still the Parent with a stroke replied;
Till all the medicine he prepared was dealt,
And every bone the precious influence felt;
Till all the panting flesh was red and raw,
And every thought was turned to fear and awe;
Till every doubt to due respect gave place —
Such cures are done when doctors know the case.

   'Oh! I shall die — my father! do receive
My dying words; indeed I do believe;   520
The books are lying books, I know it well,
There is a devil, oh! there is a hell;
And I'm a sinner: spare me, I am young,
My sinful words were only on my tongue;
My heart consented not; 'tis all a lie:
Oh! spare me then, I'm not prepared to die.'

   'Vain, worthless, stupid wretch!' the Father cried,
'Dost thou presume to teach? art thou a guide?
Driveller and dog, it gave the mind distress

530 To hear thy thoughts in their religious dress;
     Thy pious folly moved my strong disdain,
     Yet I forgave thee for thy want of brain:
     But *Job* in patience must the man exceed,
     Who could endure thee in thy present creed;
     Is it for thee, thou idiot, to pretend
     The wicked cause a helping hand to lend?
     Canst thou a judge in any question be?
     Atheists themselves would scorn a friend like thee. –

        'Lo! yonder blaze thy worthies; in one heap
540 Thy scoundrel-favourites must for ever sleep:
     Each yields its poison to the flame in turn,
     Where whores and infidels are doomed to burn;
     Two noble faggots made the flame you see,
     Reserving only two fair twigs for thee;
     That in thy view the instruments may stand,
     And be in future ready for my hand:
     The just mementos that, though silent, show
     Whence thy correction and improvements flow:
     Beholding these, thou wilt confess their power,
550 And feel the shame of this important hour.

        'Hadst thou been humble, I had first designed
     By care from folly to have freed thy mind;
     And when a clean foundation had been laid,
     Our priest, more able, would have lent his aid;
     But thou art weak, and force must folly guide,
     And thou art vain, and pain must humble pride:
     Teachers men honour, learners they allure;
     But learners teaching, of contempt are sure;
     Scorn is their certain meed, and smart their only cure.'

INFANCY

Who on the new born Light can back return
And the first Efforts of the Soul discern? –
Waked by some sweet maternal Smile, no more
To sleep so long or soundly as before.
Yet cannot Memory reach with all her Power
To that new Birth, that Life-awakening Hour.
No! all the Traces of her first Employ
Are keen perceptions of the Senses' Joy
And their Distaste and what they could impart –
That Figs were luscious and that Rods had Smart.   10

But though the Memory in that dubious Way
Looks to the Dawn and Twilight of her Day
And thus encounters in the doubtful View
With Imperfection and Distortion too,
Can she not tell us as she looks around
Of Good and Evil which the most abound?

Alas! and what is earthly Good? 'tis lent
Evil to hide, to soften, to prevent
By Scenes and Shows that Cheat the wandering Eye
While the more pompous Misery passes by;   20
Shifts and Amusements that awhile succeed,
And Heads are turned that Bosoms may not bleed.
For what is Pleasure, that we toil to gain?
'Tis but the slow or rapid flight of Pain.

Set Pleasure by and there would yet remain
For every Nerve and Sense the sting of Pain;
Let Pain abide and fear no more the Sting,

And whence your Hopes and pleasures can ye bring?
No! there is not a Joy beneath the Skies
That from no Grief nor Trouble shall arise.

Why does the Lover with such Rapture fly
To his dear Mistress? — he shall show us why —
Because her Absence is such Cause of Grief
That her sweet Smile alone can yield Relief.
Why then, that smile is pleasure — true, but still
'Tis but the Absence of the former ill:
For married, soon at will he comes and goes,
Then pleasures die and Pains become repose
And he has none of these and therefore none of those.

Yes, looking back as early as I can
I see the Griefs that seize their Subject, Man
That in the weeping Child their early Reign began;
And though he softens and is absent since,
He still controls me like my lawful Prince.
Joys I remember like phosphoric light
Or Squibs and Crackers on a Gala Night
(And if ye ask what Pain do these subdue
I say the Impatience of the eager Crew,
Ardent if unindulged, rebellious too).
Joys are like Oil: if thrown upon the Tide
Of flowing Life they mix not nor subside;
Griefs are like Waters on the River thrown,
They mix entirely and become its own,
Mix as the Bodies when to Earth we trust,
And Griefs with Minds commix as sure as Dust with Dust.

Of all the Good that grew of early Date
I can but parts and Incidents relate:
A Guest arriving, or a borrowed Day
From School, or Schoolboy triumph at some play:
And these from Pain may be deduced, for these
Removed some ill and hence their power to please.

But it was Misery stung me in the Day
Death of an Infant Sister made his Prey;
For then first met and moved my Early fears,
A Father's Terrors and a Mother's tears.
Though greater Anguish I have since endured –
Some healed in part some never to be Cured –
Yet there was something in that first born ill,
So new and strange that Memory feels it still,
Though Death and sad Varieties of Woes   70
Have mocked my Plans and baffled my Repose.

Lydia perhaps who laughs the whole day long
Would tell her Slaves and Subjects I was wrong,
For she remembers Time has brought her Fun,
And knows not what besides her Power has done.
Where little Cares and petty pleasures come
'Tis hard to show the Balance or the Sum;
And where the feelings are obtuse, the Mind
Not yet awakened and the Judgement blind,
Where Health is blooming and where Comfort lives,   80
You have the whole that Fate when favouring gives.
Yet would not Lydia take the Joy and Pain
Of the past Life, live o'er the Past again;
Or if she would, it is that she is weak
And lets her Fancy not her Judgement speak.

That my first Grief, but Oh! in after years
Were other Deaths that called for other tears.
No! that I cannot, that I dare not paint,
That patient Sufferer, that enduring Saint,
Holy and lovely – but all Words are faint.   90
But here I dwell not – let me while I can
Go to the Child and lose the Suffering Man,
For then was not the dread and dismal Time
When Care and Grief were Armed by Sin and Crime;
There was no Juliet in the World I knew
To call me vilest and to name me true.

*

Well I remember in the Days that we
So much admire, the Days of Infancy,
One – Emblematic of my Life – I view,
100   That was most pleasing and most stormy too.
Sweet was the Morning's breath, the inland Tide,
And Our Boat gliding where alone could glide
Small Craft, and they oft touched on either Side.
It was my first-born Joy, I heard them say
'Let the Child go, he will enjoy the Day',
For Children ever feel delighted when
They take their portion and enjoy with Men.
Give him this Pleasure that the old partake
And he will his peculiar Joy forsake.

110   That common Herbage that beside us grew
Not fair alone but gay and fragrant too;
The Linnet chirped upon the Furze as well
To my young Ear as sings the Nightingale:
Without was Paradise because within
Was a keen relish and no trace of Sin.

A Town appeared and where an Infant went
Can they determine, on themselves intent?
I lost my Way and my Companions me
And all their Comforts and Tranquillity.
120   Mid-day it was and as the Sun declined
The early rapture I no more could find.
The Men drank much to whet the Appetite
And growing heavy drank to make them light,
Then drank to relish Joy, then further to excite.
Their Cheerfulness did but a Moment last,
Something fell short or something overpast.
The Lads played idly with the Helm and Oar,
And nervous Ladies would be sat on Shore,
Till civil Dudgeon grew and peace would smile no more.

130   Now on the colder Water faintly shone
The sloping Light, the cheerful Day was gone;

Frowned every Cloud and from the gathered Frown
The Thunder burst and Rain came pattering down.
My torpid Senses now my fears obeyed
When the fierce Lightning on the water played;
Now all the freshness of the Morning fled,
My Spirits burdened and my Heart was dead.
The female Servants showed a Child their fear,
And Men full wearied wanted Strength to cheer;
And when at length the dreaded Storm went past   140
And there was peace and Quietness at Last
'Twas not the Morning's Quiet – It was not
Pleasures revived but Miseries forgot.
It was not Joy that new commenced her Reign
But mere relief from Wretchedness and Pain.

In Life's Advance, Events like this I knew;
So they commenced and so they ended too.
Even Love himself, that Promiser of Bliss,
Made his best Days of Pleasure end like this:
He mixed his Bitters in the Cup of Joy   150
Nor gave a Bliss uninjured by Alloy.

All promise they, all Joy as they began!
And these grew less and vanished as they ran!
Errors and Evils came in many a Form,
The Mind's Delusion and the Passions' Storm.
The promised Joy that, like the Morning, rose
Broke on my View, grew clouded in its close.
Friends who together in the Morning sailed
Parted ere Noon and Solitude prevailed.

TALES OF THE HALL

BOOK XIII
DELAY HAS DANGER

Morning Excursion – Lady at Silford, who? – Reflections on Delay – Cecilia
and Henry – The Lovers contracted – Visit to the Patron – Whom he finds
there – Fanny described – The yielding of Vanity – Delay – Resentment –
Want of Resolution – Further Entanglement – Danger – How met –
Conclusion.

Three weeks had passed, and Richard rambles now
Far as the dinners of the day allow;
He rode to Farley Grange and Finley Mere,
That house so ancient, and that lake so clear:
He rode to Ripley through that river gay,
Where in the shallow stream the loaches play,
And stony fragments stay the winding stream,
And gilded pebbles at the bottom gleam,
Giving their yellow surface to the sun,
And making proud the waters as they run:
It is a lovely place, and at the side
Rises a mountain-rock in rugged pride;
And in that rock are shapes of shells, and forms
Of creatures in old worlds, of nameless worms,
Whose generations lived and died ere man,
A worm of other class, to crawl began.

There is a town called Silford, where his steed
Our traveller rested – He the while would feed
His mind by walking to and fro, to meet,

10

He knew not what adventure, in the street: 20
A stranger there, but yet a window-view
Gave him a face that he conceived he knew;
He saw a tall, fair, lovely lady, dressed
As one whom taste and wealth had jointly blessed;
He gazed, but soon a footman at the door
Thundering, alarmed her, who was seen no more.

'This was the lady whom her lover bound
In solemn contract, and then proved unsound:
Of this affair I have a clouded view,
And should be glad to have it cleared by you.'   30

So Richard spake, and instant George replied,
'I had the story from the injured side,
But when resentment and regret were gone,
And pity (shaded by contempt) came on.

'Frail was the hero of my tale, but still
Was rather drawn by accident than will;
Some without meaning into guilt advance,
From want of guard, from vanity, from chance;
Man's weakness flies his more immediate pain,
A little respite from his fears to gain;   40
And takes the part that he would gladly fly,
If he had strength and courage to deny.

'But now my tale, and let the moral say,
When hope can sleep, there's Danger in Delay.
Not that for rashness, Richard, I would plead,
For unadvised alliance: No, indeed:
Think ere the contract – but, contracted, stand
No more debating, take the ready hand:
When hearts are willing, and when fears subside,
Trust not to time, but let the knot be tied;   50
For when a lover has no more to do,
He thinks in leisure, what shall I pursue?
And then who knows what objects come in view?
For when, assured, the man has nought to keep

His wishes warm and active, then they sleep:
Hopes die with fears; and then a man must lose
All the gay visions, and delicious views,
Once his mind's wealth! He travels at his ease,
Nor horrors now nor fairy-beauty sees;
60   When the kind goddess gives the wished assent,
No mortal business should the deed prevent;
But the blessed youth should legal sanction seek
Ere yet the assenting blush has fled the cheek.

'And – hear me, Richard, – man has reptile-pride
That often rises when his fears subside;
When, like a trader feeling rich, he now
Neglects his former smile, his humble bow,
And, conscious of his hoarded wealth, assumes
New airs, nor thinks how odious he becomes.

70   'There is a wandering, wavering train of thought
That something seeks where nothing should be sought,
And will a self-delighted spirit move
To dare the danger of pernicious love.

———————

First be it granted all was duly said
By the fond youth to the believing maid;
Let us suppose with many a sigh there came
The declaration of the deathless flame; –

And so her answer – 'She was happy then,
Blessed in herself, and did not think of men;
80   And with such comforts in her present state,
A wish to change it was to tempt her fate;
That she would not; but yet she would confess
With him she thought her hazard would be less;
Nay, more, she would esteem, she would regard express:
But to be brief – if he could wait and see
In a few years what his desires would be.' –

Henry for years read months, then weeks, nor found
The lady thought his judgement was unsound;

'For months read weeks,' she read it to his praise,
And had some thoughts of changing it to *days*.   90

And here a short excursion let me make,
A lover tried, I think, for lovers' sake;
And teach the meaning in a lady's mind
When you can none in her expressions find:
Words are designed that meaning to convey,
But often *Yea* is hidden in a *Nay*!
And what the charmer wills, some gentle hints betray.
Then, too, when ladies mean to yield at length,
They match their reasons with the lover's strength,
And, kindly cautious, will no force employ   100
But such as he can baffle or destroy.

As when heroic lovers beauty wooed,
And were by magic's mighty art withstood,
The kind historian, for the dame afraid,
Gave to the faithful knight the stronger aid.

A downright *No!* would make a man despair,
Or leave for kinder nymph the cruel fair;
But '*No!* because I'm very happy now,
Because I dread the irrevocable vow,
Because I fear papa will not approve,   110
Because I love not – No, I cannot love;
Because you men of Cupid make a jest,
Because – in short, a single life is best.'
A *No!* when backed by reasons of such force,
Invites approach, and will recede of course.

Ladies, like towns besieged, for honour's sake,
Will some defence or its appearance make;
On first approach there's much resistance made,
And conscious weakness hides in bold parade;
With lofty looks, and threatenings stern and proud,   120
'Come, if you dare,' is said in language loud,
But if the attack be made with care and skill,
'Come,' says the yielding party, 'if you will;'

Then each the other's valiant acts approve,
And twine their laurels in a wreath of love. –

We now retrace our tale, and forward go, –
Thus Henry rightly read Cecilia's No!
His prudent father, who had duly weighed,
And well approved the fortune of the maid,
Not much resisted, just enough to show
He knew his power, and would his son should know.

'Harry, I will, while I your bargain make,
That you a journey to our patron take:
I know her guardian; care will not become
A lad when courting; as you must be dumb,
You may be absent; I for you will speak,
And ask what you are not supposed to seek.'

Then came the parting hour, and what arise
When lovers part! expressive looks and eyes,
Tender and tear-full, – many a fond adieu,
And many a call the sorrow to renew;
Sighs such as lovers only can explain,
And words that they might undertake in vain.

Cecilia liked it not; she had, in truth,
No mind to part with her enamoured youth;
But thought it foolish thus themselves to cheat,
And part for nothing but again to meet.

Now Henry's father was a man whose heart
Took with his interest a decided part;
He knew his Lordship, and was known for acts
That I omit, – they were acknowledged facts;
An interest somewhere; I the place forget,
And the good deed – no matter – 'twas a debt:
Thither must Henry, and in vain the maid
Expressed dissent – the father was obeyed.

But though the maid was by her fears assailed,
Her reason rose against them, and prevailed;

Fear saw him hunting, leaping, falling — led,
Maimed and disfigured, groaning to his bed;
Saw him in perils, duels, — dying, — dead.   160
But Prudence answered, 'Is not every maid
With equal cause for him she loves afraid?'
And from her guarded mind Cecilia threw
The groundless terrors that will love pursue.

She had no doubts, and her reliance strong
Upon the honour that she would not wrong:
Firm in herself, she doubted not the truth
Of him, the chosen, the selected youth;
Trust of herself a trust in him supplied,
And she believed him faithful, though untried: 170
On her he might depend, in him she would confide.

If some fond girl expressed a tender pain
Lest some fair rival should allure her swain,
To such she answered, with a look severe,
'Can one you doubt be worthy of your fear?'

My lord was kind, — a month had passed away,
And Henry stayed, — he sometimes named a day;
But still my lord was kind, and Henry still must stay:
His father's words to him were words of fate —
'Wait, 'tis your duty; 'tis my pleasure, wait!'   180

In all his walks, in hilly heath or wood,
Cecilia's form the pensive youth pursued;
In the grey morning, in the silent noon,
In the soft twilight, by the sober moon,
In those forsaken rooms, in that immense saloon;
And he, now fond of that seclusion grown,
There reads her letters, and there writes his own.

'Here none approach,' said he, 'to interfere,
But I can think of my Cecilia here!'

But there did come — and how it came to pass   190
Who shall explain? — a mild and blue-eyed lass; —
It was the work of accident, no doubt —

The cause unknown – we say, 'as things fall out;' –
The damsel entered there, in wandering round about:
At first she saw not Henry; and she ran,
As from a ghost, when she beheld a man.

She was esteemed a beauty through the hall,
And so admitted, with consent of all;
And, like a treasure, was her beauty kept
From every guest who in the mansion slept;
Whether as friends who joined the noble pair,
Or those invited by the steward there.

She was the daughter of a priest, whose life
Was brief and sad: he lost a darling wife,
And Fanny then her father, who could save
But a small portion; but his all he gave,
With the fair orphan, to a sister's care,
And her good spouse: they were the ruling pair –
Steward and steward's lady – o'er a tribe,
Each under each, whom I shall not describe.

This grave old couple, childless and alone,
Would, by their care, for Fanny's loss atone:
She had been taught in schools of honest fame;
And to the Hall, as to a home, she came,
My lord assenting: yet, as meet and right,
Fanny was held from every hero's sight,
Who might in youthful error cast his eyes
On one so gentle as a lawful prize,
On border land, whom, as their right or prey,
A youth from either side might bear away.
Some handsome lover of the inferior class
Might as a wife approve the lovely lass;
Or some invader from the class above,
Who, more presuming, would his passion prove
By asking less – love only for his love.

This much experienced aunt her fear expressed,
And dread of old and young, of host and guest.

'Go not, my Fanny, in their way,' she cried,
'It is not right that virtue should be tried;
So, to be safe, be ever at my side.'   230

She was not ever at that side; but still
Observed her precepts, and obeyed her will.

But in the morning's dawn and evening's gloom
She could not lock the damsel in her room;
And Fanny thought, 'I will ascend these stairs
To see the chapel, – there are none at prayers;
None,' she believed, 'had yet to dress returned,
By whom a timid girl might be discerned:'
In her slow motion, looking, as she glides,
On pictures, busts, and what she met besides,   240
And speaking softly to herself alone,
Or singing low in melancholy tone;
And thus she rambled through the still domain,
Room after room, again, and yet again.

But, to retrace our story, still we say,
To this saloon the maiden took her way;
Where she beheld our youth, and frightened ran,
And so their friendship in her fear began.

But dare she thither once again advance,
And still suppose the man will think it chance?   250
Nay, yet again, and what has chance to do
With this? – I know not: doubtless Fanny knew.

Now, of the meeting of a modest maid
And sober youth why need we be afraid?
And when a girl's amusements are so few
As Fanny's were, what would you have her do?
Reserved herself, a decent youth to find,
And just be civil, sociable, and kind,
And look together at the setting sun,
Then at each other – What the evil done?   260

Then Fanny took my little lord to play,
And bade him not intrude on Henry's way:

'O, he intrudes not!' said the youth, and grew
Fond of the child, and would amuse him too;
Would make such faces, and assume such looks –
He loved it better than his gayest books.

When man with man would an acquaintance seek,
He will his thoughts in chosen language speak;
And they converse on divers themes, to find
If they possess a corresponding mind;
But man with woman has foundation laid,
And built up friendship ere a word is said:
'Tis not with words that they their wishes tell,
But with a language answering quite as well;
And thus they find, when they begin to explore
Their way by speech, they knew it all before.

And now it chanced again the pair, when dark,
Met in their way, when wandering in the park;
Not in the common path, for so they might,
Without a wonder, wander day or night;
But, when in pathless ways their chance will bring
A musing pair, we do admire the thing.

The youth in meeting read the damsel's face,
As if he meant her inmost thoughts to trace;
On which her colour changed, as if she meant
To give her aid, and help his kind intent.

Both smiled and parted, but they did not speak –
The smile implied, 'Do tell me what you seek:'
They took their different ways with erring feet,
And met again, surprised that they could meet;
Then must they speak – and something of the air
Is always ready – ''Tis extremely fair!'

'It was so pleasant!' Henry said; 'the beam
Of that sweet light so brilliant on the stream;
And chiefly yonder, where that old cascade
Has for an age its simple music made;
All so delightful, soothing, and serene!

Do you not feel it? not enjoy the scene?
Something it has that words will not express,
But rather hide, and make the enjoyment less: 300
'Tis what our souls conceive, 'tis what our hearts confess.'

Poor Fanny's heart at these same words confessed
How well he painted, and how rightly guessed;
And, while they stood admiring their retreat,
Henry found something like a mossy seat;
But Fanny sat not; no, she rather prayed
That she might leave him, she was so afraid.

'Not, sir, of you; your goodness I can trust,
But folks are so censorious and unjust,
They make no difference, they pay no regard   310
To our true meaning, which is very hard
And very cruel; great the pain it cost
To lose such pleasure, but it must be lost:
Did people know how free from thought of ill
One's meaning is, their malice would be still.'

At this she wept; at least a glittering gem
Shone in each eye, and there was fire in them,
For as they fell, the sparkles, at his feet,
He felt emotions very warm and sweet.

'A lovely creature! not more fair than good,   320
By all admired, by some, it seems, pursued,
Yet self-protected by her virtue's force
And conscious truth – What evil in discourse
With one so guarded, who is pleased to trust
Herself with me, reliance strong and just?'

Our lover then believed he must not seem
Cold to the maid who gave him her esteem;
Not manly this; Cecilia had his heart,
But it was lawful with his time to part;
It would be wrong in her to take amiss   330

A virtuous friendship for a girl like this;
False or disloyal he would never prove,
But kindness here took nothing from his love:
Soldiers to serve a foreign prince are known,
When not on present duty to their own;
So, though our bosom's queen we still prefer,
We are not always on our knees to her.
'Cecilia present, witness yon fair moon,
And yon bright orbs, that fate would change as soon
340   As my devotion; but the absent sun
Cheers us no longer when his course is run;
And then those starry twinklers may obtain
A little worship till he shines again.'

The father still commanded 'Wait awhile,'
And the son answered in submissive style,
Grieved, but obedient; and obedience teased
His lady's spirit more than grieving pleased:
That he should grieve in absence was most fit,
But not that he to absence should submit;
350   And in her letters might be traced reproof,
Distant indeed, but visible enough;
This should the wandering of his heart have stayed;
Alas! the wanderer was the vainer made.

The parties daily met, as by consent,
And yet it always seemed by accident;
Till in the nymph the shepherd had been blind
If he had failed to see a manner kind,
With that expressive look, that seemed to say,
'You do not speak, and yet you see you may.'

360   O! yes, he saw, and he resolved to fly,
And blamed his heart, unwilling to comply:
He sometimes wondered how it came to pass,
That he had all this freedom with the lass;
Reserved herself, with strict attention kept,
And care and vigilance that never slept:

'How is it thus that they a beauty trust
With me, who feel the confidence is just?
And they, too, feel it; yes, they may confide,' —
He said in folly, and he smiled in pride.

'Tis thus our secret passions work their way,   370
And the poor victims know not they obey.

Familiar now became the wandering pair,
And there was pride and joy in Fanny's air;
For though his silence did not please the maid,
She judged him only modest and afraid;
The gentle dames are ever pleased to find
Their lovers dreading they should prove unkind;
So, blind by hope, and pleased with prospects gay,
The generous beauty gave her heart away
Before he said, 'I love!' — alas! he dared not say.   380

Cecilia yet was mistress of his mind,
But oft he wished her, like his Fanny, kind;
Her fondness soothed him, for the man was vain,
And he perceived that he could give her pain:
Cecilia liked not to profess her love,
But Fanny ever was the yielding dove;
Tender and trusting, waiting for the word,
And then prepared to hail her bosom's lord.

Cecilia once her honest love avowed,
To make him happy, not to make him proud;   390
But she would not, for every asking sigh,
Confess the flame that waked his vanity;
But this poor maiden, every day and hour,
Would, by fresh kindness, feed the growing power;
And he indulged, vain being! in the joy,
That he alone could raise it, or destroy;
A present good, from which he dared not fly,
Cecilia absent, and his Fanny by.

O! vain desire of youth, that in the hour
Of strong temptation, when he feels the power,   400

And knows how daily his desires increase,
Yet will he wait, and sacrifice his peace,
Will trust to chance to free him from the snare,
Of which, long since, his conscience said, beware!
Or look for strange deliverance from that ill,
That he might fly, could he command the will!
How can he freedom from the future seek,
Who feels already that he grows too weak?
And thus refuses to resist, till time
Removes the power, and makes the way for crime:
Yet thoughts he had, and he would think, 'Forgo
My dear Cecilia? not for kingdoms! No!
But may I, ought I not the friend to be
Of one who feels this fond regard for me?
I wrong no creature by a kindness lent
To one so gentle, mild, and innocent;
And for that fair one, whom I still adore,
By feeling thus I think of her the more;'
And not unlikely, for our thoughts will tend
To those whom we are conscious we offend.

Had Reason whispered, 'Has Cecilia leave
Some gentle youth in friendship to receive,
And be to him the friend that you appear
To this soft girl? – would not some jealous fear
Proclaim your thoughts, that he approached too near?'

But Henry, blinded still, presumed to write
Of one in whom Cecilia would delight;
A mild and modest girl, a gentle friend,
If, as he hoped, her kindness would descend –
But what he feared to lose or hoped to gain
By writing thus, he had been asked in vain.

It was his purpose, every morn he rose,
The dangerous friendship he had made to close;
It was his torment nightly, ere he slept,
To feel his prudent purpose was not kept.

True, he has wondered why the timid maid
Meets him so often, and is not afraid;
And why that female dragon, fierce and keen,
Has never in their private walks been seen;
And often he has thought, 'What can their silence mean?   440

'They can have no design, or plot, or plan, –
In fact, I know not how the thing began, –
'Tis their dependence on my credit here,
And fear not, nor, in fact, have cause to fear.'

But did that pair, who seemed to think that all
Unwatched will wander and unguarded fall,
Did they permit a youth and maid to meet
Both unreproved? were they so indiscreet?

This sometimes entered Henry's mind, and then,
'Who shall account for women or for men?'   450
He said, 'or who their secret thoughts explore?
Why do I vex me? I will think no more.'

My Lord of late had said, in manner kind,
'My good friend Harry, do not think us blind!'
Letters had passed, though he had nothing seen,
His careful father and my Lord between;
But to what purpose was to him unknown –
It might be borough business, or their own.

Fanny, it seemed, was now no more in dread,
If one approached, she neither feared nor fled: 460
He mused on this, – 'But wherefore her alarm?
She knows me better, and she dreads no harm.'

Something his father wrote that gave him pain:
'I know not, son, if you should yet remain; –
Be cautious, Harry, favours to procure
We strain a point, but we must first be sure:
Love is a folly, – that, indeed, is true, –

But something still is to our honour due,
So I must leave the thing to my good Lord and you.'

470   But from Cecilia came remonstrance strong:
'You write too darkly, and you stay too long;
We hear reports; and, Henry, — mark me well, —
I heed not every tale that triflers tell; —
Be you no trifler; dare not to believe
That I am one whom words and vows deceive:
You know your heart, your hazard you will learn,
And this your trial — instantly return.'

'Unjust, injurious, jealous, cruel maid!
Am I a slave, of haughty words afraid?
480   Can she who thus commands expect to be obeyed?
O! how unlike this dear assenting soul,
Whose heart a man might at his will control!'

Uneasy, anxious, filled with self-reproof,
He now resolved to quit his patron's roof;
And then again his vacillating mind
To stay resolved, and that her pride should find:
Debating thus, his pen the lover took,
And chose the words of anger and rebuke.

Again, yet once again, the conscious pair
490   Met, and 'O, speak!' was Fanny's silent prayer;
And, 'I must speak,' said the embarrassed youth,
'Must save my honour, must confess the truth:
Then I must lose her; but, by slow degrees,
She will retain her peace, and I my ease.'

Ah! foolish man! to virtue true nor vice,
He buys distress, and self-esteem the price;
And what his gain? — a tender smile and sigh
From a fond girl to feed his vanity.

Thus, every day they lived, and every time
500   They met, increased his anguish and his crime.

Still in their meetings they were ofttimes nigh
The darling theme, and then passed trembling by;
On those occasions Henry often tried
For the sad truth – and then his heart denied
The utterance due: thus daily he became
The prey of weakness, vanity, and shame.

But soon a day, that was their doubts to close,
On the fond maid and thoughtless youth arose.

Within the park, beside the bounding brook,
The social pair their usual ramble took;   510
And there the steward found them: they could trace
News in his look, and gladness in his face.

He was a man of riches, bluff and big,
With clean brown broad-cloth, and with white cut wig:
He bore a cane of price, with riband tied,
And a fat spaniel waddled at his side:
To every being whom he met he gave
His looks expressive; civil, gay, or grave,
But condescending all; and each declared
How much he governed, and how well he fared.   520

This great man bowed, not humbly, but his bow
Appeared familiar converse to allow:
The trembling Fanny, as he came in view,
Within the chestnut grove in fear withdrew;
While Henry wondered, not without a fear,
Of that which brought the important man so near:
Doubt was dispersed by – 'My esteemed young man!'
As he with condescending grace began –

'Though you with youthful frankness nobly trust
Your Fanny's friends, and doubtless think them just;   530
Though you have not, with craving soul, applied
To us, and asked the fortune of your bride,
Be it our care that you shall not lament
That love has made you so improvident.

'An orphan maid – Your patience! you shall have
Your time to speak, I now attention crave; –
Fanny, dear girl! has in my spouse and me
Friends of a kind we wish our friends to be,
None of the poorest – nay, sir, no reply,
540   You shall not need – and we are born to die:
And one yet crawls on earth, of whom, I say,
That what he has he cannot take away;
Her mother's father, one who has a store
Of this world's good, and always looks for more;
But, next his money, loves the girl at heart,
And she will have it when they come to part.'

'Sir,' said the youth, his terrors all awake,
'Hear me, I pray, I beg, – for mercy's sake!
Sir, were the secrets of my soul confessed,
550   Would you admit the truths that I protest
Are such – your pardon' –
                              'Pardon! good, my friend,
I not alone will pardon, I commend:
Think you that I have no remembrance left
Of youthful love, and Cupid's cunning theft?
How nymphs will listen when their swains persuade,
How hearts are gained, and how exchange is made? –
Come sir, your hand' –
                              'In mercy, hear me now!'
'I cannot hear you, time will not allow:
You know my station, what on me depends,
560   For ever needed – but we part as friends;
And here comes one who will the whole explain,
My better self – and we shall meet again.'

'Sir, I entreat' –
                    'Then be entreaty made
'To her, a woman, one you may persuade;
A little teasing, but she will comply,
And loves her niece too fondly to deny.'

'O! he is mad, and miserable I!'
Exclaimed the youth; 'But let me now collect
My scattered thoughts, I something must effect.'

Hurrying she came – 'Now, what has he confessed, 570
Ere I could come to set your heart at rest?
What! he has grieved you! Yet he, too, approves
The thing! but man will tease you, if he loves.

'But now for business: tell me, did you think
That we should always at your meetings wink?
Think you, you walked unseen? There are who bring
To me all secrets – O, you wicked thing!
Poor Fanny! now I think I see her blush,
All red and rosy, when I beat the bush;
And hide your secret, said I, if you dare! 580
So out it came, like an affrightened hare.

'Miss! said I, gravely; and the trembling maid
Pleased me at heart to see her so afraid;
And then she wept; – now, do remember this,
Never to chide her when she does amiss;
For she is tender as the callow bird,
And cannot bear to have her temper stirred; –
Fanny, I said, then whispered her the name,
And caused such looks – Yes, yours are just the same;
But hear my story – When your love was known 590
For this our child – she is, in fact, our own –
Then, first debating, we agreed at last
To seek my Lord, and tell him what had passed.'

'To tell the Earl?'
                    'Yes, truly, and why not?
'And then together we contrived our plot.'

'Eternal God!'
                'Nay, be not so surprised, –
In all the matter we were well advised;
We saw my Lord, and Lady Jane was there,

And said to Johnson, "Johnson, take a chair;"
600   True, we are servants in a certain way,
But in the higher places so are they;
We are obeyed in ours, and they in theirs obey —
So Johnson bowed, for that was right and fit,
And had no scruple with the Earl to sit —
Why look you so impatient while I tell
What they debated? — you must like it well.

'"Let them go on," our gracious Earl began;
"They will go off," said, joking, my good man:
"Well!" said the Countess, — she's a lover's friend, —
610   "What if they do, they make the speedier end" —
But be you more composed, for that dear child
Is with her joy and apprehension wild:
O! we have watched you on from day to day,
"There go the lovers!" we were wont to say —
But why that look?'
               'Dear Madam, I implore
A single moment!'
               'I can give no more:
Here are your letters — that's a female pen,
Said I to Fanny — "'tis his sister's, then,"
Replied the maid. — No! never must you stray;
620   Or hide your wanderings, if you should, I pray;
I know, at least I fear, the best may err,
But keep the by-walks of your life from her:
That youth should stray is nothing to be told,
When they have sanction in the grave and old,
Who have no call to wander and transgress,
But very love of change and wantonness.

'I prattle idly, while your letters wait,
And then my Lord has much that he would state,
All good to you — do clear that clouded face,
630   And with good looks your lucky lot embrace.

'Now, mind that none with her divide your heart,

For she would die ere lose the smallest part;
And I rejoice that all has gone so well,
For who the effect of Johnson's rage can tell?
He had his fears when you began to meet,
But I assured him there was no deceit:
He is a man who kindness will requite,
But injured once, revenge is his delight;
And he would spend the best of his estates
To ruin, goods and body, them he hates;   640
While he is kind enough when he approves
A deed that's done, and serves the man he loves:
Come, read your letters – I must now be gone,
And think of matters that are coming on.'

Henry was lost, – his brain confused, his soul
Dismayed and sunk, his thoughts beyond control;
Borne on by terror, he foreboding read
Cecilia's letter! and his courage fled;
All was a gloomy, dark, and dreadful view,
He felt him guilty, but indignant too: –   650
And as he read, he felt the high disdain
Of injured men – 'She may repent, in vain.'

Cecilia much had heard, and told him all
That scandal taught – 'A servant at the Hall,
Or servant's daughter, in the kitchen bred,
Whose father would not with her mother wed,
Was now his choice! a blushing fool, the toy,
Or the attempted, both of man and boy;
More than suspected, but without the wit
Or the allurements for such creatures fit;   660
Not virtuous though unfeeling, cold as ice
And yet not chaste, the weeping fool of vice:
Yielding, not tender; feeble, not refined;
Her form insipid, and without a mind.

'Rival! she spurned the word; but let him stay,
Warned as he was! beyond the present day,

Whate'er his patron might object to this,
The uncle-butler, or the weeping miss –
Let him from this one single day remain,
And then return! he would to her, in vain;
There let him then abide, to earn, or crave
Food undeserved! and be with slaves a slave.'

Had reason guided anger, governed zeal,
Or chosen words to make a lover feel,
She might have saved him – anger and abuse
Will but defiance and revenge produce.

'Unjust and cruel, insolent and proud!'
He said, indignant, and he spoke aloud.
'Butler! and servant! Gentlest of thy sex,
Thou wouldst not thus a man who loved thee vex;
Thou wouldst not thus to vile report give ear,
Nor thus enraged for fancied crimes appear;
I know not what, dear maid! – if thy soft smiles were here.'

And then, that instant, there appeared the maid,
By his sad looks in her approach dismayed;
Such timid sweetness, and so wronged, did more
Than all her pleading tenderness before.

In that weak moment, when disdain and pride,
And fear and fondness, drew the man aside,
In this weak moment – 'Wilt thou,' he began,
'Be mine?' and joy o'er all her features ran;
'I will!' she softly whispered; but the roar
Of cannon would not strike his spirit more;
Even as his lips the lawless contract sealed
He felt that conscience lost her seven-fold shield,
And honour fled; but still he spoke of love,
And all was joy in the consenting dove.

That evening all in fond discourse was spent,
When the sad lover to his chamber went,
To think on what had passed, to grieve and to repent:

670

680

690

700

Early he rose, and looked with many a sigh
On the red light that filled the eastern sky;
Oft had he stood before, alert and gay,
To hail the glories of the new-born day:
But now dejected, languid, listless, low,
He saw the wind upon the water blow,
And the cold stream curled onward as the gale
From the pine-hill blew harshly down the dale;
On the right side the youth a wood surveyed,
With all its dark intensity of shade;   710
Where the rough wind alone was heard to move,
In this, the pause of nature and of love,
When now the young are reared, and when the old,
Lost to the tie, grow negligent and cold —
Far to the left he saw the huts of men,
Half hid in mist, that hung upon the fen;
Before him swallows, gathering for the sea,
Took their short flights, and twittered on the lea;
And near the bean-sheaf stood, the harvest done,
And slowly blackened in the sickly sun;   720
All these were sad in nature, or they took
Sadness from him, the likeness of his look,
And of his mind — he pondered for a while,
Then met his Fanny with a borrowed smile.

Not much remained; for money and my Lord
Soon made the father of the youth accord;
His prudence half resisted, half obeyed,
And scorn kept still the guardians of the maid:
Cecilia never on the subject spoke,
She seemed as one who from a dream awoke;   730
So all was peace, and soon the married pair
Fixed with fair fortune in a mansion fair.

Five years had passed, and what was Henry then?
The most repining of repenting men;
With a fond, teasing, anxious wife, afraid
Of all attention to another paid;

Yet powerless she her husband to amuse,
Lives but to intreat, implore, resent, accuse;
Jealous and tender, conscious of defects,
She merits little, and yet much expects;
She looks for love that now she cannot see,
And sighs for joy that never more can be;
On his retirements her complaints intrude,
And fond reproof endears his solitude:
While he her weakness (once her kindness) sees,
And his affections in her languor freeze;
Regret, unchecked by hope, devours his mind,
He feels unhappy, and he grows unkind.

'Fool! to be taken by a rosy cheek,
And eyes that cease to sparkle or to speak;
Fool! For this child my freedom to resign,
When one the glory of her sex was mine;
While from this burden to my soul I hide,
To think what Fate has dealt, and what denied.

'What fiend possessed me when I tamely gave
My forced assent to be an idiot's slave?
Her beauty vanished, what for me remains?
The eternal clicking of the galling chains:
Her person truly I may think my own,
Seen without pleasure, without triumph shown:
Doleful she sits, her children at her knees,
And gives up all her feeble powers to please;
Whom I, unmoved, or moved with scorn, behold,
Melting as ice, as vapid and as cold.'

Such was his fate, and he must yet endure
The self-contempt that no self-love can cure:
Some business called him to a wealthy town
When unprepared for more than Fortune's frown;
There at a house he gave his luckless name,
The master absent, and Cecilia came;
Unhappy man! he could not, dared not speak,

But looked around, as if retreat to seek:
This she allowed not; but, with brow severe,
Asked him his business, sternly bent to hear;
He had no courage, but he viewed that face
As if he sought for sympathy and grace;
As if some kind returning thought to trace:
In vain; not long he waited, but with air,
That of all grace compelled him to despair,
She rang the bell, and, when a servant came,   780
Left the repentant traitor to his shame;
But, going, spoke, 'Attend this person out,
And if he speaks, hear what he comes about!'
Then, with cool courtesy, from the room withdrew,
That seemed to say, 'Unhappy man, adieu!'

Thus will it be when man permits a vice
First to invade his heart, and then entice;
When wishes vain and undefined arise,
And that weak heart deceive, seduce, surprise;
When evil Fortune works on Folly's side,   790
And rash Resentment adds a spur to Pride;
Then life's long troubles from those actions come,
In which a moment may decide our doom.

'PEASANTS DRINKING' BY MISS FORD

'Tis said, how falsely let these Figures prove,
They best can paint a Scene who most can love;
Yet here behold a Coarse and vulgar Tribe
Drawn by her Hand who can the Scene describe,
Her Taste and Virtue scorn – What Things displease,
Will on the Mind with stronger Influence seize,
Or how could One so gentle truly draw
Scenes that she saw not, or with Hatred saw.

See! how each potent Draught the Spirit cheers
How free from Care each Son of Toil appears;
Lord of himself and freest of the Free,
He tells how Statesmen rule and how would he;
Untaught to read, unable well to stand,
He yet would rule and rectify the Land;
Then gives his Toast as he reforms the State,
'Be Great Men honest, honest men be great;'
And loudly shouting round the noisy Room,
He staggering goes to tyrannize at home.

Such is the Scene her playful Hand has traced
The pleasing Effort of a genuine Taste;
  So the great Master of the Tragic-Page
Who gave his Lears and Hamlets to the Stage,
Could to his Knaves and Coxcombs Language give
And bid his Touchstone and Malvolio live.

THE FLOWERS

1

Custom has been, time out of mind
    With Rose or Lily to compare
Our favourite maid! We love to find
    And say she is so sweet and fair.
And Violets from the sun retired
    Whose fragrance scents the passing gale
Are in their still retreats admired
    As lasses in their lowly Vale

2

'Tis well but may we not our views
    Extend, and still a likeness find?
Flowers are of many forms and hues
    Of many a Class of many a kind.
Not all are like the Rose, not all
    Are like the Lily passing fair
Come then the sister beauties call
    And let us see how like they are

3

See first where spring these favourite flowers
    The rocky Glen, the Wild has some
Others are raised in sheltering bowers
    And some in common hedgerows bloom
The open plain the furrowed land
    The wide brown heath the seaside sand.

4

And thus are tribes of Females fixed
   These in the Wild, the Wood, the Glen
Those with the World's proud people mixed
   And in the seats of wealthier men
Or in laborious lots of Life
   The Shepherd's Lass, the Seaman's Wife

5

See Mary like the Primrose wild
30   Retiring not but placed from view
All unaffected Nature's child
   No stately form no sprightly hue
Her has no great admirer found
   She pleases but the Swains around.

6

But take this Primrose from its seat
   Take Mary from her humble lot
Let both the appropriate training meet
   And change of both the rustic lot
They take a different air and name
40   The Polyanthus and the Dame
Improved, perhaps it may be said
   But not the Primrose or the Maid

7

Some Flowers are famed for early bloom
   And have their triumphs for the year
But soon their beauty finds a Tomb
   They charm, they fade, they disappear
They have their day, they have their doom
   None of the faded glories hear

Some to a second season last
    But live upon the honours past. 50

8

But Flowers there are of nobler fame
    Who live when other Flowers decay
Year after year they please the same
    The same the beauties they display
Time to all other charms severe
    Respects the beauty planted here

9

So 'tis with many a lovely face
    Admired its season, every Eye
Attracted to the favourite place
    That so much beauty can supply 60
The season flies, and every grace
    And glory with the season fly
The Annuals of the Sex, though some
    A second year with luck may bloom

10

But there are charms that long abide
    Through years that other Charmers kill
Through winter's frown through summer's pride
    They flourish and are beauties still
Perennials, they compel our praise
    The Rutlands of their happier days 70

11

See with what mighty care and cost
    The fair Mimosa keeps alive
Expose her but to one night's frost

And not a beauty will survive
And when you wear the tender thing
    And take the utmost care you can
It is in vain, you cannot bring
    Your nurseling to the gaze of man
No! he must this with caution view
    And if he put a finger forth
It shrinks away, as if it knew
    Itself of a surpassing worth

80

12

So was the tender Abra reared
    With such attention skill and cost
As if the wondering parents feared
    An atom of her should be lost.
She never felt the cold rough seas
    That flaccid nerves and tendons brace
She never felt the morning breeze
    That blows such freshness in the face
She sits in her own drawing room
    Where only her admirers come
And there they all agree in this
    That none is half so fair as Miss
And Miss the kindness to repay
    Thinks none are so polite as they

90

13

Descending we the Nettle view
    Armed with an hundred thousand stings
Who to such plant has likeness? Who
    Such pain creates, such trouble brings
Yet let us not be much alarmed
    We are not by the Nettle harmed
For grasp it as you've heard before
    Boldly and it will sting no more

100

14

Such is Corinna, she is sharp
   And joy to her her sharpness brings
She has the mind that loves to carp
   And suck out blame from harmless things
She never tries to soothe or please
   But deals in waspish repartees   110
She has no beauty but she lives
   In some repute for giving pain
Rejoicing in the pain she gives
   By hints that sting, or worse that stain
Wit 'tis esteemed, but no indeed
   'Tis poison in a wicket weed
But strong and sharp if your reply
   Corinna's sting, and venom die

15

The Plant that we the Climber call
   And in our bowers with care dispose   120
Mounts quickly oer the lofty wall
   And spreads her branches where she goes
Will her abundant flowers produce
   With great display and little use

16

So Martha climbs ambitious dame
   By all she reaches, foes or friends,
Though from the very dust she came
   She to the very height ascends
And mounted thus she stretches forth
   Her riches and displays her worth,   130

17

But climbers have no native strength
   They must upon their props rely
With these they fail and must at length
   Drop on the ground to get supply
From earth's bare bosom where they feed
   And mix with every vulgar weed.

18

So will the lofty Martha droop
   Should her supporters fail or die
For aid will to the humble stoop
   And to the poorest refuge fly
High as she rose will sink as deep,
   And show that pride who climbs can creep

19

Thou art the very wormwood Ruth
   Art bitter, blossomless, and grey
But thou hast virtues and in truth
   Will last, when brighter flowers decay
Thy hair is silvered and thy look
   Proclaim thee, let not man despise
Thou art not by the seasons shook,
   Thou drawest no idle herd of flies
No gaudy insects light by thee
   But one there comes who knows thy worth
His aid and helper thou shalt be
   Who calmly takes, and bears thee forth
Thou very bitter art, 'tis true
   But thou art very wholesome too.

20

Who is that Tulip who can show
   Colours of that transcendent kind?
Thou Daphne, thine the kindred glow
   That stately form in thee we find   160
How do all eyes thy charms explore
   Admire and pass and look no more
Pity that one so praised and known
   Should call no single grace her own
The heath flower bruised by Shepherds feet
   Is far less fine but far more sweet.

21

Deep is the Poppeys blushing red;
   Ah! take it from our joyous bowers
With baneful Dew its flower is fed
   Until replete with deadly powers   170
Its heavy influence round is shed
   That ease and cheerfulness oerpowers
No being loves it, all would hate
   Did it not men intoxicate
Ah! Lais, thou art like that Herb
   Its baneful properties are Thine
So formed the reason to disturb
   So gaudy, flimsy, flaunting fine
And yet thou hast the witchcraft too
   That can the sense of man subdue   180

22

Yon roving Woodbine, now behold
   How she her flexile beauty flings
On all supporters, young and old
   On hedge row thorns and baser things
As Phillis with each decent charm
   Will hang on every offered arm

23

But spite of this if you can bind
　　These roving branches round a tree
If Phillis can an Husband find
　　Both pleasant in their way may be
But then to have the pleasure last
　　You watch them well and hold them fast.

24

See Larkspurs, blooming on that bed
　　'Twas wisdom to assemble these
Their different looks! their pale and red
　　Borrow and lend a power to please
So nymphs in many a pleasant dress
　　In our assemblies take their place
And when together, All confess
　　They lend by turns and borrow grace
What one alone, had failed to do,
　　They make a very pretty view

25

Then we have Sunflowers large and tall
　　Who spread their beauty to the day
And we have Daisies neat and small
　　Pinks, bright and smart and Pansies gay
And there are Lilies of the Vale
　　So sweet, so pure, so fresh, so pale
Of modest growth and humble kind
　　But very scarce, and hard to find
Of some of these go where you may
　　You find a likeness every day
Whilst some are rare and boast a place
　　An Habitat that few can trace

26

Come let us look discretely round
   In fear let us the charmers view
The prizes may no doubt be found
   The blanks Alas! are many too
Much care it asks, to seek, to shun,
   For choose we must and choose but one   220

27

Shall we the blooming Rose select
   There's beauty modesty and grace
What more in flower can man expect
   What more in woman's lovely race?
Alas! and yet her beauties all
   Charm but a day and fade and fall.

28

Say in the Myrtle shall we find
   Resemblance to the favourite maid
There's nothing of a sweeter kind
   To Man's approving eye displayed.   230
It loves the shade and yet the sun
   No sweeter blossom smiles upon
A poet's brow it loves to bind
   But other wreaths are there entwined
All seasons it alone will brave
   To spend its freshness oer his grave
But where shall we this Fair behold?
   Ah! that the Muse will not unfold –

POSTHUMOUS TALES

THE FAMILY OF LOVE

In a large town, a wealthy thriving place,
Where hopes of gain excite an anxious race;
Which dark dense wreaths of cloudy volumes cloak,
And mark, for leagues around, the place of smoke;
Where fire to water lends its powerful aid,
And steam produces – strong ally to trade: –
Arrived a Stranger, whom no merchant knew,
Nor could conjecture what he came to do:
He came not there his fortune to amend,
He came not there a fortune made to spend;
His age not that which men in trade employ:
The place not that where men their wealth enjoy;
Yet there was something in his air that told
Of competency gained, before the man was old.
He brought no servants with him: those he sought
Were soon his habits and his manners taught –
His manners easy, civil, kind, and free;
His habits such as agèd men's will be;
To self indulgent; wealthy men like him
Plead for these failings – 'tis their way, their whim.

His frank good-humour, his untroubled air,
His free address, and language bold but fair,
Soon made him friends – such friends as all may make,
Who take the way that he was pleased to take.
He gave his dinners in a handsome style,

10

20

And met his neighbours with a social smile;
The wealthy all their easy friend approved,
Whom the more liberal for his bounty loved;
And even the cautious and reserved began
To speak with kindness of the frank old man,   30
Who, though associate with the rich and grave,
Laughed with the gay, and to the needy gave
What need requires. At church a seat was shown,
That he was kindly asked to think his own:
Thither he went, and neither cold nor heat,
Pains or pretences, kept him from his seat.
This to his credit in the town was told,
And ladies said, ' 'Tis pity he is old:
Yet, for his years, the Stranger moves like one
Who, of his race, has no small part to run.'   40
No envy he by ostentation raised,
And all his hospitable table praised.
His quiet life censorious talk suppressed,
And numbers hailed him as their welcome guest.

'Twas thought a man so mild, and bounteous too,
A world of good within the town might do;
To vote him honours, therefore, they inclined;
But these he sought not, and with thanks resigned;
His days of business he declared were past,
And he would wait in quiet for the last;   50
But for a dinner and a day of mirth
He was the readiest being upon earth.

Men called him Captain, and they found the name
By him accepted without pride or shame.
Not in the Navy – that did not appear:
Not in the Army – that at least was clear –
'But as he speaks of sea-affairs, he made,
No doubt, his fortune in the way of trade;
He might, perhaps, an India-ship command –
We'll call him *Captain* now he comes to land.'   60

The Stranger much of various life had seen,
Been poor, been rich, and in the state between;
Had much of kindness met, and much deceit,
And all that man who deals with men must meet.
Not much he read; but from his youth had thought,
And been by care and observation taught:
'Tis thus a man his own opinions makes;
He holds that fast, which he with trouble takes:
While one whose notions all from books arise,
70   Upon his authors, not himself, relies –
A borrowed wisdom this, that does not make us wise.

Inured to scenes, where wealth and place command
The observant eye, and the obedient hand,
A Tory-spirit his – he ever paid
Obedience due, and looked to be obeyed.
'Man upon man depends, and, break the chain,
He soon returns to savage life again;
As of fair virgins dancing in a round,
Each binds another, and herself is bound,
80   On either hand a social tribe he sees,
By those assisted, and assisting these;
While to the general welfare all belong,
The high in power, the low in number strong.'

Such was the Stranger's creed – if not profound,
He judged it useful, and proclaimed it sound;
And many liked it: invitations went
To Captain Elliot, and from him were sent –
These last so often, that his friends confessed,
The Captain's cook had not a place of rest.
90   Still were they something at a loss to guess
What his profession was from his address;
For much he knew, and too correct was he
For a man trained and nurtured on the sea;
Yet well he knew the seaman's words and ways, –
Seaman's his look, and nautical his phrase:

In fact, all ended just where they began,
With many a doubt of this amphibious man.

  Though kind to all, he looked with special grace
On a few members of an ancient race,
Long known, and well respected in the place: 100
Dyson their name; but how regard for these
Rose in his mind, or why they seemed to please,
Or by what ways, what virtues – not a cause
Can we assign, for Fancy has no laws;
But, as the Captain showed them such respect,
We will not treat the Dysons with neglect.

  Their Father died while yet engaged by trade
To make a fortune, that was never made,
But to his children taught; for he would say
'I place them – all I can – in Fortune's way.'   110

  James was his first-born; when his father died,
He, in their large domain, the place supplied,
And found, as to the Dysons all appeared,
Affairs less gloomy than their sire had feared;
But then if rich or poor, all now agree,
Frugal and careful, James must wealthy be:
And wealth in wedlock sought, he married soon,
And ruled his Lady from the honey-moon:
Nor shall we wonder; for, his house beside,
He had a sturdy multitude to guide,   120
Who now his spirit vexed, and now his temper tried;
Men who by labours live, and, day by day,
Work, weave, and spin their active lives away:
Like bees industrious, they for others strive,
With, now and then, some murmuring in the hive.

  James was a churchman – 'twas his pride and boast;
Loyal his heart, and 'Church and King' his toast;
He for Religion might not warmly feel,
But for the Church he had abounding zeal.

  Yet no dissenting sect would he condemn,   130
'They're nought to us,' said he, 'nor we to them;

'Tis innovation of our own I hate,
Whims and inventions of a modern date.

'Why send you Bibles all the world about,
That men may read amiss, and learn to doubt?
Why teach the children of the poor to read,
That a new race of doubters may succeed?
Now can you scarcely rule the stubborn crew,
And what if they should know as much as you?
Will a man labour when to learning bred,
Or use his hands who can employ his head?
Will he a clerk or master's self obey,
Who thinks himself as well-informed as they?'

These were his favourite subjects – these he chose,
And where he ruled no creature durst oppose.

'We are rich,' quoth James; 'but if we thus proceed,
And give to all, we shall be poor indeed:
In war we subsidise the world – in peace
We christianise – our bounties never cease:
We learn each stranger's tongue, that they with ease
May read translated Scriptures, if they please;
We buy them presses, print them books, and then
Pay and export poor learnèd, pious men;
Vainly we strive a fortune now to get,
So taxed by private claims, and public debt.'

Still he proceeds – 'You make your prisons light,
Airy and clean, your robbers to invite;
And in such ways your pity show to vice,
That you the rogues encourage, and entice.'

For lenient measures James had no regard –
'Hardship,' he said, 'must work upon the hard;
Labour and chains such desperate men require;
To soften iron you must use the fire.'

Active himself, he laboured to express,
In his strong words, his scorn of idleness;

From him in vain the beggar sought relief –
'Who will not labour is an idle thief,
Stealing from those who will;' he knew not how
For the untaught and ill-taught to allow,
Children of want and vice, inured to ill,   170
Unchained the passions, and uncurbed the will.

 Alas! he looked but to his own affairs,
Or to the rivals in his trade, and theirs:
Knew not the thousands who must all be fed,
Yet ne'er were taught to earn their daily bread;
Whom crimes, misfortunes, errors only teach
To seek their food where'er within their reach,
Who for their parents' sins, or for their own,
Are now as vagrants, wanderers, beggars known,
Hunted and hunting through the world, to share   180
Alms and contempt, and shame and scorn to bear;
Whom Law condemns, and Justice, with a sigh,
Pursuing, shakes her sword and passes by. –
If to the prison we should these commit,
They for the gallows will be rendered fit.

 But James had virtues – was esteemed as one
Whom men looked up to, and relied upon.
Kind to his equals, social when they met –
If out of spirits, always out of debt;
True to his promise, he a lie disdained,   190
And e'en when tempted in his trade, refrained;
Frugal he was, and loved the cash to spare,
Gained by much skill, and nursed by constant care;
Yet liked the social board, and when he spoke,
Some hailed his wisdom, some enjoyed his joke.
To him a Brother looked as one to whom,
If fortune frowned, he might in trouble come;
His Sisters viewed the important man with awe,
As if a parent in his place they saw:
All lived in Love; none sought their private ends;   200
The Dysons were a Family of Friends.

His brother David was a studious boy,
Yet could his sports as well as books enjoy.
E'en when a boy, he was not quickly read,
If by the heart you judged him, or the head.
His father thought he was decreed to shine,
And be in time an eminent Divine;
But if he ever to the Church inclined,
It is too certain that he changed his mind.
He spoke of scruples, but who knew him best
Affirmed, no scruples broke on David's rest.
Physic and Law were each in turn proposed,
210   He weighed them nicely, and with Physic closed.

He had a serious air, a smooth address,
And a firm spirit that ensured success.
He watched his brethren of the time, how they
Rose into fame, that he might choose his way.

Some, he observed, a kind of roughness used,
And now their patients bantered, now abused:
220   The awe-struck people were at once dismayed,
As if they begged the advice for which they paid.

There are who hold that no disease is slight,
Who magnify the foe with whom they fight.
The sick was told that his was that disease
But rarely known on mortal frame to seize;
Which only skill profound, and full command
Of all the powers in nature could withstand.
Then, if he lived, what fame the conquest gave!
And if he died – 'No human power could save!'

230   Mere fortune sometimes, and a lucky case,
Will make a man the idol of a place –
Who last, advice to some fair duchess gave,
Or snatched a widow's darling from the grave,
Him first she honours of the lucky tribe,
Fills him with praise, and woos him to prescribe.

In his own chariot soon he rattles on,
And half believes the lies that built him one.

But not of these was David: care and pain,
And studious toil prepared his way to gain.
At first observed, then trusted, he became 240
At length respected, and acquired a name.
Keen, close, attentive, he could read mankind,
The feeble body, and the failing mind;
And if his heart remained untouched, his eyes,
His air, and tone, with all could sympathise.

This brought him fees, and not a man was he
In weak compassion to refuse a fee.
Yet though the Doctor's purse was well supplied,
Though patients came, and fees were multiplied,
Some secret drain, that none presumed to know, 250
And few e'en guessed, for ever kept it low.
Some of a patient spake, a tender fair,
Of whom the doctor took peculiar care,
But not a fee: he rather largely gave,
Nor spared himself, 'twas said, this gentle friend to save.
Her case consumptive, with perpetual need
Still to be fed, and still desire to feed;
An eager craving, seldom known to cease,
And gold alone brought temporary peace. –

So, rich he was not; James some fear expressed, 260
Dear Doctor David would be yet distressed;
For if now poor, when so repaid his skill,
What fate were his, if he himself were ill!

In his religion, Doctor Dyson sought
To teach himself – 'A man should not be taught,
Should not, by forms or creeds, his mind debase,
That keep in awe an unreflecting race.'
He needed not what Clarke and Paley say,
But thought himself as good a judge as they;
Yet to the Church professed himself a friend, 270

And would the rector for his hour attend;
Nay, praise the learnèd discourse, and learnèdly defend.
For since the common herd of men are blind,
He judged it right that guides should be assigned;
And that the few who could themselves direct
Should treat those guides with honour and respect.
He was from all contracted notions freed,
But gave his Brother credit for his creed;
And if in smaller matters he indulged,
'Twas well, so long as they were not divulged.

Oft was the spirit of the Doctor tried,
When his grave Sister wished to be his guide.
She told him, 'all his real friends were grieved
To hear it said, how little he believed:
Of all who bore the name she never knew
One to his pastor or his church untrue;
All have the truth with mutual zeal professed,
And why, dear Doctor, differ from the rest?'

''Tis my hard fate,' with serious looks replied
The man of doubt, 'to err with such a guide.' –
'Then why not turn from such a painful state?' –
The doubting man replied, 'It is my fate.'

Strong in her zeal, by texts and reasons backed,
In his grave mood the Doctor she attacked:
Culled words from Scripture to announce his doom,
And bade him 'think of dreadful things to come.'

'If such,' he answered, 'be that state untried,
In peace, dear Martha, let me here abide;
Forbear to insult a man whose fate is known,
And leave to Heaven a matter all its own.'

In the same cause the Merchant, too, would strive;
He asked, 'Did ever unbeliever thrive?
Had he respect? could he a fortune make?
And why not then such impious men forsake?'

'Thanks, my dear James, and be assured I feel,
If not your reason, yet at least your zeal;
And when those wicked thoughts, that keep me poor,
And bar respect, assail me as before
With force combined, you'll drive the fiend away,
For you shall reason, James, and Martha pray.'   310

But though the Doctor could reply with ease
To all such trivial arguments as these, –
Though he could reason, or at least deride,
There was a power that would not be defied;
A closer reasoner, whom he could not shun,
Could not refute, from whom he could not run;
For Conscience lived within; she slept, 'tis true,
But when she waked, her pangs awakened too.
She bade him think; and as he thought, a sigh
Of deep remorse precluded all reply.   320
No soft insulting smile, no bitter jest,
Could this commanding power of strength divest,
But with reluctant fear her terrors he confessed.
His weak advisers he could scorn or slight,
But not their cause; for, in their folly's spite,
They took the wiser part, and chose their way aright.

Such was the Doctor, upon whom for aid
Had some good ladies called, but were afraid –
Afraid of one who, if report were just,
The arm of flesh, and that alone would trust.   330
But these were few – the many took no care
Of what they judged to be his own affair:
And if he them from their diseases freed,
They neither cared nor thought about his creed:
They said his merits would for much atone,
And only wondered that he lived alone.

The widowed Sister near the Merchant dwelt,
And her late loss with lingering sorrow felt.
Small was her jointure, and o'er this she sighed,

340 That to her heart its bounteous wish denied,
Which yet all common wants, but not her all, supplied.
Sorrows like showers descend, and as the heart
For them prepares, they good or ill impart;
Some on the mind, as on the ocean rain,
Fall and disturb, but soon are lost again —
Some, as to fertile lands, a boon bestow,
And seed, that else had perished, live and grow;
Some fall on barren soil, and thence proceed
The idle blossom, and the useless weed;
350 But how her griefs the Widow's heart impressed,
Must from the tenor of her life be guessed.

Rigid she was, persisting in her grief,
Fond of complaint, and adverse to relief.
In her religion she was all severe,
And as she was, was anxious to appear.
When sorrow died restraint usurped the place,
And sate in solemn state upon her face,
Reading she loved not, nor would deign to waste
Her precious time on trifling works of taste;
360 Though what she did with all that precious time
We know not, but to waste it was a crime —
As oft she said, when with a serious friend
She spent the hours as duty bids us spend;
To read a novel was a kind of sin —
Albeit once Clarissa took her in;
And now of late she heard with much surprise,
Novels there were that made a compromise
Betwixt amusement and religion; these
Might charm the worldly, whom the stories please,
370 And please the serious, whom the sense would charm
And thus indulging, be secured from harm —
A happy thought, when from the foe we take
His arms, and use them for religion's sake.

Her Bible she perused by day, by night;
It was her task — she said 'twas her delight;

Found in her room, her chamber, and her pew,
For ever studied, yet for ever new –
All must be new that we cannot retain,
And new we find it when we read again.

    The hardest texts she could with ease expound,   380
And meaning for the most mysterious found,
Knew which of dubious senses to prefer:
The want of Greek was not a want in her; –
Instinctive light no aid from Hebrew needs –
But full conviction without study breeds;
O'er mortal powers by inborn strength prevails,
Where Reason trembles, and where Learning fails.

    To the church strictly from her childhood bred,
She now her zeal with party-spirit fed:
For brother James she lively hopes expressed,   390
But for the Doctor's safety felt distressed;
And her light Sister, poor, and deaf, and blind,
Filled her with fears of most tremendous kind.
But David mocked her for the pains she took,
And Fanny gave resentment for rebuke;
While James approved the zeal, and praised the call,
'That brought,' he said, 'a blessing on them all:
Goodness like this to all the House extends,
For were they not a Family of Friends?'

    Their sister Frances, though her prime was past,   400
Had beauty still – nay, beauty formed to last;
'Twas not the lily and the rose combined,
Nor must we say the beauty of the mind;
But feature, form, and that engaging air,
That lives when ladies are no longer fair.
Lovers she had, as she remembered yet,
For who the glories of their reign forget?
Some she rejected in her maiden pride
And some in maiden hesitation tried,
Unwilling to renounce, unable to decide.   410

One lost, another would her grace implore,
Till all were lost, and lovers came no more:
Nor had she that, in beauty's failing state,
Which will recall a lover, or create;
Hers was the slender portion, that supplied
Her real wants, but all beyond denied.

When Fanny Dyson reached her fortieth year,
She would no more of love or lovers hear;
But one dear Friend she chose, her guide, her stay;
And to each other all the world were they;
For all the world had grown to them unkind,
One sex censorious, and the other blind.
The Friend of Frances longer time had known
The world's deceits, and from its follies flown.
With her dear Friend, life's sober joys to share
Was all that now became her wish and care.
They walked together, they conversed and read,
And tender tears for well-feigned sorrows shed:
And were so happy in their quiet lives,
They pitied sighing maids, and weeping wives.

But Fortune to our state such change imparts,
That Pity stays not long in human hearts;
When sad for others' woes our hearts are grown,
This soon gives place to sorrows of our own.

There was among our guardian Volunteers
A Major Bright – he reckoned fifty years:
A reading man of peace, but called to take
His sword and musket for his country's sake;
Not to go forth and fight, but here to stay,
Invaders, should they come, to chase or slay.

Him had the elder Lady long admired,
As one from vain and trivial things retired;
With him conversed; but to a Friend so dear,
Gave not that pleasure – Why? is not so clear;
But chance effected this: the Major now

Gave both the time his duties would allow;
In walks, in visits, when abroad, at home,
The friendly Major would to either come.
He never spoke – for he was not a boy –
Of ladies' charms, or lovers' grief and joy.   450
All his discourses were of serious kind,
The heart they touched not, but they filled the mind.
Yet – oh, the pity! from this grave good man
The cause of coolness in the Friends began.
The sage Sophronia – that the chosen name –
Now more polite, and more estranged became.
She could but feel that she had longer known
This valued friend – he was indeed her own;
But Frances Dyson, to confess the truth,
Had more of softness – yes, and more of youth;   460
And though he said such things had ceased to please,
The worthy Major was not blind to these:
So without thought, without intent, he paid
More frequent visits to the younger Maid.

Such the offence; and though the Major tried
To tie again the knot he thus untied,
His utmost efforts no kind looks repaid, –
He moved no more the inexorable maid.
The Friends too parted, and the elder told
Tales of false hearts, and friendships waxing cold;   470
And wondered what a man of sense could see
In the light airs of withered vanity.

'Tis said that Frances now the world reviews,
Unwilling all the little left to lose;
She and the Major on the walks are seen,
And all the world is wondering what they mean.

Such were the four whom Captain Elliot drew
To his own board, as the selected few.
For why? they seemed each other to approve,
And called themselves a Family of Love.   480

These were not all: there was a Youth beside,
Left to his uncles when his parents died:
A Girl, their sister, by a Boy was led
To Scotland, where a boy and girl may wed –
And they returned to seek for pardon, pence, and bread.
Five years they lived to labour, weep, and pray,
When Death, in mercy, took them both away.

Uncles and aunts received this lively child,
Grieved at his fate, and at his follies smiled;
490 But when the child to boy's estate grew on,
The smile was vanished, and the pity gone.
Slight was the burden, but in time increased,
Until at length both love and pity ceased.
Then Tom was idle; he would find his way
To his aunt's stores, and make her sweets his prey:
By uncle Doctor on a message sent,
He stopped to play, and lost it as he went.
His grave aunt Martha, with a frown austere,
And a rough hand, produced a transient fear;
500 But Tom, to whom his rude companions taught
Language as rude, vindictive measures sought;
He used such words, that when she wished to speak
Of his offence, she had her words to seek.
The little wretch had called her – 'twas a shame
To think such thought, and more to name such name.

Thus fed and beaten, Tom was taught to pray
For his true friends: 'but who,' said he, 'are they?'
By nature kind, when kindly used, the Boy
Hailed the strange good with tears of love and joy;
510 But, roughly used, he felt his bosom burn
With wrath he dared not on his uncles turn;
So with indignant spirit, still and strong,
He nursed the vengeance, and endured the wrong.
To a cheap school, far north, the boy was sent:
Without a tear of love or grief he went;
Where, doomed to fast and study, fight and play,

He stayed five years, and wished five more to stay.
He loved o'er plains to run, up hills to climb,
Without a thought of kindred, home, or time;
Till from the cabin of a coasting hoy,   520
Landed at last the thin and freckled boy,
With sharp keen eye, but pale and hollow cheek,
All made more sad from sickness of a week.
His aunts and uncles felt – nor strove to hide
From the poor boy, their pity and their pride:
He had been taught that he had not a friend,
Save these on earth, on whom he might depend;
And such dependence upon these he had,
As made him sometimes desperate, always sad.

  'Awkward and weak, where can the lad be placed,   530
And we not troubled, censured, or disgraced?
Do, Brother James, the unhappy boy enrol
Among your set; you only can control.'
James sighed, and Thomas to the Factory went,
Who there his days in sundry duties spent.
He ran, he wrought, he wrote – to read or play
He had no time, nor much to feed or pray.
What passed without he heard not – or he heard
Without concern, what he nor wished nor feared;
Told of the Captain and his wealth, he sighed,   540
And said, 'how well his table is supplied:'
But with the sigh it caused the sorrow fled;
He was not feasted, but he must be fed,
And he could sleep full sound, though not full soft his bed.

  But still, ambitious thoughts his mind possessed,
And dreams of joy broke in upon his rest.
Improved in person, and enlarged in mind,
The good he found not he could hope to find.
Though now enslaved, he hailed the approaching day,
When he should break his chains and flee away.   550

Such were the Dysons: they were first of those
Whom Captain Elliot as companions chose;
Them he invited, and the more approved,
As it appeared that each the other loved.
Proud of their brothers were the sister pair,
And if not proud, yet kind the brothers were.
This pleased the Captain, who had never known,
Or he had loved, such kindred of his own:
Them he invited, save the Orphan lad,
560   Whose name was not the one his Uncles had;
No Dyson he, nor with the party came –
The worthy Captain never heard his name;
Uncles and Aunts forbore to name the boy,
For then, of course, must follow his employ.
Though all were silent, as with one consent,
None told another what his silence meant,
What hers; but each suppressed the useless truth,
And not a word was mentioned of the youth.

Familiar grown, the Dysons saw their host,
570   With none beside them: it became their boast,
Their pride, their pleasure; but to some it seemed
Beyond the worth their talents were esteemed.
This wrought no change within the Captain's mind;
To all men courteous, he to them was kind.

One day with these he sat, and only these,
In a light humour, talking at his ease:
Familiar grown, he was disposed to tell
Of times long past, and what in them befell –
Not of his life their wonder to attract,
580   But the choice tale, or insulated fact.
Then, as it seemed, he had acquired a right
To hear what they could from their stores recite.
Their lives, they said, were all of common kind;
He could no pleasure in such trifles find.

They had an Uncle – 'tis their father's tale –
Who in all seas had gone where ship can sail,
Who in all lands had been, where men can live;
'He could indeed some strange relations give,
And many a bold adventure; but in vain
We look for him; he comes not home again.'   590

'And is it so? why then, if so it be,'
Said Captain Elliot, 'you must look to me:
I knew John Dyson' – Instant every one
Was moved to wonder – 'knew my Uncle John!
Can he be rich? be childless? he is old,
That is most certain – What! can more be told?
Will he return, who has so long been gone,
And lost to us? Oh! what of Uncle John?'

This was aside: their unobservant friend
Seemed on their thoughts but little to attend;   600
A traveller speaking he was more inclined
To tell his story than their thoughts to find.

'Although, my Friends, I love you well, 'tis true,
'Twas your relation turned my mind to you;
For we were friends of old, and friends like us are few;
And though from dearest friends a man will hide
His private vices in his native pride,
Yet such our friendship from its early rise,
We no reserve admitted, no disguise;
But 'tis the story of my friend I tell,   610
And to all others let me bid farewell.

'Take each your glass, and you shall hear how John,
My old companion, through the world has gone;
I can describe him to the very life,
Him and his ways, his ventures, and his wife.'

'Wife!' whispered all; 'then what his life to us,
His ways and ventures, if he ventured thus?'
This, too, apart; yet were they all intent,
And, gravely listening, sighed with one consent.

620   'My friend, your Uncle was designed for trade,
To make a fortune as his father made;
But early he perceived the house declined,
And his domestic views at once resigned;
While stout of heart, with life in every limb,
He would to sea, and either sink or swim.
No one forbad; his father shook his hand,
Within it leaving what he could command.

     'He left his home, but I will not relate
What storms he braved, and how he bore his fate,
630 Till his brave frigate was a Spanish prize,
And prison-walls received his first-born sighs,
Sighs for the freedom that an English boy,
Or English man, is eager to enjoy.

     'Exchanged, he breathed in freedom, and aboard
An English ship, he found his peace restored;
War raged around, each British tar was pressed
To serve his king, and John among the rest;
Oft had he fought and bled, and 'twas his fate
In that same ship to grow to man's estate.
640 Again 'twas war: of France a ship appeared
Of greater force, but neither shunned nor feared;
'Twas in the Indian Sea, the land was nigh,
When all prepared to fight, and some to die;
Man after man was in the ocean thrown,
Limb after limb was to the surgeon shown,
And John at length, poor John! held forth his own. –

     'A tedious case – the battle ceased with day,
And in the night the foe had slipped away.
Of many wounded were a part conveyed
650 To land, and he among the number laid;
Poor, suffering, friendless, who shall now impart
Life to his hope, or comfort to his heart?
A kind good priest among the English there
Selected him as his peculiar care;

And, when recovered, to a powerful friend
Was pleased the lad he loved to recommend;
Who read your Uncle's mind, and, pleased to read,
Placed him where talents will in time succeed.

'I will not tease you with details of trade,
But say he there a decent fortune made, –   660
Not such as gave him, if returned, to buy
A duke's estate, or principality,
But a fair fortune: years of peace he knew,
That were so happy, and that seemed so few.

'Then came a cloud; for who on earth has seen
A changeless fortune, and a life serene?
Ah! then how joyous were the hours we spent!
But joy is restless, joy is not content.

'There one resided, who, to serve his friend,
Was pleased a gay fair lady to commend;   670
Was pleased to invite the happy man to dine,
And introduced the subject o'er their wine;
Was pleased the lady his good friend should know,
And as a secret his regard would show.

'A modest man lacks courage; but, thus trained,
Your Uncle sought her favour and obtained:
To me he spake, enraptured with her face,
Her angel smile, her unaffected grace;
Her fortune small indeed; but "curse the pelf,
She is a glorious fortune in herself!"   680
"John!" answered I, "friend John, to be sincere,
These are fine things, but may be bought too dear.
You are no stripling, and, it must be said,
Have not the form that charms a youthful maid.
What you possess, and what you leave behind,
When you depart, may captivate her mind;
And I suspect she will rejoice at heart,
Your will once made, if you should soon depart."

'Long our debate, and much we disagreed;
690   "You need no wife," I said – said he, "I need;
I want a house, I want in all I see
To take an interest; what is mine to me?"
So spake the man, who to his word was just,
And took the words of others upon trust.
He could not think that friend in power so high,
So much esteemed, could like a villain lie;
Nor, till the knot, the fatal knot, was tied,
Had urged his wedding a dishonoured bride.
The man he challenged, for his heart was rent
700   With rage and grief, and was to prison sent;
For men in power – and this, alas! was one –
Revenge on all, the wrongs themselves have done;
And he whose spirit bends not to the blow
The tyrants strike, shall no forgiveness know,
For 'tis to slaves alone that tyrants favour show.

'This cost him much; but that he did not heed;
The lady died, and my poor friend was freed.
"Enough of ladies!" then said he, and smiled;
"I've now no longings for a neighbour's child."
710   So patient he returned, and not in vain,
To his late duties, and grew rich again.
He was no miser; but the man who takes
Care to be rich, will love the gain he makes:
Pursuing wealth, he soon forgot his woes,
No acts of his were bars to his repose.

'Now John was rich, and old and weary grown,
Talked of the country that he calls his own,
And talked to me; for now, in fact, began
My better knowledge of the real man.
720   Though long estranged, he felt a strong desire,
That made him for his former friends inquire;
What Dysons yet remained, he longed to know,
And doubtless meant some proofs of love to show.

His purpose known, our native land I sought,
And with the wishes of my Friend am fraught.'

    Fixed were all eyes, suspense each bosom shook,
And expectation hung on every look.

    '"Go to my kindred, seek them all around,
Find all you can, and tell me all that's found;
Seek them if prosperous, seek them in distress,   730
Hear what they need, know what they all possess;
What minds, what hearts they have, how good they are,
How far from goodness – speak, and no one spare,
And no one slander: let me clearly see
What is in them, and what remains for me."

    'Such is my charge, and haply I shall send
Tidings of joy and comfort to my Friend.
Oft would he say, "If of our race survive
Some two or three, to keep the name alive,
I will not ask if rich or great they be,   740
But if they live in love, like you and me."

    ''Twas not my purpose yet awhile to speak
As I have spoken; but why further seek?
All that I heard I in my heart approve;
You are indeed a Family of Love:
And my old friend were happy in the sight
Of those, of whom I shall such tidings write.'

    The Captain wrote not: he perhaps was slow,
Perhaps he wished a little more to know.
He wrote not yet, and while he thus delayed,   750
Frances alone an early visit paid.
The maiden Lady braved the morning cold,
To tell her Friend what duty bade be told,
Yet not abruptly – she has first to say,
'How cold the morning, but how fine the day; –
I fear you slept but ill, we kept you long,
You made us all so happy, but 'twas wrong –

So entertained, no wonder we forgot
How the time passed; I fear me you did not.'

760   In this fair way the Lady seldom failed
To steer her course, still sounding as she sailed.

'Dear Captain Elliot, how your Friends you read!
We are a loving Family indeed;
Left in the world each other's aid to be,
And join to raise a fallen family.
Oh! little thought we there was one so near,
And one so distant, to us all so dear:
All, all alike; he cannot know, dear man!
Who needs him most, as one among us can –
770   One who can all our wants distinctly view,
And tell him fairly what were just to do:
But you, dear Captain Elliot, as his friend,
As ours, no doubt, will your assistance lend.
Not for the world would I my Brothers blame;
Good men they are: 'twas not for that I came.
No! did they guess what shifts I make, the grief
That I sustain, they'd fly to my relief;
But I am proud as poor; I cannot plead
My cause with them, nor show how much I need;
780   But to my Uncle's Friend it is no shame,
Nor have I fear, to seem the thing I am;
My humble pittance life's mere need supplies,
But all indulgence, all beyond denies.
I aid no pauper, I myself am poor,
I cannot help the beggar at my door.
I from my scanty table send no meat;
Cooked and recooked is every joint I eat.
At Church a sermon begs our help, – I stop
And drop a tear; nought else have I to drop;
790   But pass the out-stretched plate with sorrow by,
And my sad heart this kind relief deny.
My dress – I strive with all my maiden skill
To make it pass, but 'tis disgraceful still;

Yet from all others I my wants conceal,
Oh! Captain Elliot, there are few that feel!
But did that rich and worthy Uncle know
What you, dear Sir, will in your kindness show,
He would his friendly aid with generous hand bestow.

'Good men my Brothers both, and both are raised
Far above want – the Power that gave be praised!   800
My Sister's jointure, if not ample, gives
All she can need, who as a lady lives;
But I, unaided, may through all my years
Endure these ills – forgive these foolish tears.

'Once, my dear Sir – I then was young and gay,
And men would talk – but I have had my day:
Now all I wish is so to live, that men
May not despise me whom they flattered then.
If you, kind Sir –'
          Thus far the Captain heard,
Nor save by sign or look had interfered;   810
But now he spoke; to all she said agreed,
And she conceived it useless to proceed.
Something he promised, and the Lady went
Half-pleased away, yet wondering what he meant;
Polite he was and kind, but she could trace
A smile, or something like it, in his face;
'Twas not a look that gave her joy or pain –
She tried to read it, but she tried in vain.

Then called the Doctor – 'twas his usual way –
To ask 'How fares my worthy friend today?'   820
To feel his pulse, and as a friend to give
Unfee'd advice, how such a man should live;
And thus, digressing, he could soon contrive,
At his own purpose smoothly to arrive.

'My Brother! yes, he lives without a care,
And, though he needs not, yet he loves to spare:
James I respect; and yet it must be told,

His speech is friendly, but his heart is cold.
His smile assumed has not the real glow
Of love! – a sunbeam shining on the snow.
Children he has; but are they causes why
He should our pleas resist, our claims deny?
Our father left the means by which he thrives,
While we are labouring to support our lives.
We, need I say? my widowed Sister lives
On a large jointure; nay, she largely gives; –
And Fanny sighs – for gold does Fanny sigh?
Or wants she that which money cannot buy –
Youth and young hopes? – Ah! could my kindred share
The liberal mind's distress, and daily care,
The painful toil to gain the petty fee,
They'd bless their stars, and join to pity me.
Hard is his fate, who would, with eager joy,
To save mankind, his every power employ;
Yet in his walk unnumbered insults meets
And gains 'mid scorn the food that chokes him as he eats.

'Oh! Captain Elliot, you who know mankind,
With all the anguish of the feeling mind,
Bear to our kind relation these the woes
That e'en to you 'tis misery to disclose.
You can describe what I but faintly trace –
A man of learning cannot bear disgrace;
Refinement sharpens woes that wants create,
And 'tis fresh grief such grievous things to state;
Yet those so near me let me not reprove –
I love them well, and they deserve my love;
But want they know not – Oh! that I could say
I am in this as ignorant as they.'

The Doctor thus. – The Captain grave and kind,
To the sad sale with serious looks inclined,
And promise made to keep the important speech in mind.

James and the Widow, how is yet unknown,

Heard of these visits, and would make their own.
All was not fair, they judged, and both agreed
To their good Friend together to proceed.
Forth then they went to see him, and persuade –
As warm a pair as ever Anger made.
The Widow lady must the speaker be:
So James agreed; for words at will had she;
And then her Brother, if she needed proof,   870
Should add, ' 'Tis truth:' – it was for him enough.

'Oh! sir, it grieves me' – for we need not dwell
On introduction: all was kind and well. –
'Oh! sir, it grieves, it shocks us both to hear
What has, with selfish purpose, gained your ear –
Our very flesh and blood, and, as you know, how dear.
Doubtless they came your noble mind to impress
With strange descriptions of their own distress;
But I would to the Doctor's face declare,
That he has more to spend and more to spare,   880
With all his craft, than we with all our care.

'And for our Sister, all she has she spends
Upon herself; herself alone befriends.
She has the portion that our father left,
While me of mine a careless wretch bereft,
Save a small part; yet I could joyful live,
Had I my mite – the widow's mite – to give.
For this she cares not; Frances does not know
Their heartfelt joy, who largely can bestow.
You, Captain Elliot, feel the pure delight,   890
That our kind acts in tender hearts excite,
When to the poor we can our alms extend,
And make the Father of all Good our friend;
And, I repeat, I could with pleasure live,
Had I my mite – the widow's mite – to give.

'We speak not thus, dear Sir, with vile intent,

Our nearest friends to wrong or circumvent;
But that our Uncle, worthy man! should know
How best his wealth, Heaven's blessing, to bestow;
900   What widows need, and chiefly those who feel
For all the suffering which they cannot heal;
And men in trade, with numbers in their pay,
Who must be ready for the reckoning-day,
Or gain or lose!' –
   – 'Thank Heaven,' said James, 'as yet
I've not been troubled by a dun or debt.'
– The Widow sighed, convinced that men so weak
Will ever hurt the cause for which they speak;
However tempted to deceive, still they
Are ever blundering to the broad high-way
910   Of very truth: – But Martha passed it by
With a slight frown, and half-distinguished sigh –

'Say to our Uncle, sir, how much I long
To see him sit his kindred race among:
To hear his brave exploits, to nurse his age,
And cheer him in his evening's pilgrimage;
How were I blessed to guide him in the way
Where the religious poor in secret pray,
To be the humble means by which his heart
And liberal hand might peace and joy impart!
920   But now, farewell!' – and slowly, softly fell
The tender accents as she said 'farewell!'

The Merchant stretched his hand, his leave to take,
And gave the Captain's a familiar shake,
Yet seemed to doubt if this was not too free,
But, gaining courage, said, 'Remember me.'

Some days elapsed, the Captain did not write,
But still was pleased the party to invite;
And, as he walked, his custom every day,
A tall pale stripling met him on his way,
930   Who made some efforts, but they proved too weak,

And only showed he was inclined to speak.
'What would'st thou, lad?' the Captain asked, and gave
The youth a power his purposed boon to crave,
Yet not in terms direct — 'My name,' quoth he,
'Is Thomas Bethel; you have heard of me.' —
'Not good nor evil, Thomas — had I need
Of so much knowledge: — but pray now proceed.' —

'Dyson my mother's name; but I have not
That interest with you, and the worse my lot.
I serve my Uncle James, and run and write,   940
And watch and work from morning until night;
Confined among the looms, and webs, and wheels,
You cannot think how like a slave one feels.
'Tis said you have a ship at your command, —
An' please you, sir, I'm weary of the land,
And I have read of foreign parts such things,
As make me sick of Uncle's wheels and springs.'

'But, Thomas, why to sea? you look too slim
For that rough work — and, Thomas, can you swim?'
That he could not, but still he scorned a lie,   950
And boldly answered, 'No, but I can try.' —
'Well, my good lad, but tell me, can you read?'
Now, with some pride he answered, 'Yes, indeed!
I construe Virgil, and our usher said,
I might have been in Homer had I stayed,
And he was sorry when I came away,
And so was I, but Uncle would not pay;
He told the master I had read enough,
And Greek was all unprofitable stuff;
So all my learning now is thrown away,   960
And I've no time for study or for play;
I'm ordered here and there, above, below,
And called a dunce for what I cannot know;
Oh, that I were but from this bondage free!
Do, please your honour, let me go to sea.'

'But why to sea? they want no Latin there;
Hard is their work, and very hard their fare.'

'But then,' said Thomas, 'if on land, I doubt
My Uncle Dyson soon would find me out;
970   And though he tells me what I yearly cost,
'Tis my belief he'd miss me were I lost.
For he has said, that I can act as well
As he himself – but this you must not tell.'

'Tell, Thomas! no, I scorn the base design,
Give me your hand, I pledge my word with mine;
And if I cannot do thee good, my friend,
Thou may'st at least upon that word depend.
And hark ye, lad, thy worthy name retain
To the last hour, or I shall help in vain;
980   And then the more severe and hard thy part,
Thine the more praise, and thou the happier art.
We meet again – farewell!' – and Thomas went
Forth to his tasks, half angry, half content.

'I never asked for help,' thought he, 'but twice,
And all they then would give me was advice;
My Uncle Doctor, when I begged his aid,
Bade me work on, and never be afraid,
But still be good; and I've been good so long,
I'm half persuaded that they tell me wrong.
990   And now this Captain still repeats the same,
But who can live upon a virtuous name,
Starving and praised? – "have patience – patience still!"
He said and smiled, and, if I can, I will.'

So Thomas rested with a mind intent
On what the Captain by his kindness meant.

Again the invited party all attend,
These dear relations, on this generous Friend.
They ate, they drank, each striving to appear
Fond, frank, forgiving – above all, sincere.

Such kindred souls could not admit disguise,　　　　　1000
Or envious fears, or painful jealousies;
So each declared, and all in turn replied,
''Tis just indeed, and cannot be denied.'

　　Now various subjects rose, – the country's cause,
The war, the allies, the lottery, and the laws.
The widowed Sister then advantage took
Of a short pause, and, smiling softly, spoke:
She judged what subject would his mind excite –
'Tell us, dear Captain, of that bloody fight,
When our brave Uncle, bleeding at his gun,　　　　　1010
Gave a loud shout to see the Frenchmen run.'

　　'Another day,' – replied the modest host;
'One cannot always of one's battles boast.
Look not surprise – behold the man in me!
Another Uncle shall you never see.
No other Dyson to this place shall come,
Here end my travels, here I place my home;
Here to repose my shattered frame I mean,
Until the last long journey close the scene.'

　　The Ladies softly brushed the tear away;　　　　　1020
James looked surprise, but knew not what to say;
But Doctor Dyson lifted up his voice,
And said, 'Dear Uncle, how we all rejoice!'

　　'No question, Friends! and I your joy approve,
We are, you know, a Family of Love.'

　　So said the wary Uncle, but the while
Wore on his face a questionable smile,
That vanished, as he spake in grave and solemn style –

　　'Friends and relations! let us henceforth seem
Just as we are, nor of our virtues dream,　　　　　1030
That with our waking vanish. – What we are
Full well we know – to improve it be our care.
Forgive the trial I have made: 'tis one

That has no more than I expected done.
If as frail mortals you, my Friends, appear,
I looked for no angelic beings here,
For none that riches spurned as idle pelf,
Or served another as he served himself.
Deceived no longer, let us all forgive;
1040   I'm old, but yet a tedious time may live.
This dark complexion India's suns bestow,
These shrivelled looks to years of care I owe;
But no disease ensures my early doom, –
And I may live – forgive me – years to come.
But while I live, there may some good be done,
Perchance to many, but at least to One.' –

Here he arose, retired, returned, and brought
The Orphan boy, whom he had trained and taught
For this his purpose; and the happy boy,
1050   Though bade to hide, could ill suppress, his joy. –

'This young relation, with your leave, I take,
That he his progress in the world may make –
Not in my house a slave or spy to be,
And first to flatter, then to govern me; –
He shall not nurse me when my senses sleep,
Nor shall the key of all my secrets keep,
And be so useful, that a dread to part
Shall make him master of my easy heart; –
But to be placed where merit may be proved,
1060   And all that now impedes his way removed.

'And now no more on these affairs I dwell,
What I possess that I alone can tell,
And to that subject we will bid farewell.
As go I must, when Heaven is pleased to call,
What I shall leave will seem or large or small,
As you shall view it. When this pulse is still,
You may behold my wealth, and read my will.

'And now, as Captain Elliot much has known,
That to your Uncle never had been shown,
From him one word of honest counsel hear –   1070
And think it always gain to be sincere.'

─────────────

Whether, if I had not been encouraged by some proofs of public favour, I should have written the Poem now before the reader, is a question which I cannot positively determine; but I will venture to assert, that I should not, in that case, have committed the work to the press; I should not have allowed my own opinion of it to have led me into further disappointment, against the voice of judges impartial and indifferent, from whose sentence it had been fruitless to appeal: the success of a late publication, therefore, may fairly be assigned as the principal cause for the appearance of this.

When the ensuing Letters were so far written, that I could form an opinion of them, and when I began to conceive that they might not be unacceptable to the public, I felt myself prompted by duty, as well as interest, to put them to the press; I considered myself bound by gratitude for the favourable treatment I had already received, to show that I was not unmindful of it; and, however this might be mixed with other motives, it operated with considerable force upon my mind, acting as a stimulus to exertions naturally tardy, and to expectations easily checked.

It must nevertheless be acknowledged, that although such favourable opinion had been formed, I was not able, with the requisite impartiality, to determine the comparative values of an unpublished manuscript, and a work sent into the world. Books, like children, when established, have doubtless our parental affection and good wishes; we rejoice to hear that they are doing well, and are received and respected in good company: but it is to manuscripts in the study, as to children in the nursery, that our care, our anxiety, and our tenderness are principally directed: they are fondled as our endearing companions; their faults are corrected with the lenity of partial love, and their good parts are exaggerated by the strength of parental imagination; nor is it easy even for the more cool and reasonable among parents, thus circumstanced, to decide upon the comparative merits of their offspring, whether they be children of the bed or issue of the brain.

But, however favourable my own opinion may have been, or may still be, I could not venture to commit so long a Poem to the press without some endeavour to obtain the more valuable opinion of less partial judges: at the same time, I am willing to confess that I have lost some portion of the timidity once so painful, and that I am encouraged to take upon myself the decision of various points, which heretofore I entreated my friends to decide. Those friends were then my council, whose opinion I was implicitly to follow; they are now advisers, whose ideas I am at liberty to reject. This will not, I hope, seem like arrogance: it would be more safe, it would be more pleasant, still to have that reliance on the judgment of others; but it cannot always be obtained; nor are they, however friendly disposed, ever ready to lend an helping hand to him whom they consider as one who ought by this time to have cast away the timidity of inexperience, and to have acquired the courage that would enable him to decide for himself.

When it is confessed that I have less assistance from my friends, and that the appearance of this work is, in a great measure, occasioned by the success of a former; some readers will, I fear, entertain the opinion that the book before them was written in haste, and published without due examination and revisal: should this opinion be formed, there will doubtless occur many faults which may appear as originating in neglect: Now, readers are, I believe, disposed to treat with more than common severity those writers who have been led into presumption by the approbation bestowed on their diffidence, and into idleness and unconcern, by the praises given to their attention. I am therefore even anxious it should be generally known that sufficient time and application were bestowed upon this work, and by this I mean that no material alteration would be effected by delay: it is true that this confession removes one plea for the errors of the book, want of time; but, in my opinion, there is not much consolation to be drawn by reasonable minds from this resource: if a work fails, it appears to be a poor satisfaction when it is observed, that if the author had taken more care, the event had been less disgraceful.

When the reader enters into the Poem, he will find the author retired from view, and an imaginary personage brought forward to describe his Borough for him: to him it seemed convenient to speak in the first person; but the inhabitant of a village in the centre of the kingdom, could not appear in the character of a residing burgess in a large sea-port; and when, with this point, was considered what relations were to be given, what manners delineated, and what situations described, no method appeared to be so convenient as that of borrowing the assistance of an ideal friend: by this means the reader is in some degree kept from view of any particular place, nor will he perhaps be so likely to determine where those persons reside, and what their connections, who are so intimately known to this man of straw.

From the title of this Poem, some persons will, I fear, expect a political satire, – an attack upon corrupt principles in a general view, or upon the customs and manners of some particular place: of these they will find nothing satirized, nothing related. It may be that graver readers would have preferred a more historical account of so considerable a Borough – its charter, privileges, trade, public structures, and subjects of this kind; but I have an apology for the omission of these things, in the difficulty of describing them, and in the utter repugnancy which subsists between the studies and objects of topography and poetry. What I thought I could best describe, that I attempted; – the sea, and the country in the immediate vicinity; the dwellings, and the inhabitants; some incidents and characters, with an exhibition of morals and manners, offensive perhaps to those of extremely delicate feelings, but sometimes, I hope, neither unamiable nor unaffecting: an election indeed forms a part of one letter, but the evil there described is one not greatly nor generally deplored, and there are probably many places of this kind where it is not felt.

From the variety of relations, characters, and descriptions which a

BOROUGH affords, several were rejected which a reader might reasonably expect to have met with: in this case he is entreated to believe that these, if they occurred to the author, were considered by him as beyond his ability, as subjects which he could not treat in a manner satisfactory to himself. Possibly the admission of some will be thought to require more apology than the rejection of others: in such variety, it is to be apprehended, that almost every reader will find something not according with his ideas of propriety, or something repulsive to the tone of his feelings; nor could this be avoided but by the sacrifice of every event, opinion, and even expression, which could be thought liable to produce such effect; and this casting away so largely of our cargo, through fears of danger, though it might help us to clear it, would render our vessel of little worth when she came into port. I may likewise entertain an hope, that this very variety, which gives scope to objection and censure, will also afford a better chance for approval and satisfaction.

Of these objectionable parts many must be to me unknown, of others some opinion may be formed, and for their admission some plea may be stated [. . .]

The Poor are here almost of necessity introduced, for they must be considered, in every place, as a large and interesting portion of its inhabitants. I am aware of the great difficulty of acquiring just notions on the maintenance and management of this class of our fellow-subjects, and I forbear to express any opinion of the various modes which have been discussed or adopted: of one method only I venture to give my sentiments, that of collecting the poor of an hundred into one building: This admission of a vast number of persons, of all ages and both sexes, of very different inclinations, habits and capacities, into a society, must, at a first view, I conceive, be looked upon as a cause of both vice and misery; nor does any thing which I have heard or read invalidate the opinion; happily, it is not a prevailing one, as these houses are, I believe, still confined to that part of the kingdom where they originated.

To this subject follow several Letters describing the follies and crimes of persons in lower life, with one relation of an happier and more consolatory kind. It has been a subject of greater vexation to me than such trifle ought to be, that I could not, without destroying all appearance of arrangement, separate these melancholy narratives, and place the fallen Clerk in Office at a greater distance from the Clerk of the Parish, especially as they resembled each other in several particulars; both being tempted, seduced, and wretched. Yet are there, I conceive, considerable marks of distinction: their guilt is of different kind; nor would either have committed the offence of the other. The Clerk of the Parish could break the commandment, but he could not have been induced to have disowned an article of that creed for which he had so bravely contended, and on which he fully relied; and the upright mind of the Clerk in Office would have secured him from being guilty of wrong and robbery, though his weak and vacillating intellect could not preserve him from infidelity and profaneness. Their melancholy is nearly alike, but not its consequences. *Jachin* retained his belief, and though he hated life, he could never be induced to quit it voluntarily; but *Abel* was driven to terminate his misery in a way which the unfixedness of his religious opinions rather accelerated than retarded. I am therefore not without hope, that the more observant of my readers will perceive many marks of discrimination in these characters.

The Life of *Ellen Orford*, though sufficiently burdened with error and misfortune, has in it little besides which resembles those of the above unhappy men, and is still more unlike that of *Grimes*, in a subsequent Letter. There is in this character cheerfulness and resignation, a more uniform piety, and an immoveable trust in the aid of religion: this, with the light texture of the introductory part, will, I hope, take off from that idea of sameness which the repetition of crimes and distresses is likely to create. The character of *Grimes*, his obduracy and apparent want of feeling, his gloomy kind of misanthropy, the progress of his madness, and the horrors of his imagination, I must leave to the judgment and observation of my readers. The mind here exhibited, is one untouched by pity, unstung by remorse, and uncorrected by shame: yet is this hardihood of temper and spirit broken by want, disease, solitude and disappointment, and he becomes the victim of a distempered and horror-stricken fancy. It is evident, therefore, that no feeble vision, no half-visible ghost, not the momentary glance of an unbodied being, nor the half-audible voice of an invisible one, would be created by the continual workings of distress on a mind so depraved and flinty. The ruffian of *Mr Scott** has a mind of this nature: he has no shame or remorse: but the corrosion of hopeless want, the wasting of unabating disease, and the gloom of unvaried solitude, will have their effect on every nature; and the harder that nature is, and the longer time required to work upon it, so much the more strong and indelible is the impression. This is all the reason I am able to give, why a man of feeling so dull should yet become insane, and why the visions of his distempered brain should be of so horrible a nature [. . .]

Long as I have detained the reader, I take leave to add a few words on the subject of imitation, or, more plainly speaking, borrowing. In the course of a long poem, and more especially of two long ones, it is very difficult to avoid a recurrence of the same thoughts, and of similar expressions; and, however careful I have been myself in detecting and removing these kind of repetitions, my readers, I question not, would, if disposed to seek them, find many remaining. For these I can only plead that common excuse – they are the offences of a bad memory, and not of voluntary inattention; to which I must add, the difficulty (I have already mentioned) of avoiding the error: this kind of plagiarism will therefore, I conceive, be treated with lenity: and of the more criminal kind, borrowing from others, I plead, with much confidence, 'not guilty'. But while I claim exemption from guilt, I do not affirm that much of sentiment and much of expression may not be detected in the vast collection of English poetry: it is sufficient for an author, that he uses not the words or ideas of another without acknowledgement, and this, and no more than this, I mean, by disclaiming debts of the kind; yet resemblances are sometimes so very striking, that it requires faith in a reader to admit they were undesigned. A line in the second letter,

And monuments themselves memorials need,

was written long before the author, in an accidental recourse to Juvenal, read –

Quandoquidem data sunt ipsis quoque fata sepulchris.

Sat. x. 146.

* Marmion.

and for this I believe the reader will readily give me credit. But there is another apparent imitation in the life of *Blaney* (Letter XIV), a simile of so particular a kind, that its occurrence to two writers at the same time must appear as an extraordinary event; for this reason I once determined to exclude it from the relation; but, as it was truly unborrowed, and suited the place in which it stood, this seemed, on after-consideration, to be an act of cowardice, and the lines are therefore printed as they were written about two months before the very same thought (prosaically dressed) appeared in a periodical work of the last summer. It is highly probable, in these cases, that both may derive the idea from a forgotten but common source; and in this way I must entreat the reader to do me justice, by accounting for other such resemblances, should any be detected.

I know not whether to some readers the placing two or three Latin quotations to a Letter may not appear pedantic and ostentatious, while both they and the English ones may be thought unnecessary. For the necessity I have not much to advance; but if they be allowable, (and certainly the best writers have adopted them), then, where two or three different subjects occur, so many of these mottoes seem to be required: nor will a charge of pedantry remain, when it be considered that these things are generally taken from some books familiar to the school-boy, and the selecting them is facilitated by the use of a book of common-place: yet, with this help, the task of motto-hunting has been so unpleasant to me, that I have in various instances given up the quotation I was in pursuit of, and substituted such English verse or prose as I could find or invent for my purpose.

APPENDIX 2: PREFACE TO *TALES*

That the appearance of the present Volume before the Public is occasioned by a favourable reception of the former two, I hesitate not to acknowledge; because, while the confession may be regarded as some proof of gratitude, or at least of attention, from an Author to his Readers, it ought not to be considered as an indication of vanity. It is unquestionably very pleasant to be assured that our labours are well received; but, nevertheless, this must not be taken for a just and full criterion of their merit: publications of great intrinsic value have been met with so much coolness, that a writer who succeeds in obtaining some degree of notice, should look upon himself rather as one favoured than meritorious, as gaining a prize from Fortune, and not a recompense from desert; and, on the contrary, as it is well known that books of very inferior kind have been at once pushed into the strong current of popularity, and are there kept buoyant by the force of the stream, the writer who acquires not this adventitious help, may be reckoned rather as unfortunate than undeserving; and from these opposite considerations it follows, that a man may speak of his success without incurring justly the odium of conceit, and may likewise acknowledge a disappointment without an adequate cause for humiliation or self-reproach.

But were it true that something of the complacency of self-approbation would insinuate itself into an author's mind with the idea of success, the sensation would not be that of unalloyed pleasure: it would perhaps assist him to bear, but it would not enable him to escape the mortification he must encounter from censures, which, though he may be unwilling to admit, yet he finds himself unable to confute; as well as from advice, which at the same time that he cannot but approve, he is compelled to reject.

Reproof and advice, it is probable, every author will receive, if we except those who merit so much of the former, that the latter is contemptuously denied them; now of these, reproof, though it may cause more temporary uneasiness, will in many cases create less difficulty, since errors may be corrected when opportunity occurs; but advice, I repeat, may be of such a nature, that it will be painful to reject, and yet impossible to follow it; and in this predicament I conceive myself to be placed. There has been recommended to me, and from authority which neither inclination nor prudence leads me to resist, in any new work I might undertake, an unity of subject, and that arrangement of my materials which connects the whole and gives additional interest to every part; in fact, if not an Epic Poem, strictly so denominated, yet such composition as would possess a regular succession of events, and a catastrophe to which every incident should be subvervient, and which every character, in a greater or less degree, should conspire to accomplish.

In a Poem of this nature, the principal and inferior characters in some degree resemble a General and his Army, where no one pursues his peculiar objects and adventures, or pursues them in unison with the movements and grand purposes of the whole body; where there is a community of interests and a subordination of actors: and it was upon this view of the subject, and of the necessity for such distribution of persons and events, that I found myself obliged to relinquish an undertaking, for which the characters I could command, and the adventures I could describe, were altogether unfitted.

But if these characters which seemed to be at my disposal were not such as would coalesce into one body, nor were of a nature to be commanded by one mind, so neither on examination did they appear as an unconnected multitude, accidentally collected, to be suddenly dispersed; but rather beings of whom might be formed groups and smaller societies, the relations of whose adventures and pursuits might bear that kind of similitude to an Heroic Poem, which these minor associations of men (as pilgrims on the way to their saint, or parties in search of amusement, travellers excited by curiosity, or adventurers in pursuit of gain) have, in points of connection and importance, with a regular and disciplined Army.

Allowing this comparison, it is manifest that while much is lost for want of unity of subject and grandeur of design, something is gained by greater variety of incident and more minute display of character, by accuracy of description, and diversity of scene: in these narratives we pass from gay to grave, from lively to severe, not only without impropriety, but with manifest advantage. In one continued and connected Poem, the Reader is, in general, highly gratified or severely disappointed; by many independent narratives, he has the renovation of hope, although he has been dissatisfied, and a prospect of reiterated pleasure should he find himself entertained.

I mean not, however, to compare these different modes of writing as if I were balancing their advantages and defects before I could give preference to either; with me the way I take is not a matter of choice, but of necessity: I present not my Tales to the Reader as if I had chosen the best method of ensuring his approbation, but as using the only means I possessed of engaging his attention.

It may probably be remarked that Tales, however dissimilar, might have been connected by some associating circumstance to which the whole number might bear equal affinity, and that examples of such union are to be found in *Chaucer*, in *Boccace*, and other collectors and inventors of Tales, which considered in themselves are altogether independent; and to this idea I gave so much consideration as convinced me that I could not avail myself of the benefit of such artificial mode of affinity. To imitate the English Poet, characters must be found adapted to their several relations, and this is a point of great difficulty and hazard: much allowance seems to be required even for *Chaucer* himself, since it is difficult to conceive that on any occasion the devout and delicate *Prioress*, the courtly and valiant *Knight*, and '*the pouré good Man the persone of a Towne*,' would be the voluntary companions of the drunken *Miller*, the licentious *Sompnour*, and 'the *Wanton Wife of Bath*,' and enter into that colloquial and travelling intimacy which, if a common pilgrimage to the shrine of *St Thomas*, may be said to excuse, I know nothing beside (and certainly nothing in these times) that would produce such effect. *Boccace*, it is true, avoids all difficulty of this kind, by not assigning to the ten relators of his hundred Tales any marked or peculiar characters; nor, though there are male and female in company, can the sex of the narrator be distinguished in the narration.

To have followed the method of *Chaucer*, might have been of use, but could scarcely be adopted, from its difficulty; and to have taken that of the Italian writer, would have been perfectly easy, but could be of no service: the attempt at union therefore has been relinquished, and these relations are submitted to the Public, connected by no other circumstance than their being the productions of the same Author, and devoted to the same purpose – the entertainment of his Readers.

It has been already acknowledged, that these compositions have no pretensions to be estimated with the more lofty and heroic kind of Poems, but I feel great reluctance in admitting that they have not a fair and legitimate claim to the poetic character: in vulgar estimation, indeed, all that is not prose, passes for poetry; but I have not ambition of so humble a kind as to be satisfied with a concession which requires nothing in the Poet, except his ability for counting syllables; and I trust something more of the poetic character will be allowed to the succeeding pages, than what the heroes of the *Dunciad* might share with the Author: nor was I aware that by describing, as faithfully as I could, men, manners, and things, I was forfeiting a just title to a name which has been freely granted to many whom to equal, and even to excel, is but very stinted commendation.

In this case it appears that the usual comparison between Poetry and Painting entirely fails: the Artist who takes an accurate likeness of individuals, or a faithful representation of scenery, may not rank so high in the public estimation, as one who paints an historical event, or an heroic action; but he is nevertheless a painter, and his accuracy is so far from diminishing his reputation, that it procures for him in general both fame and emolument: nor is it perhaps with strict justice determined that the credit and reputation of those verses, which strongly and faithfully delineate character and manners, should be lessened in the opinion of the Public, by the very accuracy which gives value and distinction to the productions of the pencil.

Nevertheless, it must be granted that the pretensions of any composition to be regarded as Poetry, will depend upon that definition of the poetic character which he who undertakes to determine the question has considered as decisive; and it is confessed also that one of great authority may be adopted, by which the verses now before the Reader, and many others which have probably amused and delighted him, must be excluded: a definition like this will be found in the words which the greatest of Poets, not divinely inspired, has given to the most noble and valiant Duke of Athens –

> 'The Poet's eye, in a fine frenzy rolling,
> Doth glance from Heaven to Earth, from Earth to Heaven;
> And, as Imagination bodies forth
> The forms of things unknown, the Poet's pen
> Turns them to shapes, and gives to airy nothing
> A local habitation, and a name.'*

Hence we observe the Poet is one who, in the excursions of his fancy between heaven and earth, lights upon a kind of fairy-land in which he places a creation of his own, where he embodies shapes, and gives action and adventure to his ideal offspring; taking captive the imagination of his readers, he elevates them above the grossness of actual being, into the soothing and pleasant atmosphere of supra-mundane existence: there he obtains for his visionary inhabitants the interest that engages a reader's attention without ruffling his feelings, and excites that moderate kind of sympathy which the realities of nature oftentimes fail to produce, either because they are so familiar and insignificant that they excite no determinate emotion, or are so harsh and powerful that the feelings excited are grating and distasteful.

Be it then granted that (as *Duke Theseus* observes) '*such tricks hath strong Imagination*,' and that such Poets '*are of imagination all compact*;' let it be further conceded, that theirs is a higher and more dignified kind of composition, nay, the only kind that has pretentions to inspiration; still, that these Poets should so entirely engross the title as to exclude those who address their productions to the plain sense and sober judgment of their Readers, rather than to their fancy and imagination, I must repeat that I am unwilling to admit – because I conceive that, by granting that right of exclusion, a vast deal of what has been hitherto received as genuine poetry would no longer be entitled to that appellation.

All that kind of satire wherein character is skilfully delineated, must (this criterion being allowed) no longer be esteemed as genuine

* Midsummer Night's Dream, Act V. Scene 1.

Poetry; and for the same reason many affecting narratives which are founded on real events, and borrow no aid whatever from the imagination of the writer, must likewise be rejected: a considerable part of the Poems, as they have hitherto been denominated, of *Chaucer* are of this naked and unveiled character; and there are in his Tales many pages of coarse, accurate, and minute, but very striking description. Many small Poems in a subsequent age, of a most impressive kind, are adapted and addressed to the common sense of the Reader, and prevail by the strong language of truth and nature: they amused our ancestors, and they continue to engage our interest, and excite our feelings by the same powerful appeals to the heart and affections. In times less remote, *Dryden* has given us much of this Poetry, in which the force of expression and accuracy of description have neither needed nor obtained assistance from the fancy of the writer; the characters in his *Absalom* and *Ahitophel* are instances of this, and more especially those of *Doeg* and *Ogg*, in the second part: these, with all their grossness, and almost offensive accuracy, are found to possess that strength and spirit which has preserved from utter annihilation the dead bodies of *Tate*, to whom they were inhumanly bound, happily with a fate the reverse of that caused by the cruelty of *Mezentius*; for there the living perished in the putrefaction of the dead, and here the dead are preserved by the vitality of the living. And, to bring forward one other example, it will be found that *Pope* himself has no small portion of this actuality of relation, this nudity of description, and poetry without an atmosphere; the lines beginning '*In the worst inn's worst room*,' are an example, and many others may be seen in his Satires, Imitations, and above all in his Dunciad: the frequent absence of those '*Sports of Fancy*,' and '*Tricks of strong Imagination*,' have been so much observed, that some have ventured to question whether even this writer were a Poet; and though, as *Dr Johnson* has remarked, it would be difficult to form a definition of one in which *Pope* should not be admitted, yet they who doubted his claim, had, it is likely, provided for his exclusion by forming that kind of character for their Poet, in which this elegant versifier, for so he must be then named, should not be comprehended.

These things considered, an Author will find comfort in his

expulsion from the rank and society of Poets, by reflecting that men much his superiors were likewise shut out, and more especially when he finds also that men not much his superiors are entitled to admission.

But in whatever degree I may venture to differ from any others in my notions of the qualifications and character of the true Poet, I most cordially assent to their opinion, who assert that his principal exertions must be made to engage the attention of his Readers; and further, I must allow that the effect of Poetry should be to lift the mind from the painful realities of actual existence, from its everyday concerns, and its perpetually-occurring vexations, and to give it repose by substituting objects in their place which it may contemplate with some degree of interest and satisfaction: but what is there in all this which may not be effected by a fair representation of existing character? nay, by a faithful delineation of those painful realities, those every-day concerns, and those perpetually-occurring vexations themselves, provided they be not (which is hardly to be supposed) the very concerns and distresses of the Reader? for when it is admitted that they have no particular relation to him, but are the troubles and anxieties of other men, they excite and interest his feelings as the imaginary exploits, adventures, and perils of romance; – they soothe his mind, and keep his curiosity pleasantly awake; they appear to have enough of reality to engage his sympathy, but possess not interest sufficient to create painful sensations. Fiction itself, we know, and every work of fancy, must for a time have the effect of realities; nay, the very enchanters, spirits, and monsters of *Ariosto* and *Spenser* must be present in the mind of the Reader while he is engaged by their operations, or they would be as the objects and incidents of a Nursery Tale to a rational understanding, altogether despised and neglected: in truth, I can but consider this pleasant effect upon the mind of a Reader, as depending neither upon the events related (whether they be actual or imaginary), nor upon the characters introduced (whether taken from life or fancy), but upon the manner in which the Poem itself is conducted; let that be judiciously managed, and the occurrences actually copied from life will have the same happy effect as the inventions of a creative fancy; while, on the other hand, the imaginary persons and incidents to which the Poet has given '*a local habitation, and a name*', will make, upon the concurring feelings of the Reader, the same impressions with those taken from truth and nature, because they will appear to be derived from that source, and therefore of necessity will have a similar effect.

Having thus far presumed to claim for the ensuing pages the rank and title of Poetry, I attempt no more, nor venture to class or compare them with any other kinds of poetical composition; their place will doubtless be found for them.

A principal view and wish of the Poet must be to engage the mind of his Readers, as, failing in that point, he will scarcely succeed in any other: I therefore willingly confess that much of my time and assiduity has been devoted to this purpose; but, to the ambition of pleasing, no other sacrifices have, I trust, been made, than of my own labour and care. Nothing will be found that militates against the rules of propriety and good manners, nothing that offends against the more important precepts of morality and religion; and with this negative kind of merit, I commit my Book to the judgment and taste of the Reader – not being willing to provoke his vigilance by professions of accuracy, nor to solicit his indulgence by apologies for mistakes.

If I did not fear that it would appear to my readers like arrogancy, or if it did not seem to myself indecorous to send two volumes of considerable magnitude from the press without preface or apology, without one petition for the reader's attention, or one plea for the writer's defects, I would most willingly spare myself an address of this kind, and more especially for these reasons; first, because a preface is a part of a book seldom honoured by a reader's perusal; secondly, because it is both difficult and distressing to write that which we think will be disregarded; and thirdly, because I do not conceive that I am called upon for such introductory matter by any of the motives which usually influence an author when he composes his prefatory address.

When a writer, whether of poetry or prose, first addresses the public, he has generally something to offer which relates to himself or to his work, and which he considers as a necessary prelude to the work itself, to prepare his readers for the entertainment or the instruction they may expect to receive, for one of these every man who publishes must suppose he affords – this the act itself implies; and in proportion to his conviction of this fact must be his feeling of the difficulty in which he has placed himself: the difficulty consists in reconciling the implied presumption of the undertaking, whether to please or to instruct mankind, with the diffidence and modesty of an untried candidate for fame or favour. Hence originate the many reasons an author assigns for his appearance in that character, whether they actually exist, or are merely offered to hide the motives which cannot be openly avowed; namely, the want or the vanity of the man, as his wishes for profit or reputation may most prevail with him.

*

Now, reasons of this kind, whatever they may be, cannot be availing beyond their first appearance. An author, it is true, may again feel his former apprehensions, may again be elevated or depressed by the suggestions of vanity and diffidence, and may be again subject to the cold and hot fit of aguish expectation; but he is no more a stranger to the press, nor has the motives or privileges of one who is. With respect to myself, it is certain they belong not to me. Many years have elapsed since I became a candidate for indulgence as an inexperienced writer; and to assume the language of such writer now, and to plead for his indulgences, would be proof of my ignorance of the place assigned to me, and the degree of favour which I have experienced; but of that place I am not uninformed, and with that degree of favour I have no reason to be dissatisfied.

It was the remark of the pious, but on some occasions the querulous author of the *Night Thoughts*, that he had 'been so long remembered, he was forgotten;' an expression in which there is more appearance of discontent than of submission: if he had patience, it was not the patience that *smiles at grief*. It is not therefore entirely in the sense of the good Doctor that I apply these words to myself, or to my more early publications. So many years indeed have passed since their first appearance, that I have no reason to complain, on that account, if they be now slumbering with other poems of decent reputation in their day – not dead indeed, nor entirely forgotten, but certainly not the subjects of discussion or conversation as when first introduced to the notice of the public, by those whom the public will not forget, whose protection was credit to their author, and whose approbation was fame to them. Still these early publications had so long preceded any other, that, if not altogether unknown, I was, when I came again before the public, in a situation which excused, and perhaps rendered necessary some explanation; but this also has passed away, and none of my readers will now take the trouble of making any inquiries respecting my motives for writing or for publishing these Tales or verses of any description: known to each other as readers and authors are known, they will require no preface to bespeak their good will, nor shall I be under the necessity of soliciting the kindness which experience has taught me, endeavouring to merit, I shall not fail to receive.

*

There is one motive – and it is a powerful one – which sometimes induces an author, and more particularly a poet, to ask the attention of his readers to his prefatory address. This is when he has some favourite and peculiar style or manner which he would explain and defend, and chiefly if he should have adopted a mode of versification of which an uninitiated reader was not likely to perceive either the merit or the beauty. In such case it is natural, and surely pardonable, to assert and to prove, as far as reason will bear us on, that such method of writing has both; to show in what the beauty consists, and what peculiar difficulty there is, which, when conquered, creates the merit. How far any particular poet has or has not succeeded in such attempt is not my business nor my purpose to inquire: I have no peculiar notion to defend, no poetical heterodoxy to support, nor theory of any kind to vindicate or oppose – that which I have used is probably the most common measure in our language; and therefore, whatever be its advantages or defects, they are too well known to require from me a description of the one, or an apology for the other.

Perhaps still more frequent than any explanation of the work is an account of the author himself, the situation in which he is placed, or some circumstances of peculiar kind in his life, education, or employment. How often has youth been pleaded for deficiencies or redundancies, for the existence of which youth may be an excuse, and yet be none for their exposure. Age too has been pleaded for the errors and failings in a work which the octogenarian had the discernment to perceive, and yet had not the fortitude to suppress. Many other circumstances are made apologies for a writer's infirmities; his much employment, and many avocations, adversity, necessity, and the good of mankind. These, or any of them, however availing in themselves, avail not me. I am neither so young nor so old, so much engaged by one pursuit, or by many, – I am not so urged by want, or so stimulated by a desire of public benefit, – that I can borrow one apology from the many which I have named. How far they prevail with our readers, or with our judges, I cannot tell; and it is unnecessary for me to inquire into the validity of arguments which I have not to produce.

*

If there be any combination of circumstances which may be supposed to affect the mind of a reader, and in some degree to influence his judgment, the junction of youth, beauty, and merit in a female writer may be allowed to do this; and yet one of the most forbidding of titles is 'Poems by a very young Lady,' and this although beauty and merit were largely insinuated. Ladies, it is true, have of late little need of any indulgence as authors, and names may readily be found which rather excite the envy of man than plead for his lenity. Our estimation of title also in a writer has materially varied from that of our predecessors; 'Poems by a Nobleman' would create a very different sensation in our minds from that which was formerly excited when they were so announced. A noble author had then no pretensions to a seat so secure on the 'sacred hill,' that authors not noble, and critics not gentle, dared not attack; and they delighted to take revenge by their contempt and derision of the poet, for the pain which their submission and respect to the man had cost them. But in our times we find that a nobleman writes, not merely as well, but better than other men; insomuch that readers in general begin to fancy that the Muses have relinquished their old partiality for rags and a garret, and are become altogether aristocratical in their choice. A conceit so well supported by fact would be readily admitted, did it not appear at the same time, that there were in the higher ranks of society men, who could write as tamely, or as absurdly, as they had ever been accused of doing. We may, therefore, regard the works of any noble author as extraordinary productions; but must not found any theory upon them; and, notwithstanding their appearance, must look on genius and talent as we are wont to do on time and chance, that happen indifferently to all mankind.

But whatever influence any peculiar situation of a writer might have, it cannot be a benefit to me, who have no such peculiarity. I must rely upon the willingness of my readers to be pleased with that which was designed to give them pleasure, and upon the cordiality which naturally springs from a remembrance of our having before parted without any feelings of disgust on the one side, or of mortification on the other.

*

With this hope I would conclude the present subject; but I am called upon by duty to acknowledge my obligations, and more especially for two of the following Tales:— the Story of Lady Barbara, in Book XVI and that of Ellen in Book XVIII. The first of these I owe to the kindness of a fair friend, who will, I hope, accept the thanks which I very gratefully pay, and pardon me if I have not given to her relation the advantages which she had so much reason to expect. The other story, that of Ellen, could I give it in the language of him who related it to me, would please and affect my readers. It is by no means my only debt, though the one I now more particularly acknowledge; for who shall describe all that he gains in the social, the unrestrained, and the frequent conversations with a friend, who is at once communicative and judicious? — whose opinions, on all subjects of literary kind, are founded on good taste, and exquisite feeling? It is one of the greatest 'pleasures of my memory' to recall in absence those conversations; and if I do not in direct terms mention with whom I conversed, it is both because I have no permission, and my readers will have no doubt.

The first intention of the poet must be to please; for, if he means to instruct, he must render the instruction which he hopes to convey palatable and pleasant. I will not assume the tone of a moralist, nor promise that my relations shall be beneficial to mankind; but I have endeavoured, not unsuccessfully I trust, that, in whatsoever I have related or described, there should be nothing introduced which has a tendency to excuse the vices of man, by associating with them sentiments that demand our respect, and talents that compel our admiration. There is nothing in these pages which has the mischievous effect of confounding truth and error, or confusing our ideas of right and wrong. I know not which is most injurious to the yielding minds of the young, to render virtue less respectable by making its possessors ridiculous, or by describing vice with so many fascinating qualities, that it is either lost in the assemblage, or pardoned by the association. Man's heart is sufficiently prone to make excuse for man's infirmity; and needs not the aid of poetry, or eloquence, to take from vice its native deformity. A character may be respectable with all its faults, but it must not be made respectable by them. It is grievous when genius will condescend to place strong and evil spirits in a commanding view, or excite our pity and admiration for men of talents, degraded by crime, when struggling with misfortune. It is but too true that great and wicked men may be so presented to us, as to demand our applause, when they should excite our abhorrence; but it is surely for the interest of mankind, and our own self-direction, that we should ever keep at unapproachable distance our respect and our reproach.

I have one observation more to offer. It may appear to some that a minister of religion, in the decline of life, should have no leisure for such amusements as these; and for them I have no reply; – but to those who are more indulgent to the propensities, the studies, and the habits of mankind, I offer some apology when I produce these volumes, not as the occupations of my life, but the fruits of my leisure, the employment of that time which, if not given to them, had passed in the vacuity of unrecorded idleness; or had been lost in the indulgence of unregistered thoughts and fancies, that melt away in the instant they are conceived, and '*leave not a wreck behind.*'

NOTES

Unless otherwise stated the text of a poem is taken from the first printed edition.

The following abbreviations have been used:

1807	*Poems. By the Rev. George Crabbe*, LL.B., 1807.
1834	*The Poetical Works of the Rev. George Crabbe: With his Letters and Journals, and his Life, by his Son*, 8 vols., 1834. Vol. I is referred to as *Life*.
New Poems (1960)	*New Poems by George Crabbe*, ed. A. Pollard, 1960.
CPW	*George Crabbe: The Complete Poetical Works*, ed. N. Dalrymple-Champneys and A. Pollard, 1988.
Selected Letters	*The Selected Letters and Journals of George Crabbe*, ed. T. C. Faulkner, 1985.
Critical Heritage	*George Crabbe: The Critical Heritage*, ed. A. Pollard, 1972.
ODEP	*Oxford Dictionary of English Proverbs*.

FRAGMENT, WRITTEN AT MIDNIGHT (p. 1)

Published *1834*, where it is dated 'Aldborough 1779' and taken from one of 'Mr Crabbe's early note-books'. Addressed to the Greek sun-god Apollo, as the god of both poetry and medicine. Crabbe argues with himself about the relation between his two vocations. Line 3 ('fourfold powers') refers to his claim to skill as surgeon, apothecary, obstetrician and physician (lines 29–30 must refer to a diploma from a Scottish University).

THE VILLAGE (p. 3)

Published 1783. Early version probably written (and possibly published) by August 1781. Revised under the influence of Burke and Johnson; final ninety-five lines added after death of patron's brother, Lord Robert Manners, on 24 April 1782. Book I, lines 109–30, are 'the verses in which he, some months after [after February 1781], expressed the gloomier side of his feelings on quitting his native place – the very verses, he had reason to believe, which first satisfied Burke that he was a true poet' (*Life*, p. 46).

The first-person narrative of departure (I. 109–30), the local landscape and vegetation (I. 63–78), the 'lessening shore' and the 'fierce tide' (I. 126, 127) point to the environs of Aldborough, and Crabbe's direct experience, as the basis for his initial attack on neo-classical pastoral poetry. The rest of Book I (from 135), and Book II, are geographically less specific, though I. 135 ff. may have the dependent villages round Belvoir Castle in mind, and II. 113 ff. eulogize Belvoir's owners. The focus of Crabbe's attack on pastoral is equally wide (or blurred). References to a shepherd in Virgil's *Eclogues* ('Corydons', I. 12), to a tributary of the Po, near where Virgil lived ('Mincio's banks', I. 15) and to a character who stands for Virgil in the first eclogue ('TITYRUS', I. 16) are specific; but it is not clear how far Virgil's poetry (and classical culture) must be rejected along with its modern imitators, whether there was once a golden age, or how far Crabbe wishes to generalize about rural reality from his own experience of it. Book I, lines 15–20, are Johnson's unsuccessful attempt to clarify these issues, confused in Crabbe's original version which ran as follows: 'In fairer scenes, where peaceful pleasures spring,/ Tityrus, the pride of Mantuan swains might sing:/ But charmed by him, or smitten with his views,/ Shall modern poets court the Mantuan muse?/ From Truth and Nature shall we widely stray,/ Where Fancy leads, or Virgil led the way?'

Earlier eighteenth-century works such as Pope's *Pastorals* (1709) and Shenstone's *Rural Elegance* (1750) are most vulnerable to Crabbe's attack but the allusion in I. 305 to Goldsmith's *Deserted Village* (1770) indicates the attack's diffuseness. Poetry is the centre of a wider target, 'the deliberate idealization of the English labourer in almost all eighteenth-century discussion of him, which allowed the Pastoral to flourish and the poor to starve' (J. Barrell and J. Bull, *Penguin Book of English Pastoral Verse*, 1974, p. 379). Elements of Crabbe's indignant realism can be found in Langhorne's *The Country Justice* (1774–7); of his attack on pastoral in Churchill's *Prophecy of Famine* (1763); of both in Stephen Duck's *The Thresher's Labour*, 1735 ('honest DUCK', I. 27).

Contemporary reaction was mixed: Crabbe had gone too far in the right direction, painting only 'the dark side of the landscape'. Edmund Cartwright anticipated modern views in identifying ideological conflicts between the encomium to Manners and the rest of the poem, between Books I and II (*Critical Heritage*, 44, 42–4). The reputation of poet and poem survived into the nineteenth century through successive republication of I. 230–319 and II. 85–104 in *Elegant Extracts*. For republication in *Poems* (1807) Crabbe excluded the by then dangerously radical I. 144–5, modified the sexual frankness of II. 59–60, and added a note to the end of Book I apologizing 'for the insertion of a circumstance by no means common' (the failure of a parson to turn up for a poor man's funeral): the *Anti-Jacobin Review* congratulated him on his apology (*Critical Heritage*, 52). Modern attempts to make sense of the poem's shifts of focus and attitude include R. B. Hatch, 'George Crabbe and the Tenth Muse', *Eighteenth Century Studies*, 7 (1974), pp. 274–94; R. Williams, *The Country and the City*, 1973, pp. 90–95.

THE HALL OF JUSTICE (p. 20)

Epigraph i. Ovid, *Ex Ponto*, I. iv. 7–8: 'I admit that this is the work of the years, but there is yet another cause – anguish and constant suffering.' (Crabbe has 'dolor' where Loeb has 'labor', normally translated as 'labour'.) Epigraph ii. Maximianus, *Elegies*, i. 137–8: 'Eyes, once laughing, now with a perpetual fount of tears, bewail their punishment by night and by day.'

Published *1807*. Probably written 1798, as 'Aaron, or The Gipsy', with only slight subsequent revision. Text here from second edition of *Poems* (1808). Hatch describes it as 'blunt and argumentative . . . closer to the style of *The Village* than the objective probing attitude of 'The Parish Register' (R. B. Hatch, *Crabbe's Arabesque: Social Drama in the Poetry of George Crabbe*, 1976, p. 38). Francis Jeffrey's review of *Poems* in the *Edinburgh Review* for April 1808 was typical in praising the poem, together with Crabbe's other experiment in closet-drama 'Sir Eustace Grey', for its 'mastery over the tragic passions of pity and horror' (*Critical Heritage*, p. 60). Hatch (*Crabbe's Arabesque*, pp. 38–49) describes its anguished exploration of poverty and crime, its social morality remarkably open-minded (especially towards natural law ideology in I. 9–16). The question of punishment is perhaps evaded by turning the magistrate into a kind of priest (II. 127–42). Crabbe is conventional in seeing gypsies as a threat to normality (see also 'The Lover's Journey', 141–95; and 'Sir Eustace Grey', 292–9, where gypsies are associated with slaves, dunghills, and badger's holes); but he is daring in presenting such a radical (in II. 39–44, an Oedipus-like) confusion of the kinship order.

SIR EUSTACE GREY (p. 29)

Epigraph. Seneca, *Hercules Furens*, 1070: 'mixing the false with the true'.

Published in *Poems*, 1807. Probably written in the winter of 1804–5, subsequently revised; Crabbe's son claims that 'it was during a great snowstorm that, shut up in his room, he wrote almost *currente calamo* his "Sir Eustace Grey"' (*Life*, 262). Text here from second edition of *Poems* (1808). Praised by reviewers for its tragic force, one of the most widely popular of Crabbe's poems in his lifetime, catering for a more romantic taste than his couplet-poems. Letters of 30 October 1817 and 25 November 1822, both to Mary Leadbeater, speak of later poems (not published in his lifetime) 'in the manner of Sir Eustace Grey', attempting 'the Description of a kind of Hallucination or Insanity' (*CPW*, i. 706). 'The Insanity of Ambitious Love' (1816), 'The World of Dreams' (1817?) and 'Where am I now? I slept to wake again' (1819?) are of this kind, which may be influenced by experience with opium (Alethea Hayter, *Opium and the Romantic Imagination*, 1968, pp. 165–90). The epigraph may indicate that Crabbe as well as Sir Eustace are mixing the false and the true (fiction and non-fiction): his wife's sufferings and his own dreams of persecution and degradation, 'such as would cure vanity for a time in any mind where they could gain admission' (*Selected Letters*, p. 221), are certainly an influence together with literary and religious sources. Many poets had described the Northern Lights as 'streamers' (220, 227). Given the context – the justified fear of madness, a theology combining predestination and guilt – 'drank' in line 305 precisely echoes lines 47–8 of Cowper's 'The Castaway', 1799 (published 1803), 'he drank/ The stifling wave, and then he sank'. Crabbe's footnotes to lines 160–63 and 188 refer us to King Nebuchadnezzar's vision of divine punishment (Daniel 4: 13 ff.) and to Christiana's (*Pilgrim's Progress*, part ii). *CPW* (i. 707) notes that *Pilgrim's Progress* also provides much of the imagery and the form (an interpolated song) for the 'sainted Preacher's' words (348–71) which were published as a hymn in various nonconformist and evangelical collections after Crabbe's death.

THE BOROUGH (p. 43)

Epigraph on title-page: 'Paulo Majora Canamus'. Virgil, *Eclogues*, IV. i. 'Let us sing a somewhat loftier strain.'

Published 1810, as *The Borough, a Poem in Twenty-Four Letters*, with Dedication to the Duke of Rutland, and Preface (see Appendix 1). Written 1804–9, probably incorporating some earlier character sketches. Text here from the second edition, 1810. 'A residing burgess in a large sea-port' (Appendix 1, p. 460) describes his borough to an inland friend in a series of letters: i. General Description ii. The Church iii. The Vicar – The Curate Etc. iv. Sects and Professions in Religion v. Elections vi. Professions – Law vii. Professions – Physic viii. Trades ix. Amusements x. Clubs and Social Meetings xi. Inns xii. Players xiii. The Alms-House and Trustees xiv. Inhabitants of the Alms-House – Blaney xv. Inhabitants of the Alms-House – Clelia xvi. Inhabitants of the Alms-House – Benbow xvii. The Hospital and Governors xviii. The Poor and their Dwellings xix. The Poor of the Borough – The Parish-Clerk xx. The Poor of the Borough – Ellen Orford xxi. The Poor of the Borough – Abel Keene xxii. The Poor of the Borough – Peter Grimes xxiii. Prisons xxiv. Schools. Crabbe's defensive Preface warns against expecting 'a political satire, – an attack upon corrupt principles' or an 'historical account' and seeks to justify the potentially offensive treatment of, especially, religious sects and 'the follies and crimes of persons in lower life' (Appendix 1, pp. 460–61).

'The reader is in some degree kept from view of any particular place' (Appendix 1, p. 460). Widely assumed to be Crabbe's native Aldborough, which certainly 'helped me to my Scenery and some of my Characters' (*Selected Letters*, p. 308), the semi-generic and semi-fictional seaport is a montage of elements taken from towns and villages in eastern Suffolk (W. K. Thomas, 'Crabbe's *Borough*: the process of montage', *University of Toronto Quarterly*, xxxvi, 1967, pp. 181–92).

Reviewers noted the lack of interaction between characters in different Letters. The appearance of 'our late Vicar' from Letter iii, in Jachin's story (xix. 1, 227–8, 265, 299–300) is unusual. Even favourable reviews criticized the poem's lack of 'composition', of moral or constructional unity. Jeffrey's enthusiastic review of *Poems* had set the terms for favourable comment on Crabbe's work in his lifetime: he praised the 'force, and truth of description' of poetry which 'exhibits the common people of England pretty much as they are' by contrast with 'Mr Wordsworth and his associates [who] show us something that mere observation never yet suggested to anyone'. But in the *Edinburgh Review* for April 1810 Jeffrey now balked at the representation of the 'depraved, abject, diseased and neglected poor ... whom everyone despises, and no one can either love or fear' (he has the stories grouped as 'The Poor of the Borough' especially in mind); perhaps misled by the number of Letters (twenty-four was the traditional number of books in an Epic) he expressed a 'very strong desire to see Mr Crabbe apply his great powers to the construction of some interesting and connected story'. Robert Grant in the *Quarterly Review* for November 1810 condemned Crabbe's low-life realism as 'essentially hostile to the highest exercise of the imagination' (*Critical Heritage*, pp. 92, 99, 118). Benjamin Britten's opera *Peter Grimes* (1945), which brings Peter Grimes and Ellen Orford and others together in a single meaningful action, may provide what Crabbe's contemporary critics wanted. More recently Hatch (*Crabbe's Arabesque*, pp. 52–113) and J. McGann have admired the poem because it rejects a consolatory integration of elements: 'it has no plot . . . "the borough" as the work's scene of order clearly exists in an incongruent relation to the literary idea of 24' (George Crabbe: Poetry and Truth', *London Review of Books*, 16 March 1989).

Letters xix–xxii, grouped as 'The Poor of the Borough', together with Letters iii and xiii–xvi, are the first of Crabbe's full-length tales in rhyming couplets. The 'poor' here are not labourers or servants but people desperate to preserve some precarious status: Jachin is parish-clerk (curate), Abel Keene has been a teacher, and Ellen Orford becomes one, Peter Grimes is a Master, a 'needy Tradesman' (xxii. 62). Peter takes money as well as apprentices from the 'Workhouse-clearing Men' (xxii. 60); Ellen has more than once 'shared the Allotments of the Parish Poor' (xx. 255) and her children are removed into parish care; Abel has to apply 'for Town-relief' (xxi. 171) and Jachin pilfers from his own offertory box because he feels too poor for his station. Obsessively puritanical beliefs contribute to Jachin's downfall; predestinarian Calvinism leads to the suicides of Abel Keene and Ellen Orford's husband. Anti-religious freethinking helps one of Ellen's sons along the road to destruction (xx. 274–7) and is an element in Peter Grimes's rebellion against his pious father (xxii. 6–11, 14–27), while the clerks' Voltairean freethinking (xxi. 15–32) tempts Abel Keene from 'the narrow Way' (xxi. 216). Abel Keene moves straight from atheism to Calvinism, the similarity between the extremes made explicit in the description of him as one of the 'Converts' to 'Unbelief' (xxi. 35, 36). But the analogies between the four Letters underline their separation: the sea appears in all these stories but the people do not mix. Jachin, Abel Keene and Peter Grimes are driven to wander on the beach and by the same muddy estuary, but they never appear in one another's stories.

LETTER XIX THE POOR OF THE BOROUGH: THE PARISH-CLERK
(p. 43)

Epigraph i. Juvenal, *Satires*, xiv. 176–8: 'For the man who wants wealth must have it at once; what respect for laws, what fear, what sense of shame is to be found in a miser hurrying to be rich?'

Epigraph ii. Juvenal, *Satires*, xiii. 217–22: 'In the night, if his troubles grant him a short slumber, and his limbs, after tossing upon his bed, are sinking into repose, he straightway beholds the temple and the altar of the God whom he has outraged; and what weighs with chiefest terror on his soul, he sees you in his dreams; your awful form, larger than life, frightens his quaking heart and wrings confession from him.'

Epigraph ii suggests that Jachin's name (the name of one of the two pillars in the porch of the temple of Solomon) is symbolic, perhaps for him and his parents, as well as for Crabbe. Crabbe demonstrates his belief in the recurrence of human types and situations and his pleasure in his own revival of the verse tale by alluding to Chaucerian formulae (2, 230–31) including the obsolete 'hight', 'Churl' and 'lewd' (illiterate); lines 44–51 allude to Dryden's 'Character of a Good Parson, imitated from Chaucer' lines 106–7. The 'book-taught' Jachin (18) is good at 'reasoning' (213, 292), at winning arguments with others and with himself. But his reading, which includes Bunyan (lines 36–9 and Crabbe's note may refer to passages in *Christ, a complete Saviour*, 1692), compares unfavourably with proverbial wisdom. '"A foolish Proverb says, *The Devil's at home*"', says Jachin (56) but the proverbial 'many a Pittance makes a worthy Heap' (170) and *'Practice makes perfect'* (209) accurately describe the progress of Jachin's self-deception and his implicit evasion of 'Thou shalt not steal' (*ODEP*, pp. 181, 510, 856; Exodus 20:15).

LETTER XX THE POOR OF THE BOROUGH: ELLEN ORFORD (p. 53)

Epigraph i. *King Lear*, IV. iii. 16–17. Gentleman, of Cordelia.
Epigraph ii: source unknown (Crabbe?).

The attack on sentimental and gothic fiction (11–119) does for storytelling what the attack on pastoral did for the poetry of rural life in *The Village*: modern pastoral poems are 'mechanic echoes of the Mantuan song', characters in modern novels are 'Creatures borrowed and again conveyed/ From Book to Book – the Shadows of a Shade' (19–20). Crabbe's good-humoured parodic summary of popular fiction is, as *CPW* notes, made up of specific references, to the following: *Darnley Vale, or, Emilia Fitzroy*, by Elizabeth Bonhote, 1789 (34); *Maple Vale, or the History of Miss Sidney*, Anon, 1791 (34); *Henry*, by Richard Cumberland, 1795 (36); *The Monk*, by M. G. Lewis, 1796 (49–50); *A Sicilian Romance*, 1790, and *The Mysteries of Udolpho*, 1794, by Ann Radcliffe (51–2 and 59–91); *Louisa, or the Cottage on the Moor*, by Elizabeth Helme, 1787 (92–9); *Celestina* (sic), by Charlotte Smith, 1790 (100–112, and Crabbe's note). The absence of nineteenth-century novels from this list may indicate the taste of Crabbe or his narrator, or an early date for the composition of all or part of this poem.

Ellen's story, as she tells it, displays the 'Ruin sudden' and 'Misery strange' (22) characteristic of real life, rather than the logic, the meaningful pattern, of 'Plots' and 'Histories' (28). Her religious belief is ratified by Crabbe (124–5) but it is probably true that the poem's final pious lines, 'which in Wordsworth would be consoling, are in Crabbe perfectly shocking because nothing in the narrative justifies them' (McGann, 'The Anachronism of George Crabbe' in *The Beauty of Inflections*, 1985, pp. 294–312, 301). The introduction of Ellen as the 'Heroine' (31, 123 and Epigraph ii) recalls the introduction of Catherine Morland in *Northanger Abbey* (begun 1797–8, published 1818), but is differently ironic since Ellen does display a kind of heroism (whereas Catherine does end the novel with a happy marriage like a fictional heroine). The sentimental novel in which we are temporarily led to believe that 'the fond Lover is the Brother too' (106) contrasts with Ellen's never-resolved suspicion that her own 'Idiot-Girl' (309) has been seduced by 'that sick-pale Brother' (314).

LETTER XXI THE POOR OF THE BOROUGH: ABEL KEENE (p. 65)

Epigraph i. Ovid, *Heroides*, ix. ('Deianira to Hercules') 23–4: 'You began better than you end; your last deeds yield to your first; the man you are and the child you were are not the same.'
Epigraph ii. 1 Timothy. 4:1.

'Abel' is an Old Testament name, like 'Jachin'. It is symbolic for his sister, and presumably for his parents, as well as for Crabbe (93–5). The sister's metaphoric description of him as 'unhappy suicide' (Abel as his own fratricidal brother, Cain) comes literally true. Crabbe's Preface nicely describes the similarities and differences between the 'Clerk in Office' – Abel and the 'Clerk of the Parish' – Jachin (Appendix 1. p. 462). James Montgomery in the *Eclectic Review* for June 1810 (*Critical Heritage*, pp. 101–2) attacked Crabbe's 'illiberality towards the "enthusiasts"' (he cites lines 267–89, 298–308); Crabbe replied with a long footnote to the second edition arguing that he has one specific case in mind (the author of 'A Cordial for a Sin-Despairing Soul', to which line 269 alludes).

LETTER XXII THE POOR OF THE BOROUGH: PETER GRIMES (p.75)

Epigraph i. Scott, *Marmion* (1808) II. xxii. 1–7.

Epigraph ii. *Richard III*, V. iii. 205–6. Richard.

Epigraph iii. *Macbeth*, III. iv. 77–81. Macbeth.

The name 'Peter Grimes' is shared by father and son and is a compound of the New Testament fisherman-Disciple and 'blackens, befouls' (*OED*). The son is like a father in that when he becomes a Master he stands *in loco parentis* to his apprentices. 'Cabined' (2) means lodged, but may also suggest, negatively, 'cabined, cribbed, confined' (*Macbeth*, III. iv., as Epigraph iii). Specific Aldborough originals have been suggested for Grimes and the landscape (*CPW*, i. p. 749), and contemporary reviewers cited the analogous case of Elizabeth Brownrigg, executed in 1767 for beating one of her pauper apprentice midwives to death. Dorothy George says that at least in London 'the disappearance of an apprentice was too common a thing to provoke suspicion' (*London Life in the Eighteenth Century*, 1925, p. 225). Social factors such as the 'Workhouse-clearing' system (60) seem only to have facilitated an unexplained sadism. Crabbe's uncertainty is repeated in the Preface: 'the character of *Grimes* . . . I must leave to the judgment and observation of my readers' (Appendix 1. p. 462). Readers have always found this a fearful tale but James Montgomery's view that it is also a 'masterpiece' is now general. For modern explorations of its troubling power see Hatch, *Crabbe's Arabesque*, pp. 104–13, and Edwards, *George Crabbe's Poetry on Border Land*, pp. 145–65.

TALES (p. 87)

Published 1812, with Dedication to Isabella, Dowager Duchess of Rutland, and Preface (see Appendix 2). Text here taken from the second edition (1812).

The Preface is Crabbe's major statement of intention as a poet, a strong and subtle manifesto for his own work, written in response to criticism of *The Borough*. Responding to what he took to be Jeffrey's demand that he should write a modern epic, Crabbe suggests that modern social reality and his own talents require a looser unity among his tales: 'if these characters which seemed to be at my disposal were not such as would coalesce into one body, nor were of a nature to be commanded by one mind, so neither on examination did they appear as an unconnected multitude' (Appendix 2, p. 466). It is not clear whether Crabbe has *The Borough* or *Tales* in mind here since the characters in *Tales* (whether we take 'characters' to mean people or descriptions of people) may well be 'an unconnected multitude'; though J. L. Swingle argues for a deliberate pattern of similarity and difference among this 'family of tales', resembling Blake's *Songs of Innocence and of Experience*

('Late Crabbe in Relation to the Augustans and Romantics: the temporal
labyrinth of his *Tales in Verse*, 1812', *ELH* 42, 1975, pp. 580–94). The
volume is also united by constant reference to Shakespeare, signalled in the
Preface. The Preface seems only to defend his own right to the title of poet
in a hostile environment, citing Chaucer, Dryden and Pope as poetic
ancestors; but Crabbe subtly suggests that this is in fact the English
mainstream by distinguishing the passage he quotes from Duke Theseus's
speech on imagination (*A Midsummer Night's Dream*, V. i. 12–17: a talismanic
passage for contemporary Romantic opinion) from the views of its author,
'the greatest of Poets, not divinely inspired' (Appendix 2, p. 469; see
McGann, 'The Anachronism of George Crabbe', pp. 295–7). All but one of
the tales' epigraphs are from Shakespeare and there are additional significant
allusions to *Macbeth* ('The Struggles of Conscience'), *King Lear* ('Resent-
ment', 'The Brothers'), *Measure for Measure* ('The Confidant'), *The Taming
of the Shrew* ('The Wager'). See G. R. Hibbard, 'Crabbe and Shakespeare'
in *Renaissance and Modern Essays for Vivian da Sola Pinto's seventieth
birthday*, ed. G. R. Hibbard, 1966. New Testament parables, as indirect
narrative answers to general moral questions, provide a model as important as
the tale-sequences (by Chaucer, Boccaccio) cited in the Preface. Phrases from
the parables, such as to 'pass by on the other side' (see 'Procrastination', line
349), are among numerous popular proverbial phrases at work in the tales.

The milieu of most of the tales is provincial southern English, upper and
middle class, in the two decades prior to 1812. Specific real-life sources for
many characters, places and incidents are suggested in *Life*, *1834* and
elsewhere; some are mentioned below; for full details see *CPW*. Crabbe's
note to the first tale, 'The Dumb Orators' (p. 95), makes its action the
earliest of the sequence and the most specifically and pointedly datable. In
the rest of the volume, the war with France comes and goes in the
background, domestic warfare in distinctively pre-industrial households
occupies the foreground: an active link between public and personal power-
struggles is sometimes implied, especially in 'The Dumb Orators', 'The
Frank Courtship' and the stories of free-thinking intellectuals. Models for
Crabbe's religious and political dissenters and their sects can sometimes be
traced but are frequently composites and are in part consonant with Anglican
and 'anti-jacobin' stereotypes: M. Butler's *Jane Austen and the War of Ideas*
(1975), though it does not mention Crabbe, is a good guide to these. An
alternative view to Crabbe's of political and religious dissent in this period
can be found in E. P. Thompson, *The Making of the English Working Class*
(1963). The value of identifying real-life sources for Crabbe's characters is
debated by G. Edwards ('Crabbe's So-Called Realism', *Essays in Criticism*,

xxxvii, 4, 1987, pp. 303–20) and F. Whitehead ('Crabbe, "Realism", and Poetic Truth', *Essays in Criticism*, xxxix, 1, 1989, pp. 29–46). Crabbe's own position, in a letter to Mary Leadbeater dated 1 December 1816, seems to be that he does and does not transform his models: 'Yes! I will tell you readily about my Creatures, whom I endeavoured to paint as nearly as I could and *dare* for in some Cases I dared not. This you will readily admit: besides, Charity bade me be cautious: Thus far you are correct. There is not one of whom I had not in my Mind the Original, but I was obliged in most Cases to take them from their real Situations and in one or two Instances, even to change the Sex and in many the Circumstances . . . I do not know that I Could paint merely from my own Fancy and there is no Cause why we should. Is there not Diversity sufficient in Society? and who Can go, even but a little into the assemblies of our fellow Wanderers from the Way of perfect Rectitude, and not find Characters so varied and so pointed that he need not call upon his Imagination?' (*Selected Letters*, p. 203).

The pattern of capitalization of the initial letters of nouns is still erratic, but different from previous volumes and more purposeful. It focuses our attention on the status, as titles, of the words used to designate social and kinship roles ('Mother', 'Poet', 'Farmer', 'Maid', 'Aunt'). Crabbe was probably not involved in the drastic move from upper to lower case in the 1820 and subsequent editions (see Swingle, 'Late Crabbe'; Edwards, 'Crabbe's So-Called Realism').

Reviewers noted the shift in Crabbe's subject matter towards the 'middling classes of society' and Jeffrey, in the *Edinburgh Review* for November 1812, urged those classes to read the tales. *Tales* was Crabbe's most popular volume in his lifetime, and represented a convergence between the social positions of author, characters and readers. One probable reader was Fanny Price (herself named after a character in 'The Parish Register') whose possession of *Tales* signals that the action of *Mansfield Park* (1814) is contemporary with its writing and that Austen feels Crabbe to be her true contemporary.

TALE I THE DUMB ORATORS; OR, THE BENEFIT OF SOCIETY (p. 87)

Epigraph i. *As You Like It*, II. vii. 155–7. Jaques on 'the justice', fifth of his 'seven ages'.

Epigraph ii. *King John*, IV. ii. 235. King John to Hubert. (Crabbe alters 'had' [i.e. would have] to 'hath').

Epigraph iii. *King John*, II. i. 463–4. Bastard, of Hubert.

Epigraph iv. *2 Henry VI*, IV. ii. 72, 173–4. Dick, the butcher; Jack Cade.
Epigraph v. *Twelfth Night*, V. i. 373–4. Feste to Malvolio.

The epigraph from *Twelfth Night* introduces a preoccupation of this poem and the whole volume with 'the phenomenon of change, the temporal condition of human life' (Swingle, 'Late Crabbe', p. 582) though the extent of this poem's interest in *historical* change is unusual. Crabbe's note to line 264 prompts us to date the action of the poem: Bolt's visit to the radical club probably follows the founding of the Corresponding Societies in 1792 and precedes the Seditious Meetings Act of 1795. His complaint that the law is soft on traitors (430–34) may refer to the acquittal of radical leaders on charges of High Treason in 1794. One of the acquitted, John Thelwall, deprived of his London lecture rooms by the 1795 Act, toured East Anglia in 1796 lecturing on 'ancient history' (see lines 315–16) and is the probable model for Hammond. For Thelwall's own account, see *A Narrative of the late Attrocious Proceedings at Yarmouth* (1796). But Hammond is a composite radical. The phrase 'King of himself' (203) represents an anarchist ideal echoed by Gwyn, the Gentleman Farmer (iii. 252), by the drunken peasant in 'Peasants Drinking', and later, positively, by Shelley's ideal of 'man/ Equal, unclassed, tribeless, and nationless,/ Exempt from awe, worship, degree, – the king/ Over himself' ('Prometheus Unbound', 1820. III. iv. 193–7). 'The original of Justice Bolt was Dr Franks, of Alderton, on the Norfolk coast – a truly worthy man, but a rather pompous magistrate' (*1834*, iv. 155).

TALE II THE PARTING HOUR (p. 102)

Epigraph i. *Cymbeline*, I. IV. 25–8, 33–5. Imogen to Pisanio, of Posthumus.
Epigraph ii. *Comedy of Errors*, V. i. 298–300. Egeon to his son, Antipholus of Ephesus.
Epigraph iii. *Comedy of Errors*, V. i. 345–6. Aemilia, Abbess at Ephesus, to her husband Egeon.
Epigraph iv. *Othello*, I. iii. 131–4, 136–7. Othello to Duke of Venice and Senators (Crabbe substitutes 'she', Desdemona, for 'he', her father).
Epigraph v. *Henry VIII*, IV. ii. 21–3. Griffith (quoting Wolsey) to Katherine (Crabbe has 'fate' for 'state').

The 1820 edition, which reduces the number of upper-case initials but leaves 'Time' standing (11), emphasizes the theme of time announced by the second epigraph; but at the expense of the theme of human classification emphasized by upper-case terms such as 'Pair' (15, 19) 'Maid' (41), 'Matron' (59) and by the riddling description of Allen and Judith (18–25). The link between the discussion of storytelling (1–14) and the subsequent story is analysed by Edwards (*Border Land*, pp. 167–95) and by J. Hillis Miller ('The Ethics of Reading: vast gaps and parting hours', in *American Criticism in the Poststructuralist Age*, ed. da Konigsberg, 1981, pp. 19–41). A possible source for part of the poem is Crabbe's own fourth brother, William, discovered by an Aldborough sailor on the Honduran coast in 1803 (*1834*, iv. 175); the poem is itself a source for Tennyson's plot – and for 'Philip' as the name of the rival – in 'Enoch Arden' (1864).

TALE III THE GENTLEMAN FARMER (p. 117)

Epigraph i. *Merchant of Venice*, II. vii. 24–7. Prince of Morocco, to himself, choosing the casket (Crabbe removes the proper name).
Epigraph ii. *Much Ado About Nothing*, I. i. 224–7. Benedick.
Epigraph iii. *Macbeth*, V. iii. 47. Macbeth, to the Doctor.
Epigraph iv. *Henry VIII*, iv. ii. 41–2. Katherine, of Wolsey.

References to Thomas Paine (203; Crabbe may be thinking of *The Age of Reason*, 1794–5), to threshing machines (10), to agricultural 'improvers' (13), and to fears of foreign invasion (390) place the action firmly post-1790. Crabbe the natural historian uses the language of natural history – of 'genus' and 'species' – to define Gwyn (19–36). He is one of Crabbe's many self-deceiving free-thinkers who reject external rules and rulers in favour of 'rules my reason and my feelings give' (165). His intellectual mentors (198–205) are agnostics (Gibbon and Hume) and deists (Bolingbroke and Paine). As usual, Crabbe aims to show that the man who believes he can be 'King of him' (252) will end up dependent on his dependants. Gwyn marries Rebecca despite a previous opposition to marriage that may allude to William Godwin's *Political Justice* (1793): Godwin was widely ridiculed by conservatives for his subsequent marriage (to Mary Wollstonecraft, in 1797). Like Abel Keene and many others, Gwyn moves straight from free-thinking to a fanatical form of religious dissent.

TALE IV PROCRASTINATION (p. 133)

Epigraph i. *Henry VIII*, II. iv. 22–3. Queen Katherine to the King ('I have been to you a true and humble wife').
Epigraph ii. *Merchant of Venice*, III. ii. 252–4. Bassanio to Portia ('. . . all the wealth I had/ Ran in my veins').
Epigraph iii. *Richard III*, V. iii. 98–101. Derby to Richmond.

Epigraph iv. *2 Henry IV*, V. v. 50. Henry to Falstaff.
Epigraph v. *Much Ado About Nothing*, IV. i. 101–3. Claudio to Hero.

Brought up in a seaport, Crabbe would know numerous examples of returning wanderers, from experience, hearsay and folk-song. It is a recurrent motif in his tales ('The Parting Hour', 'The Brothers') as well as providing the structural principle of *Tales of the Hall* and the 'Farewell and Return' sequence in *Posthumous Tales*. Catherine Lloyd in 'The Parish Register' was an earlier version of Dinah, displacing sexual desire into possessions and piety. Dinah's pious talk – line 222 refers to the Anglican Burial Service, 'In the midst of life we are in death' – is brilliantly undermined by the appearance of the parable of the Good Samaritan in the final lines ('A Levite, when he was at the place, came and looked on him, and passed by on the other side', *Luke* 10:32).

TALE V THE PATRON (p. 144)

Epigraph i. *All's Well That Ends Well*, I. i. 84–98. Helena, of Bertram (Crabbe substitutes 'she' and 'her' for 'he' and 'his').
Epigraph ii. *Cymbeline*, V. iv. 127–9. Posthumus.
Epigraph iii. *The Tempest*, v. i. 114–16. Alonso to Prospero ('. . . and, since I saw thee').

Crabbe continues his critique of the romantic imagination through a story which suggests that love, poetry and mental breakdown are of imagination all compact. John's description of his romantic 'Dream' and its horrible outcome in reality (654–63) closely parallel the fearful transformations in Crabbe's poems of nightmare hallucination such as 'Sir Eustace Grey' and 'The World of Dreams'. Crabbe's son suggests that his father's 'painful circumstances' and 'sensations of wounded pride' as chaplain to the Duke of Rutland at Belvoir Castle lie behind the representations of 'the nature of a literary dependant's existence in a great lord's house' (*Life*, p. 113). But the references to '*Rutland's Duchess*' (241) and to working on the 'London [not the Slaughden] quays' (568) cleverly say (to the volume's dedicatee as well as to other readers) that the differences between author and protagonist are as real as the similarities. Walter Scott identified his own past self with the 'admirably painted young poet' (*Selected Letters*, p. 90). The relationship between John and Lady Emma may be a source for Harriet Martin and Emma in Austen's *Emma* (1816).

TALE VI THE FRANK COURTSHIP (p. 166)

Epigraph i. *Much Ado About Nothing*, II. i. 46–9. Beatrice to Hero.
Epigraph ii. *King Lear*, II. ii. 96–7. Cornwall, of (the dissembling) Kent.

Epigraph iii. *Hamlet*, III. i. 144–7. Hamlet to Ophelia (he may be aware that she has been set there as a trap for him by Claudius and Polonius).

Epigraph iv. *Much Ado About Nothing*, III. i. 107–8. Beatrice, overhearing Ursula and Hero (both dissembling).

The private ritual in which the sect pay homage to a concealed picture of Oliver Cromwell (51–64) is said to have been 'the actual consolation of a small knot of Presbyterians in a country town, about sixty years ago' (*1834*, iv. p. 267). But the description of them as 'an independent race' (35) hints at Independents (Congregationalists), and 'Friends' (67, 123) suggests Quakers. Though unclear in this respect, this is Crabbe's most historically conscious poem. The wars against regicide revolutionary France (1793–1815) are an important unspoken context for these descendants of English seventeenth-century revolutionaries and regicides. More explicitly, the poem explores the part played in the present by images of the biblical and seventeenth-century past. Edwards discusses linguistic and behavioural quotation in the poem, including the epigraphs (*Border Land*, pp. 197–215).

TALE VII THE WIDOW'S TALE (p. 181)

Epigraph i. *A Midsummer Night's Dream*, I. i. 132–5, 137, 139, 141–2. Lysander to Hermia.

Epigraph ii. *As You Like It*, II. iv. 29–31. Silvius to Corin.

Epigraph iii. *As You Like It*, III. v. 61. Rosalind (as Ganymede) to Phebe, of Silvius.

Crabbe's recurrent criticism of popular fiction is here like Austen's *Northanger Abbey* in showing Nancy's perception of reality systematically deformed by the characters and plots of romantic fiction. But the brain-washing is so thorough that its source in fiction needs only a brief mention (112–15). Her delusions exist as a belief in 'heroes' and in the power of love to cross the barriers of social class defended by parental 'tyrants' (163–70, 198–211, 248–50, 313–14, 351–5). The tale the widow tells – a cautionary tale from her own real life designed to help Nancy accept her true social position – is implicitly contrasted with romantic fiction and perhaps embodies some of Crabbe's own purposes as a storyteller.

TALE VIII THE MOTHER (p. 194)

Epigraph i. *As You Like It*, III. v. 37, 40. Rosalind (as Ganymede) to Phebe ('What though you have no beauty').

Epigraph ii. *Much Ado About Nothing*, II. i. 229–31. Benedick to Don Pedro, of Beatrice (incorrect attribution).

Epigraph iii. *As You Like It*, IV. iii. 68–70. Rosalind (as Ganymede) to Silvius, of Phebe.

Epigraph iv. *All's Well That Ends Well*, V. iii. 2–4. King of France to Countess of Rossillion, of Bertram and Helena.

Epigraph v. *All's Well That Ends Well*, V. iii. 67: King to Bertram. 15, 17–19: Lafew to King and Countess, of Bertram.

In this 'domestic war' (233), the tyrant-parent of Nancy Moss's romantic fantasies in 'The Widow's Tale' comes to life in the 'sovereign will' of Lucy's mother (234). Similarly, Swingle argues ('Late Crabbe', pp. 588–9), the mother – who 'would rule, and *Lucy* must obey' (218) – offers a counter-example to the apparent conclusion of 'The Wager' that ''Tis easiest dealing with the firmest mind' (xviii. 297).

TALE IX ARABELLA (p. 205)

Epigraph i. *A Midsummer Night's Dream*, I. i. 74, 76–8. Theseus to Hermia.

Epigraph ii. *Measure for Measure*, II. iv. 119–20. Isabella to Angelo.

Epigraph iii. *Much Ado About Nothing*, III. i. 109. Beatrice, after overhearing Hero and Ursula (both dissembling).

'A surgeon of Ipswich had an addition to his family just as he had obtained the consent of a young lady to marry him. The breaking off of the match, by the good principle and delicacy of the intended bride, gave rise to much difference of opinion at the time and suggested this tale' (*1834*, v. p. 5). Crabbe's opinion of Arabella Rack's conduct is at least nuanced. The tale, and the criticism of 'single blessedness' in the first epigraph, warn us not to generalize from Lucy's virginal and single blessedness at the end of 'The Mother'. But Crabbe's note to line 337 alerts us to, and does not resolve, uncertainty. The intellectuals whom Arabella 'could converse with' (32) are Hannah Moore (1745–1832) and Elizabeth Montague (1720–1800). The 'boast' that slaves could be freed by being brought to England (314–15) refers to Lord Mansfield's 1772 judgement in the case of the slave James Somerset.

TALE X THE LOVER'S JOURNEY (p. 216)

Epigraph i. *King John*, III. iii. 34–6. King to Hubert.

Epigraph ii. *A Midsummer Night's Dream*, V. i. 7–8. Theseus to Hippolyta.

Epigraph iii. *Two Gentlemen of Verona*, I. iii. 84–7. Proteus.
Epigraph iv. *The Taming of the Shrew*, V. i. 115–16. Lucentio to Baptista and others on his marriage to Baptista's daughter, Bianca.

'It was in his walks between Aldborough and Beccles, that Mr Crabbe passed through the very scenery described in the first part of "The Lover's Journey"; while near Beccles, in another direction, he found the contrast of rich vegetation introduced in the latter part of the tale' (*Life*, pp. 32–3). Crabbe told Scott that the description of the gypsies (lines 141–95) was based on a drawing by his younger son which 'I have nearly copied' (*Selected Letters*, p. 97). Lines 232–43 suggest a neo-classical landscape painting such as might hang in the 'rural mansions' it contains (line 241). The second epigraph is from an earlier part of Duke Theseus's speech on imagination quoted in the Preface (Appendix 2, p. 469). The link between the lover and the poet which the epigraph announces is most direct in the names of literary lovers which John and Susan give to each other ('Laura' from Petrarch, 'Orlando' from Ariosto and from Shakespeare's pastoral *As You Like It*). Edwards (*Border Land*, pp. 70–75) argues that Crabbe's theory of visual perception (lines 1–17) raises wider problems of social cohesion which the subsequent story explores. The best context for the poem is provided by David Simpson's *Wordsworth and the Figuring of the Real* (1982) which does not mention Crabbe or his poem but says that for Wordsworth 'It is the mind that sees, not the eye' (p. xi).

TALE XI EDWARD SHORE (p. 228)

Epigraph i. *Henry V*, II. ii. 128, 130–7. King Henry to Cambridge, Scroop, Grey.
Epigraph ii. *King Lear*, IV. vi. 280–83. Gloucester, with Edgar.

Crabbe's analysis of the domestic wreckage wrought by freethinking intellectuals. Howard Mills contrasts the affair between Edward Shore and his friend's wife with a comparable incident in the Shelley circle (real-life romantic free-thinkers) in 1811; 'Crabbe could not diagnose the romanticism that fuses with individual character and directs one's life' (*George Crabbe: Tales, 1812 and other selected poems*, 1967, p. xx). The description of Shore as a person who 'unfixed, unfixing looked around,/ And no employment but in seeking found' (47–8), together with other positive uses of the word 'fix' (121, 228, 449) may be contrasted with Blake's affirmation of 'she who burns with youth and knows no fixed lot' in *Visions of the Daughters of Albion* (1791–2), Plate 5.

TALE XII 'SQUIRE THOMAS: OR, THE PRECIPITATE CHOICE (p. 243)

Epigraph i. *King Lear*, II. ii. 71–3. Kent (dissembling) to Cornwall.
Epigraph ii. *Richard III*. II. ii. 151–3. Richard to Buckingham. ('my Prophet, my dear Cousin').
Epigraph iii. *Much Ado About Nothing*, II. iii. 253–4. Benedick, of Beatrice.
Epigraph iv. *3 Henry VI*, I. iv. 141–2. Duke of York to Queen Margaret.
Epigraph v. *The Winter's Tale*, II. ii. 31–3. Paulina to Emilia of Leontes and Hermione.
Epigraph vi. *Twelfth Night*, II. ii. 27. Viola, of 'Cesario's' effect on Olivia.

One of many tales ('Peter Grimes', 'The Gentleman Farmer', 'Jesse and Colin', 'Advice', 'The Wager') which explore the reversible relationship between rulers and ruled within the household. The Squire is the victim of his wife and his 'more than servant' both of whom turn out to be his 'kindred' (64, 293). Harriot is 'like *Jephtha*'s Daughter, but in different state' (325): both are sacrificed to a father's determination to recapture his birthright, but Harriot is forced to marry a man she hates, Jephtha's daughter to die a virgin (Judges 11: 1–40). The poem is among a number which, despite apparent ideological differences, recall features of Godwin's *Caleb Williams* (1794): the exploration of the master-servant dialectic, and the atmosphere of paranoid (but possibly justified) suspicion, are common to poem and novel; the Squire's discovery that the servant had not really lost his way (130–41, 286–7) resembles Caleb's discovery that Mr Forrester, in whose village he found himself when he lost his way, is really on Falkland's side.

TALE XIII JESSE AND COLIN (p. 255)

Epigraph i. *The Merry Wives of Windsor*, II. ii. 290–93. Ford, of his wife and Falstaff.
Epigraph ii. *Macbeth*, V. i. 46–7. Gentlewoman to Doctor, of Lady Macbeth.
Epigraph iii. *The Merchant of Venice*, II. iii. 2. Jessica to Launcelot.
Epigraph iv. *The Merchant of Venice*, I. ii. 5–7. Nerissa to Portia.

Jesse's experience in the household of the wealthy Lady leads her to accept her lot as farmer Colin's wife in the way that Nancy Moss is led by the widow to accept farmer Harry in 'The Widow's Tale'. But Swingle notes the difference, in the different value the two tales seem to put on 'prudence': Nancy is shown that no 'joys from Love unchecked by Prudence flow' (vii. 211), while Jesse 'led by prudence' (58) is led astray into misery

and confusion ('Late Crabbe', p. 588). The poem is interested in the ways
people are put in classes (social classes, mental categories) and named (see
especially, lines 8, 15–20, 102, 133–6, 341–8, 355–66). The final couplet is
consequently nice in the way it turns the couple's names into a class (Jesse
seems to keep her own name within the marriage).

TALE XIV THE STRUGGLES OF CONSCIENCE (p. 271)

Epigraph i. *Richard III*, V. iii. 192–5. Richard.
Epigraph ii. *The Merchant of Venice*, II. ii. 25, 26–7. Launcelot Gobbo.
Epigraph iii. *Macbeth*, III. i. 1, 2–3. Banquo, of Macbeth .('Thou hast it
now, King, Cawdor, Glamis, all/ As the Weird Women promis'd;').
Epigraph iv. *Macbeth*, V. iii. 40–45. Macbeth to the Doctor.
Epigraph v. *Richard III*, iii. 179–80. Richard.

The peculiar status of 'conscience' is emphasized (deliberately?) by the
variation in its physical appearance: sometimes italicized like the proper
names, not always given an initial capital. As a female personification it
helps to form a *ménage à trois* with the Fulhams. Their conflicts are often
described in terms of 'wars' (99) and battles for 'sovereign' power (346); and,
as Conscience becomes increasingly like a real person for Fulham, allusions
to *Macbeth* start to surface. Two of the epigraphs are from *Macbeth* and the
poem refers to a dagger (467), a disrupted banquet (470) and a power that
can 'murder sleep' (489).

TALE XV ADVICE; OR, THE 'SQUIRE AND THE PRIEST (p. 287)

Epigraph i. *Henry V*, I. i. 56–8. Canterbury, of Henry V as Prince Hal.
Epigraph ii. *Richard III*, IV. ii. 28–30. Richard.
Epigraph iii. *The Tempest*, II. i. 108–9. Alonso to Gonzalo and Antonio.

Frank Whitehead notes that 'about half the livings in England and Wales
were in the gift of one of the landowning families' and suggests that 'the
"patriot's zeal" [line 48] ... with which the squire claims to have persisted
in churchgoing in the face of the old rector's denunciation of him from the
pulpit irresistibly recalls the account in *The Annual Register* for 1793 of the
unwonted queues of carriages outside churches by means of which "the
upper ranks of society" manifested their hostility to "the irreligious and
profligate doctrines" of the French Revolution, while the resemblances
between James's Evangelical preacher and the Cambridge clergyman Charles
Simeon also suggest a date in the 1790s' ('Crabbe, 'Realism', and Poetic

Truth', pp. 45–6). The particularly systematic use of upper-case initial letters for terms denoting social and kinship roles may indicate a sociological intention here.

TALE XVI THE CONFIDANT (p. 300)

Epigraph i. *Othello*, III. iii. 175–7. Othello to Iago.
Epigraph ii. *1 Henry IV*, II. iii. 46–8. Lady Percy to Hotspur.
Epigraph iii. *Measure for Measure*, II. ii. 107–9. Isabella to Angelo.

No close source for the story of the Caliph has been identified. Whether wholly Crabbe's invention or not, he uses it imaginatively to revive a dead metaphor of biblical origin used, in the traditional sexual context, earlier in the poem (91–2, 209–10, 271–2). Charles Lamb adapted the plot for his tragi-comedy *The Wife's Trial* (1827). Hazlitt, in the *Atlas* for 20 September 1829, noted that 'Mr Crabbe is an original writer; but it is to be hoped he will have few followers. Mr Lamb, by softening the disagreeableness of one of his tales, has taken out the sting' (*Works*, ed. P. P. Howe, 1934, xx. p. 276).

TALE XVII RESENTMENT (p. 318)

Epigraph i. *2 Henry IV*, IV. iv. 31–3, 36. King Henry to Clarence, of Prince Hal.
Epigraph ii. *Julius Caesar*, I. ii. 269–72. Casca to Brutus.
Epigraph iii. *King Lear*, III. ii. 68–71. Lear, to Fool.

Crabbe has changed the gender in the first epigraph. The third epigraph is echoed by lines 399–420 (especially 417–18) which allude also to *Lear*, II. iv. (especially to lines 290–92).

TALE XVIII THE WAGER (p. 333)

Epigraph i. *The Taming of the Shrew*, V. ii. 56. Tranio to Petruchio, of Katherine.
Epigraph ii. *The Taming of the Shrew*, II. i. 295–6. Petruchio to Tranio and Gremio, of Katherine.
Epigraph iii. *The Taming of the Shrew*, V. ii. 66–7. 69. Petruchio to Hortensio and others.
Epigraph iv. *The Taming of the Shrew*, II. i. 160–61. Petruchio to Hortensio and others.

As the epigraphs suggest, the poem alludes systematically to *The Taming of the Shrew*, with Clubb's wife as Katherine. Other explorations of power-relations in marriage, not included in this edition, include 'The Preceptor Husband', 'The Natural Death of Love' (*Tales of the Hall*, ix, xiv) and 'The Equal Marriage' (*Posthumous Tales*, iii).

TALE XIX THE CONVERT (p. 343)

Epigraph i. *The Merry Wives of Windsor*, I. iii. 15–17. Falstaff to Bardolph. 16–18.
Epigraph ii. *The Winter's Tale*, IV. iii. 84–5. Autolycus, to Clown.
Epigraph iii. *The Merry Wives of Windsor*, II. ii. 22–4. Falstaff to Pistol.
Epigraph iv. *Henry V*, I. i. 27–9. Canterbury, of Henry's response, as Prince Hal, to his father's death.
Epigraph v. *Macbeth*, V. iii. 22–6. Macbeth.

'This tale was suggested by some passages in that extraordinary work *The Memoirs of the Forty-five First Years of the Life of James Lackington, Bookseller, Written by Himself*, 1791' (*1834*, v. 155). John Dighton is probably a Methodist, converted from dissipation as was Lackington. But Dighton's early life (his unknown paternity, the preoccupation with his name) is Crabbe's work, helping to link religious conversion to wider questions of insecure identity. Crabbe's preoccupation with Dighton's 'name' (1, 7, 15, 17, 311, 372, 446) would draw him to passages in the *Memoir* such as: 'My master's eldest son George happened to go and hear a sermon by one of Mr Wesley's preachers . . . He persuaded himself that he had passed through the *New Birth*, and was quite sure that his name was registered in the book of life, and (to the great grief of his parents) he was in reality become a new creature' (pp. 30–31). The link between family-name, trade-name and paternity (134–5, 366–75, 426–7) suggests the first chapters of *Dombey and Son* (1848) but capital letters are not used here with Dickens's precision.

TALE XX THE BROTHERS (p. 357)

Epigraph i. *King Lear*, I. ii. 175–8. Edmund, of Edgar.
Epigraph ii. *As You Like It*, I. i. 17–18. Orlando to Adam, of Oliver.
Epigraph iii. *As You Like It*, IV. iii. 136–7, 138. Oliver, to Celia and Rosalind.

This story of the 'Landman' and his 'Seaman' brother is anticipated in *The Borough*, xvii. 114–37. Crabbe does not tell us that the speaker of the third epigraph is brother to the speaker of the second; but the three epigraphs, taken together, may in any case imply that a relationship (close but distant) between brothers can be like the relationship between early and late stages in the life-history of an individual. This analogy may explain why Crabbe based *Tales of the Hall* on the meeting of two long-separated brothers.

TALE XXI THE LEARNED BOY (p. 370)

Epigraph i. *The Merchant of Venice*, II. ii. 183–4. Gratiano to Bassanio.
Epigraph ii. *As You Like It*, II. vii. 146–8. The second of Jaques's 'seven ages'.
Epigraph iii. *The Merry Wives of Windsor*, IV. i. 75–6: Mistress Page to Evans, of William. 77: Evans to Mistress Page, of William.
Epigraph iv. *Julius Caesar*, IV. i. 36–9. Antony to Octavius, of Lepidus.
Epigraph v. *2 Henry VI*, III. iii. 11. Cardinal to King Henry.

The volume ends with the violent punishment of the pathetically rebellious Stephen Jones and the burning of his licentious books, apparently with Crabbe's approval. The 'shiftless' Stephen (130), a weaker version of the rootless intellectual Edward Shore, succumbs to most of the influences Crabbe regards as vicious: religious fanaticism (117–25), literary romances and anti-clerical rationalists (299–302, 332–3) and pornography (380–85). The first four epigraphs together announce the theme of learning as imitation; Stephen mugs up a role in life from books and bad company (334–51; 289–96 and 481–8). The beating teaches him to know his proper place, gets him speaking the right lines.

INFANCY (p. 387)

Published *1834*; excerpts in *Life*. Reconstructed here from the sometimes illegible Murray Archive manuscript; annotations above title read 'Dec 12 1814/ March 27th 1815/ Past [?] – my own Life [in Crabbe's cypher]/ April 16. 1816./ Col. Houlton's [cypher]'. Marginalia at lines 96–7 read 'The Morning of Life, Orford Exp/ The early voyage – the early days'. The River Alde joins the sea at Orford. Lines 45–9 may refer to firework displays over the water (hence 'Crew') and so to the boating expedition with its 'civil Dudgeon' (129). The wealthy 'Lydia' (72–85) seems to be an invention but the context (vanity, and wealth) suggests an echo of 'Lydia's Monarch' (Croesus) in Johnson's *Vanity of Human Wishes* (1749), line 313. But

Crabbe may not be so sure as Johnson that vanity (mirror-gazing) is vain (self-defeating) for everybody: the manuscript hesitates between 'Fancy' and 'Feeling' in line 85. Lines 95–6 refer cryptically to *Romeo and Juliet*, III. iii. 99–107. Lines 97–8 may refer to popular commonplace or to a current climate of opinion but there may also be specific echoes – e.g. lines 41–2, 92 – of Wordsworth's 1807 'Ode' ('There was a time').

TALES OF THE HALL (p. 392)

Published 1819, with Dedication to Duchess of Rutland, and Preface (see Appendix 3). Twenty-two tales, selected by Crabbe from a series begun in 1814. Originally entitled 'Remembrances' and then 'Forty Days, A Series of Tales told at Binning Hall'; final title possibly suggested by Murray. For history of the title, and selection and sequence of tales, see *Selected Letters* (pp. 246, 250–58, 264) and *CPW*, ii. pp. 710–15.

Crabbe's most ambitious attempt to embed his tales in a linking narrative. He now does attempt to 'imitate the English Poet [Chaucer]' by finding 'characters . . . adapted to their several relations' (Preface to *Tales*, Appendix 2, p. 467). Two half-brothers, George and Richard, 'both past middle age, meet together for the first time since their infancy, in the Hall of their native parish, which the elder and richer [George] had purchased as a place of retirement for his declining age – and there tell each other their own history, and then that of their guests, neighbours, and acquaintances' (Francis Jeffrey, *Edinburgh Review*, July 1819, *Critical Heritage*, p. 235). George is moderately tory, Richard was once a slightly radical whig. Reviews noted that Crabbe's characters were now 'more elevated in station' (as was Crabbe) and 'milder and more amiable'. The *Monthly Review*, November 1819, compared 'the verbose garrulity of metrical conversation, every-day talking in rhyme' with 'the conciseness and the classical precision which marked his earlier couplets' (*Critical Heritage*, p. 273).

BOOK XIII DELAY HAS DANGER (p. 392)

Title and line 44 allude to proverb 'Delays are Dangerous' (*ODEP*, p. 176; see also *Parish Register*, ii. Epigraph and lines 1–18). 'Farley' (3) is Crabbe's normal spelling of 'Farleigh' Castle, Wilts., home of the Houlton family. Crabbe wrote to Colonel Houlton, 5 August 1816: 'never did any kind Beings in your Situation of Life and surrounded by Friends of your own Class, show such repeated and unwearied Affection to a Man situated as I am and almost standing alone in Society, at least at the Time when I had first the Happiness of seeing that dear Seat of Hospitality and Cheerfulness' (*Selected Letters*, p. 192). Edwards (*Border Land*, pp. 19–33) describes Fanny and Henry as young people standing alone in the society of an aristocratic household, on a 'border land' (219) between classes, families and stages in the life-cycle. In this study of social stratification Crabbe links social and natural-historical meanings of the word 'class' (221–3, 16; the Pforzheimer Library manuscript experiments with 'A later Worm of higher Class' for line 16); R. Williams puts Crabbe's use of 'class' in context in *Keywords: A Vocabulary of Culture and Society*, 1976, pp. 51–9). Jeffrey thought the poem 'one of the best managed of all the tales', admiring the 'long and finely converging details by which the catastrophe is brought about' (*Critical Heritage*, pp. 236–7).

'PEASANTS DRINKING' BY MISS FORD (p. 416)

Published *CPW*, 1988. Probably written 1823, one of a number – requested by the Dowager Duchess of Rutland – on drawings by young ladies. Transcribed here from a fair copy, probably not in Crabbe's hand, enclosed in a letter to the Dowager Duchess dated 24 December 1823, now in the Belvoir Archive. The drawing not identified, the artist probably one of the daughters or nieces of Thomas Ford, Vicar of Melton Mowbray. The image of the drunken, illiterate (and male) labourer shouting radical slogans was a commonplace of conservative polemic. For variations on 'Lord of himself' (11) see 'The Dumb Orators' (line 203), 'The Gentleman Farmer' (line 252).

THE FLOWERS (p. 417)

Published *New Poems* (1960). Written between 1819 and 1826. Transcribed here from fair copy in Murray Archive, with lines 3 and 155 punctuated from earlier Murray Archive manuscript. Probably intended for Sarah Hoare's album. Crabbe right to think it has 'some originality' (*CPW*, iii. p. 409) despite similarities to the 'humanization and cataloguing' of plants in Erasmus Darwin's *Loves of the Plants* (1789), itself probably influenced by Crabbe's *Library*, 1781 (D. King-Hele, *Erasmus Darwin and the Romantic Poets*, 1986, pp. 163–9). Personal allusions are to Crabbe's first patroness, the Duchess of Rutland (70) and to the evil effects of opium (167–80). The principal allusion is to customary comparison-making, in the naming of girls (Rose, Lily, Myrtle etc.) and in proverbs such as 'he that handles a nettle tenderly is soonest stung', 'the fairest rose at last is withered', 'a myrtle among nettles is a myrtle still', 'the highest climbers have the greatest falls' (*ODEP*, pp. 348, 684, 552, 357).

POSTHUMOUS TALES (p. 426)

Published *1834*. Crabbe wrote to George jun., 24 October 1831, 'So you have been reading my almost forgotten stories – Lady Barbara and Ellen [*Tales of the Hall*, xvi, xviii] . . . I have to observe that there are, in my recess at home, where they have been long undisturbed, another series of such stories – in number and quantity sufficient for an octavo volume; . . . they may hereafter . . . be worth something to you' (*Selected Letters*, pp. 377–8). Twenty-two tales, written between 1815 and 1827, of which seventeen (vi–xxii) are grouped as 'Farewell and Return'. Reviews were lukewarm; *1834* did little to revive Crabbe's flagged popularity. New literary comparisons appeared: the *Edinburgh Review*, January 1835, noted the 'clear and microscopic observation of ordinary existence, delineated, as it is, with the marvellous exactness of Miss Austen's novels, and carried into a variety of regions where she durst never venture'; J. G. Lockhart in the *Quarterly Review*, October 1834, suggested that 'the example of Lord Byron's "Corsair" and "Lara" had not, we suspect, been lost upon him' (*Critical Heritage*, pp. 318–19, 347).

TALE II THE FAMILY OF LOVE (p. 426)

Written 1826–7. Manuscript versions in Murray Archive and Victoria and Albert (Forster Collection) entitled 'The Family of Friends' (that and eventual title used by Dysons to describe themselves). Part of the plot anticipated in 'The Parish Register' iii. 731–800. But the poem, one of Crabbe's last and longest, is a new departure, drawing on his experience of industrial (woollen cloth manufacturing) Trowbridge with its recently established factories based on steam-power (see lines 1–6, 120–25, 534) and its industrial 'murmuring' (125). References to the Bible Society founded in 1804 (134–5), the Volunteers formed to combat French invasion and internal subversion in 1793 and 1812 (435–40) help to put the poem's main action firmly in the nineteenth century. *1834* may derive lines 167–71 from the Forster manuscript, which had however experimented with the very different: '"Who what he earns not takes is but a Thief/ Stealing from those who can" – he [James] never knew/ How first the Evil in men's Nature grew/

Urging them What they did, with Pain and Dread to do.' The Murray manuscript has 'and forced' for 'urging'. A crowded social milieu, urban nineteenth-century class tensions, sustained disguise, a social philosophy of philanthropy and social reconciliation: the combination is Dickensian. Lockhart thought it 'perhaps the best tale in this volume' (*Critical Heritage*, p. 319).

INDEX OF TITLES

INDEX OF FIRST LINES